Coerte Felske was born in New York City in 1960. He was educated at Dartmouth College and Columbia University. He has worked as a screenwriter in Hollywood. Both his previous novels, *Word* and *The Shallow Man*, are currently in production at New Line Cinema. He lives in Manhattan.

For more information about Coerte Felske, visit his website at: www.forwhat.com

The millennium girl

Coerte Felske

HEADLINE

First published in 1999
by HEADLINE BOOK PUBLISHING

First published in the USA in 1999
by St Martin's Press

10 9 8 7 6 5 4 3 2 1

ISBN 0 7472 6313 2

Typeset by Avon Dataset Ltd, Bidford-on-Avon, Warks

Printed and bound in Great Britain by
Clays Ltd, St Ives plc

HEADLINE BOOK PUBLISHING
A division of the Hodder Headline Group
338 Euston Road
London NW1 3BH

www.headline.co.uk
www.hodderheadline.com

This book is dedicated to the Old Mill House,
Club Lane, Quogue, Long Island

acknowledgments

Ginny and Andy Anderson, Honoré de Balzac, Peter and Najma Beard, Mark Ciardi, Bruce Cox, Mike De Luca, Ulf Ekberg, Arthur and Dorothy Felske, Alan Finkelstein, Kevin Gannon, Gordon Gray, Michael Gruber, Niko Hansen, Jimmy and Kitty Hewitt, Richard Johnson, Owen Laster, Carolyn Manetti, Dorsey Mills, Roger Morrison, John Mosley, Bill Mullally, Jeremy Nussbaum, Maya Perez, Chuck Pfeifer, Scott Rosenberg, Luca Rossi, Emma S., Randy Schindler, Melanie Spear, Carey Stokes, Taki Theodorocopoulos, Bill Tonelli, Frederique and Michiel van der Wal, Ellen von Unwerth, Lance Valdez, Nick Wechsler, Charles Winslow, and Sandra Zita.

I offer special thanks to my editor, Charlie Spicer, and to Sally Richardson for their tremendous enthusiasm and support.

*W*omen are those sweetly smiling angels with
pensive looks, innocent faces, and cash-boxes for hearts.

—HONORÉ DE BALZAC,
Cousin Bette, 1846

I never worked so hard in my life
to get rich without working.

—MINER,
Leadville Gold Mine (near Aspen), Colorado,
circa 1877

new york yum

It was late August and I was sun-splashed St Raphaël blond. I was riding high in the sky on my transatlantic flight from Nice to New York. And I was returning to the United States happily. Finally, I was going off-Tour, meaning I had just completed the Tour's last leg. I was coming home.

It had been quite a summer. It had been quite a year, for that matter. If I go strictly by the calendar, it started in Gstaad at Christmas, Aspen at New Year's, and then St. Bart's through the end of January. I spent February in Palm Beach, March in St. Moritz and Los Angeles, April in Marbella and Paris, May in Cannes and Monaco, June in the Hamptons, July in St Tropez, and August in Ibiza – give or take a little excursion here and there.

Now, for sure, there's always some new hot spot, hamlet, or festival that becomes very chic each year, meaning it welcomes all Walletmen. London, for instance, is very good now in September and October. In which case, I'll go off-Tour and follow, providing I don't have any other previous engagement. And even if I do, I'll weigh the potential for each and make my decision.

Or there are certain private enclaves or Must Go private parties to attend where the men are very generous. After all, my life's blood is the Bigger, Better Deal and I follow the Green. But, basically, that is the Tour. The Digger Tour, to be specific.

By the way, that was my name – the Tour – for this special year-round circuit. The girls didn't use it. In fact, you'll never hear it from anyone else. But, well, all I can say is, welcome to my world.

And when the summer comes to a close, I always return to New York City. It is my home base. I usually stay here for the duration of the fall until Christmas, when I return to Gstaad and Aspen and go back on Tour.

The year was 1999. I was excited to be coming home, I truly was.

The fall in New York is just about the nicest season in any town. It reminded me of all the beautiful clothes I could wear – the assortment of wool slacks, sweaters, and suits; the new ready-to-wear collections; the holiday charity balls and galas with all their New York society pageantry; the loop around Central Park on my Rollerblades while listening to my U2 *Joshua Tree* tape; and the men. Oooooh, the men.

From all over the globe, the men come to New York in September. They arrive from their summers looking all tan and dastardly. Love that. And they bullshit their little buns off, telling little lies, making little promises they never intend to keep, and they spend. They spend nicely. Mmmmm. I called it New York Yum. September in New York is like April in Paris. Only better. Why? I like dollars more than the Euro.

2

Come all ye Walletmen, come all!

It's a bumper sticker my Digger pal **Earning Every Penny** had made for me. And it's matted across my refrigerator door in my Trump Tower apartment. I have Native American nicknames for all the Tour gals. And they're not all sweet ones. I'm talking the names and the girls. I apply the Indian coinings to hide their real identities. I don't want to expose anybody. The gals are getting enough exposure already, if you know what I mean. I started nicknaming after I saw the movie *Dances With Wolves*. There's **Travels With Men**, **I'm in a Pinch**, **Snake in Her Pants**, **Operation:** *I Do*, **No Deposit, No Return**, and **Ellen B. Generous**, as well as others.

I employ this nomenclature as a part of my heritage too. I'm a quarter Native American myself from the southwestern Zuni tribe, with another quarter English, another quarter Brazilian, and another quarter Eskimo. I'm a real mutt. Until the mid-sixties, you would have hated to be me. But nineties beauty-worship saved me. Not that I am beautiful, but I am pretty good-looking. Or so they say.

I have big green eyes the color of cool jades. I'm five feet seven inches tall, which is not leaf-eater size, but it's not gnomelike either. I have chestnut hair but I change color just about every six weeks. At that moment I was sun-bleached from the salty Mediterranean waters. I had my lips tattooed a deeper red, which also gives me a more pronounced lip line. I can dash out of the house, and from thirty feet you'd think I was wearing lipstick. It's the only cosmetic surgery I've ever had. I have nice full breasts and an ass that's high, tight, firm, and about the size of a grapefruit.

I'm not a hooker in the traditional sense, but I do live off men. The simple reason is, why shouldn't I? With the deck stacked against the women of the world the way it is, and always will be, why shouldn't I take what I can while I can? But more on that later.

My name is Bodicea, but most people call me Bo. I don't always go by my real name. I've been Joey and Tish and Wanda and Celeste. But that's when I go into my Fake Mode, which is fairly often. Several times a day, in fact. Sometimes I get lost in my Fake Mode. That's when it gets really scary.

I'm rather proud of my name. Boadicea was a British queen. Hers was my mother's favorite romantic tale growing up, even though it's a sad one. In 60 A.D., when the Romans ruled Britannia, the Roman army annexed Boadicea's kingdom and tortured her and raped her daughters. So Boadicea led a bloody revolt against them. Boadicea's troops fought valiantly. She killed herself so as not to be captured by the enemy. Queen Boadicea became known as the Warrior Queen.

My grandmother taught my mother about all the princesses and goddesses. And me too. I think knowing that I was named after a warrior queen helped with my early self-esteem. I didn't have much else to latch it onto. I had a father and a mother and one sister. My sister has a daughter named Maximilia, whom I adore. I was born somewhere in Ohio, and it's not that I don't know where. But you don't, so why should I bother to tell you?

When my plane touched down, I sat upright from my first-class-you-bet-seat and waited by the exit door. I always travel first-class. It's one of the business's perks. Eventually the door was opened, and I marched swiftly out of the gate, to the awaiting crowd of greeters. You see, I had an appointment. And I was late.

I found my driver holding up a placard that said MS. WANDA PARK. The name derived from a Beverly Hills street – Wanda Park Drive – up in the Benedict Canyon area. Sonny Bono used to live up there. I use different names a lot. I never give away more than I have to. I learned that lesson the hard way.

My driver retrieved my bags and drove me straight into Manhattan to the Lowell Hotel on Sixty-third Street. I love the Lowell. Husbands love it too. It's the Carlyle, but with more privacy. I'm a privacy freak. I'm sure you understand.

The desk clerk, who looked like a Gertrude, was ready for me.

'Mr. Hamilton asked me to tell you to join him at Le Bilboquet across the street,' she said.

'Fine,' I said without showing any surprise.

I was staying in Giles Hamilton's room. He's an English guy **Travels With Men** introduced me to. Usually, I stay away from introductions from other Diggers. They're normally satisfying some need of their own at your expense. It's a cutthroat world, it really is. Which means it's more than cutthroat. It's downright mean. I don't recommend it unless you have the stomach for it. The frail need not apply. If women weren't so jealous of one another, we'd be the rulers of the planet.

I usually stay away from English men. It's only my opinion, but I've found them to be somewhat cold, sexually underdeveloped, and rather cheap. There is nothing worse to a Digger than the tag *cheap*. It's the worst thing you could say about a man. Bad sense of humor, okay. Small penis, whatever. Ugly, so what. But cheap – yuck. It's a five-letter word, only to be outdone by its six-letter cousin, prenup. *Bastard* cousin, that is.

I took a quick bath, but used lots of bath gel. I always use the entire bottle. I just love to have the bubbles rise up and give me a suds collar. The bathrooms at the Lowell are the best. There's lots of marble and gold fixtures. And the in-house lotions. Yum.

I toweled off and got dressed. I was Prada. I was Gucci. I was Fogal. I was Manolo. I was Chanel for accessories and Tiffany for trim. Like usual, I was anything I wanted to be.

that little voice

Sometimes I think I'm a man. Not that there's any kind of genetic crossover, like I'm caught in between the two worlds. My body, and it is mine, prickles and surges with femininity, as well as hosts the required monthly letdown. But I really think like one. I'm not a woman professional. I am not a childbearer. I'm not a clothes-washer. I'm not great in the kitchen. I'm a hunter and a gatherer. Plain and simple.

Let me get this out of the way. All women are wildly insecure. This is not to say that men are not. But it is overly true for us, especially in this decade of model-mania and the über-slim ideal. And I was particularly frothing. Of course, in my case, these kinds of womanly worries were business-related. But it's like that for all the women I know, even the galactically beautiful, which I am not.

You wonder if you're not pretty enough, not thin enough, if your boobs are sagging too much to the left, or to the right. These thoughts take up most of your time. And if you're a prospector in search of the Precious, you're plagued by them. If you're making money off your good curves, you think about your curves. Incessantly.

I was constantly dashing to powder rooms; catching sight of my reflection in store glass windows; inspecting other women on the street and making comparative, and sometimes shattering, mental notes; in addition to flash-checking myself in my mirrored compact, Chanel *bien sûr*. I never tired of what I saw either. It's almost as though I was afraid from one minute to the next I was going to lose what I had. Like some wicked fairy godmother was going to wave a wand over me and it was all going to vanish.

Let it suffice to say that as soon as I set foot out the door, no matter how I looked, no matter what I was wearing, no matter where I was, or whose place I was staying at – whenever I go somewhere, anywhere, my mind is chatted up by That Little Voice which is always whispering some stroke of inadequacy in my ear. It's usually that I'm not something *enough*, whatever that something is.

That day was no different.

sugar daddy saturday

I forgot to tell you, I came back to New York on Friday night for a reason. Why? The next day was Saturday. Sugar Daddy Saturday. I was very excited.

Sugar Daddy Saturdays happen all over the globe on the finest shopping streets. Rodeo Drive, of course, in Beverly Hills, Avenue Foch in Paris, Via Roma in Rome, Calle de Serrano in Madrid, Bond Street in London, and Madison Avenue in New York. And why Saturday? Saturday is the first day Walletmen are available to spread their leather. They've been working all week, remember? Today's their day, which means it's your day. Saturday was my favorite day of the week.

Though a Londoner, Giles knew the New York routine. The Lowell and Le Bilboquet were a perfect play for a pay-for gal. It's why he chose them. How did he know? How do you think? They're both catty-corner to Madison Avenue. The play involves a little bath, a little bistro brunch, and a little jaunt up the avenue. All your favorite stores are there. And you already know what they have in stock. For designer clothes, you've received the videotape of their latest show. And you've already been in the store – at least three times. And if you haven't been in town for a while, you've seen the other chain boutiques in the other high-shop cities – so you know what to order or what questions to ask.

I'll make the distinction right now between a prostitute and a Digger. And I know it sounds self-serving, because many people believe that they are one and the same. That is not true. What is true is, there's a fine line between them. And in the modern era, the millennium era that is, there's little distinction between the two.

The primary difference is, the prostitute is someone who sleeps with people she doesn't know for money. The gold digger has targeted a guy and wants to keep him for a long-term thing – not just the five-hundred-dollar one-shot deal. And hopefully it ends in getting your life paid for – the way I enjoyed it – or *marriage*, but that depends on the goals of the individual Digger.

In addition, as a Digger, the relationship you're looking for involves emotions. The prostitute wants the quick one-time transaction, maybe with repeat business. But she'll opt for no emotions, thank you very much.

The prostitute also gets paid *before* the sexual act. A Digger gets paid afterward. And it's in the form of 'shopping money,' credit card usage, or 'kitty' and 'puppy' funds. You could say the prostitute is smarter that way – to get paid up-front. But the Digger, I feel, still retains a little more dignity than just the ho doing the corner flesh hustle. The Digger gets wined and dined and romanced somewhat. She is appealed to more as a woman. The prostitute is treated more like a beast.

The Digger is known to be more educated and attractive, with obvious exceptions. Hookers are more crude and crudely do it for money. It doesn't matter who the men are, as long as they pay up. Diggers check out a guy. And the better the Digger, the more selective she is.

And digging is definitely safer. There are no pimps to pay off or fear. You work for yourself and depend on your own ingenuity for survival.

Let me also add that, emotionally, sometimes there is no difference at all between the two. As a Digger, you can still feel like a whore – and that's never fun.

If the Walletman is a cheapie, however, sometimes a Digger is forced to be more aggressive and force the action. This could include relegating yourself to traditional prostitute behavior. For instance, occasionally you have to perform a little clip. You may have to rifle through his clothes in the morning or at some point. Some of these guys can process their being with you as a result of their own irresistibility. Especially if they've already achieved orgasm. In such cases, you have to fend for yourself.

The male ego is just about the most sensitive thing – next to your own. They have their own version of That Little Voice. And if a guy is rich – and he must be, or you wouldn't be with him – he takes his self-esteem from that, and sometimes it can result in a whopping, oversized ego. It can make him conveniently forget the little things, like why you're there with him in the first place. Other times, the fact that if he wasn't rich, you wouldn't be interested in him may eat him up. In which case, his generosity is also affected. So you take a little initiative. Bo knows initiative.

Whichever, most Walletmen always have tons of cash on hand. In their dressers, in their hotel bureaus, in their suitcases, and in their clothes. I'm talking the Western Walletmen anyway. The Muslim Men – Kuwaitis, Brunei guys, Saudis – never have any cash on them. They let their servants do the spending. More on them later.

I apologize for my scattered delivery. I have a tendency to ramble, and for that I am sorry. But there's so much to tell. There really is. And I want to tell it.

Anyway, I emerged from the Lowell feeling refreshed and squeaky clean. I glided across the street and slipped inside Le Bilboquet. It's one of those chic, high-visibility French bistros preferred by the European set. Brunching men there usually aren't the generous types, with the occasional exception. It's a scene. And you must stay away from scenes. But I already had my Walletman.

I saw Giles. But he wasn't alone. **Check the Passport** was with him. That put me on alert immediately. The usual thoughts went through my head. **Check the Passport** was your classic Tour bitch. She had a reputation for homing in on turf – mine and everyone else's. I wondered how the two of them had met. I was kind of miffed.

Giles stood up seemingly unaware of the problem. **Check the Passport** turned around and gave me that pasted-on smile, so falsely cheery, like we'd been college roommates. I kept my cool. We exchanged phony greetings. I played it soft and sweet with Giles. **Check**

the Passport I gave my best frost. I wanted an answer. Then I got it.

'I didn't think you were coming . . .' Giles explained.

'Oh, really? Didn't you get my message?'

'You called me at the hotel?'

'No, on your mobile.'

'Oh, sorry, I turned it off. I didn't check the messages.'

Whatever, I thought. And beamed down at her.

'We just met,' she said.

'Yeah,' Giles said. 'At the door.'

'How nice . . . Giles, I'm not really in the mood for French food.'

And that was all I needed to say. One cab later we were on our way to Le Cirque 2000.

'Isn't Le Cirque French?' Giles asked.

'But it's owned by Italians.'

Giles knew I was perturbed by the confrontation with **Check the Passport**. Eventually I calmed. And I probably wouldn't have even suggested the change in venue had it not been for her. But she was one of the worst. She had connived and weaseled and snaked her way through America and Europe and the Middle East. Some reputations were worse, but not many. She'd spent a lot of time in Abu Dhabi, which enabled her to stockpile cash. The Arabs are very generous, after all. The most generous. Anyhow, **Check the Passport** now lives off that cache like some trust-fund kid and just bops in to the little Digger spots once in a while, pretending she was to the manner born. And, boy, wouldn't I love to show the world her passport, all foreign stamps included, to show everyone where her manner-born money came from. I disliked **Check the Passport**. Immensely. After all, she was a Scorpio Dog. Yuck!

star blast

Le Cirque 2000 had quite a draw. Politicians, socialites, celebrities, traveling businessmen, and unknown Walletmen and Diggers padding the leather in between. We were seated in a nice booth near Henry and Nancy Kissinger.

Our brunch chatter wasn't stimulating. Giles wasn't very talkative. Maybe he was still wondering about **Check the Passport**, I thought. I'm always wary of a man's mood, especially when his attention span drops out of sight just after he's met some other bombshell. You have to reel him back in. A simple little 'I saw Simon in Ibiza' usually does the trick. You know, a little reference to a close friend of his. Just to make him wonder a bit.

After the teaser, Giles was postured forward in his chair ready to listen to anything I had to say. In fairness to him, though, I think he'd had a lot to drink the night before. He told me he'd gone to VIP's strip club. Walletmen are so predictable. Rest assured, if you're not there to be with them, they're fulfilling the same needs somewhere with someone else. Whether it's at a club, with a dirty magazine, on hotel smut channels, or two-timing with beauts like **Check the Passport**. They can never get enough. That's why you should never care deeply about them. Even though sometimes you'd really like to.

Giles was bald with some whitish side patches. He wasn't bad in bed for an Englishman. He was actually somewhat open-minded. He loved the strap-on, traveled with it, and we used it generously. His body was fuzzy but firm, with a little rim of softness in the middle. He was as white as a ghost, as most limeys are, but I didn't care, really. Whenever we got together, it was always dark anyway. White-white flesh is pretty scary but, hey, that's what light switches are for.

I ordered the gazpacho. That Little Voice kept me in salads and soup. And black stockings that whish when you walk, of course.

Giles did tell me about his daughters, however, both of whom are older than me. See, Giles is seventy-one. You may think that is old, and I guess it is. But old men are much more dependable. And generous. And I'm sure you know by now that *generous* is the operative word. He treated me very well. I considered him rather un-English in that regard.

After he gave me his family update, I gave him my astrological bit. Giles was a Gemini Rooster and he was worried about a recent business dealing. So I imparted to him what I'd learned during my previous night's in-flight magazine horoscope study.

'I think you should avoid pushing too hard, Giles. I know you want to push things through, but a more relaxed approach would benefit you. Take your time. . . .'

I loved talking astrology. Especially blending the Eastern and the Western zodiacs. You can really spy on a person if you know his or her combined signs. I read daily from Suzanne White's *The New Astrology*. It's a textbook that describes every sign combination. All 144. It even lists celebrity examples – always fun. As for me, I'm a Capricorn Snake just like Martin Luther King, Muhammad Ali, and Aristotle Onassis. It's a sign that gives me a lot to work with.

I'll explain.

My character is spectrally diverse. I have a garish side, a trendy side, a sexually liberated side, a street-smart side, a side that purposefully blends with the upper classes, and a side that gives no priority to social distinctions. I could be a young Pamela Harriman on Rollerblades or Anna Nicole Smith at the Piping Rock Club. I'm not a chameleon as much as I'm open-minded. Three of my moons are in Libra, so *voilà*. You have to be able to switch social-class gears accordingly. I truly believe that's what it takes to make it as a woman at Century's End. It's just too competitive. I was adaptable and spontaneous and I lived my life hour to hour.

Anyhow, I wrote down every Walletman's sign. Whenever we had an appointment, I would study his latest horoscope offerings in the monthly magazines as well as the morning papers. Eventually, we'd have some sort of life discussion, at which time I would advise him, given what I knew and what I'd read already. Or I'd give it to him right on the phone as I secretly read from the paper. He, of course, would see my offering as some form of uncut spirituality that surged from my soul. Not common for a pay-for gal. That always helps. Even in the art of gold digging, it's the little things that make the difference.

But it wasn't a con, really. I am spiritual. You may think because of my chosen vocation that my moral fiber isn't very strong or fibrous, but that's not true. I have morals. And spiritual fortifications. To judge me solely by my fat-cat yearnings I think would be a mistake.

I've been hearing forever that you have to be some sort of saint if you want to embrace God. And if you're not exhibiting such saintly goodness at all times, you're a hypocrite. I think as overpopulation continues and we exhaust the world's precious resources, life and work get increasingly competitive. And as we get pushed closer to the edge, and more density and stress pervades society, you have to be prepared to do things – simple Darwinian things – that you may not have had to in previous times. I'm not talking about acting out your own depraved version of the Ten Commandments. But simple and practical survival techniques are essential. At the same time, you can't lose yourself and your moral standing. I think you should be spiritual but practical. That's what I am. Call it practically spiritual. Or spiritually practical. It all means *Do what you can for yourself and do what you can for God*. This is my formula for living at Century's End.

In any case, every man I've ever known wants to talk about his life. They just don't know who to tell.

Sometimes they're reluctant to tell colleagues because colleagues will try to profit from such a showing of weakness. They can't tell their wives because often the problems are with the wives themselves. In this way, you can become their cherished confidante.

In addition to needing a good listener, men want to be told what to do – whether they listen or not. And I must say I believed in astrology, and I felt I gave good advice. So this kind of feature added to my package. Not only was I a sex kitten with bells, I was a spiritual sex kitten with bells.

I know I sound somewhat antsy and giddy, but that's how I was that day and I want to give you the closest representation of my moods and their fluctuations. I think if you understand my mind, you'll understand me. And I want you to, I really do.

Let's not forget, when I was shopping, or on the verge of it, that's exactly how I felt. Nothing excited me more. I mean, to score a new Prada bag in the afternoon or some new Jourdans in the twilight hours before din, now, that's really living. Free-spreeing fills you with the nicest highs. Of course, it can be dangerous. By that I mean it can be addictive and druglike.

I would say it's akin to the way men get addicted to sex and womanizing. They achieve a similar high when they experience a new sexual partner or conquest. It's a challenge for a man to make it on intimate terms with a woman. Women aren't that gratified with a new partner, generally speaking. All we have to do is show up. And three-quarters of the men will want a liaison after simple hellos. Men are easy to get for the first time. And successive times. It's landing them for a lifetime that's the challenge. And the essence of my story.

the ten-year window

'B o!' I heard shouted out with a giggle sidecar.

I looked up and she was a cutie. **Every Little Bit Helps** had curves that haunted you all year. And a blond mane like Rapunzel. She was truly a statement broad. She was also one of the few girls on the Tour I liked. She was my buddy. She was a Taurus Goat. We were very compatible. We'd had some history too. In the realm of hot-spot, resort-related juicy stuff.

'Hi, baby.'

'Wow, I can't believe you're here. This is Jasper.'

And he was worth looking at too. He was about thirty-five and had a nice blazer on, T-shirt beneath, and jeans. I immediately nailed him to thirty grand a year. Nevertheless, he was a real cutie-pie.

'Jasper said they were open for brunch, but I didn't think so.'

'We've been here for brunch before,' I said to her.

Every Little Bit Helps was so sexy. She was busty, tall, thin, and always wrong. *Sexy.*

'Oh, right,' she said, and we both laughed at that. We had our reasons.

I introduced them both to Giles. 'Why don't you join us?' he asked.

'Wow,' she said airily. Sure, she had helium head. But she always meant well. As well as she could, anyway. We're all trying to survive, remember.

I patted the seat next to me. 'Mind if Jasper sits next to me?' I asked **Every Little Bit**.

'Only if I can sit by your friend.'

'Settled,' Giles said, a tad enthusiastically.

And we proceeded to have a marvelous lunch. I liked Jasper. He was a writer of what he called 'preppy fiction,' though I hadn't heard him correctly the first time.

'Did you say pop fiction?' I asked. 'I like that.'

'Uh, no.' And he repeated his version.

'Oh,' I said trying not to seem less enthusiastic. But I sensed he knew I was. I asked him the title of his latest book.

'*To Die in Black Tie*,' he said. I told him I liked the title.

'I also write magazine articles with a satirical slant to them,' he added to give his career statistics more weight.

'He's my Plato,' **Every Little Bit** remarked.

'Yeah,' Jasper quipped.

At that moment, she leaned in to me. 'I called him my *play toy*, but he misunderstood me. He thought I said *Plato*. So we kept it.'

I laughed at that, though I wasn't surprised. Knowing **Every Little Bit** and her previous beaux, I knew Jasper was some form of toy. In fairness to him, he was intelligent and had a decent sense of humor. And he was very handsome. He had that typical arm-wrestle going on with the world, a world that hadn't yet begun to appreciate him. It would eventually. I could feel it.

'My first book had elements of my family in it. Similar elements. It was reviewed well but . . .'

'But what? That's great.'

'Yeah, but it was kind of Vanilla Boy writes about his hometown.'

'What would you like to write about?'

'I don't know. I just don't know. I mean, I have a few ideas. But there's not enough – grit – to the stories.'

'Not yet . . .'

He smiled at me for taking that kind of initiative with him, then recoiled again and sipped on his Bloody Mary. He seemed down, didn't he? He was very handsome.

To yank him out of his shell, I inquired about his birth date to ascertain his zodiac data. I found that Jasper was a Libra Rat.

'Great sign for a writer,' I remarked immediately. I'd had a boyfriend in London who was a Libra Rat, so I knew the combination well. In addition, I had a lot of Libra in my chart. Next to my sun sign, Capricorn, Libra was my greatest influence.

'Really?' he asked with a touch of skepticism.

'Wouldn't kid you.'

'Or are you just saying that?'

'Would you consider Eugene O'Neill, Thomas Wolfe, Truman Capote, and T.S. Eliot good company?'

He smiled at me. 'Yes, I would.' And his smile hung around and not surprisingly.

'Oscar Wilde, F. Scott Fitzgerald, William Faulkner, Nietzsche, John Lennon, Gore Vidal – all Librans,' I added.

He only nodded, but his mood had been bettered. Hearing that he had astro similarities to such creative heavyweights made him feel good. I could tell. Even though he was not a follower of the zodiac. Sometimes you'll take any connection to greatness you can.

'I don't know anything about astrology,' he confessed. 'So tell me. What makes Librans good writers?'

'They understand all viewpoints, almost to a maddening degree.'

'Why maddening?'

'Occasionally you want them to take a stand. But they don't like confrontation. In general.'

Jasper was the kind of guy you could love to death, love to be with, love to have on your arm, love to take you places, love to make love to, and love to make babies with. I could never have been with him. He was a one-way ticket to the Forest Where Dreams Have Died – an awful place. He was good for a small Manhattan apartment, a modest farmhouse north of the highway in the Hamptons (the so-so section), a trip to the Islands once a year, and a station wagon as the second car. *Ouch*. At peak, he would net a hundred grand, and still he was ten years away from making that. Why would I want a husband who's making a tenth of a million when I'm thirty-eight? Yes, I'm twenty-eight. Shhhhhhhhhhhhhhh . . .

Anyhow, Jasper? Groan, groan. It would be against everything I stood for. And it would simply destroy the Ten-Year Window philosophy, the Digger Magna Carta.

Let me explain. Women have ten years to make their move. Ten years. That's all.

Let's start by saying the world is an unfair place – genetically, biologically, and with respect to gender. We all know men hold their looks better than women. And they have no reproductive worries. From ages twenty to thirty, women are at their peak aesthetically. Plus or minus a few years depending on the God-given genetic talent and makeup of the woman. Within those ten years it is imperative for her to find her mate, a mate who can support her and, if she's smart, support her like a queen. After all, who likes doing without? So that ten-year period is one of, and *it must be*, intensified life, the likes of which a man will never experience. A woman must scratch, climb, screw, and crawl to get what she wants. It may take adopting some unsavory methods, and I'm not talking about lies. I'm talking about serious behind-the-back, in-the-closet, while-she's-away, while-he's-away kind of stuff. Now, of course, men have been calling us bitches for centuries for this kind of seemingly merciless behavior. But let's not forget. We're constructed differently in terms of our biology. We hold the key to life. And we can't wait for ever to do it. A man can. He can wait and wait and hold out and play around through millennia and back. But we cannot. If we're in a stalled situation like an emotional or marital gridlock with present company, we have to make a move. We'd be foolish not to. It's the mistake too many women make. Men can't judge us as they judge themselves – in terms of fairness, honesty, and integrity. It would be like giving a man only ten years to make money. Can you imagine the scrambling? All the deceptions and dirty dealings?

Murder rates would be up hugely.

If we, as women, find the right guy, no matter what age, and he wants to commit, fine. There's no need to spread it around. But if he wants to fly around like Peter Pan, he can, and should, expect a swift kick in the heart, when all the buzzing around is done. Enough said.

With respect to Jasper, and the unfortunate fact that he had only ninety-nine out of one hundred essential qualities, it was clear he just didn't make the cut.

'How did you two meet?' I asked.

And his peaceful, confident reaction to the question let me know he had no idea who he was dealing with with respect to **Every Little Bit Helps**. When a guy knows something dark and gossipy is up, his reaction is tense, paranoid, and he squirms a little. And often he will explain in so many words how really unattached he is to her. Because he knows *you know* and he doesn't want to seem as if he's embraced all the lies he's been told by her, thereby making him look like a fool. Men hate looking like fools.

Jasper, however, didn't show even the slightest trace of anxiety.

'We met in New York last Christmas,' he said proudly. 'See the silver heart I gave her?'

'Elsa Peretti no doubt . . .'

'How did you know?'

'Just a lucky guess,' I said. 'Tell me, Jasper, how long have you been together?'

'Since then,' he said with a smile. An innocent smile.

'You're a sweet guy,' I said to him. And he was. And

let's get something straight. It's not as though Jasper was some wildly naive boy with an Upper East Side haircut incapable of any keen judgments. I could tell from the description of his writing, his table wit, and his tepid cynicism that he was familiar with some forms of the darker corner of life. It's just that he wasn't familiar with all of them. Better for him. But one day I was certain he'd have That Face. It's so painful, I don't even want to explain it right now.

Jasper offered to cover the tab, but Giles wouldn't let him. Jasper didn't put up a fight. We got in our car and left the two of them outside the restaurant on Park. Jasper and **Every Little Bit Helps** had some discussion about seeing a movie, and I think **Every Little Bit** opted to see *Titanic*, a movie Jasper had already seen. But I wasn't sure.

What the movie was, that is.

every little bit helps

I opened the door with one hand on the doorknob and the other clutching a preposterously superior vintage of champagne.

'Hi, baby.'

You see, the highlight of our Le Cirque brunch had been when I followed **Every Little Bit** into the bathroom; we giggled and delicately French-kissed, and I informed her that Giles had asked her to join us later that afternoon and that he was very generous.

I handed her the bottle and the flute so she could pour for herself. As she poured, I grabbed the elastic of her tight black skirt and peeled it down past her knees. She then stepped out of it with a dancer's hop and a performer's smile. She was wearing underwear, if you can call it that. She had an amazing figure. And Bo knows figures.

'Beautiful Girl with a Handful,' I joked, referring to her inability to protect herself from the undressing. It was some kind of mock newspaper headline.

She giggled. 'Wow,' she said. And Giles, seated on the couch, a smile that was half joy, half disbelief streaking across his face. He loosened his tie.

You could see **Every Little Bit**'s blondies through the minuscule black lace panties. I sent a series of kitten kisses up her leg as she took a long draw of champagne. We both giggled.

Then I tugged her panties down and they gave way. All the way to the carpet, in fact. She stepped out of them like she knew what she was doing. She had nicely painted toes that resembled rubies in a row.

'An hour ago I hadn't even met you, and now you're seeing my pussy,' she said provocatively to Giles.

Giles by now had a handle on himself. He was very excited.

I took **Every Little Bit** by the hand and guided her over to where Giles was seated. She lowered herself to her knees.

'The carpet's so soft,' she noted.

I stood behind her, palming her busty chest with both hands over her tight spandex top. I then peeled it up. She didn't have a bra on. Full breasts with ten-pence nipples released and hung invitingly before him.

Every Little Bit unzipped him and unearthed his member and extended it through the hole of his pants. She then took another mouthful of champagne. Without swallowing, she bent low and took him whole. His eyes nearly rolled back into the street. And when I dipped low behind her and began to kiss her, they did.

Giles didn't say much that afternoon. Until we all woke up in bed together three hours later. Then got dressed. And then launched an attack on Madison Avenue. I got two dresses and two pair of Manolo

Blahnik shoes. I also put myself on a waiting list at Hermès for a Kelly bag. **Every Little Bit Helps** got the latest, just-arrived lingerie at La Perla, a suit at Gucci, and superior toiletries. And Giles, of course, got a seat wherever we shopped. He was over seventy, don't forget. Then we went back to the Lowell and discovered just a little bit more about one another.

It was sweet, he was happy, we were very happy, and it was Saturday. The way Sugar Daddy Saturdays ought to be.

Bo knows Saturdays too.

three-way dreams

Let's get one thing straight. I'm not a grazer. Not that I have any problems with it. I feel people should express themselves sexually however they wish. But to me, lesbian sex just is not the kind of sex I grew up on or with or derive my utmost pleasure from. But in the nineties, sexual mores have changed. It has become fashionable for women to engage in same-sex sexuality. It has sent the ripple effect through society. Even the uptight roamers on Madison Avenue were doing it. I called the era Lesbian Chic, or someone did anyway. It is a marked cultural departure. And not surprisingly, requests for the Three-Way had been pouring in on Tour all year long. As a Digger, you have to adapt. For this reason I duly added it to my repertoire. It was purely a business decision.

Beyond just keeping up with the cultural rat race, the Three-Way scenario became a great ploy that translated into raw dollars. I can't tell you how important it is to give a Walletman the feeling that there was always the possibility of engaging in a little Three-Way. *Eventually.* It would make him all the more interested and generous along the way. I would never act on it immediately, of course. It was a teaser. I would string him along with Three-Way Dreams. Eventually, however, I'd have to make good on the promise.

How did I do it? I'd get a girl whose company I enjoyed, like **Every Little Bit Helps**, **Show Me You Mean It**, a brunette stunner, or the **Three-Minute Princess**, a strawberry-blond girl with a grapefruit-tree body. I'm sure you can guess what the **Three-Minute Princess** excelled at. I would simply tell them I needed help in a little smoocherella. One would be onboard in no time. After all, men getting Three-Way are very generous. Of course, if one of them needed me, I would oblige as well – provided, obviously, the fat cat was no fat-cat rat and had a pleasant record of generosity. During the act or acts, we would giggle and laugh and joke and pretend we absolutely loved it. And show like we were really getting off. But really we'd be faking it all the way. Believe it or not, we always felt a little bit embarrassed no matter how many times we engaged in it. Some of the girls truly were grazers and did enjoy it, but it's like everything else, either you do or you don't. It wasn't my thing. It was fun, though. And very profitable. The most profitable.

Before I proceed any further, I want you to know there are two types of Diggers: those who want the immediate full conjugal union, meaning marriage, and those who have an abundance of men and strategically alternate them for the quick cash-and-carry payoffs. But age dictates this as well. When you're just starting out, the quick hits can be more attractive, as you've just stepped out of your teens and you want to live a little. You travel the world with no worries. It can be very exciting.

It depends on the girl too, however. She may just have it set in her mind to marry now and marry rich. She may not want to play around. Whichever, if the right fat cat comes along with the right offer, I don't care what type you are, you'll sign on. It's what I would consider smart behavior. Take it now. Don't wait. Because those last few years of the Ten-Year Window can be pretty hard and pretty desperate ones. Ones you may never recover from.

napoleon

I live in a cute two-bedroom apartment on the thirty-fourth floor of Trump Tower. My rent is $4,800 a month. At least that's what the lease says. In actuality, it is paid for by – none other than Giles Hamilton. He's a good friend of Donald Trump's and he bought the apartment in the early eighties. So, you see, after a full summer of my galavanting around on the circuit, Giles had good reason to want to see me.

It's quite a nice arrangement, actually. All I have to do is take care of Giles whenever he's in town. Or any of his business associates. It's not a hooker thing. His associates will just call to take me out on dates. And then I decide if (a) they are generous and (b) I like them enough to go to bed with them. And they always are. Generous, that is. All his friends are rich, of course, so that's not an issue. I've only gone to bed with one of them, but I can't remember if we did it or just played around. I do remember he was married and had no tots.

My apartment has a great view. And mirrors everywhere. Trump had put them in to give an apartment like mine a further sense of space. I kept them there to give any guest a further sense of immortality.

It was late September and I was asphalt-jungle red. The month had been pretty active so far. I had enough Walletmen on my current roster to go twelve days without a repeat. But I didn't work it that way. I would go in two- or three-day intervals. But I was busy pretty much every night of the week. When I got a little tired, or when I wasn't sustaining any good moods, I'd take a day or two off.

Like that morning. I was lying in bed watching *Regis and Kathie Lee* and putting a few thoughts to my previous evening. *Some men are so weird* was the gist.

Napoleon came running in and hopped on my bed. I lifted the comforter and let him tuck his feet inside. We spooned for the rest of the show. Yes, Napoleon was gay and still is. He was wearing boxers with Jason Priestley heads on them.

'Tell me about last night,' he said excitedly.

'I was with the Senator,' I said.

'The one who's into pain and humiliation?'

'Is there any other?'

'Do tell, *s'il tu plaît.*'

Napoleon loved my stories.

'He's so hard to figure. We drive around in the limo and I tell him what a loser he is, and then I whap and spank him for a while. And he loves it,' I cued up.

'*He really loves it!*' we both sent out in chorus. It was our Sally Field Oscar-acceptance-speech cheer.

'Doesn't he want to have sex?'

'Sometimes. But for the most part, he just wants to

be degraded. After the circle around town, we went to the Vault.'

'On the West Side Highway?'

'Yeah.'

'What did he do?'

'Well, I dragged him around on a leash and he stayed behind me crawling like a little poodle. He had to obey my orders.'

'Is he generous?'

'Is that a serious question?'

'Are you going to see him again tonight?'

'No. He's traveling. We're going to meet in Greenwich next month.'

I know you're wondering who Napoleon is. Napoleon Dieudonne is the love of my life. This is not to say we were lovers. That would never have happened. Napoleon is my best friend and confidant. He is also my father, my mother, my brother, my sister, and my shrink all wrapped into one five-foot-six-inch frame. Which is to say he is my family. These millennium days, you take family wherever you can.

Napoleon is half French, thirty years old, and an aspiring psychologist or psychiatrist, I'm not really sure which. But he was studying at New York University. He paid for his schooling by being a hairstylist on television-commercial shoots. He's great with hair. He was schooled in France and came to the States after dropping out of university. He's very sexy, and when he's speaking English, his French accent just kills you.

Napoleon had had a rough childhood like me, even though we came from entirely different backgrounds.

He was from a wealthy Palm Beach family – the Merriweathers. That may not sound rough, but it was. His father, Townsend Merriweather, inherited big railroad bucks and married a French socialite named Estelle Dieudonne from Brittany, and they live in one of those huge Ocean Boulevard houses right near the Estée Lauder compound. They do the European social circuit as well as ride the Double ET, the Eastern Establishment triangle – Greenwich, Palm Beach, and Southampton.

Sadly, Napoleon had been cut off financially by his father because of, if you can believe it, his homosexuality. The father is a wretched man. I think Napoleon's mother had offered to help him from time to time, but Napoleon was too proud. Though I advised him to play the game, he wouldn't listen. I respected Napoleon immensely, however, for his stance.

His sister is a preppy little thing named, of all things, Go Go. I swear. She goes to the University of Virginia. And she didn't send him a dime either. Yes, Napoleon kept his mother's maiden name, Dieudonne. It means 'God-given.' I loved the sound of it. Besides, he thought being gay and having the name Merriweather would be overdoing it.

digger with a logo

A couple of years back, Napoleon had been barely squeaking by, so I gave him my apartment while I was away on Tour. It became a permanent thing. In case you're wondering, it's the reason Giles and I cavorted in hotels. I would always tell him I was redecorating and the place was a mess, or my mother was in town, which was a more sizable fib because she lives in Ohio and is incapacitated. But Larry, the manager at Trump Tower, had become my pal, as I'd fixed it that he'd never say a word. I had gotten him a night with **Ellen B. Generous**. She'd owed me one and therefore did the deed. Apparently, she drank heavily to do it. Larry's not the most attractive guy and has a condition that is very tough on a woman – overactive sweat glands.

In any case, our housing arrangement was good for Napoleon as well as for me. Why? In those days, I was his only patient. But it's not because he couldn't get any others. It's that he felt there was more than enough to work with, with me. He didn't need anyone else. He felt the life and times were reflected through me and my life experience. He loved all the delectable stories with all the frothing and depraved psychologies. It was like having his own practice with tons of colorful clients right in his own home. Napoleon really helped me. In fact, he saved my life.

I'll never forget the day he said to me, 'You know, you're the Millennium Girl.'

'What's that?' I asked, a little skeptical. You know, it didn't sound so wonderful. What I was doing didn't seem nearly as triumphant as the 'Millennium Girl' sounded.

'You're the woman uniquely qualified to handle life in America at Century's End.' See? That's his term, *Century's End*, too. Or so he thought. I knew it was the title of a Donald Fagen song. But I didn't ever tell him. In any case, I liked the term. I used it with fat cats. It made me sound as though I had a sociological handle on things.

'Is that good?' I asked at the time.

'I don't know if it's good. But it's pretty cool.'

He even bought me a stack of personal calling cards with THE MILLENNIUM GIRL: BY APPOINTMENT ONLY printed on them. And a nice logo he designed himself with my favorite evening color scheme – black with a touch of gold. Gold represents getting everything you've always wanted. And black symbolizes the color of night, the time of day when you seal the deal and get it. I was a Digger with a Logo. It sounded pretty turn-of-the-century to me.

'You go where Holly Golightly feared to tread,' he always said.

Napoleon was the one who had urged me to tell my

life story, my full story. He made me write it down. It's
what you're reading. I'm sorry my Reminiscence is
structured haphazardly. That's what we call my story.
My Reminiscence. I guess you could say it's part diary,
part spontaneous ramblings, and part chronicled history.
Anyway, you know when you're telling a story and you
just have too much to tell? You say things like *meanwhile,
at the same time, nevertheless,* and *oh yeah, I forgot this part.*
I wrote things down as I remembered them. There is no
great order. And I repeat. It is a patchwork-quilt-style
presentation, and for that I apologize. But in the end,
you'll have the full story. And then you can judge its
significance for yourself. Or don't. But please, bear with
me.

Oh, and by the way, whenever I wrote, I always used
red pen. And I bought pens by the box. I used Flairs,
ballpoints, razor points, Magic Markers. All in that one
color. Red. It wasn't because it was a sexy color, or fiery,
or the color of lipstick or passion or cherries. The fact is,
if you glare long enough at red, when you look away
you see its primary opposite, green. I wanted to see
green as much as possible. On a daily basis. Yes, I was
that focused.

Anyhow, Napoleon felt that I had to get my story off
my chest if I wanted to move forward and get on with
my life. To 'evolve,' as he put it. It was therapy. And
doing it as I have done, it has been very therapeutic.
There's no doubt I'd seen the need to move forward. As
a woman, if you're not moving forward, you're actually
moving backward, even if you're standing still. Because
you're not getting any younger. Status quo is death to a

woman. Especially a single woman, with no inheritance or lottery check in sight.

Anyway, Napoleon, that's right. Here I am, rambling again. Yes, Napoleon is gay and we lived happily together in Trump Tower.

'A guy named Jasper called you.'

'Oh,' I said without enthusiasm.

'Love the name. He sounds cute.'

'He is. But that's all.' Then I told Napoleon Jasper's stats, meaning statistics. 'I told him to call me anytime. He believed me.'

'Snowman potential?'

'No.'

'Who is he?'

I told Napoleon how Jasper and I had met. That he was this Libra Rat, bleeding heart, romantic writer hopelessly in love with **Every Little Bit Helps**. And that he called me from time to time to talk about her and how she seemed 'distant' of late.

'It's always *distant*, isn't it?' Napoleon noted.

'The survey says: forty-three points. It's the People's Choice favorite. Either that or *distracted*. Or *preoccupied*.'

' "I need some space" isn't bad,' he added.

'Well, how about she just had bathtub sex with an eighty-year-old man, the one who's putting her in that nice tight Alaia he loves to see her in? *Boring*.'

'He thinks she's something she's not?'

'How about: everything she's not.'

'He couldn't think she's smart.'

'That I doubt. She may have the greatest body in town, but smart didn't get a ride. God, we're being deliciously bitchy this morning. Seen John?'

'Don't ask.'

'Please, tell me, tell me.'

Like Jasper, Napoleon was hopelessly in love. Unfortunately, it was with a very hetero rascal named John Summers. John had grown up in the Midwest somewhere. I didn't really like him. He was an account executive for an advertising agency in New York and was pretty much the definition of the young, shallow, urban womanizer the nineties and any other decade since cities began have been known for. I mean, rural America has womanizers too. But they are nothing like the city breed, where the psychologies are more jaded and the ruses more complex. Besides, in the city there are so many places to hide. I guess that goes for Diggers too.

Obviously, I'd never date a guy like him. Those types don't have to get generous for it. Not yet anyway. But it's not that. I just didn't like him. He wasn't a good spirit, meaning he wasn't a good person. From what I'd heard, he was all take and no give.

I'd never met him but I'd heard all the stories. I'd seen his picture too. Of course, Napoleon had his photo. Believe it or not, Napoleon had followed John, unbeknownst to him, to Orlando one weekend. He toured Disney World with him from thirty paces away. When they went on the Splash Mountain ride, Napoleon got the gimmicky Disney photo – you know, the action group photo of the big logframe boat as it falls perilously down that descent. Napoleon was sitting two rows behind John. It was actually a cute shot. I hadn't considered the trip stalking, but it was close. And sweet. That's how I saw it. Napoleon would never have hurt John. He'd have died if John had ever known of his galactic crush on him.

There was some family scandal involved with John too. You see, Napoleon originally heard of him through his sister, Go Go, whom John had slept with. In fact, John had been Go Go's first guy ever. And after that one-night stint, he dumped her flat. He handled it so poorly, and ever since, Mr Merriweather has wanted to kill shallow John. Anyhow, Go Go later told Napoleon some of John's intimate details – the fact that John was well endowed, for starters. Wildly so. He was legendary. It had made even me a little more interested in him. But not by much. That was not enough. It never had been.

That's when it all started heating up for Napoleon. Every time I saw him, he gave me dour John updates. 'I saw him at Indochine with the flavor du jour.'

'Ms **Cherry for Your Thoughts**?'

I could only sigh. 'Bo, when is he going to go snowman?' he droned.

Let me explain. A snowman was Napoleon's sweet term for a gay guy. I liked it and we used it often. It's a nice way of putting it, I think, and it stays under the radar from all the politically incorrect freaks who think you want to bash their choice of sexual preference. No one knew what a snowman was. It comes from all those holiday snowmen you've seen all your lives in store windows, on front lawns, and on Christmas cards. You know, the ones with the coal eyes, the carrot nose, and the sickly sweet curve of a mouth that just looks so gay.

Anyhow, Napoleon could talk publicly on the subject with impunity. He'd say things like 'There's a snowman over left' or 'Do you know the forecast? It calls for snow' or just a simple 'Bundle up.' It would all indicate there was a snowman nearby. Because, let's face it, Napoleon was sadly single and, therefore, constantly on snowman alert, searching for his true love. I loved Napoleon. He was my best friend in the world.

'You think I should let John know?' Napoleon asked.

'About your crush on him?'

Napoleon would say silly things like that to scare himself. To just propose the juiciness of the idea. It made him tingle. Me too. Normally, I indulged him. But not in this case. 'No way.'

'Why not?'

'He's your classic homophobe. He'd see you as a spotty rash from then on.'

'But maybe it'll give me some closure.'

'You want closure?'

Then he smiled wide. And kicked his legs up in the air – kind of like he was running upside down. 'Oooooooooooooh,' he said with a squirm, no doubt intoxicated by imagining the charged, dramatic event. And other ones too, I'm sure. In case it's hazy, Napoleon loved drama.

Like I said, I loved Napoleon. How could you not?

'Want to go shopping?' I proposed.

'Love. For who?'

'My niece.'

'You mean us.'

'Of course I mean *us*. . . .'

the three-minute princess

The **Three-Minute Princess** called in very upset. I'd known **Three Minutes** for a couple of years. She was a sugar sweet from Pensacola, Florida. A Miami Walletman had introduced us at a polo match in Palm Beach. I liked the **Three-Minute Princess**. I considered her a friend. She took care of me after I'd had a corrected pregnancy from some Master of the String-Along. Masters of the String-Along are the worst, by the way. You know the type – claims to love children, wants to meet your parents, then when you get pregnant, he manipulates you into not having the kid, and then you find out he's made half a dozen girls have abortions before you.

Anyhow, **Three Minutes** had nursed me through it by taking me down to her native Florida Panhandle town. So I tried to help her out whenever I could.

'Where are you?' I asked.

'Los Angeles.'

Already I knew what was coming, just based upon her choice of town. 'How's it going?'

'Not well.'

'Are you broke?'

'Just about.'

'What's wrong?'

'I don't know. It's not working out.'

And I employed a suspicious tone. '**Three Minutes**, are you being smart?'

'Each guy I meet is a dead end. They just want sex after dinner.'

You see, it wasn't that the **Three-Minute Princess** wasn't bright, she was . . . she just was short of common sense. There's a big difference. She'd get money guys but would always lose them. They'd dump her after a few rolls. Or she'd get no-bank hucksters who would use her. The reality is, she wasn't playing The Game right. And The Game is based purely on common sense.

'Have you been following the Checklist?'

'I try to, yeah. But sometimes it doesn't apply. These guys are used to getting what they want. It's girls, girls, girls out here. Everywhere I go. And a lot are prettier than me. And if you don't put out, well . . .'

'That's L.A. It's very competitive.'

It's precisely why I stayed away from it. Don't get me wrong. Los Angeles is a money town. It had beaucoup entertainment bucks. But it's also a Sex for Less town. A lot of guys who are holding out there don't want to pay for it – to the extent that it's worth it or not at all! – because there are just too many women to choose from. You have aspiring actresses and models in addition to the hooks and Diggers like us. They're all vying for the same men. And if a girl is going for the fame-celebrity thing, she'll give up the sex for less, or free. It forces you to work that much harder. And that's if you're really in the circle of legitimate Walletmen.

Los Angeles is a tricky place too. It's a con-artist town and always has been. Often guys give the impression of wealth when they don't have a pot to piss in. There's no doubt about it. Los Angeles and New York are our two financial centers, but New York has always been more up-front with its bucks. In New York if a guy is really holding, you know about it. It's written in the papers and it rolls off tongues. In Los Angeles you never really know what you're getting unless you give the Walletman the full Checklist press.

'Did you dump that music-business guy, I hope?'

'No. He's still in the picture. The little picture.'

'How little?'

'Well, we had sex a few times.'

'Was he generous?'

'No. He took me to an awards show, though.'

And I got miffed. And not because I was, because I wasn't. She was just another No-Daddy Kid who needed to be scolded for anything to sink in. 'Hey, **Three Minutes**,' I said. 'Get real!'

'But—'

'Zip it! You can't work it that way.'

Then she got quiet. Real quiet. Until I heard her begin to sob. I let her for half a minute or so.

'What happened, honey?' I asked eventually.

'He dumped me.'

'He dumped you?'

'Didn't you get him hooked on you emotionally?'

'Obviously not.' And she was crying now.

You see, that is the secret to successful gold digging. You must get the guy involved with you on an emotional level. Or you're just another sex object with no leverage. You need leverage. And that comes in the form of an emotional tie, as deep as you can get it. Along the lines of a whale harpoon buried in his chest.

'Oh, baby. Are you in love with him?'

'Y-y-yes.'

I truly felt sorry for the **Three-Minute Princess**. She just wasn't getting it right.

'Baby, calm down. It's all going to work out. Are you okay?'

'I'm okay,' she said, and blew her nose into a handkerchief.

'Now wipe your nose. Did you wipe it?'

'Uh-huh.'

'Now listen. You cannot get involved emotionally with these guys the way you do. You have to get *him* hooked emotionally. Or you're dead. He'll never get generous if you give up the ghost like that. Never give of yourself like that – all the sex as well as your heart. He'll dump you flat every time. Is he American?'

'Uh-huh.'

'American men *especially*. But most men too. Are you listening, baby?'

'Uh-huh.'

'Don't uh-huh. Get out of the sandbox.'

'Okay,' she whimpered.

'Men are not getting married these days. Right?'

'Right.'

That is true. The statistics are pretty bleak. Older men

aren't hitching up the way they used to. Usually they've already been married once, have had kids already, and have paid out a big settlement. They don't want to do it again. And young men have been waiting longer and longer to hitch up. And young men have never been as generous as older men anyway. And usually not as rich. These are things I learned in the field – in America and abroad.

'So you have to get what you can, while you can. Right?'

'Right.'

'And to do that, no emotions.'

'No emotions,' she repeated.

'Remember the rule I taught you?'

'Yes.'

'What is it?'

'*It's not who you know, it's who you blow.*'

'No!' I cried out. '*As soon as you start to feel, take a plane.*'

'Oh, right.'

'And what does that mean?'

'If I start falling in love with a guy, take off for a while.'

'Until when?'

'Until the feeling goes away.

'That way, you'll tug on his emotional strings, you'll keep the power over him, he'll still want you, and he'll be more generous on top of it. And if you're lucky, it'll last a year or two. It's like an athlete's contract. That's what you're looking for. And it only comes from an emotional bond. And it prevents you from putting all your eggs in one basket and letting him steal away the peak years of your life.'

She blew her nose again. 'I don't know, Bo. Maybe I'm just too sensitive for this stuff.'

'Hey, **Three Minutes**. Snap out of it! If you're too sensitive, you've got to show tough. Or get out. It's the only way. Make them pay for it. You deserve it. And always have backup. Do you have backup?'

'Well . . .'

'Did you meet his wealthy friends?'

'Yeah, there are a couple of guys I like.'

'How old?'

'One is about forty-five.'

'Is he generous?'

'Well, he hasn't given me a lot of money. But we've gone out a lot.'

'Dinner is nothing – zilch.'

'I know. But he bought me some shoes on Rodeo.'

'Shoes . . .'

'And we're going places.'

'Where?'

'Well, we're going to Gstaad.'

'Great. When?'

'Next week –'

'October? Are you crazy?'

'What's wrong with that? We had a great time in St Tropez.'

'When was that?'

'April.'

'So let me get this right. He goes to St Tropez in April and Gstaad in October. You know who this guy is?'

'Yeah. Maurice.'

'No. He's Low-Season Boy. The kind of guy who goes to hot spots when they're not hot. When the towns are dead and hotel rates are cut in half. It's like a two-for-one vacation, most likely paid for by his company. And you got one pair of shoes, and he got near-free sex with you for two weeks. Next he'll take you to Aspen in July.'

'He doesn't go to Aspen. He doesn't like it.'

'Where does he go?'

'He goes to Breckenridge.'

'Naturally,' I groaned. 'It's fifty percent cheaper.'

'Hey, Bo, don't be so hard on me. It was the only time he could go to Gstaad.'

'It's *Gstaad*. You pronounce the *g*. Why?'

'Just 'cause.'

'Tell me.'

She hesitated. 'No.'

'**Three Minutes**, tell me.'

And she sighed. She knew I wouldn't like the answer. 'He's going through a divorce.'

This was disturbing. '**Three Minutes**. What are you doing?'

'Don't yell at me!'

I calmed myself. But it was so frustrating.

'Honey, haven't you listened to anything I've told you? If he's about to go through a divorce settlement, where is the money going to be for you?' And I had to groan again.

'I'm really trying, Bo. Really. But it's hard out here.'

'I know. What about the other guy?'

'Well, he has his own company.'

'Did you visit it?'

'Yes. It's big.'

'What about his house?'

'He lives in a condo.'

It was painful. I couldn't listen anymore. The reasoning here is a close cousin to the guy getting divorced. Obviously, if he's living in a condo, he's put all his money into his new company – and again, where's the money for you? I'd had enough. The **Three-Minute Princess** was just not getting it. So . . .

'I've got to go.'

'Bo, where are you going?'

'Keep an eye on your mailbox,' I shot back and hung up.

I decided to send the **Three-Minute Princess** a plane ticket. But not to New York. She wasn't playing The Game right, and New York was a professional Digger's town. She needed some training. So where did I send her? London, of course. It was where I'd trained. It's not that the things needed to be learned weren't right here in the good old US of A, but the great advantage of England was, they spoke the same language and, more important, nobody had any tabs on you. You could operate under the Reputation Radar and make all your mistakes overseas and nobody would learn about them. Because, don't forget, reputation is everything for a Digger. Once someone gets a whiff of the fact that you're in search of the Green, the news passes like the flu in the R train. Fast.

In England, the **Three-Minute Princess** could

reinvent herself in an environment that had some good ideas on education and had elements of sophistication, as well as the privacy aspects. All this would make her stock price rise. She'd be more worldy and, I hoped, more savvy. So when she came to America, she'd be new, fresh, gorgeous blood. As well as prepared. The **Three-Minute Princess** needed all that if she was going to succeed.

walletman city

If a girl is going to make Digging a serious business, if she wants a nest of Walletmen from which to choose – or she wants to hit that one home run with one guy – there are a few simple rules she must adhere to. First, she has to know where to go. The big international business cities are the best. Paris, London, Hong Kong, New York. This is where the Western world's richest men flock. So, follow the Green.

As I said before, in America the best cities are New York and Los Angeles. Again, it's where most of the country's wealthy men live. I chose New York over Los Angeles because I found New York Walletmen to be a more dependable group. The L.A. Walletmen have more of a playboy flair. I consider L.A. to be like one big playpen filled with men who have never grown up. They just want to extend their childhoods as long as possible. This is not to say you couldn't hit the mother lode in Los Angeles, but these are the sweeping trends I've seen and you would do yourself a favor to heed the demographics.

In addition, there's better class of girl in New York.

They're usually more sophisticated. And the men expect them to be. Out-and-out tarts get laughed at in New York. In L.A. they're received warmly. That's the way I saw it, anyhow.

By the way, if you're wondering why I employ English terms like *tarts*, it is because of my foreign-study years in London. But more on them later.

Once you've chosen one of the Digger capitals, then you must be dressed for the role. You have to look rich, to sound rich, to seem as if you are rich, and to know rich – so that you can blend in seamlessly and effortlessly with the rich. Let's not forget that these men are not stupid people, for the most part. Or they wouldn't have made all that money. Or inherited it and held on to it. And if they've lost it, it's a no-brainer – you're not hanging around with them anyway.

Clothes are very important. It is imperative for a Digger to dress the part. There are clothes for wives and clothes for mistresses. You have to have clothes from the 'mistress' shops. By mistress shops I mean the reigning top designers of oven-mitt-hot, sexy clothes. We're talking Gucci, Prada, Helmut Lang, Dolce & Gabbana, Rifat Ozbek, Alaia, etc. You want classic but sexy. The wives tend to go for just plain classic. They've already landed their man, after all, and had a kid or two with him. They don't need to flaunt. Unless they're trying to spark up an affair. So they shop at Bergdorf's and Saks and wear Bill Blass, Carolina Herrera, Oscar de la Renta, Valentino for the small-boned, Scaasi, Ralph Lauren – the more safe and boring attire. For their feet it's Ferragamo across the board and Helene Arpels.

Again, the mistresses are a bit more daring with Manolo Blahnik and Patrick Cox and the occasional Jourdan.

Don't worry about lingerie. Whether La Perla or Victoria's Secret or Frederick's of Hollywood or the Pleasure Chest, it all works. Guys will not complain. Classless lingerie is like classless fellatio. At this point of intimacy, who cares? In fact, some of the sleazier stuff can be a real hit. It really depends on the individual taste of the Walletman. Overall, it's safe to start with the expensive stuff, and dress down from there.

I know it's very fashionable to mix lesser labels (as in thrift-shop finds) with designer clothes, but I had had so many shabby castoffs in my youth that I just couldn't bear to go back to that. I mean, I almost died when two classmates saw my mother having me try on a dress in the window of the Salvation Army in nearby Kopple. The dress was synthetic in the color of a cola Slurpee. I was teased mercilessly, of course. These days I'll stick to the fresh labels. I'm sure you understand.

Don't forget the baby shops for the best in sexy, I'm All Here, close-fitting clothing. Baby TSE for cashmere, Parker's for lingerie, and Petite Bateau for camisoles and tight-and-teeny T-shirts.

Once you've dressed the part, then you've got to find the right guy. And the right guy means one thing. Making sure he has the goods – bank. Real bank. And every country in the Western world has lists of wealthy and influential people. In America, of course, there's the Fortune 500, the Forbes 400, *Premiere* magazine's Top 100 Entertainment Executives, etc. I stay away from the moguls and entertainment guys, however, Again, they're less dependable than the East Coast big-business guys.

Your primary sources of information on this, believe it or not, are readily available. You can look up any company on the Internet and find out what business the men are involved in, what the company's earnings are, and who the other heavies at the company are. And it's not only CEOs. Presidents are welcomed too.

Once you've targeted your Walletman or -men, then you find out what places he likes to frequent – where he likes to have drinks, dinner, where he works out, if at all. Anything. Find out whatever you can on the personal side. It takes time, and patience is definitely a virtue. Remember: you're in it for the long run. So don't blow it with ill-conceived ruses, stupid entrances, and botched meetings. Be smart.

Your Digger pals can help too. They also can try to screw you. Most do. But sometimes you can get an introduction. Or use a Walletman on your active roster to meet others. That is the best way to get to know someone you've been targeting. Introductions. And once you're introduced, you're golden. You've already studied up on him and can work the conversation to your favor. Don't let him know you know much about him. A crucial mistake. A good Walletman can sniff out a Digger easily. Remember, rich men are like beautiful women. They get overtures all the time.

All I'm saying is, you shouldn't have a problem communicating with your target. You can talk business with him if he's the type who enjoys it. Or you can stick to lighter fare – brainless stuff like movies and sex. After all, many Walletmen after a long workday or work week just want to relax. They don't want to be challenged or forced to talk business. So read and react.

Then you use your sexuality like a stringed instrument. You've got the womanly thing – the curves, the lips, the body. After two martinis, they'll most certainly want to have sex. So play with it. Give it up or don't depending on the guy and depending on what you want out of him. If you're looking to get married, don't give up the ghost. Not yet. But for the long-term, nonexclusive arrangement, once you've started doing it, and he's not a playboy, as your research has made sure of, you're on your way. All you have to do is have enough sex with him to get him emotionally attached, and you're in for a series of big, generous paydays. And if you're smart, you'll save. For that day when you decide you want to change your strategy and link up for good.

by way of the rich

The absolute best way to land a Walletman is to infiltrate his private circles. To do this, you must target the exclusive communities. Some preferred Eastern Establishment communities are Greenwich, Connecticut; Bedford, New York; East Hampton, Long Island; Palm Beach, Florida. Out West, it's Beverly Hills, Bel-Air, Pacific Palisades, Newport Beach, La Jolla, etc. Every state and city has its upper-crust communities. But New York and California have their upper-upper.

In the cities, you have to frequent the nicest hotels and restaurants. You've got to be in close proximity to the business world. You can't be support staff like a secretary or a gofer. That goes for leisure time too. Even more so. You have to play on his playing fields and playgrounds. You can't just play in a nightclub.

If it's the Old Guard, meaning old-money families you're targeting, get invited to their country clubs. Take up skiing, golf, and the racquet sports – tennis, squash, paddle tennis. The gambling games are good to know too. Backgammon, baccarat, blackjack, poker, and bridge if he's really old.

Even more selectively, learn to ride a good horse. You can learn to play polo or foxhunt. **Travels With Men** is well on her way to landing the fat-cat man of her dreams because she successfully infiltrated the foxhunting circuit in Pennsylvania. She became adopted by them. She altered her Walletman's mind-set by sleeping with one of his friends when he was 'insensitive' to her, and it was just enough to get her fat cat to give up the kitty. She's got the rock already. They're expecting too. **Travels** was really good.

Personally, I'm scared of horses.

But not all Diggers have the talent for this. Yes, it's Darwinian with Diggers too. The really successful ones usually have some form of empowerment already. They've attended the right colleges, or they once did have money but now it's all gone. These types hold an advantage. They know the world already. But make no mistake, they're digging, just like the rest of us.

The point is, the more you can act, or at least appear, rich and to the manner born, the more chance you have at landing the dashing single Walletman Son who's been getting family pressure all his life to marry his own kind. It's drilled into these guys' heads from early on – often by suspicious ex-Digger Mothers. You know the types – the ones who clawed and maneuvered and dished it out on a platter through their twenties and eventually landed the big kahuna and, ever since, have been overly wary of every other girl's intentions toward their sons, while sweetly and conveniently forgetting their own rocky climb. Digger Mothers are very adept at sniffing out other Diggers. It's as though they have night goggles for the breed. After all, they see the Digger in themselves. And they don't necessarily like what they see. If they're this type, they are the ultimate obstacle. Beware of Digger Mothers.

Stay with your own kind is the formula the Walletmen parents give to their offspring. So, the Walletman Son is conditioned to look for his own kind, in the nicest possible, pretty, and presentable package. This is where all your hopeful education and any adopted and mimicked breeding can come into play.

walletman checklist

If you're not talented enough to be able to go the way of the rich, you have to take the more pedestrian approach. And to target, you have to know the public places frequented by affluent society – the bars, hotels, and restaurants. It's not difficult. Even cabbies could tell you in most towns. They know where their grudge flashpoints lie.

How do you know if a guy is holding? There are some very simple ways to check out a guy. It is imperative to do so. It saves time. Otherwise, you end up wasting valuable hours of those precious Window years on guys who are cut-rate, five-figure con men. Many guys try to fake big-time wealth to score the quick roll in the hay, and it's as easy to spot as a bad nose job.

First of all, you start with the watch. Bulgari, Cartier, and gold Rolexes. Any guy with a Timex, Swiss Army brand, the kind Jasper the writer had – forget it. Granted, having one of these items can be deceiving. A guy could have inherited a nice one. Or spent all his money on one. But as it goes for the rest of the list requirements, you must put the guy through the full Checklist. If he survives the full test, there's a good chance he's the real thing and you're going to want to date him. Then you use subtle psychological ruses to decipher real bank potential and his all-important generosity index.

After the watch, it's the shoes. Gucci, Bally, Magli, Crisci, Armani, bust.

Next, the business card. If they don't have a business card, or it's flimsy, meaning simple two-toned black-and-white, see ya. Anybody can get a black-and-white card at any cheap place. Business cards have to be multicolored, or have at least two colors, and a decent logo. Not something generic like a hooked fish or a sunset. If he's got money, he'll pay for his own memorable design for his company.

On the business card, the potential Walletman must be listed as chief operating officer, CEO, or at least president. No vice presidents, because there're thousands of them. If you're going to go the route of the VP, you might as well just order a beer at a happy-hour bar and wait for random passers-by. Or a pub in London. Pubs have the cheapest men.

Yet if a guy has a card with just his name on it, a calling card, that's a good sign. He doesn't need to give you a number – because everybody knows him, knows what company he runs or owns, and he can easily be contacted. He won't even write his number on the back. Receiving the calling card is an invitation to call him, and you'll know where to do so. An oversize, multi-colored business card is the best.

Fourth is the suit. It has to be Armani. Or Bijan if he's Arab. No Versace or Hugo Boss. And don't be deceived by the tie. Because many nickel-and-dimers will buy an expensive Versace, Chanel, or Hermès tie and make the suit look expensive. Having said that, Chanel ties are great. A man with a Chanel tie, that says something about him. Because most men don't even know they make ties. But they do. And they're beautiful. Forget Hermès. Every thin-wallet Wall Street hack has learned in the first three months of his training program that Hermès ties are the sophisticated standard, which has made them overworn, obsolete, and unsophisticated. It means nothing. It means a corner long dog with kraut. Their H belts too. Hermès is out.

This is not to say there are not some world-class bank folk who wear Hermès. In America, the WASPy club types have been wearing Hermès ties for years. But the WASP phenomenon is a little tricky, especially with the really wealthy old families. Old money plays money down. Like those club members in New York, for instance – the University Club, the Racquet Club, and the Brook Club in the city, the Piping Rock Club on the Island, and the Maidstone Club and the Meadow Club in the Hamptons. And sometimes old money is all gone, in which case they're just riding a name. Even if the old money is still there, often they're downright cheap. So beware of the wealthy WASP.

But that's where your research comes in. You'll know who the big-bank heavies of the Old Guard are from your study of New York's society registers, charity committees, etc. Ditto for other cities and towns.

Let me make this clear. Landing a fat cat is not a lot of guesswork born of hazy pipe-dream theories. It is a science. Gold digging has rules and parameters and laws and counterlaws. To make it happen, you have to be on top of it. You have to be informed. That means reading the monthly business periodicals, studying the all-significant lists – the Fortune 500, the Forbes 400 – as well as the daily gossip columns and society pages. I knew the lists by heart, for the most part.

This all means getting yourself a laptop and taking notes. That's if you want to do this right. It's just like a business – knowing who your customers are, where to find them, how to approach them, how to advertise your product, how to get them to pay for your product as opposed to that of the competition – and crush the competition along the way.

Fifth – and this is so important – when you call the number on the business card, a secretary must answer. No voice mail. And you have to be careful. Always inquire delicately. Certainly say you're someone else. Especially if it's his main secretary. And if the secretary is mean, all the better. Attitude comes from the feeling of power that being the point guy or gal for a financial heavyweight brings. When I make contact with a flaming bitch as a secretary, I am a happy gal.

If it's the receptionist, however, you can be a bit more daring. And if you do get voice mail, check the voice mail names from A to Z to see how many people are in the company. If you live in the city where the company is located, you should visit the company and see what kind of operation it is. I mean, who knows who this guy purports to be?

Sixth, a serious Walletman must own a house or

houses, with at least five bedrooms or more. No apartments unless it's New York, and then only on the nicest avenues – Fifth, Madison, and Park Avenues above Fifty-seventh Street. It shows they're generous, at least with themselves, and that's a start.

Seventh, you have to find out who your Walletman knows and how well. To accomplish this, it serves you well to name-drop and see how he responds to the names you're mentioning. To see if they're intimidated by names like Bill Gates or if they're warm to them. Any guy who says Bill Gates is an ass, or gets weird, you know is not holding. He's jealous. I call it the Bill Gates Litmus Test. Of course, it's not exclusive to Bill Gates. It could mean any guy on the Fortune 500 list. Or whatever standard the country you're operating in uses. If a Walletman is casual at the mention of a big-bank peer, or is complimentary, then he's obviously not threatened and doesn't feel inadequate.

In addition, see how many guys he knows on the List. Drop names like Carl Icahn, Ron Perelman, and Warren Buffet. Always remember: rich people know one another.

These are obviously not laws, but they are the initial, cursory steps to finding out whether or not a Walletman is full of it or not. I'll also add, Donald Trump is not a name to drop, for obvious reasons. He's asked for and received so much publicity that he means a lot of different things to a lot of people, whether rich or bank-bust.

There is also the list of Don't Bothers. For instance, any of the reputed playboy Walletmen, stay away from.

Anyone who knows them too. Those types are a dead end. You know, the ones who give big parties at big resorts for loads of people they barely know. It's just a girl roundup. And the guys who round up are not generous. They just use and dump you. You want quiet but single or married or recently divorced or separated men. Not playboys.

Anyone who's been to a party at the Playboy Mansion, forget it. They want the quick-and-easy, one-night, hump-and-dump kind of thing.

Anyone who's ever dated a supermodel, forget it. Their standards of beauty are so out of line, it's not worth the time. Plus they're usually in it for the ego. For the name of the girl. Not because they really care about her. They're not generous either.

And never date a guy who owns a Ferrari. Never. Like model daters, they're only in it for the look. Those guys are not real. They don't have to pay for it. And they won't.

Men who date businesswomen are not good either. Because they're used to being with women who are independent. They obviously like not having to pay for her. In essence, they won't take care of you.

Obviously any guys with tattoos, forget it. They have no bank. Or bank potential.

Anyone who's dated a stripper is okay. Because strippers are real women. And a man who respects real women will respect you. They're usually pleasant guys. And generous guys. They're used to taking care of women.

Ideally, you want men who have a capacity for, or

show some vulnerability. These are the types who will get emotionally attached to you. That emotional bond is tied to the generosity index. In addition, believe it or not, when a Digger starts having sex regularly with someone, it's difficult for her not to get emotionally attached. Somewhat anyway. And if that happens, which you should not allow, but if it does, you certainly want your feelings reciprocated. Or you're in trouble.

Personally, I've been in a phase where I only date married men. It gives me my independence, I have emotional attachments with them – meaning them for me – and the generosity just flows smoothly from them *to* me.

Eight, you should find out where the Walletman has traveled. He must have traveled extensively. To Hong Kong, especially. Hong Kong is the key to real business-men. London too. And New York, of course.

Walletmen must be comfortable with the private-plane thing – they either have or have had one, or rent frequently. If a Walletman scoffs at private-plane usage – go back to the Bill Gates Litmus Test.

And when they fly, they fly first-class. Only. No exceptions. A guy who flies economy – I don't think so.

Nine, you have to see where a Walletman lives, his living space, in what town or suburb, in what section, on what street. But you have to see it during the day. At night it's not uncommon for them to be physically all over you. Though you're just doing research, he will equate your coming home with him with a consensual free flesh ride.

You also want a guy who's neat, not some joker who's

got shit everywhere. No maids, no money.

Ten, you must remember what he tells you. The specifics, the little things. And make sure he stays true to it. If you start catching him in little lies, bail. There's a reason he's lying, and you don't want to waste the time to find out why. Of course, you should be pretty well prepared on the subject of big-business heavies – the company's business, how it started as a business, where he went to college, his age roughly – so if he starts to brag, name-drop, and expound on things you know are not true, the same story. See ya.

Eleven, cars are deceiving. Mercedes, Porsches, Rolls-Royces, and Bentleys are the preferred brands and can be indicators of wealth, but they also can be a screen. Some guys will pump all their money into their cars, especially in Los Angeles.

In the end the easiest and most dependable Walletmen are the Golden Oldies, meaning the seventy-plus group – they're so appreciative, and the older they get, the more generous they get. In the younger age ranges, you have a better time of it with the guys who aren't physically gifted. They're a little overweight or not handsome. These are the guys who can't land the killer babes consistently. They can be very generous. The reasoning is, the more gifted the guy, the more he has going for him and the less generous he can afford to be.

the bill gates litmus test

It was the second week in October and I was toasted almond. My car had picked me up at noon. It had taken just over an hour to get to Greenwich. We'd charged up the Hutchinson River Parkway without much delay. The leaves were splendid. They were yellow and orange and brown and all the psychedelic versions in between. The leaves were the one thing that reminded me of my hometown in Ohio. And that was all.

It was a little overcast when we pulled into the grounds of the Greenwich Polo Club. Rain wouldn't halt play. It would just make people a little wetter. And it would turn the afternoon into a tent event. I brought my pearl-handled theater umbrella just in case. I was wearing a fall suit by Ralph and a Chanel print silk scarf.

My driver dropped me off at the courtesy booth. I gave the woman my name. She was a nice-looking WASPer with a flair cut and thin lips with little miserly wrinkles attacking them.

'Bodicea Lashley, I'm sure it's here somewhere,' she said politely. Then the tension in her face released suddenly. 'Ah, you're the guest of Senator Thayer.'

'Yes,' I said with a smile.

Though the weather was forboding, the stands were rather packed. It was the last Sunday of the polo season, and the game's winner would receive the coveted Mercedes Cup. A team called Two Pines was playing White Birch.

I gazed into the stands. There wasn't a lot of poverty there. It was a sea of Greenwich and Manhattan society. They were all dressed immaculately in designer week-ender clothes. The ladies had elegant floral dresses or suits or slacks. The men had tweed jackets, blazers, and polo shirts with turned-up collars.

I spotted **Travels With Men** and her beau. **Travels** had successfully infiltrated the horsey circuit, as I mentioned before. Now she just blended in with all the affluent color. Her guy looked pretty handsome. And he wasn't that old. I wondered when she was getting married. Or if in fact he was a Master of the String-Along. He looked like it. I watched him not watch the polo match. He was too busy scanning the crowd. He was either a social climber or a social sex freak – or both. I needed to know his star data to get a better idea. At the same time, **Travels** was a real pro. She knew what she was doing, meaning she knew not to go too long without his delivering. And she knew how to kick him around good if he wavered. She had those Marriott eyes. The kind that would book a room in the time it took to carve out a lemon twist. *What a couple* was a final thought.

I didn't see my friend, so I hesitated about venturing

into the stands. And then the rain fell and made up my mind for me. I did a quick step beneath one of the huge hospitality tents that had been erected at the side of the field. I stepped up to the bar and ordered a white wine. Then I moved back out to the edge of the tent. I watched the match from there.

I enjoyed watching polo. I loved hearing the thunderous sound of the hooves as the horses dashed up and down the field. I found it powerful. And sexy. It was a flash of greens and whites and browns and mud, and mallets hitting balls and, well – doubly sexy. Many of the players were dark and handsome Argentinians or other South American nationalities. Triply sexy. They were often hired ringers, given big contracts to play with lesser American players. They were usually playboys, however. And I stayed away from playboys. Besides, the bank they made was decent but wasn't exceptional. Now, the owners of the teams and stables – well, that was a different story.

'Are you Bo?'

'Uh, Bodicea is my name, yes.'

He was well-groomed, frosted and silvery at the temples, had a nice WASPy commuter's face, with a hairline that was holding its ground, and a spiffy tweed jacket. Not bad, I thought. It was worth a cheery smile.

'I'm William Pomeroy,' he said.

The name meant nothing to me. Not in my personal files, nor from my years of research. 'Have we met?'

'Yes. We met in London several years ago.'

'That sounds about right. I was a student there.'

Guys often claim to have met you, but really, the

truth of the matter is, they saw you from afar and wanted to meet you but never did. Or they've never even seen you at all. The way this guy was glowing, I sensed he had seen me before and had liked what he saw. As I wasn't sure, I played along. In fact, I put him to the test – the Checklist – which is always an amusing pastime. It came second nature to me by now.

I scanned William Pomeroy's wrist, but a white cuff with gold links was covering his watch.

'Do you have the time, William?'

And he jerked his wrist out and shoved back the cuff to tell me. The flash response didn't bother me. He was immediately giving, which demonstrated a lack of composure. Which usually translates to infrequent sex. It could mean he's unhappily married. I didn't see a band, however. But men often don't wear them when they're out. But I did spot a nice platinum Rolex as he told me the time.

I thanked him. 'That must have been several years ago,' I added.

I then spied his feet. He had a pair of black Guccis with a buckle atop. . . .

'It was. Ninety-four, I believe.'

'Good memory.'

'Well, I was working abroad a lot that year. I saw you a few times, actually. But even if it had been just for a quick glimpse one night, you are memorable, Bo.'

I considered that remark either the cheesy crap of an El Cheapo or he was out of practice, again meaning married or just separated. I didn't like the cheese, but the married part was, again, acceptable.

'What do you do, Mr Pomeroy?'

'Bill. Please.'

'Okay, Bill.'

Bill told me he worked for an insurance company that specialized in policies for the elderly. We chatted for a while. I sensed he was a Taurus.

'I like your jacket,' I remarked. And I felt it and let my finger drag slowly off it.

'I got it in Scotland.'

'It's beautiful.' And I meant it. I could tell that the jacket was custom-made of the finest Scottish wool. Obviously, it wasn't one of the designer labels listed earlier. But it still showed some class as well as a desire to spend.

Bill Pomeroy had made it through three items on the Checklist. Watch, shoes, jacket.

After some more chatter about his company, I asked him. 'Do you have a business card, Bill?'

He said he did, and handed it to me. We traded simple getting-to-know-you smiles.

Bill's business card was nicely presented with strong lettering that claimed he was the president of the company. It had a classy red-and-black logo. Bill was checking out.

Then I gave him the Litmus Test.

'Is your company listed on the New York Stock Exchange?'

'No. It's still privately owned.'

And his expression had an unspoken message to it that I liked. It said he owned it. I hadn't been sure before. But I liked the discretion. It showed a certain composure and sense of class. And a lack of needing to impress. Which means he was comfortable with his wealth, which means he may have had it for a while. And it was sizable enough to make him comfortable.

'It's amazing what's been happening on Wall Street,' I continued. 'The Dow?'

'Incredible. You follow the market?'

'I do. I have several investments.'

'May I ask which?'

'Two cancer-cure companies and a new one that services impotence relief.'

'The drug stocks.' He looked impressed.

'No Microsoft, though.'

'That story is amazing.'

'He's a genius, don't you think?'

'Genius.'

'Do you think they'll get nailed in all this antitrust talk?'

'I'm not sure. But Gates, well. I've always thought he was a little less than ruthless. So you never know. It comes back around sometimes.'

'Really.'

'I mean, look at all the cutting down of the competition he's responsible for. You think how many people he's put to work. But think about how many he's made go unemployed.'

And that was a check mark against Bill Pomeroy. He seemed to be praising Gates at first. But the grudge garble came soon after. We kept up the business chatter, though, and he was kinder on Icahn and Buffet and Redstone. And he truly lauded Eisner. And he told me a tale about renting several G-4s. So the results weren't entirely tallied on Bill Pomeroy yet. I wondered if **Travels With Men** knew him.

Now, I grant you, this Checklist stuff is not gospel or law or any kind of exact science. It is purely a simplistic, preliminary gauge to deduce the extent of a man's wealth. And it is not always accurate. There are many wealthy men out there with swollen egos who can't give credit to other success stories. Some are just incapable of praising others. Whether it's their kids or their wives. Everyone is a forever competitor. But if a guy has a real problem with Bill Gates or any of the other captains of industry, it's an indicator of some sort. If you combine it with other data, it could mean anything from he's broke to he has a few million. But clearly if he doesn't own or use private planes and he bristles at the mention of other business titans, it's a good indication that he is not holding big bank.

Bill Pomeroy and I shook hands. He told me to give him a call. After all, I did express an interest in an insurance policy for my mother. I wasn't really keen on one. But I'd left myself the option, for other obvious reasons.

Though I sensed he was a Taurus Rooster, I didn't try to confirm it. That would have been asking too much too fast. Sometimes I will ask at a first meeting. It depends on the situation. In the case of Bill Pomeroy, I wanted him to buzz off on his impression of me that I was familiar with the business world. That was far stronger than letting him think I had a nice ass and a nice smile and enjoyed astro talk. It gave me more respect. Certainly, I would ask him during our next encounter, provided the research I would do on him made him worthy of that next encounter. There's only so much of the Checklist you can accomplish in person. The rest is purely investigative.

Besides, that was all there was time for. I'd seen my date sidling up to the bar and looking over our way. It was a suitable time to end the discussion. I walked up to him.

'Hi, Bo.'

'Hello, Senator.'

And he kissed me like his ex-wife's fellow PTA colleague. I didn't consider his cool demeanor strange. He was in politics, remember?

Senator Owen Thayer was a tall and lean man who had a ruggedly handsome face like he'd played football in those years before they had face masks. And he had. It gave his face this cozy, weathered look like that of an old barn.

'I've been looking all over for you.'

'You found me.' And I smiled the smile he was known to appreciate.

it's all about character

We left the polo match after the third chukker. The Senator had a limousine and a driver named Mike. Once we got on the parkway, we had Mike slide down the partition that separated us from him.

'Get on your knees,' I started off with.

He did. Then I commanded him to take off his pants. He did that too.

I whacked him on his bare behind, then started in with the lowly stuff.

'You're garbage.'

'I know.'

'You're nothing. . . .' And I smacked him again. Hard. Then again, harder.

'I'm sorry. . . .'

'You're a bad man. . . .'

'I'm very bad. . . .'

'You're worse than bad. Don't you dare get up! You're not worthy of getting up. Kneel!'

'But –'

'Shut your mouth. You're nothing. Aren't you?'

'I'm nothing.'

'Louder!'

'I'm nothing!'

'And you're a piece of shit.'

'And I'm a piece of shit!'

Then I smacked him across the face. 'Shut up! You're not worthy of speaking to me. Now come over here. . . .'

'Right now?'

'Now! On your hands and knees! Crawl. Now whimper like a dog.'

He did. He was good at that. He must have had lots of pooches growing up.

'Put a paw under my dress. *And don't look at me!*'

I let myself retire against the backrest of the seat.

'That's right. Now kiss.'

When his eyes raised slightly and caught mine, I whacked him in the face, hard. 'I said, Don't look at me!' His head bowed. 'Now pull down my hose. Pull them down. And keep your eyes closed. That's right.'

And I grabbed his face in one hand, gripping him by his lower jaw and shoved his face into me.

'Now kiss it! You piece of garbage! Kiss it and love it. Say you love it!'

'I love it!'

'Tell me what a piece of trash you are!'

'I'm nothing!'

I whapped him in the face.

'I'm trash!' he adjusted.

'That's right! Now just kiss. And suck. That's right. Kiss . . . you're going to dive.'

'No!'

I smacked him.

'Don't breathe until I say so. . . .'

Then I held the back of his head with both my hands and shoved him forward. His face was planted in me.

I didn't let him take another breath for another thirty-five seconds.

'You're such a loser. . . .'

the brush

We spent the weekend at the Old Lyme Inn in Lyme, Connecticut. It was the Senator's favorite place. It was our favorite place too. It had a spa and was very discreet. We staggered our check-ins and had separate suites, of course. But we were rarely separate. We alternated rooms with great aplomb.

If you did it right, a weekend at the Inn was just about the best forty-eight hours of sex and pampering you could ever imagine. And when and if you wanted to emerge, the October foliage outside was something to behold. It was all multicolored and gorgeous. Walking through the tree line was the closest thing to an all-natural acid trip, though I've never tried the drug. It made for an uncommon surreal setting.

We took our last afternoon walk in the woods just after brunch on Sunday. We were holding hands. I was pretty sore. But it wasn't my privates that were hurting. It was my hands from all the disciplinary treatment I'd administered to him. It was funny. The Senator could romantically alternate from holding hands and hugging like we were at a county fair to taking a dark tour down degradation lane. The Senator was very versatile.

'How are you feeling, Bo?'

'No surprises. I've had a wonderful weekend.'

'Are you happy?'

I considered that to be an odd thing for the Senator to ask. He made conversational stabs into emotional states only when he was feeling a little overworked. And though our two days were demanding, it wasn't exactly high stress and toil. My flash analysis indicated something else was afoot.

'No more than usual. And no less. Why?'

'Are you planning to get married?'

'Eventually.'

We walked onward.

'Don't tell me you're going to propose to me,' I said in jest.

Just then the Senator stopped in his tracks. And he looked down at his shoe. A yellow leaf had stuck to the toe. He scraped it away with his other shoe.

'I can't see you anymore,' he said.

I'll never forget that leaf. It's imprinted for ever on my psyche. Not because the news was so dramatic. I had never been in love with the Senator. Nor did I think we'd be in each other's lives for as long as we were. After all, a Ten-year Window year is like five normal years.

That leaf. It was just one of those quirky things. The leaf, then the delivery of news.

'Oh?'

'I'm sorry. Are you surprised?'

I was, as you know, less so than I was letting onto. 'Well, I am, I guess.'

He grasped my hand. 'As you know, it's an election year and there's a lot of work to be done. I'm going to be traveling a lot. The race looks like it's going to be a tight one.'

And that's when I went into my Daddy-Daughter mode. It started by my taking my hand back from him.

'I should have known,' I said with a mildly bitter edge.

'Should have known what?'

'I never thought you really cared about me.'

'Bo, don't say that. Of course I do.'

'No, don't give me that, Owen. I gather you've found someone else.'

'No. That's not the case.'

'God, why are you such a man? Blah, blah, blah.'

'Bo . . .'

'No, leave me be.'

And I advanced off to have my own teary private moment. He came up from behind me, of course. And put his hands on my shoulders. My face was covered in my hands.

'It's my entire life in a nutshell,' I said, my head still bowed as if I were addressing the bright leaves on the ground.

'What is?'

'Tell me this, Owen. Did you ever love me?'

'You know I cared for you. And still do.'

my little threats

Eventually I broke out from my covered face, with water rimming my eyes. My expression was one I'd worked on. It was cold, ruthless, calculating, and mean. I'd used it to my advantage before. I wasn't trying to play down my upset. Rather, I was promoting it. In all its glory. It was a face that made men scared. Especially prominent men. The types who have something to lose. Implied in that face were all My Little Threats. I didn't have to verbalize My Little Threats. Not with a face like that. By looking at my face, any man could see into his future, one that could be highlighted by headlines – the unwanted kind – lawyers, courtrooms, embarrassments, and beyond.

Not that I'd ever carry out whatever was implied, in My Little Threats. After all, my life depended on my reputation. And secrecy. And discretion. That's if I ever wanted to get the rest of my life paid for in the way I wanted to. My Little Threats were just insurance policies.

'What do we do now?' I asked with a steely gaze.

He looked at me sharply. The implication, of course, was, How are you going to take care of me? Meaning,

What type of severance pay?

As I looked at the Senator, his expression was confused and dumb. He understood fully what I was saying, but he was playing his version of a face too. It was a silent negotiation. You see, the more open to my demands he was at the outset, the more he'd have to cough up. If he showed resistance, however, it would already get me thinking about less and a compromise.

But I wasn't going to be timid. Or silently intimidated.

'We're going to have to finish this, Owen.'

'How do you mean?'

'You can't just dump me . . . .'

As I looked at him, once again I saw my father's face. It was a situation I'd seen myself in many times before. It was easy to substitute my father's face for a Walletman's. It was like an acting exercise I could call upon at any time. And get a damn good performance. The themes were the same – *no love, abandonment, how could you do this*? Any conversation I'd yearned to have with my father and never did, I had with my Walletmen at the time of tiff, quarrel, or breakup. It made the confrontations easy. Especially the anger part. I could immediately draw from my past and throw a flash fit down on someone like the Senator at a moment's notice.

'You never treated me right.'

'Bo . . .'

'After all the sordid and humiliating stuff you made me do.'

'I'm sorry you feel that way.'

'You hate me, don't you?'

The Senator's face was getting more of a beaten look.

It knocked the hell out of the artificial dumbfounded one he'd had before. Which is what I was after. The reality was, now he didn't know what was coming at him. Or where it was coming from. But like most Walletmen, and men in general for that matter, I'm sure he chalked it up to the Impossibility of Woman thing. But the dramatics made it no less real.

Of course, I then cried. And heaved. And he held me. And I kept it going strong until he filled my ears with the sweet music I'd been waiting and hoping for.

'Don't worry. I'll take care of you.' It sounded like vintage Frank from the *Hit Parade* years.

'*Don't worry/ I'll take care of you . . .*' La-la-la, boo-boopy-do.

And he did. But before he did, I screwed the hell out of him one more time.

When you're abandoned as a child, there's so much psychological treasure there, so much mileage you can get out of it. This is, of course, if you get beyond the crippling part and see the past as an essential positive. If you use it properly, it can make you stronger. You must be in control of your past. Not *it* in control of *you*. You must make your past obey you. It can drive you to win great battles. I'd learned to activate my demons at a moment's notice. Using them in this way was the greatest lesson I ever learned. I made my demons work for me. It made me pretty darn tough.

One more thing. On the drive back to New York, the Senator claimed there was a friend of his who had always wanted to meet me. He described him as the owner of an insurance company and claimed that he was very wealthy. And generous. Bill Pomeroy had been a friend of the Senator's after all. And the Senator was trying to pass me on to him. I wasn't upset, really. It was all a part of The Game. A crucial part. It's how you kept business flourishing.

Then the Senator cut me a check for twenty grand. I slipped out of the limo and walked up the sidewalk. I had smiles for everyone. I entered my building feeling just about as light as a goose feather.

brunei baby

It was late October and I was jet black with a white stripe. For Halloween, of course. I was feeling a little PMS-y. And bloated. And pimply. And crampy. And weak. And vulnerable. I had those hot and cold flashes. I wanted to hug someone. Napoleon was away on a TV-commercial production. I started to worry about my life somewhat. I had several spontaneous cries. That Little Voice was having a field day.

Then, **At These Prices** called in from Brunei. She kind of hit me with no underclothing, so to speak. She was a California blonde from some valley somewhere. Not the famous one near Los Angeles. She usually called in every couple of weeks. She was kind of lonely for America. She'd ask about everyone and what was happening. And she missed her boyfriend. But she was making a mint. Twenty-five thousand dollars a week. And jewels. She would constantly say, 'At these prices, how can I leave?' I must confess I was jealous. I had some money banked, but not that much. Maybe thirty grand. Total. You try to save. But it's tough. My overhead was about four thousand dollars a month. That included my wardrobe allowance, travel, the occasional order-in, car services, hair, nails and feet, spontaneous purchases – always the real killers – a biannual check to Father Rollins, as well as the tab at my mother's nursing home in Cleveland. So I had to be careful.

Let's get this straight. **At These Prices** was not gold digging. She was out-and-out working as a prostitute. I didn't have any prostitute friends, and it's not that I didn't like them. Or felt superior to them. I've always claimed a woman or a man should do whatever he or she wants with his or her body. But **At These Prices** I knew from previous days on the Tour. She was constantly trying to get me to join her over there. I could never do it. But she told me all about it. It was fascinating. And depressing. I remember the conversations like yesterday. So much so, I wished I hadn't taken the calls.

'Come on, Bo. You won't have to work for two years. You'll be able to rest easy and not worry about the future. You'll have it taken care of – so you don't make any desperate moves.'

'I'm sorry, **At These Prices**, but Brunei is a desperate move.'

'Is it any different going from man to man in New York? You're doing the same thing with them. But getting *less* money.'

'But they get emotionally involved with me. And I get used to them. And I like them. I can't just let unknown guys from foreign countries have their way with me. I'm not that hard.'

'Just consider yourself like a model who's putting up

with all the career hassles so that she can afford a life
she really cares about. And, you know, no one ever
finds out. The Arabs don't talk. And neither do you.'

I sighed.

'Look. What are you doing now that's so great?' she
asked.

I didn't have an answer.

'A few years from now, when you look back on it,
you may wish you took my advice. What do you have
to lose?'

My soul, was my answer. Instead, I was weak, so I said
something different, along the lines of *How does it work*?

'Mark my words, Brunei is a totally unique experience. There's only one way to get there. It's if you know
someone who's been hired by someone who works for
the Prince.'

'Who are . . .?'

'In every city in every major country there are talent
scouts. They're like model scouts. In L.A., there's one or
two people. And New York, London, the Philippines,
Brazil, Hong Kong – one or two people. These talent
scouts are pretty sleazy. They're usually madams, or
women who hang out at the Playboy Mansion. But you
can't go to them; they come to you. They say, literally,
"Would you like to come to Brunei?" Then you get an
interview.'

I was painting my toenails at the time of this chat and
I had to stop. I couldn't keep a line. This chatter was too
unsettling.

'Once a month these talent scouts make "movies."
They get a room somewhere in a hotel or private house,

they set up a movie camera – and they shoot film. You have to bring a bathing suit, a prom dress, or an evening gown – the Prince is very tacky, he likes tacky things – and it's not about what you look like. They like every type of girl. They have a lot of beauty queens, but for as many beauty queens as I've seen, they've had a lot of ugly girls. Did you see the Prince's women?'

'I did. On *Sixty Minutes* or some news magazine.'

'Okay. He likes women like that. Short, fat girls. The tall, thin ones are for all his business friends. But the ones he keeps are darker, Arab- and Asian-looking.'

'Is this a year-round thing, or is it seasonal like "I did the winter in Brunei"?'

'It's year-round. They take girls all year. They have girls living in the palace in Brunei. So, what happens is, first you find the talent scouts, then you have to go on film or videotape.'

'Every girl who goes there is on videotape?'

'Yes.'

'And all previous years?'

'Yes.'

That seemed stupid to me. 'What would happen if these tapes were confiscated? Wouldn't the girls' reputations or careers get completely ruined?'

'No. That's the beauty of it. I can't tell you the number of young Hollywood actresses working today who have been to Brunei. No one will ever find out. It's not publicized. The Prince doesn't want anyone to know what he's up to. And the Arab men aren't even supposed to be smoking or drinking, let alone screwing whores – it's against the Muslim religion – so they don't talk either.

There's a kind of secrecy insurance.'

The depravity was pretty staggering. But I must say, it was turning me on somewhat. I was getting a tingling down inside. Real low. It was making me aroused. The thought of these dark men doing dark deeds no one ever finds out about – and the jewels that came with it. It was the *Aladdin* cartoon movie run amok in the most perverse way.

'And look what happened to Miss USA. She's so stupid. She went to Brunei. I know the madam who sent her there. Her name is Martine and she lives in Santa Barbara now. She was promised twenty-five thousand dollars a week. When she learned that she would be passed around to other guys and friends of the Prince, she freaked. And what happened? The case was thrown out. The Prince has the best deal of anyone on the planet. He has the most money and he can do whatever the hell he wants with the rest of the world. There's protection in that. For you. And your reputation.'

I wanted to kill this guy, the Prince, whoever he was. Even still, it was intriguing. 'Go on . . .' came out of me.

'So, they ask you questions like, *What are your favorite hobbies? What books do you like to read?* You have to talk about yourself. *What are your goals in life? What do you want to do?* And they videotape you in a bathing suit, the evening gown, and regular clothes. Then you take a head shot, a full-body shot – it's like being a model. You have to totally audition for the role. There are about twenty other girls there, and it's a fun day, you get to know one another – you know how many girls I've met through these interviews? You make friends, Bo.'

'Where did you do the interview?'

'It was at some madam's house.'

'In what area?'

'In Los Angeles – borderline Marina del Ray – Venice.'

I thought about these talent scouts. I was sure they kept these videotapes – for the future. *Their* future.

'They have a makeup artist and a photographer. They make you up and take the head shot.'

'Who pays for it?'

'You do.'

'How much?'

'About a hundred and seventy-five dollars.'

'The madams don't put out any money?'

At These Prices started to become annoyed with my nagging, nitpicky questions. Because I was trying to shoot holes in this arrangement however I could. I needed to, after all. It sounded too good. From a financial standpoint, anyway.

'No, Bo. It's two hundred dollars. Big deal! Can't you afford two hundred dollars to make three hundred thousand?'

I didn't answer the question. Her Brunei economics always shut me up.

'So,' she continued, 'the madam takes the tape and sends it to her contact in Brunei—'

'Don't tell me this is all top-secret. Everybody talks about everybody. I mean, I know ten girls who have supposedly done the Brunei thing.'

'Look – the girls have just as much to lose as the Prince. Nobody talks about it. Where was I?'

'The interview is sent off.'

'Okay, then you're picked. I don't know how many girls they pick at a time – but at least twenty-five. And your contact is to go for, like, six months. And the minimum you're supposed to get paid is twenty-five thousand dollars. Plus every girl is promised a Cartier watch at the end. Sometimes you get a really good one, sometimes you get a cheap one. I'm trying to be honest with you, Bo.'

I told her I was sure of that.

'Then when it's all over, you have to give forty to fifty percent of what you make in Brunei to your talent scout who sent you there.'

'How do you pay that? Do they have ways to get it from you?'

'They could,' she said, and I heard her light up. 'They could,' she repeated, and I could hear the smoke exhale. The thought of smoke and Brunei and my upset stomach was all making me sick.

'Then, after you get picked, you fly to Singapore—'

I'd had enough. I had a rush of depression. 'I can't take this now,' I said abruptly.

'Bo? What's the matter?'

I hung up. I couldn't take it anymore.

Sometimes, as a woman all it takes is one period. And you get to thinking about things and that's it – you want to change. They can be small changes like a hairstyle, the clothes, or they can be big changes. They can be as big as wanting to change your life for ever.

That's how I felt as I got off the phone with **At These Prices**. I wanted to change my life for ever. . . .

joan

I suffered anxiety that night. I tossed and turned in my bed. I wiped my face of the cold sweat that had covered it. I tried late-night support calls. **Travels With Men** was off in Pennsylvania; the **Three-Minute Princess** was unfindable in London. **More, More, More** was in, but busy. And **Show Me You Mean It** wanted to talk about herself – she fired off some tale of great, sweaty, slimy, primal-urge, freebie sex she'd had with some Neanderthal guy with blue thumbs, meaning his thumbnails had been painted blue. A freebie is sex with no financial strings. A frumbie is sex from behind. And a freebie frumbie is guy talk for a dream. Yes, my restless mind drifted to that too.

I tried to fall asleep again.

What I thought about and what I always tried to think about in stressful times was Joan. Joan was my best friend when I was growing up. She lived in a small town in Ohio. The town I grew up in. I met Joan for the first time one hot summer night when I was eight years old.

In those days, I didn't like to go to bed. I was afraid of

the night, I was afraid of the dark, and I hated to go to sleep. So to prevent myself from sleeping, I'd just lie there and stare out my bedroom window, determined not to drift off. I'd just gaze out the window, hour upon hour's end. I'd look at the stars through the trees and dream about being a little girl somewhere else. I'd dream about being a big girl somewhere else too.

But there was one night, in the summer of 1979, that I'll never forget. It was the night I saw her. It was a brilliant night. Every star in the galaxy could be seen shining brightly in the sky. The moon was there too, riding the sky very high, glowing away like a big, silver ball. As I looked out, I focused on the old maple that rose up just outside my bedroom window. I began to study the leaves in the tree and the silhouetted patterns they were making against the bright sky. That's when I saw her. She looked like Joan Crawford, my mother's favorite actress. I could see her flowing hair, her slashing cheekbones, her arched eyebrows, and the cool, go-to-hell mouth. But Joan wasn't nasty. Not at all.

I sweated some more, felt a hot flash all over my body. My face was like a space heater and could have warmed the whole room. All I could think of was, *Why me? Why me?*

If my mind wanders and loses its sensitivity to the narrative, it is because that was the way it happened and I want to give it to you that way. That night in October my head was feeling like some sort of perilous crossroads and everything was crashing into it at once – fears, hopes, bad memories, good ones, and, therefore, more painful ones. It wasn't a good time. A ghoulish nightmare would have served as relief to all this.

Joan was about twenty-five years old when I first met her. And, may I tell you without hesitation, she was a vision to behold. I watched her every night. And she watched over me. All summer long. On any given night, I couldn't wait to go to bed and see her. And talk to her. I said my prayers to her.

But the seasons changed, and the leaves began to fall. One by one. And soon she lost her nose. Then an eye. And then her mouth. Before long, her face had lost all of its features, all of its character. It grew old and splotchy. But I still talked to her. I loved Joan.

One day Joan disappeared altogether. It made me cry. I realized, and hoped, she might come back the following year when the leaves returned. I waited all year for her. The next spring the leaves came back, green as ever. But I couldn't find her. I looked and looked. I even searched in other trees in other people's yards, thinking she might have moved away, like some of my classmates had. She certainly had good reason to. There was a lot of yelling in my house. Any friend I ever invited to sleep over usually returned home before midnight.

I thought Joan might have left me for another girl's house. One day I asked Heather Jones, a girl in my third-grade class I hated, if she'd seen her. Then I accused her of stealing her. Heather and I had a fight, and I got a bad scratch under my eye. I never saw Joan again. And I never found out what happened to her. At the time, I guessed she had just died.

Though I was disappointed, I never did stop thinking about Joan, however. But I do remember making a conscious effort to avoid that maple outside my bedroom window. I think I turned my back on nature in general. I guess I felt betrayed. Cities and television and nice clothes and making money to buy them and *National Geographic* photos of faraway places received all my attention. There was no time for flowers and lakes and rope swings over rivers and all that was nature anymore. I never played with that old maple ever again.

Once I lost Joan, the Darkies kind of had their way with me. I mean, I still tried to think about her, about my conversations with her. Memories of her silhouetted face brought some temporary comfort and solace. But, like I said, the relief was only temporary. And diversionary. The Darkies soon perched themselves back on my shoulders like little gargoyles, the kind you see peering down nastily from the Notre Dame Cathedral in Paris, whispering their brand of sweet evil into my then vulnerable and impressionable young ears.

Maybe I was more susceptible to the Darkies than most. But everyone has weaknesses and must cater to them in order to overcome them. Or else they will overwhelm you. Since Joan didn't work out, I tried to find other ways. I didn't really want to tell you all this, but I suppose it would clear things up about the Darkies and me.

You see, my father had some work to do before he ran out on us. He had to get in some last whacks on my mother. For good measure. He'd come home late at night all gassed up on scotch, and if she did anything as offensive as sleep or leave the kitchen with a few plates in the sink, she'd suffer for it. He'd yank her out of bed, throw her across the room, hit her, and yell and scream. He reminded me of an evil Yogi Berra. Once I overheard him say to her, 'You never let me fuck you the way I want to fuck you.'

The guy was obviously in pain. I could see it in his face. He worked for a mining company. Then a rubber factory. He was constantly getting laid off. Either that or fired. The bitterness oozed out of him, not about what he had done with his life but what he hadn't done. As I learned later, it was pretty obvious caveman stuff. Unoriginal, is what I'm saying. But back then, when you don't know any better, it was incomprehensible. He'd get us all up, my mother included, smack us around, throw empty bottles against the fireplace, rant and rave.

I've put all that behind me, but that was when the Darkies were born – those hours after dark when I went to bed, praying we were not going to be called on for a late-night pound session. That's why I always fought off sleep. I feared going to sleep. My private little consultations and meditations with Joan were my only comfort. That was why she was my best friend. And that was why I was so sad when she left me.

I snapped out of my childhood memories and found myself making coffee in the kitchen.

Napoleon slipped out of the bathroom and joined me.

'Good morning, Bo.'

'Morning.'

I let go one more spontaneous cry. And wiped my nose. Napoleon didn't see. I felt better. Because eventually my mind would always come back to a point that really became my keepsake. I'd gotten the hell out of Fort Lowell, where all those Darkies lived. In seeing it this way, somehow my brutal childhood didn't seem so brutal after all.

And then everything was okay again.

fat cat blues

I say this now and for ever for women. *Every day is a new day*. Everything you've learned has little bearing on any event at any time. Because random acts do occur, and psychologies are very susceptible. But something cataclysmic that occurs in your life can make you not necessarily change your life but change your path, your direction – make you set your sights or target differently. That's the effect the **Three-Minute Princess**, the Senator, and **At These Prices** and her tales from Brunei had on me. They made me readjust my focus. To what?

It didn't emerge until later, however, during a discussion I had with Napoleon.

'Are you going to Aspen this year?' he asked.

'I'm not sure.'

'Why not? You go every year.'

'Well, I'm tired of the circuit.' That was true. I was twenty-eight and feeling like fifty.

'No . . .' he remarked in disbelief.

'I am, Napoleon. It's for the kiddies. I'm not a kiddy anymore.'

'You look fab. And not a day over twenty-two.'

'I don't feel fab. All this traveling. I'm tired of short-timing and short-timers. I want out.'

'You mean settle down? No. I won't let you.'

'What's wrong with settling down?'

'Oh, and let some guy get you pregnant four times, lock you up with all those babies, go out and cheat on you every night and make you miserable?'

'Well, at least I'd have the babies. And the rest of the burdens taken off.'

'Think it through, Bo.'

'I know. Men are the worst. How do I know? I'm the one they become *the worst* with. But maybe, just maybe . . . I can find one who's different.'

'Now you sound like every last idyllic romantic bimbo. Don't turn your back on all your experience.'

'But what about the lesser-known places?'

'Like?'

'Nantucket.'

'We summered there. Boring.'

'Or Montana.'

'More so.'

'Ted Turner's son goes out there.'

'Bo, come on. That kid's not going to settle down for another thirty years. Men aren't getting married. It was you who told me so. Why don't you sit down and let me do your color. How about Norma Jean platinum for the holidays?'

I ignored his well-intentioned conversational detour. 'I need a man without access. Who doesn't know about all the rest. He'll get married.'

'How do you mean?'

'Someone who's rich but doesn't know about all these other things. And doesn't want them. I search in all the wrong places. Not every guy in the world wants to screw around for ever.'

With that one, we both looked at each other. And said nothing. There it was, Convenient Mood Technologies getting the best of me. You know, how a woman can make up an on-the-spot philosophy to cover or rationalize her recent predicament or situation, a philosophy that is antithetical to all her previous philosophies and firm beliefs.

'You know the right people,' I said eventually. 'Why don't you introduce me?'

'I did, remember?'

'That guy Stockwell? I ran the simplest TRW credit check on him. He was off the charts! They practically hauled me in just because I inquired about him.'

'He comes from a wealthy family.'

'Whatever.'

'Are you really sure?'

'Am I really sure, *what*?'

'You want to settle down. All that "I want to stay independent, why have one guy who'll treat you badly when you can have twenty who treat you great?" – all that is out the window?'

It was a good question. But I was tired. And feeling old. And looking old. My daily little conferences with my compact case were telling me as much. And I knew if I continued at this pace, my time would be up. I'd be finished. The Ten-Year Window would be closed. And I'd be fighting for scraps. By scraps, I mean a-hundred-grand-a-year guys. It would be a dusty cabin in the Forest Where Dreams Have Died. And checkbook art on all the walls. Yikes!

'Maybe you need a vacation,' he said.

It all came to me at once. I knew what to do.

'Do me café caramel,' I said.

little a-frame on the prairie

The town is called Fort Lowell. Population: 4,200. It's by the Ohio River in southern Ohio, not far from the Kentucky and West Virginia borders. I'm not going to describe gorgeous rolling hills and snowy plains. Because there weren't any. It was a flat town. It was about as flat as a dime in asphalt. There used to be a rubber factory that manufactured tires. They used to call Fort Lowell 'Rubber Town.' It still had some franchises. And pretty much one of everything. Except a millionaire. Why? There was nowhere to spend what you had. And there was nowhere to make any more.

I arrived there on the second Saturday in November and I was café caramel, just as I'd selected. It was a souped-up name for my real color. Fort Lowell knew me as chestnut brown, so that's how I went. I just rewrote the name. I found café caramel to be a little sexier.

Maximilia was my favorite person in the world. She was as cute as a button the last time I'd seen her. And getting cuter. Perilously so. She was wearing black now. Everything was black. Her stockings, her sweaters, her jeans, her T-shirts, even her toothbrush. She'd discovered black two years before. Guess how? It was the last time I'd seen her. I gave her a Ralph Lauren black suede miniskirt. Sure, she loved it. She'd never even had suede clogs.

I took a cab to Vicky's house. It was my house too, actually. My father had ditched out on us early. About 1982, I think. My mother ended up in a nursing home in Cleveland. She'd had a rough life. I'm not going to say any more about it. I'm just not. Fill in the blanks on trailer-park tragedy without the trailer park. Or hot water for six of those years.

The cab glided up to Searchlight Lane. I got out and tipped the driver. It cost four dollars. It was amazing how much further a buck went in Ohio.

I dragged my bag on little wheels up the front walk.

'Aunt Bo!'

Maximilia charged out the front door and greeted me with a huge hug. I tried to pick her up as usual, but she was much taller. And heavier.

'Hi, sweetheart,' I said and kissed her with all my goodness.

'I love the sweater. See?' And she tugged down the front. It was the black V-neck from Cashmere-Cashmere I'd sent for her birthday. It was already rumpled from all the use.

I noticed Max had grown a full chest and an Uh-Oh body. Uh-oh was the thought too. She was trouble-sixteen now. And she had her aunt's curves. Somebody better chain her to the basement floor quick, I thought. And not a man either.

'What took you so long?'

'Plane was late. Where's Mom?'

'She'll be back.'

'Where'd she go? Shopping?'

'No. To the dentist.'

'On Saturday?'

We slipped inside and plopped down on the couch. Max wanted to hear everything. Where I'd been, what I'd worn, who I'd met, and what I'd said. Everywhere. Max loved me. Her mother wasn't as much of an enthusiastic supporter.

I handed her the coat. It was a black shearling.

'Oh my God,' she said.

'I wasn't sure before, but you've grown so much, I think it'll fit. Try it on.'

She did and it fit perfectly, even at the wrists.

'It's my old winter coat.'

'Where did you get it?'

'In Milan.'

'You don't want it?'

'I never wear it anymore. It looks great on you.'

She twirled a few times. Then dashed into the bathroom to inspect herself in the mirror. At that moment, Vicky stepped through the front door.

'Hi, Vick,' I said.

'Bo, look at you,' she said evenly.

We pressed cheeks together.

'Everything okay?' I asked pointedly.

'Yeah, sure. Why?' She sent me a look too, like she didn't know what I was talking about.

'Max said you went to the dentist. Did they drill?'

'Uh, no. Just a routine cleaning.'

'Look, Ma!' Max came in sliding across the floor in her socks. 'Look what Aunt Bo gave me.'

'Bo . . .' And Vicky looked at me and shook her head. She didn't like the way I spoiled Max.

'Hand-me-down,' I said.

'It's beautiful,' Vicky said as she felt the soft sleeve. Her face didn't really brighten at all, though.

And we all stood there. And did a nervous jig.

'I brought some wine . . .' I said, and extended a bag.

'Thank you. Should we open it?'

'Why not?'

'Here, Max, open the bottle and pour a glass of red wine for Aunt Bo.'

'You too?'

'No, I'm fine.'

Vicky looked tired. Her complexion was rather gray, and there were shadows beneath both eyes. Her cropped hair, which had always been bouncy, was hanging limply against her face. Whether it was her life, her job, her kid, or our past, I couldn't really be sure. But something was bringing her down. And it was hurting her. I hoped it wasn't me.

She was the greeter or maître d' or whatever they call it in Ohio, at a Western Sizzler chain restaurant the next town over. She'd been there since it opened a dozen or so years ago. Her husband, Max's father, had gone the way of our father. He'd knocked her up, they had sex a few more times, and then he was gone. I think she tracked him down, though. Or he tracked her down. He was broke and needed to pay off some landlord in Indiana. She helped him, of course. Dutifully. Like all good beaten-down and victim-playing Ohio women do. Don't get me started. I can't believe they take this shit from guys. Needless to say, she never heard from him again.

We sat there on the Brown Couch. The Brown Couch was a relic from our childhood. I was surprised Vicky had held on to it. I was also surprised it didn't smell like one giant TV dinner. It reminded me of sitting there in my Salvation Army dresses, watching noncable television with the tin-foil rabbit ears that needed to be given quarter-turn adjustments constantly for adequate reception. By the way, I had those fine, cut-rate dresses in all Gatorade colors.

I sipped on the wine and looked at the walls of that little A-frame and thought, If only these walls could talk. They had endured some difficult days.

Max was seated at my left playing with my hem, and Vicky was on my right.

'Is Eddy coming by?' Max asked.

'Yeah, later,' Vicky said.

'Who's Eddy?'

'Eddy's Mom's boyfriend.'

'He is not.'

'Is too.'

'We're just friends.'

'Friends who hump.'

'Max!'

'He's cute, Aunt Bo. And a wild one!'

'Hush, girl! And get me a glass of wine.'

'Say please.'

'Ugggh . . . Please . . .'

Max danced off into the kitchen.

'I've never really heard her speak this way. With an understanding of sex and—'

'She understands all right. She has a boyfriend.'

'Wow, both of you.'

'Yeah. The two of us. God, I hope she uses protection,' she said and got lost for several moments on a train of concern for Max.

'Has she had sex?'

'I'm not sure. I think so. She's very private.'

Then I asked her about her own beau, Eddy.

'We've been seeing each other about six months now. He works in Kopple. He's a businessman.'

'He owns a business?'

'No. He's a salesman.'

'What does he sell?'

'Tires,' she said.

'The tire business, huh?' And the sound of it made it seem even lower budget. Of course, in fairness to him, I did see him as one of the remaining titans of an industry that had gone nearly extinct in Ohio. Then I caught myself. I tried to avoid prejudging. But it was second nature to me now.

'Yeah. He's never been married. No kids. I met him in the restaurant.'

Max came back with a glass for Vicky. She took a sip first. Vicky just shook her head.

I don't know what it is, but whenever you face your family or people whom you've known all your life, all of a sudden your self, or what you think is your self, shuts down – the self that walks out of her apartment every morning in the big city and has an identity and a reputation, a self that commands a certain type of reaction from people and respect, it all just shuts down in front of these old faces. And you're stripped. You don't have those things to rely on. Those fortifications and cements. I think it's why I didn't like coming back to Fort Lowell. I felt stripped. And unprotected. And vulnerable. More so than normal. Which is saying a lot.

It's funny. Ironic, even. Because in the traditional sense, I was a much better girl when I'd lived in Ohio. By better girl, I mean behaviorally – more of a conservative girl. In that living room, I felt conservative. And there was nothing conservative about me. I felt closed down. Yet stripped. I was being maneuvered back to that old reality. And it was unsettling.

I finished my wine and announced that I was going to take a shower. I was going to wash myself back together.

a shot of nowhere

Eddy drove up in an old Ford Maverick. I didn't know there were any left. I had him pegged for thirty-eight grand a year, max. Timex watch. And I stopped the study right there. It was painful to put him on the Walletman grate. It was my sister's guy, after all. We weren't close but we were blood. I didn't bother to look at his shoes. But the Kmart clip-on bow tie practically gave me a black eye, it was so expansive, as he stepped inside the house.

But don't forget, forty grand went a few more miles in towns like Fort Lowell. After all, he had no kids. All he had was a mortgage.

'Eddy, meet Bo.'

It sounded like a bad country movie. 'Hi,' I said.

'So you're Bo.'

Oh no, I thought. Not one of these guys. The heard-a-lot-about-you type. But I told myself not to be so cynical. It wasn't my life, anyway. I had my flight out. And a place to go.

Max had gone to a movie with her boyfriend. He was quite a sight too. His name was Danny and he had the worst haircut I'd ever seen. You know, short on the side and a long ponytail in the back. I don't know where these hairstyles come from. Or who tells them they look good. If anyone.

After some very light chit-chat, the three of us motored in the Maverick to the Starfish.

'You know he has *Maximilia* tattooed on the inside of his lower lip,' Vicky said on the way over.

'I didn't.'

'Kid's a punk,' Eddy said.

'He means well,' she said in her characteristic capitulating way.

Vicky was older than me. By two years. She wasn't as pretty and didn't have the same figure. She was actually smarter, I think. But she let people get the best of her. Classic self-esteem shortage. She knew a good portion of the answers to life but she couldn't execute them. Her confidence had been grinded away early, as early as I can remember. We had the same color hair. And lips. And that was all. Vicky reminded me of my father. Their baby pictures were identical. I think he reminded her of herself too. And she resented it.

I felt sorry for Vicky, though I didn't want to. Pity is just about the most insulting thing. But I couldn't help but cringe when I thought about those high-school days we'd shared. When all the cute senior guys were after me and not her. I tried to make it up to her. I avoided situations that would hurt her. Because she didn't recover well from them. They made her go into her shell. Further into her shell. It's never easy for an older sister to have a younger one who's more popular. It can be the stuff of lifetime resentment. Of course, I had my self-esteem problems too. Fatherless families are known for that.

The Starfish was a cheesy, rustic bar, but somehow I kind of liked it. It was nice to have the pressure off. I hadn't been feeling great lately. It was good for me to get away. And not to *somewhere*. *Nowhere* is what I needed. Fort Lowell offered that. And if we had to go out, the Starfish offered that too. The ceiling was draped with low-hanging fishnets with plastic fish and marine ornaments dangling off them. There was a row of locals at the bar, and the bartender wore a sea captain's hat.

'What'll you have?' he asked us.

'Turkey Coke,' Eddy blurted out immediately. He was several prehistoric eras away from exhibiting any gentlemanly qualities. Vicky and I both ordered white wine.

Eddy angled a look at me. 'I've heard a lot about you.' He'd obviously picked up where he'd left off back at the house. Yet now, his tone was kind of leading. Leading in a way I didn't necessarily like.

'Like?'

And he smiled. Kind of.

'He doesn't know anything about you,' Vicky interjected.

I took a sip of wine. It was really bad. That was okay. It immediately indicated I'd found the *nowhere* I'd been seeking out. We moved away from the bar and sat at a nearby table.

'So, how's the tire business?' I asked him.

And then his mouth just moved, and whatever he said I didn't hear.

I didn't like this cat Eddy. I didn't like him one bit. He was handsome in a regional-soda-commercial kind of way. He had that square jaw you see in *GQ*, but the face wasn't perfectly mapped out. His eyes were too close together. I'm sure he'd milked his almost-looks to the limit wherever he'd been raised. His ego was one of those that had formed firmly from heroic deeds performed in high school, a time when it didn't matter. And he was still living off of it. I could tell. There was something brutally unevolved about him. Like evolution had passed him by.

But there was something more unsettling to me going on too. I didn't know what it was. But he was bad news. Even for Ohio. Maybe it was just that he was your classic tire salesman. I didn't really know what that was like. But at some point, no matter how myopic or dim you were, the daily responsibilities owing to a profession like that would eventually have to leave you feeling that maybe, just maybe, things in life didn't go your way. And then, watch out. It gets taken out on things. Cars, walls, wives, and kids. Thuds and smacks. Really bad homemade music. Pity the products of a household like that. And watch out for them when they grow up. How did I know? How do you think?

With respect to Eddy, it was his eyes that told the story. He had the eyes of a cheater. Like he bent the rules at everything. Monopoly, taxes, card games, relationships. The weasel type. But he was just attractive enough to get women to sleep with him. And always had been.

'What's that face?' Vicky asked me.

'Nothing,' I said.

'So what's going on in the big city?' he offered with another two-dollar smirk. He had that touchdown smile and perfect teeth, so it actually came out somewhat attractively.

'I'm happy. I live in a nice place.'

'So I've heard,' he muttered.

I looked at Vicky. 'Well, Vicky has never seen it, actually.'

'Pictures.'

'Yes, pictures.'

'You going with anyone?' And he laughed a little too.

Obviously, Vicky had told him about me. I wondered whether it was the PG, NC-17, R, or X version. To give you a benchmark, the PG version would be à la *Breakfast at Tiffany's*. You know, the fifty-dollars-for-the-powder-room-type stuff.

Not that Vicky knew either. She had an idea. And she probably assumed the X. After all, she always had painted me the brightest demon I could be. It made her feel better about herself, I'm sure.

He kept looking at me, waiting for an answer. And the more he looked, the more I wouldn't give him one. Prick.

What he did do was order another round. I waved mine off. I didn't feel like drinking with him at the table. I wanted to get out of there.

Eddy sucked down his second Turkey Coke and talked about growing up in Missouri. It took ten minutes. Then they discussed having taken a trip to Vegas and seeing

Tom Jones. My feeling was, at least he forked over for some professional entertainment. How he scored the tickets I didn't want to know. I almost died when Vicky went to the bathroom, leaving me all alone with him.

'Thought you were a drinker,' he sent out immediately.

'I'm kind of tired,' I said.

'Not exciting enough for you?' he asked in a tone indicating I thought I was the snobby Nile Queen.

I let it go.

'So – you like my sister, Eddy?'

'I like her, yeah. Nice girl.'

'You gonna marry her?'

'Hey, wait a minute now,' he said and guffawed. And then he took another swig of his glass, which was already empty. I looked off and away at the paper jack-o'-lanterns matted to the mirror behind the bar. They were still celebrating Halloween in Fort Lowell.

As I surveyed the room, I could tell that Eddy was examining my chest wares with a contaminated 100-proof glare. 'What do you care, anyway?' he chided.

I flared a look at him. And he took it and just kept on with his stupid stare of his own. He wasn't going to give in.

'You'd never go out with a guy like me, would you?'

'Would you go out with yourself?' I asked.

'Okay, okay,' he said, seemingly enjoying the retort.

'Don't sell yourself short, Eddy. But the answer is *no*. You've been dating my sister. I draw a line there.'

Then he drew the curtain. Those cheating eyes

prepared me somewhat. 'Think you're pretty tough, don't you?'

The exchange would only go down a tumultuous path, one that would upset my sister if I let my mouth fly, so I decided to add a sedative to it.

'Don't take me so seriously, Eddy.'

'Oh no?' he asked, and he held on me with some more of his ridiculous facial goop. 'How about – I don't take you seriously at all?'

'Shall we go?' Vicky said as she advanced on the table.

'If you insist,' I said. And there was no one around to appreciate my sarcasm.

When I maneuvered into the backseat of the Maverick and Eddy laid a hand on the curve of my ass and held it there a grotesque moment, I didn't say anything.

bad dreams

I went to bed that night in the guest room. Maximilia had inherited my childhood room. I was across the hall from her. And down the hall from Vicky.

I had trouble sleeping. I heard Vicky coughing and getting up to go to the bathroom repeatedly. I knew why the first time. Eddy had stayed over. He wasn't the kind of guy who would give you the night off. Especially if he'd bought you a white wine. The successive times she got up, though, I didn't know why.

As I lay in bed, I thought about my New York life. And what it held for me. I was tired of my unsettled existence. I was going to change that. As soon as I returned, I'd take the proper steps.

I dreamed wildly that night. Surreal visions, with faces I hadn't seen for years, a high-school history teacher included; an old friend named Virginia; my first boyfriend, Buddy; Vicky; my father; baby Maximilia – really strange stuff.

I was tossing and turning in bed. I felt pressure. On my waist. I was in that sleep trance that maybe wasn't sleep. That in-between state. It's like quicksand. You can't move.

Even though you want to wake up and jump out of bed, you have no control of your arms. They're inert.

And I felt pressure.

And a hand . . . down there. Near my waist. Maybe lower. I forearmed away a hand and sprang up in bed.

'Don't touch me, motherfucker!' I heard myself yell.

I saw someone standing over me. It was Eddy.

'Bo. Bo. It's me.'

'No!' And the face turned into Maximilia. It was Maximilia. She'd been rubbing my waist.

'Aunt Bo, wake up,' she whispered. 'You were dreaming.'

'Oh, God . . . you scared me.'

'Sorry,' she said. Then she mumbled, 'Danny and I had a fight.'

'Ooh, wow,' I uttered and tried to get perspective. 'What about?'

'Well, he was trying again.'

'Trying what?'

'To, you know . . .'

'I don't.'

'To do it.'

'It?'

'Yeah, *it*.'

'Oh, *it*. Right.'

And there was the answer to the discussion with Vicky earlier.

'He was being all nice and stuff, and we were making out. And I let him' – and she looked at me, and not fearing any pressure, continued – 'do stuff to me. But . . .'

'But what?'

'Not that.'

'You told him *no*?' She nodded. 'So what happened?'

'Well, first he started getting weird. He told me he didn't like my coat. Said it was ugly. It was like everything having to do with me, he was cutting down. Then he said I talk about you too much. Mean things he was saying. Really mean. And he wouldn't stop.'

'What did he say next?'

'Like, *If I liked you so much, why wasn't I more like you?*'

'Meaning?'

'Like, *Why wouldn't I do it? Why was I so high and mighty?* And, *Who was I saving myself for?*'

'Was he calling me nasty names?'

'Not at first but . . . later.'

'When, later? What did he say?'

'He said everyone knew what you did to get those fancy clothes and stuff.'

'What made him say that?'

'His mother told him. She saw you in that photo in *People* magazine with some guy named Trumpet.'

She meant Trump. 'I was with someone else who was cut out of the photo.'

'And, *Why was I such a prude?* When you were . . . like that.'

And I could now hear all his little scraps of ugliness. How I was a whore, and how much Max wanted *it*, really wanted *it*, she was just pretending she didn't. It made me seethe.

Max began to sob. I looked at her more closely. I could see she'd been crying. And then I noticed her blouse was ripped. It was one I'd given her. I shot upright. 'Are you okay, Max? What happened?'

'He pinned me down and tried to rip it off. It's my favorite shirt, Aunt Bo.'

'What happened next? Did he hurt you?'

'I got away and ran. But he chased me. And caught me, and I pushed him away and yelled at him. So he smacked me.'

'Are you hurt?' She didn't answer. I wrapped my arms around her and squeezed her tight. 'I'm so sorry.' I cradled her in my arms.

We heard some shouting coming from down the hall. The Last of the Great Tire Guys was letting his unique personality roam again.

'Close the door, sweetheart.' She did. Then she came back over and lay down next to me. 'You listen, Maximilia. And listen good. Don't ever let yourself get treated badly. By a man, or anyone. You hear me?'

She nodded.

'*Ever.*'

'What should I do?'

'With Danny? Dump him.'

She gazed into my eyes trustingly. Then she angled a look down low and tugged at the blouse. 'It's all ripped,' she said sadly.

'Don't worry. We'll get another.'

I felt her head nod. I petted her awhile. A long while. Until she drifted off. And I thought about the awful symphony of my dream. How it had started with Eddy Black Rims and ended with Danny Bad Hair. And how it was the same goddamn disgusting music. Without any discord or any note out of place. They just flowed right together. What a bonus.

breakfast

When I woke up the next morning, Maximilia was gone. I slipped down into the kitchen in a robe. Vicky was pouring a cup of coffee for me. She looked drained. Like she hadn't gotten any sleep.

'Morning, Vick.'

'Morning.' She handed me the cup without looking at me. I sat down at the kitchen table. A box of Frosted Flakes was towering in front of me.

'Where's the little one?'

'She went to see her boyfriend.'

'Did she?' That surprised me. 'Did she tell you what happened?'

'*Bo*,' and she looked at me with fiery eyes. 'Don't ever tell my child what to do.'

'Vicky—'

'Don't you walk into my house and tell my little girl what to do with her life—'

'He hit her, for God's sakes.'

'Don't interfere, Bo!'

Her voice was strained and her face was folded up. She coughed.

'I'm sorry,' I said.

Some time passed. But not that much. Vicky started sponging down the countertop.

'You have a certain way of seeing life, Bodicea, and maybe it works for you. But that child of mine is young, she's impressionable. And she worships the ground you walk on. And I don't want you putting ideas in her head.'

'I told her to get away from him.'

'That's not for you to judge.'

'Then you be the judge!'

'Don't tell me how to raise my kid!'

'Vick, he was trying to have sex with her. Against her will.'

'Who told you that?' And she was beaming at me almost violently.

'She did.'

She resumed the sponging. 'She's telling fibs.'

'She's not.'

'She is too! She wants you to think she's more grown-up! They're just kids. They have a crush on each other.'

'Ripping her blouse? That's some crush.'

'The thing is, you can't see anything that's sweet and nice anymore. You see it all as dirty. Well, that may be your life, but it's not ours.'

'Vick—'

'Who the hell are you advising her about what to do, anyway? That's like a drunk driver telling someone not to drink beer. You buy her all those racy clothes. Black this and that. Everything black. Black is dark. Some people think black is evil, you know? But you tell her it's chic. And she wears that low-cut stuff because you tell her to look sexy.'

'I don't tell her that.'

'You get her the clothes, don't you?' I remained silent. 'Then you tell her to dump the guy she cares about. You want to make a tease out of her. Is that what you want? Or do you want to make a slut out of her? Now which is it? I don't blame Danny for getting aggressive with her if she's teasing him.'

I let it go. I could tell it had hurt her. To find out that her daughter had confided in me. And not her. It was bringing up all those old memories. Only now it included the new generation. When will it ever stop? I'm sure she was thinking.

'I understand, Vick, why you're upset. I'm just trying to help,' I said. 'I won't say another word to her about what she should do, or what she needs, nothing. It's none of my business. I'm sorry.' And I slid out the doorway of the kitchen.

But that only prompted more from her. 'Oh yeah, Ms Smarty Pants? Tell me. Just what in the hell do you think she needs?'

I let out a sigh. 'A father,' I said softly.

'A father,' she scoffed.

'She needs guidance. Look what happened to us.'

'Us or you?'

'Both,' I snapped. 'When you have no father figure around, anything goes. Mothers can only do so much.'

'Fathers can only do so much. Listen to what you're saying. Have you forgotten your early life? Or has all your galavanting around romanticized it into some gorgeous fairy tale?'

'I haven't forgotten.'

'You're a dreamer, Bo. And dreamers end up—'

'What?'

'Forget it.'

'No, tell me. Like whores? Is that what you want to say?'

She looked up and over at me. Nothing came out of her mouth. Which were words enough.

'Get this straight, Vicky. I control my own destiny.'

'Oh yeah? Then how come you're not married?'

'Because that is *not* and *has never been* proof to me that you're in control. In fact, just the opposite. You're born alone and you die alone, Vicky. And no one is going to take care of you. So you'd better control your own destiny.'

'You hear yourself? You think that's a philosophy? I call it selfish. I call it caring about no one but yourself,' she declared. 'But you were always good at that.'

I stood up. 'Why are you so angry with me?'

'You talk about control. Your life is totally out of control.'

'What the hell do you know about my life?'

'I know, Bo.'

'Yeah, how?'

'I know you. You're the same as you were in high school, trying to make all the boys swarm after you. Just last night you were doing the same to Eddy.'

'Is that what he said?'

'No. It's what I say. I saw it. And I've seen it before.'

'That's bullshit, Vick.'

'It's not bullshit! It wasn't bullshit then, and it's not bullshit now! You're way too far gone!'

Just then, Maximilia charged in the kitchen crying hysterically. 'Mom!'

'Honey? What happened?'

'He—'

'Did he hurt you?'

'He tried. I ran away. He tripped me.'

'What happened?'

She looked at me and through the tears she said, 'I tried to tell him what you told me, Aunt Bo! I told him I didn't want to see him anymore.'

Vicky flared a look at me.

'And he hit me and told me I came from a family of white-trash whores!'

Vicky reached out protectively, pulling her close. Then with eyes blazing, she turned in my direction.

'I want you to leave,' she announced firmly.

I didn't argue. I called a cab. Then I packed. My flight wasn't until the next day. But I couldn't change that. And for reasons that were my own, I didn't want to.

That night I stayed in the Triple Play Motel. I called home, my home, and talked to Napoleon for an hour. I was upset. He calmed me down.

The next morning, I drove over to Vicky's. Maximilia saw me through the window, and moments later she was outside greeting me. She gave me a big hug. It felt nice.

'Sorry I caused all the trouble, Aunt Bo.'

'Honey, nothing is your fault.' We let go of each other.

'Your mother and I disagree on some things, but we love each other. Is she here?'

'No.'

I took in a deep breath of Fort Lowell air and scanned the yard. 'You tell her I love her, will you?'

'I will.'

'And don't let her marry him.'

'I won't.'

Just then, Eddy sauntered out the front door and approached us. He didn't look very happy. He looked stern. I was sure I was going to get some kind of warped earful for some reason.

'Excuse us a second, Max,' he said.

'Bye, baby. I love you.'

'Bye, Bo! And thanks for the coat.' We hugged again for a few moments, then released each other.

Eddy, I noticed, was waiting for her to fade into the house. I looked at him for no other reason than he was facing me. 'It's about your sister, Bo.'

Here we go, I thought. Mr Turkey Coke butting in on our family business. Telling me he never said anything to Vick about my coming on to him. To cover his ass. He took his time. And when he did open his mouth, I was all wrong. He had nothing to say about Vick and me. It was all about Vick. Her Saturday dentist story had been a cover.

That Monday was the day I found out her tumor was malignant.

I didn't bother to tell Eddy that I didn't know Vicky was sick at all. I did tell him not to tell Maximilia. Yet. He knew that much, God bless him.

And God bless her.

Before I slipped back into the awaiting cab, I sent eyes over to the bare old maple. I didn't wave.

After touching down in Cleveland, I dropped by the nursing home to look in on Mom. She was in the corner of a small room, looking off into space. She looked very old. There was no point in saying hello to her. She wouldn't recognize me. I crept up behind and wrapped my scarf around her. She didn't move.

I left the nursing home sooner than I'd intended. The combination of Vicky and Mom was tough. I sobbed on the way to the airport. But made myself stop.

I had to pull it together.

Needless to say, the vacation I'd been looking for, and the relaxation I'd hoped would come with it, never happened.

air religion

Warren K. Samuels is the country's eleventh-richest man. His G-4 plane was waiting for me at the Cleveland airport. He'd been meeting with the owners of the city's new football team. Warren was an old lover. We got together whenever we could. Yes, he was married. Like I said, most of my Walletmen were.

I know you're wondering whether I knew of this development before I visited Ohio. Yes, I did. Was it further incentive to go? Not really. I'd been feeling pretty low recently. In all honesty, it had been a complete coincidence. I was going to visit Max anyway. I had already decided. It only made me stay that extra day.

In addition to edging into the big-bank top ten, Warren was a huge contributor to one of the nation's largest churches. He claimed to be a very religious man. And he was. It's all he ever talked about. But he had that same bizarre sense of purity of self I'd seen in other religious supporters, even religious leaders.

Though Warren was married, he upheld an attitude that he was not an adulterer or a sinner, or that he was exhibiting any type of duplicitous behavior. We would have these romps in midair, real midflight maulings, in a back room in his private plane, and I really feel – I'm not kidding – that he thought it was okay. And if anything, I was the sinner, the temptress, the one showing all the evil colors. And it was I who needed the salvation. Like I was a modern Mary Magdalene who needed to be redeemed. And saved. And he would help me save myself by humping me. And the act of intercourse would serve to purge me of all my heathen qualities. That was the idea, anyway. His idea. At first, it was actually sexy in a strange way. I was very turned-on the first few times we performed the ritual.

Once we returned to the ground, it would be as though nothing had ever happened, of course. And his verbal ticker tape would resume with all his religious mumbo-jumbo talk. He even gave me a few religious books to convert me. The books would outline what a good woman is and what a good man is. You know, a good woman was married and faithful and walked circumspectly. Meanwhile, he was cheating on his wife, being with me. But he never saw it this way. He saw himself as doing the work of the Lord Jesus.

Sure, it was a classic case of denial. He'd throw the blame on me. He had divided up the world in his mind between good girls and bad girls. And he thought since I was a bad girl, that it was all my fault. That he was one with God and was being called upon to direct me in the ways of the Holy Spirit, even though it was during massive grunting and enthusiastic intercourse.

If you asked him what he was doing in general, he'd say, 'I'm just workin' for Jesus.' And he really believed it. Soon, of course, I found the self-delusionary aspects to be depressing. We're anything we want to be at any time, I'd guessed.

That afternoon we had to make a stop in Memphis so Warren could lunch with a Southern Baptist preacher who I also knew partook in Air Religion sexual romps with him. Not that day, however.

I, of course, had to remain on the plane. Warren didn't want anyone to know a female was flying with him.

When Warren came back from his Working-for-Jesus luncheon, we flew to New York. On that last flight our business returned to business as usual. That included Warren calling me Mommy, and me calling him Daddy. He loved the doggy-style method and spanking me. The dialogue would rip like this:

'Now, Mommy, you've got to stop being so bad.'

'Oh, I know, Daddy. I am bad.'

'Mommy, you're a slut.'

'But I'm getting better.'

'I hope so, Mommy. Take this for Jesus.'

'Give it to me, Daddy, give it to me.'

'I'm giving it to you.'

'I want it.'

'You need it! You need it! Accept Jesus as your savior!'

'I want him! Give Him to me!'

'You're a whore, Mommy!'

'Yes, I'm a whore, Daddy. But I can't help it. I like to [have sex]!'

'Yes, Mommy likes to [have sex]. You mustn't say that, Mommy.'

'But I can't help it, Daddy.'

'Take Jesus into your heart, Mommy. Lay your head on His breast.'

'[Have sex with] me, Daddy!'

'I am [having sex with] you, Mommy.'

'But really [have sex with] me. Harder.'

'Mommy! Let yourself be filled with the Holy Spirit!'

'I am. All the way!'

'All the way, Mommy!'

'Do me, Daddy!'

'Take Jesus, Mommy!'

'Jesus is so hard . . . on me, Daddy!'

'Yes, he's hard. But you're a whore!'

'I need it hard, Daddy! Or how else will I get better?'

'Take it hard, Mommy.'

'I am taking it!'

'For all your sins!'

'All of them. I'm going to hand my life over to Jesus. [Have sex with] me for Jesus.'

'I am [having sex with] you for Jesus!'

'Save me, Daddy, save me!'

And he'd writhe and moan and, well, you get the idea.

Then we'd disembark his plane and take a peaceful ride into Manhattan and he'd drop me off at Trump Tower. He'd give me puppy money for my dog too – the one he'd never seen and the one I hadn't purchased yet. Warren was very generous.

And then he'd buzz off in his dark limousine, just making more money as he drove and, of course, dreaming up new ways to serve Jesus.

That trip was no different.

Sure, it was disturbing. Though my parents weren't avid churchgoers, I attended occasionally in my youth. I even lived in a church in Chicago at one point. I had respect for the Christian religion. With Warren, I was just playing a game, albeit a depraved one. There is hypocrisy everywhere. But I saw it and heard about it more often than I cared to in the religious rank and file. And yet, it was no different in any other country. **At These Prices** taught me about the Muslims. They were supposed to hold firm to the principles of the Koran. They weren't supposed to drink, smoke, gamble, or have sex outside of wedlock. Still . . . well, you get the picture.

I think you have to find your own religion. It may draw on Christianity, it may not. But I think a strong spiritual awareness is crucial for survival. This stuff with Warren I knew was contaminated. But it was his problem. Not mine. It didn't affect my spiritual constitution in the least. Had it, I wouldn't have engaged in it at all. It was purely a money thing.

blond hair, pink roses

As soon as I stepped through the door of my apartment, the phone began to ring. Napoleon was still away. I dropped my bags and answered it.

'Hello?'

'Who is *this?*' a woman's voice blurted at me. I hated hearing that. The nerve.

'Who is *this?*' I sent back with an edge.

'This is Beverly Hamilton,' she stated. 'I own the apartment.'

'Oh, hello, Mrs Hamilton. I'm Bodicea Lashley. I've been renting the apartment.'

'And screwing my husband. Yes, I know. I want you out of there immediately.'

I was surprised, of course. I paused first. And pondered the best response. I went with the all-business angle.

'Uh, Mrs Hamilton, I'm afraid you're going to have to take that up with your husband. I have a lease.'

'You don't have anything. You're a two-bit prostitute.'

'Excuse me?'

She repeated it. Louder. And more clearly.

'Call your husband. Or call your lawyer,' I said.

'My husband is dead, you tart.'

I had no response to that. My handset clicked as someone was on call-waiting for me.

'I want you out,' she roared.

'I'm sorry about your husband, Mrs Hamilton.'

'I *bet* you are,' she finished with. Then the phone went dead.

I was stunned. I wondered why I hadn't heard the news.

Immediately, I called Larry the building manager. Larry told me that he'd tried to warn me. That had been the call-waiting click. He said she really couldn't throw me out yet. I did have a lease, after all. If she started the eviction process, it would take at least three months. But still. Shit, I thought.

Of course I gave thought to Giles Hamilton. He was a sweet man. A tear developed in my eye and spread to the other. I recalled how he used to phone Napoleon regularly to find out what color hair I had. And he'd send me flowers to match it. If I was blond, he'd send me pink roses. If I was brown, he'd send me yellow ones. If I had black hair, he'd send me white. Giles Hamilton had been good to me.

I'd like to think I added a little joy to his life before he left us too. He'd added some joy to mine. He had always treated me with respect. And he was very generous. I was proud to have known him.

Napoleon burst through the door an hour later from a television-commercial shoot in Arizona. He was as tan as a lifeguard. I told him about the regressive development. He wanted to know where he could send flowers.

Nice. Napoleon loved Giles. I think he felt as though Giles was, in some ways, the father he never had. Even though he'd never met him in person.

'What are we going to do?' he asked.

'Start looking for a new place, I guess.'

'You still wish to live with me?'

'For ever. And now more than ever.'

'It was that bad in Ohio?'

I told him everything. At the end of it he said, 'Are you ready?'

It came with a funny tone and he looked at me as if there was something sort of controversial or illicit I should be catching on to. I didn't.

'What do you mean?'

'I mean *ready*.'

And then my green eyes locked on his blues. 'The *Plan*?'

'The Plan.'

Whenever Napoleon and I had discussed The Plan previously, he would take on a troubled and disturbed look. And then he would sigh. Then look at me. And shake his head. And the notion would be called off. There was none of that in his expression now. He was all systems go. And when he lit up a cigarette to reduce tensions, I knew he was serious.

'What's your sudden change?'

He claimed it was financial. Quel *surprise*. He explained that he was worried about how he was going to pay for school and office space and all the other expenses that were going to converge on him in the spring if he didn't get serious. And The Plan, if nothing else, was unquestionably serious. 'On top of our present living situation,' he added.

'Let's do it,' I said without further questioning. 'I'll call my travel agent.'

And I did. I got two first-class seats to Palm Beach. 'Where do you want to stay?' I asked him with the agent still on the line.

'There's a benefit we want to attend at the Breakers. Why don't we stay there?'

I made the appropriate arrangements.

'You're smiling very slyly,' he remarked after I hung up the phone. 'I like that.'

'A benefit,' I repeated. 'If it's a benefit, everyone should be in a charitable frame of mind.'

And we both knew what that meant.

anybody got a better one?

Yes, it was time. Napoleon and I were going to make the announcement. It would be controversial. It would be talked about in the wealthiest of circles. But it would also change our lives in ways we already knew about. The furiously gay son of Townsend Merriweather, a man so gay that he needed asbestos pants, was going to take a bride. And he was going to write himself back into the will and family fortune. We were going to give the tale a beachy boost with news of a pregnancy.

And the sex of this love child had been determined already. And its name would be such another solar-system-sized surprise: Townsend.

We took a flight the next morning and checked into the Breakers that afternoon. At the check-in desk we bought two tickets to that evening's gala. It was a Thanksgiving Pediatric Aids Benefit.

Immediately I hit a Worth Avenue salon and changed from café caramel to Palm Beach benefit blond, which was an ash blond, actually. When I returned to our room, Napoleon was getting a jealousy-fueled phone inquisition from his latest boy toy. He presented me to him as a mystery guest just to drive the poor guy wild.

Our room was commodious enough. It had two queen-size beds. Fit for two queens. Queen Bodicea and Napoleon.

'When will your parents arrive at the party?'

'Early. If cocktails begin at six, they'll be there five minutes before. And they'll wait in the car.'

'What for?'

'My father always makes her go early. But when they get there, my mother won't go inside. They're very different people.'

I knew that, but I wanted it spelled out. I wanted all the information I could get to avoid any personality clashes or sensitive-issue speed bumps. Napoleon gave me his parents' birthdays, of course. I told him that his father was an Aquarius Pig like Ronald Reagan. He was visionary but also money- and power-hungry. His mother was a Leo Snake like Jackie O. She was strong-willed but romantically indulgent.

'My father is a caveman. My mother is very expressive. Open. Loving. She's having an affair, you know.'

I wasn't surprised. 'With who?'

'The golf pro at the club down here.'

It seemed like a time to smile, but I didn't. I wanted to see how Napoleon felt about it first. They were his parents, after all.

'How does that make you feel?' I asked him.

'I love it. Are you kidding?'

'Let's go downstairs and have a drink,' I announced.

'Yeah,' he said. 'And then get money from that pig.'

'Aquarius Pig,' I corrected him.

start spreading the news

It was a very warm night. I wore a white Oscar de la Renta gown, just like half of Palm Beach society. Napoleon had black tuxedo pants and a white dinner jacket I'd bought for him at Barneys in New York. We looked very good. For some reason I felt like getting a little tipsy. Or drunk. Or something. The last couple of months had been rather stressful. I needed a release. My New York Yum falls weren't usually stressful. But as I'd expressed after my return from Ohio, I felt that my life was changing before me. And my attitudes. I could feel the transition. Certainly marrying Napoleon and hitting the Merriweather mother lode would make for a definite transition. It would resolve some of those age-old issues that were still nagging me. Like finances for my future. I wondered how it would play out.

I also pondered what it would be like if indeed Napoleon and I had a kid. I guessed I could be artificially inseminated. But only if Napoleon wanted to. So I asked him. We were in the bar sipping on Cosmopolitans.

'Should we?'

'Should we what?'

'Have a kid.'

And he laughed out loud. 'A kid? Wow. I don't know.'

'Would you make love to me?' I asked with a smile. 'John Summers would understand.' And I added a naughtier version.

'Ooooh. I can't handle this right now.'

And we both laughed.

'I mean, you wouldn't have to. There are other ways.'

'Part of me has always wanted to.'

'Really?'

'Yes. You know that. If I were straight, you're the kind of girl who would drive me crazy. I'd probably kill you in a jealous rage.'

And he kissed me on the lips, softly and as well as any hetero could. He slid his hand under my dress and cupped my breast. He loved playing faux-hetero games. It felt nice. I felt so safe with Napoleon. It turned me on a little too.

'Oh yeah? Which part?' I asked on Cosmopolitan delay from his comment left dangling earlier.

'Wouldn't you like to know?'

I raised a glass. 'To being Mrs Bo Dieudonne . . .'

'No. Merriweather, of course.'

'Really?'

And we touched glasses.

'I suppose we could change it afterward,' he noted.

It was such a big, collossal *afterward*. We both looked at each other. The mission seemed to be calling us, and we were hearing the call.

'Shall we?' I asked.

And Napoleon extended his arm. I looped mine through it.

I must tell you. As we glided past the wall of mirrors in the lobby on our way to the cocktail reception, we looked like a couple worth a few million dollars. I was prepared for a victorious encounter. I figured the first minutes would tell the story, meaning they would make or break us. The Merriweathers had no idea we were attending the party. There was room for some real drama. The good kind.

We stepped into the Circle Dining Room, which was adjacent to the grand Venetian Ballroom. I'd been to both once before for a wedding reception. Many society functions, receptions, and significant Palm Beach events in general took place there. You started in the Circle Dining Room for drinks, then moved on to the Venetian Ballroom for dinner.

'Is your sister going to be here?'

'No. She's in school.'

Napoleon squired me through the crowd. He introduced me to people he hadn't seen in a long time. Most notably, after I'd introduced myself to a pouty young woman with my first and last name, she bluntly sent back, 'Helga.'

'Helga?' And I left it open for her to complete it with a full name.

'Of Greece,' she said.

'Oh,' I said.

Though Napoleon had been schooled in Paris, he always returned to Palm Beach for vacations. Until he ventured down that other road of personal choice. I could tell from the turning heads and odd looks from people that the sight of Napoleon with a woman, and not a faghag type of woman, was raising brows.

You see, Napoleon was keeping a constant arm around my waist. I'd told him to. And we smooched from time to time. It made us laugh. We were actually having a great time. It's how we wanted to be seen. We switched from Cosmopolitans to champagne, and our flutes were never empty. The Glorious and Beautiful. People, as elderly and brown-leather-skinned as they were, just kept filling the room. Until it was entirely jammed with high-and-mighty Palm Beach society. I didn't know what Napoleon's parents looked like. I'd seen a photo of them from when they were in their forties. Now they were in their seventies. So, who knew? Napoleon claimed they were there, though. They'd been spotted earlier. Our feeling was, we wanted them to hear about us first and then seek us out. After all, we didn't want to show any kind of agenda, direction, or strategy. We were just out to have a good time.

And then it happened.

Napoleon received a tap on the shoulder. We spun around, and there they were. Mr and Mrs Townsend Merriweather. The principals of one of the fifty richest families in America.

'Hello, Mother,' Napoleon said.

'We heard you were here!' Napoleon's mother said in a maternally explosive way. She really looked cute in a baby-blue dress and silver hoop earrings. He gave her a peck on the cheek.

'Father,' Napoleon then uttered.

And the patriarch grumbled a greeting with a stingy, gin-and-tonic half smile. I could tell he wasn't the type to ever give you a whole smile.

'Mom and Dad, meet Bodicea.'

'I can't hear,' she said, cupping an ear. 'What was your last name?'

'I didn't say it,' Napoleon said.

'Lashley,' I spoke up with.

'What a beautiful name,' she remarked.

And she inquired as to its origin. I gave her the historic connections to Bodicea and the English derivation of Lashley. And that provided Mr Merriweather with the time to carve up my body with his eyes. I wanted to say, 'We accept Viagra and MasterCard,' but held off. I didn't feel comfortable with them enough to let my sense of humor sing.

We chatted a short while, then Napoleon recounted the details of his schooling and his intention to enter into the field of psychiatry. As his mother offered some quasi-related story, I could see Napoleon shuffling his feet and giving her dead nods, all in preparation to follow her segue with the News.

But I squeezed his arm to hold on a moment. I gestured that I'd be right back.

I stepped over a few paces and extended my glass to a standing waiter holding a champagne bottle. He refilled it. At this moment, I felt a furry hand pressure my arm. I looked over.

'Hello, Bo,' a man said in an unsettling way. He was nearly bald with a disciplined look and narrow eyes. He was about my height.

In addition to his suggestive tone, this man looked at me in a certain way. As if we'd been together on some other level of experience. An intimate level. The most intimate. Or something real close. And I couldn't understand it. I didn't recognize him at all.

But close by I heard Napoleon say, 'We have some news for you.' Then he addressed me. 'Don't we, Bo?'

And I smiled and nodded. I gave a flash of a glance at Mr Merriweather, and his face was stern, as if *what kind of news could come from a snowman son?* I held up another wait-a-moment finger.

'How are you?' the man resumed.

I looked back at him. 'I'm sorry. But have we met?'

And he laughed. 'Are you joking me?'

'Do you know each other?' And now it was Mr Merriweather calling in from the wings.

'Hey there, Duke,' the man said.

Oh, shit, I thought. They're good friends. On 'Duke' terms. I processed quickly. If something had happened between me and this guy, and I wasn't sure it had, but if it had, our plan would be destroyed. The gossip would get back. Of that, I was sure. Like as soon as I turned my head. I didn't know what this guy knew, but if he knew anything about me, and then heard I was going to marry Napoleon, the son of his good friend Duke, he certainly would divulge. I got very warm all of a sudden. Even though the air-conditioning was thrusting through the place.

'So – now that we're all here,' his mother said. 'Tell us.'

At that moment, I clutched Napoleon's arm.

'Sweetheart, could you escort me to the ladies' room?'

'I was just about to tell them the news.'

'I'm really feeling faint.' And I gave him a charged look that the others couldn't see.

Napoleon looked at the rest of them. 'Uh, sure, honey.'

'Are you all right, dear?' Mrs Merriweather inquired.

'I think so.'

'We'll be right back,' Napoleon said. Though I sensed that would not be the case. And I gave a polite smile to all, and we moved off, Napoleon's arm still matted to my lower back. We marched out of sight and down the hall and slipped into the bar of the Ponce de Leon Ballroom. I ordered a martini. Sure, I was mixing.

'Who is that guy?' I asked him.

'Which?'

'The one who just joined us. With the shifty eyes. He knows your father.'

'That's Robert Paulson. He's one of my father's best friends. They go way back.'

'I think I know him.'

'What do you mean?'

'Does he go to London?'

'He has a house in Surrey, yes.'

'He's a friend of Giles Hamilton's.'

'So?'

We looked at each other. I didn't want to utter the next words. I let Napoleon have the honors.

'Did you . . .?'

'I don't know.'

'You don't know?'

'No.'

'How can you not *know*?'

'I just . . . I know I met him. And there is one friend of Giles's I slept with. But it's kind of a blur. It was not a great time for me. We were very drunk. Wait,' I said. 'Does he have kids?'

'No.'

'Neither did this guy I was with.'

'*Merde*. What are we going to do?'

I was silent.

'Okay,' Napoleon said. 'Say you did sleep with him. What does that indicate?'

'That's bad.'

'Why?'

'He'll tell your father about me, about Giles, about his night with me. And they'll know what I am, or what both of us are up to.'

'*Tu pense?*'

'Of course.'

'Okay, what if you didn't sleep with him?'

'That's better. Because the more serious Giles stuff can be denied. And I don't know to what extent he knows about Giles and me at all, anyway. Our relationship could just be viewed as an extramarital affair. Which is simple stuff. Besides, Giles was well respected.'

'Man,' he said with a sigh. 'You can't remember?'

'No.'

'What can't you remember? That you kissed him? Or gave him a blow job or fucked him?'

'I don't know anything at all.'

'Do you want to test him?'

'Now? No way. That would make it worse.'

He looked directly at me. 'So – what are you saying?'

I looked at him. My eyes began to tear. All the recent pain and difficulty just surged through me, and before I knew it, I was heaving, crying my eyes out, using cocktail napkins to preserve my makeup. Until there was no point anymore.

'It's okay, baby.'

But I knew it wasn't. Our plot had been ruined. The News would never be told. It was all over for The Plan. For now, anyway.

I told Napoleon I wanted to return to our room. He escorted me there. I told him to return to the ballroom and make points with his father. He didn't want to. I told him he at least had to tell them what 'news' he'd been preparing them for. He agreed.

I slipped out of my shoes and lay down on the bed. I swiveled my head into the pillow. And cried.

When Napoleon returned some minutes later, he was very quiet. He laid the room key and an envelope on the dresser, then took off his jacket and shirt and collapsed on the bed. He turned on the television. I turned over, snared the remote from him, and turned off the TV.

'What did you tell them?'

He was monotoned and robotlike with his response. He was obviously very disappointed. 'That I was graduating from NYU in the spring. With honors. That I was going to start my own practice. That was the "news." '

'Is that all that was said?' I asked in a leading way.

'No. My mother asked me if I was seeing you. Romantically.'

'In front of your father?'

'No.'

'What did you say?'

'I said we were good friends.'

'Good. What did she say?'

'She said she was happy for that.'

And it just burst forth from me in a rage. 'Happy for what? *That we were friends or the fact that we weren't together?*'

He looked at me. My charged, mascara-smeared face was hovering on death row over him.

'Paulson told them that I should watch out for you. That you were a "gold digger on a global scale," was the way he put it.'

I was stupefied. But that lasted only a moment. The floodgates were opened again. I resorted to bawling like an airplane baby.

'Listen, Bo. In this crowd, accusations like that are made a thousand times over on a night like this. During the party and after. It never stops. Wherever you have a collection of wealthy types, those labels are passed around like hors d'oeuvres. You know that. You know it better than I do.'

But I was on to other thoughts already. 'I hate my life, Napoleon. It's never going to work out.'

'Of course it is.'

'No. All these men. Everything for men. Men, men, men.' And words were just coming out of me. I was spitting them. 'You just run around. And they want to fuck you this way and that way. And then when they're done with you, they want you to fuck their friends. They throw parties for their business friends and they introduce you to everyone so they can fuck you. So they can make more money, because let's face it, there's no better way to show goodwill to some business associate than to present him with the new hot young fuck. No one gives a shit about you. It makes you hate yourself.'

'Bo . . .'

the rant

Napoleon was sitting up on the bed. I was out on our little deck looking out now at the dark ocean. It had little white lines of shorebreak lapping up on the beach. But it didn't have any calming effect on me. The fury kept coming. Like bile from my inner core. I stepped back into the room and had a thorough meltdown.

'It's never going to happen for me. I'm hitting the same ceiling each time. With every guy. I ruined it for myself. My past is going to kill me. Past is cancer to a woman. Not because of the actual events that make it what it is or was, but how it's perceived. I thought I'd been discreet. I thought I'd been quiet. But they find out. They always find out. And it's not like you've done anything wrong. It's not like you've done anything they haven't been doing themselves. You're just trying to find your way. You're just trying to find your way home. And they bill it as something dark, slutty, whorish, and perverted. Like you're sick or something. When, in fact, the world is stacked against you from the start.

'We run around with this highly sensitive plumbing equipment. The equipment that makes life, that gives life, that produces beautiful children. Children that can't be cared for, even though they make it into the world. Why? Because this planet is the worst. The way it starts – the men ditch out when a child is born, the women are so whacked-out that they leave babies in garbage cans. It's too much stress. Too many people. For a finite amount of resources. And let's not forget the men. They just want to fuck you this way and that way and blow jobs and from behind, and for what? Domination? Ego? We are on the run, Napoleon. Women are on the run.'

I didn't wait for him to respond. Maybe he did, for all I knew.

'And why the hell shouldn't we be? Why the hell shouldn't there be a separation of the sexes? Why the hell shouldn't women be sent spiraling into the lesbian complex? Why the hell shouldn't we get the hell out of Dodge? We can't even get the government to subsidize tampons. Rest assured, if men had periods, they'd be subsidized.'

Yes, I was paraphrasing Gloria Steinem. But so what?

'Look at the **Three-Minute Princess**. Running. My sister? Running. My niece? Trying to. My mother? Her head buckled in an attempt to. **Earning Every Penny**? Running. Me? Running. Everyone I know is running. No one is taking care of us. Us. Who give life. Us, who keep the whole show going. And we can't even get married. We're just a vast field of sperm receptacles for as long as they want. They. Men. Men are the worst.'

'Yes, they are,' Napoleon added.

'They call you a whore if you've slept with someone before them. And they call you a bitch if you don't do it with them. And they call you a whore if you have done them but you move on to someone else because they haven't taken care of you. We're whores coming and going, no matter what we do. And you know what? All that matters is that you're pretty and thin and your nails are painted and your legs are waxed so that you can at least play The Game. After all, it's the only show going. So we get all dressed up to get beaten down. We're on the defensive, and it's not going to change. It makes you hate them. Every last one of them. And, of course, they lie. And cheat. And they stick it in somewhere else whenever it suits them. And when we do it back, we get the blame for being liars. And cheats. What I'd like the data on is, who lied first? In all these tales of heartbreak and female romantic atrocities levied on men, who the hell lied first? But "that's different," the morons say. "We have a closed system. And no pregnancy can result. You women have an open system. Someone invades your space." I say bullshit! It takes two. Always. Whether you're sticking it. Or taking it. It's the same mind-set. It's having a sexual act with another party. *Basta!*'

'Bo?'

I wasn't going to let him in now. I was too furious.

'And I say, Fine! Okay. Have sex with other people. We're all animals. And maybe not lifelong monogamists. But stop blaming us!'

'You're right—'

'I have met so many people, Napoleon, and I don't have any friends.'

'You have me.'

'I don't know who to trust.'

'You can trust me.'

'Because there's no one *to* trust. As soon as another woman opens her mouth, I think, *My God, what a bullshitter*. And men, well, I believe them even less. Who can you trust? No one. It sucks. The truth is, you can trust only yourself. You're born alone and you die alone and you'd better love yourself. And do we live in a faster circle? Sure we do. New York, L.A., London. It's fast living. And maybe morals flee quicker in these environments. But the truth of the matter is, I'm from Ohio and the life there isn't much better. The same crap goes on there. All that matters is how pretty and thin you are and if your pussy is waxed. And legs and whatever . . .'

'Tell it like it is, Bo . . .' I looked at him. And it gave me a boost of momentum.

'And your parents? They don't give a shit. By the time you've come into the world, your mother has been beaten down to the point where she resents anything positive that happens in your new and fresh life. And your father will see you as a sex object or like another female puppet he can manipulate, and when he's tired of the sex with your mother, he takes off and you never see him again. So there you stand, with your knees knocking in a Salvation Army dress with a thumb stuck in your mouth and a quarter wedge chopped out of your melon and you're looking around for that man who you saw around the house in your first five years and now he's gone and you're totally confused and dazed, like *Where am I?* and you're told to do well in school and learn and sit on the john properly and you have no value systems, and any values you do cling to get sodomized by the behavior of your two in-house role models who are supposed to love you but hurt you and do everything the opposite of what those values are supposed to be. So what do you do? The little girl in the Gatorade-shade dress from nowhere with no concrete values, and you want to feel your self-esteem and beauty and power, and the only way you can do it is by attracting men who want you. So you run around the world trying to find that Asshole Daddy figure again somewhere, hoping he will take care of you and make everything right. But when you get to him, he's all fucked up by fucked-up women who've been fucked over by fucked-over men who've been fucked over by fucked-over women, and so he's not going to treat you like any kind of princess. He's going to manipulate you the same way everyone has manipulated him. And you move on with another black eye and wait for it to heal, and when it does, the whole cycle repeats itself and you want the whole goddamn thing to stop. And you want to change and you want it to change and you want to get out of it, and the harder you try to get out of it, you get sucked further back in, hoping still it will get better – and it never does. They just want to fuck you this way and that way and blow jobs and from behind, and you know what matters?'

'How pretty and thin you are and if your toes are painted and your ass is waxed,' Napoleon chimed in with.

'That's right,' I said, and stopped short, as though a

crossing guard had held up her hand at the crosswalk and made me.

And I don't know how, but the fact that Napoleon had contributed, that he had listened, and listened so keenly, keenly enough to repeat the chorus I'd been singing, made me pop out of my ranting head and made me step back and listen to my words and feel the stress wrinkles on my forehead.

And I just ... and I couldn't believe it, but I just started to laugh. And I laughed harder. And then Napoleon started to laugh too. And I walked over to the bed and curled up on it next to him and climbed on top of him and did a somersault over his body and crashed down into the gap on the floor in between the two beds. And I couldn't stop laughing. I propped myself against the bedside table, and we continued to laugh until our sides hurt.

And then I said it with all my heart. 'I love you, Napoleon.'

'I love you, Bo.'

the sermon

At this point, I was raiding the minibar. I took a vodka mini and tossed Napoleon a gin mini.

'I don't like gin.'

'Drink it,' I said firmly. 'But it's a deeper love,' I qualified.

You see, I wasn't done. Not by a long shot.

'Oh?'

'We're both outcasts, Napoleon. That's why you get me, I get you, we get each other.'

He swigged on the little bottle and then blasted out, 'We get each other!' as if we were in a Baptist church.

'It's us against the world!' I chanted.

'You tell it, girl,' he chanted back.

'You didn't want a child—'

'Amen!'

'You wanted your money!'

'Oh yeah!'

'You wanted your money your way!'

'Yeah, yeah.'

'Like me. And us. The women of the world!'

'It's your world, girl!'

We were laughing in between verses, of course. It was a nice release.

'A gold digger is more of a hooker today!'

'Your world!'

'Why? Because men aren't getting married. That's the cruel truth. So we are forced to satisfy ourselves with shorter-term situations. We have to make as much money as we can in the short periods.'

'Tell it, sister!'

'But we have to be smart—'

'Oh yeah.'

'We have to know when to kiss, when to scold, when to encourage, when to caress, when to give a humdinger, when to have sex, when to have dirty sex, when to speak up, and when to shut up!'

'Yes!'

'We're not here to rule. We're here to influence. There's power in that.'

'Go-go-go, girl!'

'We have to accept that. Just as men have to accept that they can't reproduce and give life—'

'Your world!'

'We cannot go against our biology. That's women barking up the wrong tree. We can't go against nature. Nature that is so much older—'

'Older!'

'Wiser—'

'Wiser!'

'And more powerful than us.'

'Power!'

'In ten thousand years, or a million years, if the planet

survives, maybe our biology will change or mutate.'

'Mutate!' And that sounded really funny. It took me a while to collect myself. I was curled up on the floor now, laughing and drooling into the carpet.

'As for now, we are stuck with our biological duties. But it's not stuck!'

'No, girl, no! No, stuck, no!'

'It's a privilege.'

'Privilege!'

'It's a privilege to give life.'

'Life!' I chanted louder.

'Life!'

'Love life!'

'Love life!'

And we remained gazing at each other. And then we hugged.

'And all together now,' I said with a smile.

And we did just that. We both sang it together.

'*And they just want to fuck you this way and that way and blow jobs and from behind, and you know what matters? How beautiful and thin you are!*'

And then we retired into a ball of laughter. And then he tickled me. I went crazy.

To be honest, I didn't know where it had come from. I felt as if it had been channeled through me in some way, and my lips were just delivering it. Other than the fact that I had the same astro data as Martin Luther King and I had watched all his speeches a few times over, I'd never given any kind of sermon before.

It was one of the most memorable nights of my life.

the announcement

My eyes opened. It was the middle of the night. I didn't know where I was. So I switched on the light. It was still our Breakers hotel room.

'Are you okay?' Napoleon uttered from a deep-sleep fog.

I was so awake. My subconscious had been grinding away. I could tell. 'I'm tired of playing The Game,' I said.

'I know.'

'It's time.'

He looked over at me. 'Is it?'

'It is.'

Time, of course, indicated a willingness to forgo all short-term arrangements. It was time to get married. And I was feeling the need now. My recent life had been working on me in such a way that I felt it was time. I'd saved some money, and that was all-important when it came to going long-term. Because in the marriage game, you had to have some reserves because you weren't necessarily going to take in any more money for a while. It required your own savings to live on while you targeted your man and executed your strategy.

'So you're retiring from the Tour?'

'Completely.'

I was tired of hitting little base hits. And if you're wondering why I break into sports jargon, it's because I used to watch ESPN with Buddy Farrell, my first boyfriend, the one who dumped me. In fact, he's the one who taught me about Bo Jackson, the great two-sport athlete who got hurt and lost both his playing careers by trying to do too much. And of course, *Bo knows* came from that.

Anyhow, now I was going to go long ball. I was going to hitch it up. Somewhere. But not in Europe. Not on the Tour. In America. I was an American. You couldn't take that out of me. And it was time.

He looked over at me and covered his eyes from the glaring lamp light. 'I have a surprise for you.'

'I need one.'

'But I was waiting to give it to you.'

'Now!'

'It's in the envelope.'

I got up and walked over to the bureau and picked up the envelope. It was a fancy cream-colored one. Like an invitation to a wedding or something. 'What's in it?' I asked prematurely, like a little anxious girl.

'Read it.'

'Where did you get it?

'Downstairs. From an old friend.'

Napoleon had already opened it. I just slipped it out of the envelope. And read aloud.

'Mr Pierre and Adele Lorne-August invite you to the Annual Costume Wing Ball, December fourth, 1999, at eight P.M.' I looked at Napoleon. 'The Lorne-August family? As in Bradley Lorne-August?'

'The one and only,' he said with a contorted smile. He didn't have complete control of his sleepy facial muscles yet.

I was excited. I spent the last fifteen minutes of my waking hours that night in the bathroom.

'What are you doing?' Napoleon droned finally.

And then I emerged, my face painted in slashing streaks like the Zuni Indian warrior queen I was.

'I'm ready.'

'For what?'

'War.'

And Napoleon laughed. It prompted me to smile. But only momentarily. We both knew I could not have been more serious.

The next day, as our plane taxied down the runway at JFK, I opened the envelope one more time and scanned the invitation. 'You know Bradley Lorne-August is one of my Rich Rebels,' I noted.

'I've heard you mention him once or twice. And Lawrence Dexter Fairchild will be there too.'

'*Two* of my Rich Rebels. It must be a big party.'

'Three hundred, maybe four.'

'It's being held at the Metropolitan Museum of Art.'

At that moment, I hung my looks on Napoleon. He knew what I was thinking. 'You're really going to need me now,' he said.

'Are you going to come with me as my date?'

'Sounds good to me.'

'Even though we didn't hit pay dirt down there, I had a great time,' I said about our travail in Palm Beach.

'Me too.'

I leaned over and gave him a kiss on the lips. Then he injected his tongue.

'Ugh,' I groaned.

'That was just my snowman sweetness.'

'Behave.'

'Fags get away with nothing these days.'

I reread the invite. 'December fourth. That's this weekend.'

And Napoleon just smiled. 'You can handle that.'

rich, rebellious, and ripe

For marriage, the rebel boys of wealthy families have always been my personal favorites. The Rich Rebels, as I called them, are the ones who have turned their backs on all that social stuff and look for a type of woman whose character will make their parents' skin crawl. They'll do it to spite them. And you know what? They almost always inherit the money anyway. I loved the type. Why? Because I'm a rebel myself. But more important, my breeding wasn't great. Though I had a great face and a killer bod, and am quite the bedroom gymnast, there were cracks in my armor. I mean, in my years abroad I had learned a lot. You could say I'd come a long way. But when really examined closely, I couldn't weather any concerted imposition of those rigid standards. I could hear it now. *But she's from Ohio, she never went to college, she doesn't know anyone we know, she speaks so American.*

In fairness to me, most of the society girls couldn't live up to my physical traits and superkeen people skills. Physically, in my opinion, most of those manner-born prepsters looked like Stepford Wives. That same hanging face with the blond flair cut dripping measuredly at chin length and no more. Spend an afternoon on Main Street in Greenwich, Connecticut, and watch the clones roll their bassinets by. You'll see what I mean.

I'm a survivor, don't forget. We're all survivors, the Diggers. And those real qualities of spice and adventure we bring to the table – and it is our colorful backgrounds that make us different – can be appealing to that rebellious upper-crust boy. The one who has had all those cotillions and social balls and bad, limp, and lifeless sex shoved down his throat. A wild, spontaneous chick from Nowheresville can be his dream girl.

The Rich Rebels were ripe for the taking. That was the boy for me. And I had come to that juncture in my life where I'd decided it was time to get one.

There had been three Rich Rebels who topped my short list. But **For Your Wallet Only** got to one of them. They got married the previous summer in Bermuda. Lucky gal. How did she do it? The Pregnancy Lock, of course. But get this. She faked the pregnancy and got him to relax on the protection. Since she was already 'pregnant,' he didn't worry about condom usage. That's when he seeded her for real. **For Your Wallet Only** was genius.

The Pregnancy Lock. It's the only sure way, incidentally. It's the only way.

In any case, I had five days to put myself together. Not that I usually wasn't together, but I wanted to be especially together. After all, I was a different girl now. I was The Millennium Girl. The **Digger with a Logo**. I was going to get my man – and take no prisoners doing it.

I went first for the dress because it was a Monday. The previous Sugar Daddy Saturday I was sure had robbed the stores of everything decent. I was already diving for scraps. But I didn't care. I was going to make a statement at this party. Even if I had to wear a leather thong and a ski mask.

I was looking for perfectly elegant yet sexy. Miraculously, I found it. It was a return. It was a Christmas burgundy Badgley Mischka and it made my waist seem nonexistent; my rear small, round, and tight; and my chest ready to be elected. I had the entire store area applauding. They knew me, of course, but still ... If there are things to die for, it was beyond sacrifice.

Then I sought shoes and undergarments. I bought some new high heels at Patrick Cox and new black lace undies at La Perla. When I tried on the underwear in the changing room, I even got hot. I bought some new thigh-highs at Fogal.

Then I did the body. I had a wax at Miano-Viel, my nails done by Roxanne at Warren-Tricomi, a reflexology pedicure at Allure Day Spa; I had a seaweed facial at Georgette Klinger, I had my hair trimmed at Frédéric Fekkai, and then colored Bordeaux burgundy at Louis Licari – to go with the dress, of course. Napoleon even added some lighter highlights at home.

The day of the party I had the Paradise Market send up a couple of dozen avocados for my requisite big-night guacamole bath. The Paradise Market is a veritable produce boutique and very expensive. It's where Jackie O bought her groceries. I mashed up the avocados in the tub and let the water rip. They made my skin soft as can be. And I was going to let it be touched that night. I wanted anyone who touched me to feel the softness. Of course, I arranged for the plumber to come in the morning. Guacamole baths are a mess. They always stop up the drain.

I also did my Hypnotic Scent Blend. I dotted Chanel No. 5 on my neck, I used Poison by Dior behind my ears, I used Allure by Chanel on my cleavage, I used Envy by Gucci on my wrists, and So Pretty I dotted behind my knees. And I put Champagne by Saint Laurent on my belly button – just in case. Different scents in different pulse points have a hypnotic effect on the opposite sex. And Bo knows pulse points.

Earlier in the week I'd bought Napoleon a new tuxedo at Armani. He looked dazzling in it. We were going to make the house quake, along the likes of as soon as we entered the room. Of that, I was sure.

metropolitan magnifique

And we did.

But before I tell you how we did it, I want to give you a sense of this party. Of course, the food was catered gourmet by the Four Seasons' chef. The champagne – all superior brands – never stopped coming. Peter Duchin and his orchestra played. There were several speeches given by fashion czars Oscar de la Renta, Ralph Lauren, and Valentino, as it was a high-fashion benefit. And there was dancing.

The guest list was appropriately impressive as well. All the big, boldfaced names from all the columns – Suzy, Liz Smith, Cindy Adams, Neil Travis, Page Six – were there. You had the Astors, the Whitneys, the Vanderbilts, the Mellons, the Drexels, the Peabodys, the Gettys, the Mortimers, Henry and Nancy Kissinger, Blaine and Robert Trump, Pat and William Buckley, Bill Blass, Carroll Petrie, Nan Kempner and Kenneth Jay Lane, Alfred and Judy Taubman, and on and on.

Not only were the socially revered in attendance, there were many prominent representatives of the business world – the Fortune 500 boys and their wives and mistresses.

And then you had the Children Of, the group that held my interest. I was actually somewhat nervous when we arrived. I couldn't eat. But I did down a quick glass of champagne to calm myself. Napoleon clutched my arm tightly. He could feel that I was nervous. It wasn't that I was intimidated. Or that I felt out of place. I had groomed myself to move effortlessly with the rich. I had studied their way of life for years. I'll tell you just how, later.

What had changed, however, was my attitude. I was in it for something else now. I was going to find the man to link up with for the rest of my life. I never saw Walletmen previously as anything but short-term lovers on long-term financial bases. And now that I was seeing them differently, it gave me butterflies. It was like the feeling you get as an athlete, I think, before the big game. You know how to do it, you're a pro, but you just need to get the game under way. The first ten minutes would be the worst. And they were.

I spilled champagne, I got my dress caught in someone's heel, and I made a couple of simple faux pas in conversation. The heel incident wasn't my fault, though. It was courtesy of **Smiles to Your Face**, a Tour girl I hadn't seen since Cannes in May. We'd had Côte d'Azur designs on the same guy, and that time I won out. The heel thing, however, could have been avoided. I should have seen it coming – that also shows how off my game I was at the gala's outset.

In addition to **Smiles to Your Face**, **No Deposit**, **No Return**, **The 50% Solution**, **Travels With Men**, and **Little Miss Windowshade Pants** were there. I don't know how **Little Miss** got in or who'd brought her. Obviously, some bloated guy who wanted no argument when he got home. He wouldn't get one with her. There were sluts around, but nobody handed it out like **Little Miss**. You know, the kind of girl whose pants have to come down in order to go back up. Her stout little friend **Meals on Wheels** was there too, pretending to know people. She tried to glom onto me, but I faked her with a diversionary 'My bra unhinged' and headed in the direction of the ladies' room.

As we shuffled away, Napoleon said, 'I'm not used to seeing you this way.'

'I know. What do I do now?'

'Just calm down.'

'I know, I know. How do I look?'

'*Magnifique*.'

'Really?'

'Really.'

'Tell me again.'

He did.

'And once more.'

After the third repeat, he pulled me close and kissed me on the cheek.

'Right now there are about twenty sets of male eyes looking at me like I'm the lucky guy. Everyone is looking. Husbands, wives, you name it. And it's been that way since we arrived. You look ravishing. The best I've ever seen you look.'

And I held him close and whispered in his ear, 'So what do I do?'

'Absolutely nothing. Be yourself. And let the party come to you,' he said.

It was the best advice. After he'd said it, everything became crystal clear. I freed up and unlocked my personality. I loved Napoleon.

We immediately began talking to some of his friends from Paris, as well as some women whose hair he'd cut and colored.

'Who did your hair?' he asked of one comely brunette.

'Simon.'

'Oh, I'm jealous. I thought I was the only one.'

'You were out of town, Napoleon. I'm not sure I like it.'

'Why not? It has attitude.'

'Do you think so?'

'When was it cut?'

'Today.'

'No wonder. Your hair is still in a state of shock. Give it a few days. It will be perfect.'

'Really?'

It's amazing how the women just tingled around Napoleon. If he ever wanted to give up gay living, he could have a field day. It would be *Shampoo* and beyond. He was so sexy.

'Oh God, Bo. There he is,' Napoleon said, his voice suddenly deep and serious.

'Your father?'

'No.'

And sure enough, in the distance, we saw him. It was John Summers. I looked at Napoleon, and he had gone from a countenance of cool sensuality to completely rattled. A twitch monster, even.

'Now I'm going to give some advice to *you*. Calm down. Let the party come to you.'

'Right, right.'

Dinner was a choice of filet mignon, salmon, or lemon chicken. I had some vegetables. We ate with a table that consisted mostly of successful businessmen. There wasn't a bad watch within a hundred yards. The most celebrated of the group was Morris Barton, CEO of Barton Industrial, number six on the List. He'd politely asked us to join his table. I'd met him once before with Warren Samuels.

After playing with his food, and making repeated neck-twisting maneuvers to spy on John's table, Napoleon said to me, 'What do you think of the girl he's with?'

'She looks model-y.'

'I'm dying to tell him about the new fragrance.'

'What new fragrance?'

'It's called Conversion. By Calvin Klein.'

'That's very funny. Do you have a slogan?'

'*Bien sûr*. "For the curiosity in all of us." '

'Not bad. How about "For pitchers and catchers." '

We laughed out loud like sick little politically incorrect party Rumpelstiltskins. When all the fun subsided, Napoleon sent his snow-beams back over at John. 'He's so superficial.'

Napoleon then went to the bathroom, and I chatted with Morris. He propositioned me after about four minutes. It would have been three, but he ordered a drink and squabbled over the type of vodka. His wife had become enraptured with a hairless man to her left, and Morris made good use of the time. He gave me his card under the table, and I tucked it away in my thigh-high to save for a rainy day.

I could tell Morris's wife found the bald man sexy. I'd heard he was a doctor too. The bald thing, I think, has psychological ties to the head of the penis. So if you take the head of a penis and cross it with a guy who knows your body and knows how to fix it and can pay for everything twice, now that's sexy. In essence, I agreed with her.

Then, during dessert, the most amazing thing happened. As the band launched into the after-dinner set, a young man came walking over from across the room. He had gel-slicked blond hair with a wispy bang flopping *GQ*-ly off his face. He was about five-eleven and very handsome. He looked like he played a good game of tennis. He wore a standard Brooks Brothers tuxedo, though his pants were way too short. It was as if he'd lost the real ones and had substituted. WASPs are so practical, I thought. Yet he had the funniest bow tie. It was tie-dyed.

'My name is Lawrence.'

I knew that already. It was Lawrence Dexter Fairchild, one of my Rich Rebels. 'Hello.'

'You must be Bodicea.'

'Yes.'

'What a wonderful name.'

'Thank you.'

'I just met your friend Napoleon. He's very funny.'

'Funny, yeah,' I agreed for a lack of anything better to say.

'He told me you were bored.'

'Well, not really.'

'These parties are pretty stiff. But I thought I would try and do my best to alter your frame of mind.'

'You're not off to a bad start.'

And we both laughed. Just then, the band played 'Come Fly with Me'.

'I haven't heard this song in so long,' I said. In actuality, I hadn't heard it since **Earning Every Penny**, my Digger mentor, and I used to sit around every Wednesday night, sip wine, strategize about men, and listen to vintage Sinatra. We called them our Sinatra and Strategy nights.

'Would you care to dance?' he asked.

'I would love to' – and I was so busy smiling and looking at him as he gently held my hand and guided me on the rise that I didn't finish my sentence until we stepped on the dance floor – 'dance,' I said finally.

I was floating. It was then that I did in fact see that people were looking at us, at me. It was a wonderful feeling.

And Lawrence was really good. He had all those fairy-tale moves down. Let me make this point. Women are suckers for the fairy tale. We've been conditioned to wait for the white knight ever since those early picture books were used on us. Whenever we see any traces of this kind of behavior in the opposite sex – no matter how jaded or how many men we've slept with – we become instantly drawn to it. Fairy-tale behavior is the most compelling. And Lawrence Fairchild knew how to white-knight a woman. I could tell.

At first, there were only several couples dancing. Then, as more people finished dinner, the floor filled up and became a sea of glitter and black tie. It was beautiful. The trumpets were blaring. Couples with glowing faces were twirling all around us. Or maybe that's how I saw it. Whichever, one thing couldn't be denied. It was a very smart party.

Lawrence would alternately hold me tight and then spin me with a sort of reckless abandon. He was a fabulous dancer. It was obvious he'd been sent to dancing school at an early age. But what was puzzling me was, he seemed so ordinary, so true to the norm. His parents' norm. Remember, he'd been one of my Rich Rebels. I was waiting for some sign of all the wildness I'd heard about. But that never happened. The only display of the unconventional was the bow tie. And clothes don't make the man. I was quite puzzled.

When the song was over, we stepped off the floor and Lawrence was immediately confronted by his date, who was all fake smiles. She was oozing with envy, so much so that she didn't even hear Lawrence introduce us. I turned my back to her and thanked him for the dance and told him Napoleon had my number.

I made my way across the room, maneuvering in between the tables. The room was about fifty percent louder, and it wasn't just because they were trying to talk above the music. It was the alcohol consumed that had fully reached the brains of everyone. It always turns up the volume. People become less inhibited, more animated, and shy has flown out the window. When they talk, they want to be heard.

I spotted Napoleon seated by himself two tables over from his 'lover.' He was sipping on scotch, or at least something brown. Napoleon did that only when he wanted to get drunk. Really drunk.

As I advanced on him, **No Deposit, No Return** intercepted me. She looked beautiful in the previous year's Ralph Lauren 'wedding' dress. It's not really a wedding dress. It's the white dress he always closes his fashion shows with.

'Hi, Bo.'

'Hello there, **No Deposit, No Return**. Don't you look amazing.'

'You too. Great party.'

'I'm having fun so far.'

'Have you heard from **At These Prices**?'

'Yes. She's still over there.'

And both our eyes took on that half skeptical, half jealous look that appeared to be only half skeptical. Because we certainly were jealous of the numbers **At These Prices** was talking. I'm sorry if I sound tomboyish, but whenever I've had a few kir royales. I start reverting to my Ohio playground verbiage. Kind of like the Southerner who finds her down-home twang when she's tipsy. Yes, I was tipsy.

'She says they treat her like a queen, but . . .'

'Yeah, *but* . . .' I said bluntly.

And we both laughed, not because of the weak humor but because of the alcohol.

'You going to Aspen?'

'I don't think so,' I said. 'I'm tired of it.'

'Me too.'

We politely waved each other off, and I joined Napoleon.

'Baby, what's the matter?' I asked.

'How about – my life?' he returned with an exaggerated pout.

'Come on. Dance with me.'

'He's so common.'

'Exactly.'

I looked over, and John had three girls semicircled around him as he was spinning off some fractionally significant story. And none of the girls was his date. In fact, his date was on the floor dancing with someone else. Someone *really* else.

'Isn't that John's date over there?'

'Yes.'

'And she's dancing with . . .' I didn't finish it but rather waited for Napoleon's reaction. He just smiled in an intoxicated way. It was a look of confirmation. It was the reaction I'd been awaiting, and hoping for.

Bradley Lorne-August was about six feet two inches tall, dark brown hair with a slashing and dashing hairline that sliced back sharply from the temples. Like Cary Grant's. He had an Armani tux, Gucci pumps, and a platinum Rolex. He was a knockout. With the fashion model clutching on to him, they looked like an advertisement for, well, you name it. Dashing. He was obviously a better dancer than she was, but she wasn't inexperienced. She knew enough to let him make all the moves.

'Wow,' I said.

Napoleon was still monitoring John. 'He's so vulgar...' Napoleon was very drunk now.

'Drink water,' I told him.

'No!'

'Come on.'

'He has zee biggest cock.'

'I know, I know.'

'Zee biggest. I swear.' And he took another brown gulp. 'You know what I hate?'

'What?'

'I hate being a fag.'

'I'm not going to let you play the self-loathing snowman. You hate the self-loathing snowman.'

'I know. I do hate it. Or him.' And he burped too.

'You're a good snowman.'

Even though my last comment was a logical tail to the previous exchange, he could see it only as singular now and standing alone. And his pickled brain would process it differently than what was intended, the way all textbook-drunk people do – they take your comment in and leave their face to do whatever it wants. It always involuntarily takes on that unpredictable glare. You don't know if they're going to hit you or kiss you. Then the idea you've postured takes root in their brain. And you get your response.

Napoleon broke out into an award-winning grin.

'You look beautiful,' he said.

'So do you.' And we hugged. 'I'm going to go to the bathroom.'

'No...'

I looked at him.

'I'm coming right back,' I said.

'Wait.' And he glanced over at Bradley. 'Don't ruin it.'

'What?' I tried to figure it out. I got as far as: Napoleon set me up with Lawrence. But what does that have to do with Bradley? Other than the fact that they were both one and two, or two and one, on my Rich Rebel List. In essence, I needed more information.

So I gave up and asked him.

'Bradley and Lawrence Fairchild are at the same table,' he explained. 'They are best friends. And they're very competitive.'

'Really . . .' My mind made note of that.

'When you were dancing with Lawrence, Bradley was burning eyes into the two of you. In fact, the whole table was watching, saying stuff like *Who's the girl?*'

'But . . .'

'Wait. Bradley is insecure about Lawrence. I think Lawrence stole a girlfriend or two of his. Lawrence is kind of a jerk that way. He likes to screw his friends' girlfriends. It's a challenge for him. It's what gets him off. He's very weak.'

'How do you know all this?'

'My sister – she told me.'

'Good work, hon.' Napoleon was very good at this. For the very reasons he was an aspiring psychologist. In addition, he considered himself an expert on both sexes. And he was, of sorts. 'I'm caught between,' he'd always say.

'So – wait here a moment,' he commanded.

'Maybe I shouldn't be so accessible.'

'That would be too much. Bradley is a little shy.'

'You really want me to score, don't you?'

'In the worst way. You're the breadwinner here. Or you have to bring home the bacon. Which is it?'

'Both.' We both laughed.

'By the way, I told Lawrence you were from Ohio.'

'Really. Why?'

'But I said Shaker Heights.'

I thought it over. Napoleon knew Shaker Heights was one of the more affluent areas in Ohio.

'You know people in Shaker Heights, don't you?'

I told him I did, and that was true. In essence, he was warning me so I wouldn't slip up. Best friends usually compare notes. The shy guy does it because he doesn't know any better. He doesn't know how to play the sport as well. The devious one, the one who screws his friends' girlfriends, does it as a teaser, to actually elicit more information or to set up his friend. If I'd seen this type of rivalry behavior once, I'd seen it a thousand times. It's the same with women.

The model was all giggles now on the dance floor and she'd had enough. As they passed, Bradley took a long drink of me, longer than sobriety would ever permit, and then at Napoleon. He kind of half smiled, and that was all Napoleon needed.

'You're Bradley, right?' Bradley confirmed it, of course. 'I'm Napoleon. Go Go is my sister.'

'Go Go Merriweather? Sure. Where is she?'

'She's down at UVA. still.'

And Bradley didn't even hear him. He was already

spying on me. I was a little embarrassed. But not that much.

'This is my friend Bodicea.'

'Hello. Bradley,' he said. We shook hands. He had a nice hand and a nice handshake.

He patted the seat next to me. 'May I?' he asked in a leading way.

'Please do,' I said with my best High Midnight smile.

At that moment, Napoleon got up and announced that he was headed to the bar. He asked if we'd like anything, and Bradley waited for me to order. So I did. And he did too. I was happy he did. It meant he would chat with me a little. Before Napoleon moved off, I stood and whispered a command for him to get Lawrence's astro data.

After the normal self-introductions, highlights of which included that Bradley had gone to Yale and I was from Shaker Heights, what he told me about himself was rather interesting. He wanted to be a sort of an anthropological chronicler of sorts. He wanted to travel to foreign cultures, study them, photograph and write about them.

'I'm waiting to hear back from *National Geographic*, actually.'

I told him I loved the magazine. And that was true.

'Do you subscribe?'

'I did when I was a kid. But not anymore.'

And that wasn't true. What is true is, our neighbors did. And they stacked them in their bookcase and I used to borrow them. That magazine had taken me away from my life and had brought me around the globe. It was one of the first things that got me thinking about moving out of Ohio. There were few things Bradley could have said that would have captivated me more. Not even his combined Eastern and Western astrological signs. But I was going to get them out of him anyway.

'If you don't mind my asking, when's your birthday?'

'February sixteenth.'

'And what year were you born?'

'I'm an Aquarius.'

'I know. What year?'

'Nineteen sixty-four.'

'Ah, a Dragon.'

'Am I? Is that good?'

It was very good. As in good news. To me. 'Depends what you call *good*,' I offered to him.

'What are we known for generally?'

I remember the moment so vividly. I debated whether to tell him the truth. 'You're a heartbreaker,' I said flatly.

'Am I?'

'I'm just kidding. You do like to dominate, however.' And I added a warm smile.

'I suppose I do,' he said, and sent the smile right back.

'But not in a bad way. You like to be in charge in order to help others.'

'You know all the combinations of the double zodiac?'

'All one hundred and forty-four. Want a celebrity list fro   r sign?'

          Domingo, Ayn Rand, and Stephanie of
             aybe it was Caroline.'

'No, Stephanie. You were right the first time. I know her.' He looked at me, and his faint smile remained there. He was charmed.

'I loved *The Fountainhead*,' I said.

From then on, we were abuzz with each other's company. We covered many subjects: international travel was a start. He was very impressed with my knowledge of the world. I told him I'd studied in Europe and had modeled part-time. I didn't really want to lie. Something about him made me feel ashamed. I'd become callous in this way, yet he cut through that and made me second-guess myself. But what could I do? Tell him I'd been banging wealthy old men in the world's hot spots? I still had to employ my Fake Mode.

He'd done a postgraduate fellowship in England at Cambridge University. We discussed politics – he was refreshingly not all that conservative – and we discussed literature. He quoted from books and pop songs and philosophers. He spun off something from Picasso: 'If you want to paint a table, paint a chair.'

'Explain,' I asked.

'Don't plod boringly and painstakingly through the exercise with exact representations and mimicry. Interpret it in your own way with your own vision.'

He explained to me that Sinatra's signature anthem 'My Way' was actually a French song called 'Comme d'Habitude' that had been rewritten by Paul Anka into English. I didn't know that, though I was a big Sinatra fan.

But it was the F. Scott Fitzgerald quote that really got me.

'It's what Fitzgerald called "the wise and tragic sense of life,"' he said. 'And I quote, "The sense that life is essentially a cheat and its conditions are those of defeat, and that the redeeming things are not 'happiness or pleasure' but the deeper satisfactions that come out of struggle."'

'I love—'

'Wait,' Brad said. 'He concluded, "Having learned this in theory from the lives and conclusions of great men, you can get a hell of a lot more enjoyment out of whatever bright things come your way." Great, huh?'

I surely thought so. It gave me hope, I think – that all my struggle was not in vain and for naught. I wanted to give him a humdinger right then and there. And he deserved one.

Bradley was captivating. Every time we tried to dance, we got caught up in some other tangential discussion that had pollinated from the previous subject, and it duly flowered. And kept flowering. He was very articulate. And his word selection was superb. He always seemed to find the right sledgehammer word or phrase to package his points. Since he had such a great vocabulary, I found myself searching for and choosing better words when speaking to him.

When we discussed movies, however, I almost blew the whole damn deal. I was tipsy, remember. I started telling him one of my favorite quotes attributed to Marilyn Monroe or Marlene Dietrich, I can't remember which, who said when upset with a movie she was making, 'Who do I have to fuck to get off this picture?' That was okay. He laughed. But what I did next was tell him my favorite – truly my favorite – movie. That recent *Dracula* remake by Francis Ford-whatever. I never should have told him. Understandably, he asked me why.

I sipped my glass again to give me time for a bogus response. 'Oh, I'm a sucker for those contemporary versions of old monster flicks,' I came out with.

Obviously, that wasn't the reason. What was the reason was that one scene that still makes me sizzle whenever I think about it. You know, the one where that half-man, half-beast played by Gary Oldman just totally takes, rapes, and devours the woman in the red dress on that slab in the middle of the courtyard. It's the sexiest scene I've ever witnessed. To be taken like that by a beast – in an uncompromising and unrelenting way. That's what every woman wants. To be taken passionately that way. If only . . .

Of course, I couldn't tell Bradley that. To let someone know you're turned on by cinematic bestiality enough to make it your favorite film, well, it could work wonders – but it could also have him heading for the hills.

'So tell me, Bradley. You carve quite a swath. Why don't you have a girlfriend?'

'I had a series of difficult relationships and, well, that cycle ended about a year ago. And I must say I needed time to heal. I brought a date tonight, but she's just a friend. A friend of the family, actually.'

'You mean you were set up?'

'Yeah, kind of.'

'By who?'

'My mother.'

'Your mother?'

'Yes.'

'You let her set up dates for you?'

'She means well. She's just bored.'

I was going to ask him to point her out to me but then wondered if I should alert him to the fact that I didn't know the real mavens of high society, which would tip off that I was of a different group. Right then I decided I wasn't going to pretend exaggeratedly anymore. I felt comfortable enough with him to be myself. So I asked him.

'Over there,' he said, and let his head give a directional. 'The one with the beehive hair in the burgundy dress. The color of your dress, actually. I love your dress, by the way.'

'Thank you.' And it was nice to hear that from him.

Mrs Lorne-August looked like a tough cookie. She had a stern face and a lot of jewelry dangling from her neck. And then my view of her was interrupted by another sighting that streaked across my field of vision. On the dance floor having a whale of a time was Mrs Giles Hamilton, dancing cheek to cheek with a bottle-blond slickster who must have been twenty years her junior. I'd seen her before. Giles had shown me photos, and she was in England's *Tatler* magazine all the time. It was obvious that she and her young gun had met prior to this affair and knew a lot more about each other than just the surface stuff. His smug facial glaze told me that he knew all of her, and her look indicated that she wanted more of what he already knew. A description of their relationship began with a *c*, but it was not as in *casual*. More like *carnal*.

I pondered going up to her and introducing myself for the fun of it. But I felt it could only make matters worse. We didn't need any accelerated eviction process. What was nice was the knowledge that the old stove had been getting a little nookie on the side too, just like her husband. It made me feel less guilty.

'Tell me about yourself. What have you been up to the past ten years?'

The question made me a little nervous, but he said it somewhat facetiously. So I gave it right back.

'The ten-year plan, what else?'

'No, really. I want to know all about you.' I just smiled. 'Would you like to meet for coffee later somewhere?'

'I'm sorry, Bradley, I can't tonight.'

'Can I call you?'

'Sure. Napoleon has my number.'

'I'll call you tomorrow,' he declared.

Though I nodded only casually, I liked hearing that too. Then Bradley moved back over to his table.

Normally, I would have gone with him. But I wasn't working normally anymore. The long-term arrangement is much different from the long, long, long arrangement. In addition, I knew we'd experienced a nice high from each other's company, and I wanted that to resonate in his mind overnight or over the rest of the weekend. Besides, he had brought a date. In the end, there was no point.

'Bo?'

I turned. It was Lawrence. 'Oh, hi.'

'Napoleon gave me your number.'

I smiled. 'Where is Napoleon?'

'He's over by the bar. I'm going to give you a call.'

I nodded. I told him it was nice to meet him.

I spun and saw Bradley eyeing me as Lawrence left my company. I waved and he quickly averted his gaze, as if he didn't want it known he'd been looking at me at all. I didn't like that note of music. I was going to go up to him but thought it was better not to.

I found Napoleon plopped down in a chair about to fall asleep. He was really drunk now. I revived him with a glass of water. And we left the party. Almost. And that only counts in horseshoes. And sex, of course.

Unfortunately, Napoleon had one more maneuver in him. I thought he was walking beside me toward the museum exit doors, but unbeknownst to me, he had circled back. I knew I should look for him and find him, *fast*. A drunk Napoleon was a socially dangerous Napoleon. When I did spot him, he was heading straight toward not John Summers but the model-ish date he'd brought to the party. I quickened my pace. I yanked his hand to pull him away before he could get too snowman-drunk-bitchy. But it was too late.

He leveled her with this: 'I just want you to know, sugar, I'm more of a woman than you'll ever be, and more of a man than you'll ever get!'

It was kind of brilliant in a way. And funny. But I held my laughter to when I'd yanked him away and our faces were out of sight. Of course, on the way out Napoleon was snowbeaming wildly everywhere. He proceeded to look all husbands up and down and then tell their wives they should be expecting lots of snow soon and that everyone should get out all their warm clothes.

At home I made coffee for us, and we sat up in bed and talked. I applied a cold rag to his forehead. We discussed John, of course, for the first half hour, and I assured Napoleon that John hadn't seen anything of the spectacle. Once Napoleon sobered a bit, I told him about Bradley eyeing me warily at the end as I was talking to Lawrence. 'What do you think it means?'

'Nothing. He'll call. Even more so now.'

'Those two really have a thing going. When you gave Lawrence my number, did you find out what his sign is?'

'Aries. Born in 1963.'

'Really? He doesn't seem like an Aries at all.'

'Aah, what are you saying with this star propaganda? Men. They are all so predictable. They all do the same shit. If they're not married by thirty, there's a reason. One reason. They want to fuck more pussy,' he said.

I didn't want to get into that discussion. I'd heard Napoleon go off on me *ad nauseam* about my zodiac obsession. But in fairness to me, I didn't live my life by it. It would be silly to. I used it as a soft guidepost. If I saw any traces of truth in the behavior to what I knew astrologically, I would simply raise an eyebrow. I felt it was better to have some kind of frame of reference than none at all. If the frame of reference didn't apply, I would see it that way.

'Bradley's much nicer,' I remarked. I could feel myself glowing with happiness. I was in such a good mood about meeting him. 'I feel like a sixth-grader.'

'That's good, no?'

'I guess it is.' And I noticed I had a smile on my face. I looked at Napoleon. 'Thank you.'

'It was nothing.'

'It was a perfect evening.'

thirties weakness

There's a major difference between seeking out a conjugal union with a young Walletman as opposed to an old Walletman. The age. And that is quite simple, but it says more than you think. By far and away the most generous men are the older ones. They are perfect for the short-term payoff. But in terms of marriage, they're very difficult to land, as stated previously. Divorce rates have soared and so has a woman's ability to protect herself. Half is a very real term with serious implications. Many of the older, available Walletmen will pay for you and take you shopping and fly you all over, but they may not want to hitch up again. They've done that, thank you very much. Unless they're widowers. And good widowers are not easy to find.

It's the youngsters who haven't had families that your hopes then rest upon. The problem with them is, they know they have time and tons of opportunities, and they are in the middle of that long wait, wait, wait period. And no matter how hard you hit them emotionally, even with the potency of a boxer's punch, they will still not go down. No matter what. I guess I'm talking about guys in their late twenties. Basically, any man who doesn't remember where he was when either Martin Luther King or Robert Kennedy was shot, I stayed away from.

However, with the guys in their mid to late thirties, it is possible. It has to be just the right mix of character, chemistry, looks, and sexual appetite. And timing. And sometimes they need a little push. You may have to force their hand. Don't forget, guys in their thirties are starting to feel a little older. Their hair is thinning a bit, their physique is swelling up. They don't see themselves as the mighty Don Juans they once used to be. In addition, they see their other friends dropping like flies, getting married and having kids. They attend college reunions and some of their classmates have had three kids already. They can feel left behind. Or all alone. In addition, thoughts of their demise creep into their skulls. They're approaching 'halftime.' And guys see things in ballgame terms, believe me. Thoughts of death and such begin to nag at them. And they wonder what they've accomplished so far, and how they have yet to procreate.

Don't forget, their parents are giving them a stare-down too. Wondering and waiting. There's parental pressure, and there's all the more pressure when they have pressuring parents.

It's this thirties weakness and vulnerability you're attacking. So, if you're there at the right time, at the right point of a guy's thirties weakness, then you have a chance. That was my theory.

You may be wondering why, with all my endless globe-trotting, I rarely ran into people from my travels, big parties and social functions included. After all, it could create embarrassing, and even costly, situations. I avoided it by keeping the two worlds apart. And any Digger worth her weight knows to. The older international set rarely mixes with the more conservative, younger, unmarried or recently married set. In most cities. It's just a simple age thing. Obviously, the less remote the city, the less chance of any overlap too.

If you've done your homework, which I was very diligent in doing, it makes everything a lot easier. I knew my social sets and circles. I studied them, remember? I knew the movements and migratory patterns of affluent society. I didn't worry about overlap. I'd taken care of it way before.

I must say I had a great teacher. **Earning Every Penny** taught me how to do it right. She showed me the ropes. She was adamant against spending time with the younger marriageable sets, like the Thirties Vulnerables, until you were ready. By *ready*, she meant you'd have saved enough money from your travels with older men to support the dating-and-waiting period you'd experience with the Vulnerables.

Now, of course, if an older guy did propose, you'd have to consider that proposition very carefully. Often you'd take it, because it's better to be married to an old Walletman than to have ten younger hopefuls. Because of the younger ones' tendency to wait, which goes directly against your time clock and Window pressures.

Of course, if the marriage to the older Walletman ends in divorce or a death even, hopefully you've worked it such that you get the great settlement. Then you're golden. Then you're the empowered one. And it's that much easier to marry big the second time around. And your round-two Walletman could be younger, more handsome, and have a better gene pool with which to mix – because you're bringing your own money to the table and therefore you're not as desperate. You're more of an asset. It's easy to breed with someone who's an asset.

That to me was the perfect play for the Digger without a dowry – get one. That empowered you. Whether by short-terming it and saving, or getting the settlement with an older Walletman. Empower yourself, then marry the man of your choice.

You see, I wanted to have a family. I wanted to have kids, but I wanted to have them with a young guy. I wanted to make it right for my son or daughter, to show them a proper family situation – everything I never had. I didn't want to have the ten-year-old kid whose eighty-year-old father would be slumped at the wheel dozing in between traffic lights. I wanted him to be able to enjoy his kids. And them, him.

And for the above reasons, I'd been on Tour for the past several years. To increase my holdings so I could then marry correctly. To me, that was the perfect play. Of course, when does life ever work out so seamlessly?

With respect to Bradley, I knew a few things. He was empowered, yes, by his financial standing. That gave him more time than your average thirtysomething. He also was extremely handsome – something I wasn't thrilled about. Bradley had a potential for vanity. That gave him even more time. He wasn't desperate or short of company. If you don't think these personal charac-teristics have their own little time correlation, you're deceiving yourself.

At the same time, I could tell he was bored of society and society's girls. He had said as much. That shaved off a little time. And he was a rebel. Aquarians are, generally. His sign was wildly rebellious. He could embark upon any project at any time. And he could turn his back on his parents' wishes. Or his parents could actually fuel behavior in him that would favor an unconventional choice of someone like myself. These traits I considered positives.

Now, with respect to sign, I was honest with him. He was an Aquarius Dragon. And they do like to be in charge. But that desire to dominate is not as subtle as I made it sound. It is very strong. He likes to own his lover. Why was I still interested?

He has a jealousy streak, which is his Achilles heel. And jealousy shaves off a little time like nothing else. With the right kind of guy, you can make him buckle at the altar in the ninth grade. The thought of his woman – you – stepping out and giving it up to someone else, or even worse, one of his friends, can be fully devastating. It's a known practice internationally. For instance, Italian girls love to hump the best friend in order to marry the guy they want. And they do! And you can sing it. *That's amore* . . .

Given the right set of circumstances, a jealous guy will crack like an egg. And that's where Lawrence Dexter Fairchild came in.

I didn't know how this would all play out. It was kind

of an educated crapshoot. But that's better than most odds in relationships. It was an educated gamble. Knowing what I knew, I felt that at least I had a few things going in my favor. And if it didn't work out, well, back to the drawing board. It was truly an art to land a guy of stature. And anybody who succeeds in doing it I revere immensely. And hate thoroughly.

The other thing about an Aquarius Dragon is that as the object of his attraction, you always keep your behavior mysterious. It keeps him interested. Kind of like all men. Or women, for that matter. And when it came to being mysterious, I was a monster.

I know this all sounds wildly calculating, but remember, it is a woman's business to find the right man with the right stuff. Business is a man's business, and his moves are just as calculating. We are fighting that Ten-Year Window, remember? In order to survive, we must do what we have to. That's all I felt I was doing – surviving. To get myself the best life and situation for me and my family-to-be.

Bradley did call on Sunday. Sooner than I'd anticipated. At 11 A.M. He asked me if I wanted to go to brunch at Le Cirque. I said I'd join him, but I'd rather do something more fun, like drift around SoHo. So we went to Félix on West Broadway, a European-style café. He liked the idea.

And from then on, all I can say about Bradley Lorne-August and me is, if we were becoming anything, we were becoming one thing – inseparable.

whatever you say, dear

If you desire to keep as a boyfriend, a man you've just met never sleep with him. For at least two weeks. Provided the chemistry is right. Because he'll wait. Chemistry is a very singular, particular thing. He can't find that kind of thing overnight. He could go for a one-nighter, but he'll still feel empty in the morning. Or he won't. But it still won't mean anything. And Thirties Vulnerables are looking for meaning. So you shouldn't get irked if you find out about it. Women still don't understand that guys can just have sex mindlessly without having any sentimental attachment. After all, that mindless need is how prostitution began.

In fact, more often than not, it makes men not want to see that one-nighted person again – provided it is a mindless union. Men are beasts. So are we. But the difference is, ours is an open system. During sex, someone invades our space. We take that – and we should – more seriously. Now you heard me rebel against this during my Rant in Palm Beach earlier, but basically I believe it to be true.

Now if you're getting paid nicely in terms of shopping

and gifts and things, then at least you're getting something in return for the invasion. What I'm saying is, if a man is having sex with you for sport, he'd better be paying for it. Or you're a fool.

A man, however, has an exterior system, a prong. He invades, lets go of his fluids, and goes on his merry way. And you may think that is the greatest deal in the world. Personally, however, I think men got ripped off in the equation. Sure, they get that wildly erogenous feeling with an erection. But what could be better than something plunging inside of you repeatedly? It's so savage. So primitive. And so delicious. Yum. Mmmm. And all that . . .

Besides, a woman can keep going. A guy is wiped for at least some interval of time. What I'm saying is, sexually, I never thought I, as a woman, was getting the raw end of the deal.

Whichever, a guy will wait if he's interested enough. And if he's not interested enough, who needs him anyway? I made Bradley wait. And he did.

In the meantime, we did all sorts of fun things together. We visited a deserted hotel in Montauk one weekend. It was a loud ocean, big waves, and big sweaters. Of course, we kissed. And fondled. And I let him see me change. Boy, was that a mistake. He was all over me that night. I even heard him tiptoe lightly into the bathroom so he could get rid of all that tension. I never let him know. But he was feeling the weight of our inactivity.

While we were on the beach one afternoon, Bradley asked me about my past again. It was on his mind. I guess it was partly my fault. First, it was the fact that I was a woman, of course. Men usually want to know about your past – who you've been with, who you've loved, and sometimes more personal details. And once they find out, they're also known to use it against you savagely. But also I was being somewhat mysterious. And true to form, my form, I balked at his request again.

But I did it by turning things around and asking him about his friends, Lawrence in particular. He told me they had gone through grade school as well as Choate prep school together. They were on the squash team together. And they always had competed for the same girls. But usually Bradley won out because he was more handsome and perhaps nicer. That was my read on the situation. It seemed as though Lawrence was always trying to prove himself.

Before Brad could angle the conversation back at me again, I offered, 'I'm cold. Let's go back inside.'

Over the following weeks we attended numerous parties in Manhattan and a couple in Westchester and Connecticut. They were all his friends' parties, of course. And I bonded nicely with his pals, the guys as well as the gals. With the guys I talked sports, but not enough to make them think I was a know-it-all. Rather, just enough to show I wasn't some oblivious prepster, that I had some balls. It's good to show balls as a woman. But not so much as to be threatening. With the gals I was a pistol. I'd rattle off a cheery version of my millennium feminism, and I'd find immediate support, in certain cases. Obviously, I'd never talk Digger with them. But female empowerment and self-esteem reinforcement were overall themes I championed.

I must say smart women got me. And most of Brad's female friends were smart, some were Ivy Leaguers, in fact. And some were smart with absolutely no common sense or street savvy. Those types I'd be lost on.

One night Brad invited me over to his apartment at Seventy-fourth and Park. There he popped a bottle of Cristal and gave me the Tiffany kidney-bean necklace. I'd never had the kidney bean. Did I like it? Get this straight. Anything you've never had from Tiffany's, you like. Or take back, and like its replacement.

Then he offered the choice of going to a hip, fashionista party downtown at the Spy Club or attending a dinner party of mostly married couples, some with whom he'd attended Yale University. Of course, I opted for the more boring gig. But not overtly. I made him feel like it was his decision. We were at Bradley's three-bedroom, four-thousand-dollar-maintenance, doorman building when we had our little discussion.

'Whichever,' I said.

'But how do you feel?'

'Well, we could go downtown, but . . .'

'It's a long way down, isn't it?'

'Kind of ... . But not overly so. I'm actually kind of hungry. Where will the food be better?'

'At Byron's, for sure. Let's do that.'

'Okay.'

See? Nothing pressing, nothing showing I really had a point of view on the situation. I let him be in control the way he liked. Yet, I gave him little proddings to exert my influence. That's what women in this world have to do. It's not to make all the decisions. It's to influence all the decisions. Let's face it – we can't rule. We have to carry on life. It is our biological duty. But we can influence how things are done. And we must exploit our influence over men to the fullest.

And, of course, you know why I wanted to go to his friend Byron's for dinner. It would psychologically make him feel like the thirties guy 'still dating' in front of all those marrieds. It would make him stick out. And lots of wine would probably go down and with the talk of their kids and their first words and their second-child comparisons, eventually one inebriated sod would put Brad on the hot seat.

And that's exactly what happened.

'What about you, Brad?'

'What about me?' he asked immediately on the flash defensive.

'Eventually you're going to have to pay the tax.'

'What tax?'

'The free-love tax.'

And everyone laughed. Brad got red in the face, squirmed a little; I did my best not to care – in fact, I got up and went to the bathroom.

When I returned, he clutched my hand under the table, harder than ever before. I was meaning more and more to him by the day. I could feel it. And he to me. I mean, we were on the phone until three and four in the morning every night. We talked intellectually, we talked spiritually, we talked silly, we talked movies, we talked books. We had very similar points of view on most subjects. And I learned from him. He was sharp. I needed that too in a man.

Before we left, one of his friends, Jason, whispered to me, 'You're the best woman I've ever seen him with.'

I loved hearing it.

And we still hadn't had sex yet.

all right already

But eventually I did break down. The week before Christmas. We were driving up to Greenwich in his BMW sedan for a dinner at his friends Paul and Betsy's place. My hands were fidgeting with the necklace he'd given me. I'd been fidgety for days. I was squirming in my seat too. He was so good-looking. I'd been holding back for what seemed so long. I couldn't hold back any longer.

I remember it so well. Guns N' Roses' 'Don't Cry' was playing on the cassette deck.

I touched him while he drove. It didn't take him long to get aroused. Probably about three notes of the guitar solo. Or one-tenth of an exit on the Merritt Parkway, and that's not saying much.

I opened his fly and released him. I played with the shaft and saw it flash all purple and red as oncoming cars passed. It was so hot in my hands.

I stretched across the seat, and with the parking brake wedged in my stomach, I began to lick him. For a few minutes, in fact. I wanted him to want more. I waited. And then it came.

He pressured the back of my neck and forced my mouth on him. I loved the feeling of being forced to take a man whole like that.

I drew and drew on it. It is one of my favorite things in the world. I'd go so low on him, to the base of his shaft. The head of his cock would part my tonsils and surge deep into my throat.

I heard the driver's-side window motor down. I heard money being exchanged. Brad paid the toll. I didn't care. I was busy.

'Thank you,' Brad said shyly to the tollgate attendant.

I added my hand to the act. While stroking his shaft, I sucked on the end. Guys love that. It's kind of like a masturbation blow job. Brad had a nice cock. He'd fit me nicely, I thought. It wasn't overly big, but it was thick.

As we pulled into someone's property, he exploded in my throat. Nice. He had trouble coordinating the brakes, though, and he took out a few branches of the shrubs rimming the driveway.

Dinner at the Whitmarshes' was full of the same married couples, with a few single guys. Lawrence was there, and I kissed him purposely on the lips. Brad knew why and loved it.

Brad really enjoyed my personality. So did his friends. They went out of their way to come over and flirt and tell me about their lives, their sex lives included. They confided in me. One guy, Jerome, was having trouble getting his girlfriend to do anything wild in bed.

'What are you doing for her?' I asked.

The sum total of his answer was, Not very much.

'Take her away somewhere. Get her out of her old systems that she relies on. Into something new. Unlock her valves again. The next day, buy her something. She'll more than return the favor.'

He went off nodding. It was a commonsensical silly idea, but some people forget the most obvious things. When the coast was clear, Lawrence moved in on me and offered me some coke. That was really disappointing. I'd selected him as one of my Rich Rebels, and even though my interest had waned on him severely, the fact that he was a coker was an insult to me and my character-screening and judgment abilities, which I had always been very proud of. That was how this guy showed his rebel colors. Drugs. That meant he was a loser in my book.

We missed the early part of the buffet dinner. Bradley had followed me into the bathroom. I was wearing a long black Gucci dress. He pushed me forward against the sink and ducked beneath my dress and began to taste me from behind. He licked me up and down, everywhere. My inner thighs, the back of them, my cheeks, all the way up. I was bent forward, my hands sliding on the shiny, smooth Mediterranean blue tiles of the sink. I looked at myself in the mirror. I thought of Alice in Wonderland, for whatever reason.

Damn. It feels good, I thought.

Someone knocked on the door. 'Fuck me, Brad' was my response to it.

And he did. But before he did, I took him in my mouth again. But soon after, he called it off. He lifted me up on the bathroom counter, instantaneously stretched a condom over himself, and plunged inside.

It was great to be gripping a man I really liked. And who had a nice one. And skin that didn't ball up in your hands. Let's call it tight skin. I'd forgotten about tight skin. And he had a nice round ass beneath it. I gripped it tight. When he was about to come, I sent in a little visitor. Guys love little visitors. When he did come, the spontaneous groan he emitted indicated to me he'd enjoyed himself. A lot. I liked the fact that he had. Probably as much as he did. Well, almost.

That was the first time.

It gave rise to four days of nonstop passion. Brad stopped going to his office. We just ordered in at his apartment and had sex. There were take-out cartons everywhere. Every time we contemplated a move outside, as soon as I started to get dressed, Brad got hard again. It was almost as if he'd get jealous that someone else would see me.

I called Napoleon one afternoon demanding a life preserver. He laughed and told me I deserved everything I was getting.

During our Lennonesque Bed-In for Peace – of Ass, that is – an invitation came forth that I was entirely open to.

'Why don't you come to Layford Cay for Christmas?' Brad asked me over some Vietnamese takeout.

'With your family?'

'Yes.'

'When are you going?'

'Two days before Christmas.'

'That's this Saturday.'

'I know.'

'I'm going to be with my mother. I could come maybe the day after Christmas.'

It wasn't true. I wasn't going to see my mother. Or my sister. I had done my yearly visit. It's funny, but I was the only one who did the visiting. Vicky didn't have any money, of course. But I really think if I didn't make any effort, I wouldn't ever see her. Or little Max. I sent them both Christmas presents. I got Vicky a soft and fluffy yellow Polo bathrobe. I got Max the new soft-boot Rollerblades.

Besides, going back to Fort Lowell would depress me too much. I needed to show happy. I was having a wonderful time with Brad. I was – and I really thought this was true – falling in love with him. I didn't want to upset that. It had been so long. I had been so guarded. I was dying to give it away to someone. I would wait until after Christmas to join him, however. I knew enough to do that. I certainly didn't want him to think I had noplace to go.

At the same time, I was getting worried. I'd been spending all of my time with Brad. And as we well know, time is money. But with him, I wasn't making any. And I wasn't making any elsewhere. That was the crux of the problem I discussed earlier about opting for the long, long, long-termer. Your intentions have to appear cleaner and more free of motive. I couldn't ask for money from Brad. It would show weakness at this point. Maybe at any point. Again, if we're talking long-term. If you want only short-term, ask away. It doesn't matter. But I wanted to marry Brad Lorne-August. And I had to play it cool.

In addition, I'd been spending a lot of money. My Christmas party expenses alone were almost ten thousand dollars. I'd bought Napoleon his tux as a Christmas present. I'd sent some money to Mom's nursing home and Father Rollins's church. And every third or fourth dinner with Brad, I was grabbing the check. It irked him but I wanted to show contribution. And, yes, I considered it an investment.

I'd also bought Brad a cashmere sweater. I was running low on money. I told Napoleon. But he was the eternal optimist when it came to money. Along the lines of, 'Hey, we're losing the apartment anyway. We won't have to pay rent.'

'We don't pay,' I reminded him.

'Well, we always tip the doormen.'

He said if worse came to worst – which was *now*, I thought – we could move into his sister Go Go's apartment, which was vacant. She would never allow it, but he knew how to get in.

'That's called breaking and entering, Napoleon.'

'No, no. I know the superintendent well.'

Like I said, I was feeling the pressure.

Brad sent me over the ticket to the Bahamas. I tried to pay him for it, but he insisted. I relented.

There's one thing I haven't mentioned. Lawrence Fairchild called me all the time. Beyond offering me drugs that one time, he also sent me flowers. I didn't return his calls. Though it hadn't even been three weeks, it was known to everyone in this circle of people that

Brad and I were obviously an item. We'd been listed in a couple of society columns. I guess it was making Lawrence go crazy with jealousy. I was a challenge he was unable to meet. Those kind of guys are weird. It's pretty sick, actually, what motivates them. Lawrence now turned my stomach.

The reality was, however, everything was happening so fast.

see-ya scenario

As I explained before, Aquarius Dragons like Bradley Lorne-August are jealous types. And the more time you spend with them, and the more emotionally hooked they get on you, the more they want to know what you've been up to in the years before their reign.

Brad had asked me half a dozen times by now about my past. And in fairness to him, the more I avoided telling him, the more it stoked his skeptical and jealous fires. As if I were hiding a lot. Or something. Or a lot of something.

It was time to come clean. So I gave him a whirlwind tour of my life, starting with when I ran away from home.

It was April of 1986. I was sixteen and a half. I was looking for the biggest town for the cheapest bus ticket. I'd been working after school at an A&W in nearby Kopple in order to be able to buy my own clothes. Kopple, Ohio, that is. I'd saved up two hundred eleven dollars.

I was heartbroken, of course. My boyfriend had hooked up with Shari, my best friend, over the course of a weekend.

It happened like this. I was very pretty in my teens, but I had somewhat of an ethnic look. My skin was the lightest shade of tan, part of my Eskimo and Native American heritage. Nowadays they call my looks exotic, but exotic was not and has never been a quick sell in Ohio. My features were pretty perfect but, well, I hadn't ever had a boyfriend.

I was tops in my tenth-grade class pretty much. And Buddy Farrell, the young star running back on the football team, sat next to me in English class. He wasn't the best student, and one day he asked me to help him with his research paper. It was on the life of Vince Lombardi, a hard-ass football coach. I did, in fact. And we ended up going out together. And I fell head over heels for him. And, yes, he was my first guy.

But that spring, at the annual Sadie Hawkins Dance, the mixer where the girls invite the boys, I invited him, of course. I didn't have a nice dress to wear, so I took all my savings from the A&W and bought a beautiful white prom-style dress. I went all the way to Cleveland to get it. I really couldn't afford it, but I was crazy about him. And it was my first dance.

I was so excited. I remember thinking I looked my best ever. Buddy had told me to meet him there at the dance. He was going to be late. That was okay. But when I arrived, I saw him smooching with my best friend, Shari, who had also invited him. I was devastated. I ran all the way home.

Of course, the entire school found out. Everyone pointed to me and laughed. I was a loser. And the only thing Buddy became was more of a stud. I hated him for it. He never called. And I never spoke to him again. I never spoke to Shari again either.

How many times later did I consider that episode to be part of my life in a nutshell, by the way.

I felt so embarrassed. And humiliated. I never wanted to see anybody from school again.

But that wasn't the real reason I'd decided to leave Fort Lowell. It was just the last straw. Home life had become unbearable for me. I couldn't stay there with my mother and my sister in. It was all too negative. Even days with sunshine were no fun.

My father was a louse, of course. He'd left us when I was twelve. But I wished he'd left sooner. He was a bitter man. He was usually unemployed and always home. And he hassled us. He always walked right into my bedroom. I had no privacy. He caught me naked a couple of times. I wondered if he did it on purpose. Our house only had one bathroom too. And it didn't lock. He used to barge in at any time. When I was peeing or doing feminine things, it didn't matter. When I was showering, he'd storm in and take a pee. He was awful.

Oddly, when he took off finally, I was sad. I only understood that later, though.

My mother didn't take his sudden departure well. She began drinking. She started not going to her job at the Kopple Hospital cafeteria. But before that, she'd been on us a lot. My sister, Vicky, and I fought constantly. Vicky had always been jealous of me. According to most people, she wasn't as attractive. I guess it was true, but at the time, I didn't see it like that. Anyhow, we endured simple sister-rivalry stuff like that. But I'd had enough.

The reality is, I saw my high school and Fort Lowell and everything around me as much too small. I needed a bigger yard. A bigger playground. A bigger pond. A bigger group of people to choose from. I went around with an attitude like *Is this all there is*?

It's true I wasn't the best daughter. I wasn't minding my mother very much. But I didn't really believe in her and her advice. I thought she was just wrong about a lot of stuff. She'd hit me with that 'Because I say so!' all the time. But I wanted a reason. And if I didn't get a good one, forget it. Mom never gave me any reasons. I couldn't stomach that just because she was my mother, I had to agree with her. Or listen to her. Mom did everything to make me rebel. Like Bradley, it was in my nature to rebel.

I remember hating to walk downstairs in the morning because I despised the way the living room looked. It had that big, old, dirty Brown Couch, which smelled like TV dinners. I hated the way the yard looked too. There was only one tree and no bushes, no flowers, no hedges. It was bare. So our house was propped up as though it was on one big low-class stage. I even hated the way my bedroom looked, even though I did my best to make it nice. I didn't have the money to make it look the way I wanted it to *and* buy my own clothes at the same time.

In the end, it was only my boyfriend keeping me in Fort Lowell. And when I lost him, I lost the last tie to my life there.

After school one day, I went into my history teacher's class, Mr Jacobson, and I asked him a few questions.

'What's the biggest town close to here?'

'Cleveland,' he said. I didn't like Cleveland. I didn't like its colors. Or the memory of having bought my dress there.

'I don't like Cleveland.'

'What's that?'

'Name another.'

'Chicago. It's where I'm from.'

'Really?'

And I decided to sit down in a chair opposite his desk. And I asked him everything I could about Chicago. As he spoke, I took notes.

'What are you writing?' he asked.

'Just reminding myself to pick up some bread and milk on the way home.'

'Oh.'

The next night, I was staying in the very church he had mentioned he grew up near. And that's how I met Father Rollins.

that missing latch

ather Rollins took me in. And guided me. He got me a job at a grocery store in the neighborhood. I lived at the church for nearly a year. I helped Father Rollins collect money on Sundays. Of course, I told him a few fibs. I told him my parents were dead. And I was eighteen years old. And I was from Wisconsin. I kept my real birthday but changed it to two years earlier and memorized that new date backward and forward.

I was born January 4. And being eighteen, it made me a Capricorn Cat. But I was really a Capricorn Snake, remember? Like King, Ali, and Onassis.

How did I learn all this astrological stuff? In my bedroom at the church there was a bookshelf with all sorts of old books. I tried to read some of them, but I got bored. I got bored easily. I still do. Anyway, there was one book I liked. It was on astrology. I opened it up. And I was instantly fascinated. It told me everything I wanted to know about people. All I needed to know was their birthday.

Of course, I read up on Buddy Farrell first, my boyfriend who had dumped me. Then I read up on my sister and my mother. I didn't know my father's birthday. And I didn't care, anyway. He liked to barge into my bathroom and bedroom, watch the Cleveland Browns or any other sports event on the air, and beat up Mom. That was all I needed to know about his character.

What amazed me was, it was all there. All the weird characteristics of people I knew. It was all right there in print. Of course, in my boyfriend's case, he was just a kid and therefore an immature version, so that didn't help either.

From then on, I used the book religiously. Though Father Rollins didn't know it, astrology became my religion. I felt if I could know a little more about people, then I could know whom to trust and whom not to, and I could prepare myself for their characters better. And if and when they would turn on me. And that's how I got into astrology.

My job at the grocery store was a pain. I was having a difficult time there. The owner was a big man named Rufus. He had a big wife too whose fingers met in the middle. She would stand behind the deli counter and make sandwiches for kids at lunch. But that Rufus, well, he always tried to pick me up. He'd bump into me, touch me, my arms and shoulders, smile at me. And he never brushed his teeth, I swear. I used to place tubes of toothpaste by the cash register, and he'd always say, 'Who keeps leaving the goddamn Aquafresh here?' He never got the hint, though.

One day I noticed the latch was gone on the bathroom door, so it couldn't be locked. I told him about it and he said he was going to fix it. The next day, he opened the door while I was in there. It was so embarrassing. I knew he knew I was in there. I knew he was the one who got rid of the latch too. It stayed unfixed for weeks until he finally got a new latch after I'd stopped using the facilities there. Still, I never set foot in that bathroom again.

What is it about men and bathrooms and young girls? I wondered.

I'd pretty much trusted men to a certain extent before my experiences with Buddy Farrell and Rufus Biggs. Though my father was not a great example of the gender, I hadn't ever considered him a man. He was my father. But after my experiences with Buddy and Rufus, as well as my father, I was for ever put on guard. To this day I'm always checking for that missing latch. And best girl-friends who smile to your face.

the finer things

There was one customer who came in regularly and became very important to me. I can safely say, the most important person of my life. Her name was Virginia Lashley. She used to come in to the store with her two dogs named Mason and Dixon. She was from the South and she was something to look at. I mean, when I first saw her, I was mesmerized. The way she moved, the way she dressed, the way she smelled, and the way she carried herself. I spied on her when she was in the food aisles. She often wore black and complemented it with just a trace of gold, whether a belt, pin or earrings, or an Hermès scarf. I only realized that later, when I knew what Hermès was. Her straight blond hair contrasted wonderfully against the black. She spoke as if she knew the world and had seen most of it. But not in a haughty way. In a sophisticated way.

Whenever she came in the store, old Rufus jumped through hoops to please her. She was a wealthy woman, not a millionaire but her husband was a professional baseball player. He played for one of the city's team, the Cubs. But she was educated and smart. I remember thinking she sounded like she worked for a fashion magazine, back when I thought they were the most sophisticated of all ladies. Virginia was the closest thing I'd ever seen to Jackie Kennedy. It wasn't her look. It was her way.

I met Virginia in an embarrassing way. I was outside the store crying one day. I'd been feeling lonely and sad, and on top of that, Rufus had tried to touch me again. And I guess she'd heard me as she was walking inside. She walked over and asked me why I was crying. I didn't tell her about Rufus, of course. But she sat with me on the bus bench there, and we talked for about an hour. Rufus came out once to see where I was. When he saw I was with her, he just let us be.

From then on, Rufus never laid a hand on me.

Virginia Lashley and I became friends. Whenever she came by, we would go outside and have a little chat. And she told me things. A lot of things. Our conversation covered more than America too. She told me about the world.

One day I asked her how she got to be the way she was.

'The way I am?' And she laughed. 'How do you mean?'

'Well, your hair falls so nicely, you wear the nicest clothes, you have a way of saying things.'

'Well, Bo,' she said. 'Though I'm from Atlanta, I went to school in England.'

'England?'

'Yes, London. And London, well, it's a very civilized place.'

'Civilized?'

'Yes, well, all I can say is, they do it a little better there. They know about the finer things in life. They invented them. You know America comes from the English, but America has its limitations. America is only two hundred years old. It's like a little boy who doesn't know how to dress properly yet. You know what I mean?'

I just smiled and said nothing. But I never forgot what she'd said. It was as if she'd just placed a window in my four walls of a life. And I was already looking through it.

I met Mrs Lashley's husband one day, after a baseball game we attended at Wrigley Field. That's where the Cubs played. His name was Don Lashley. He was a really nice man. And he had the firmest handshake.

But, well, Don Lashley was traded to another baseball team in San Francisco. And the Lashleys moved. Before they left, they took me to dinner at Gleason's, one of the nicest restaurants in the city. After dinner, Mrs Lashley handed me a card. Inside, it was the greatest gift I've ever received to this day. It was a plane ticket.

'Heathrow?' I asked. They both laughed.

'London,' she said.

Tears soon streamed down my face. I gave her a hug. I'd never given anyone such a hug. Not even my mother.

After the Lashleys moved from Chicago, I was sad for a long time. I missed Virginia. I wrote her all the time, though. And she wrote me back. She was much happier in San Francisco. She said it was more 'cosmopolitan' than Chicago. That's how I learned that word too.

Of course, old Rufus started up again with his touchy-feely stuff. It's how I first came to understand the power of influential friends. How they can change people's behavior. My friendship with Virginia Lashley was my protection against Rufus. And once she was gone, it was open season for him on me again.

It came to a head one day in March of that year. We were closing up and I had just finished sweeping the floor near the register. Rufus came up from behind me, spun me around, kissed me, all the while grabbing my ass. He was too strong for me. But somehow I got my hand on that Kool cigarette grocery separator bar and I conked him on the head. It was just enough to let me go. I knew it hurt. He was clumped in a fat pile holding his head. And I ran. I ran fast. That was the last time I ever saw Rufus Biggs.

I only understood later why Rufus wasn't worried about my telling his wife about his behavior, however. And why I hadn't said anything. She was the classic beaten-down, low-self-esteem number that men always prey upon. I didn't know about people with self-esteem holes yet. But I guess I sensed it somehow, though. I guess I sensed the wife wouldn't be able to do anything about her husband's misbehaving, or she wouldn't believe me, and it would just end up a big mess. That's why I didn't say anything to her, I think. Sometimes you just feel these things.

I told Father Rollins I wanted to go to England. I told him I'd saved up three hundred dollars. And I told him why I wanted to go. I told him I wanted to educate myself, that I wanted to find out about the finer things in life. He didn't say anything at first. But eventually he smiled. He understood. I didn't tell him about Rufus, though. It would have made him upset. Father Rollins then told me about an old friend of his named Sebastian who lived just outside of London. He was a rector in a church. He said Sebastian could help me.

Father Rollins also gave me three hundred dollars. I didn't want to take it, but he insisted. I told him I would pay him back, though he indicated I didn't have to. I think Father Rollins is the purest, most good-souled man I've ever met. If you didn't have faith in human beings, Father Rollins changed your mind. He did mine. I kept him in mind as a measuring stick. As well as a beloved friend.

He also gave me the astrology book he knew I'd been studying – but I didn't take it. I wanted it to be available to anyone else who came through the church trying to find their way. Just like I had. It surely helped me. I didn't want to deprive anyone else.

But at O'Hare Airport I found a book by Sydney Omarr and bought it. And then I was off on the most exciting trip I'd ever taken in my seventeen and a half years. I was so excited.

By the way, I did write to my family from time to time. I let them know I was safe. I even wrote them a postcard from the airport to let them know I was going to England. I wished them an early Merry Christmas. It was only May.

Father Rollins had phoned his rector friend Sebastian to let him know I was coming and to see if he might find me a maid's job. As soon as I arrived at the airport, I changed money just as Father Rollins instructed me, and I phoned Sebastian. Sebastian was kind of a miracle worker, like most religious people I'd met early in my life.

Anyhow, Sebastian had already found me a job at a bed-and-breakfast hotel in Earl's Court where one of the day maids had just quit and had returned to Ireland. I was to make beds and light breakfast for seventy-five pounds a week. It wasn't a lot of money, but it was the luckiest break I'd ever had. For that, I got a maid's room too, the size of a shoebox. A woman's shoebox.

For ever since, I've had a tremendous amount of respect for those who have dedicated their lives to God. I've never forgotten those early experiences with Father Rollins and Sebastian. That's why those religious freaks I met later in life didn't really bother me. I knew about the real deal.

After work one day, I wandered over to London University and scanned the bulletin boards. I was looking for an English tutor. I could pay only ten pounds a week. But I figured that anyone who just spoke proper English could help me. I was determined. I wanted to speak clearly and articulately like Virginia Lashley, don't forget. Role models are so important to kids, no matter what anyone says.

All I can say is, I had four different tutors in three weeks. The first two were men and they both wanted to screw me. I got smart with the third choice – a woman. But she made me pay first and then went to the bathroom. I never saw her again. Then when I was roaming around the halls of the university, I slipped into an auditorium and saw a play rehearsal in progress. There was a girl there playing the role of Lady Macbeth. She sounded so powerful and articulate even though her words were Shakespeare's. I waited until after the rehearsal. I approached her and introduced myself. And I told her my story.

'What's your name?'

'Bodicea Lashley. But people call me Bo.'

'People,' she repeated, my choice of word piquing her curiosity, I could tell. 'Hi, Bo. I'm Phillipa.'

'Would you like to teach me English?'

And she just laughed. It made me worried. 'How old are you, Bo?'

'Twenty-one.'

She looked at me. 'You're not a day past eighteen.'

'Seventeen and a half.' And I stood there awkwardly. 'Can you, Phillipa? Can you teach me English?'

She smiled a warm smile and just looked at me. She enjoyed looking at me. I could tell. I don't know why. I don't know if it was because my request was so out there, or so pure, or so original, or so not something anyone would ever ask her. And I don't know if the response she gave was something she was aware she'd ever give. Like we'd both pushed each other into some space or orbit or locked room we both weren't familiar with.

And then her response came back. And I liked it. 'Okay, Bo. I'll teach you English.'

I'd made my fourth friend of my new life. And don't think I hadn't been counting.

the saints-and-sinners triangle

Phillipa and I had a coffee in the school cafeteria. There she told me that she was actually the stand-in for the stand-in for the girl who had gotten the role of Lady Macbeth. The girl who received the part came down with the chicken pox, and the first alternate had broken her leg. Phillipa hadn't even been attending the university. But they'd needed someone quick, and Phillipa had played the role before. She was an out-of-work actress.

And now, an English teacher.

I offered her my ten pounds, for which she not only taught me English but gave me voice lessons. We became friends, even though I was what I was and she was thirty. She was a Pisces Goat, after all, swimming through life supersensitively. But there was more to Phillipa than met the eye. Or the simple star read.

My job at the B&B gave me my nights off, and when I wasn't reading English and Irish novels and plays, from Hardy and Joyce and Shaw and Shakespeare, or more astrology books, Oriental as well as Occidental, I'd go out and about in London with Phillipa.

Phillipa, it's fair to say, was looking to get married. She'd had enough playing around, and finances were putting too much pressure on her at a time when she wanted the pressure to ease off. And yes, it was Phillipa who taught me about the Ten-Year Window. Eventually, I coined her Native American Digger nickname, **Earning Every Penny**. But that was much later.

Phillipa would go out to Annabel's or Brown's or the Atlantic. During this period, I met a good portion of affluent London society, Giles Hamilton included. I even met Prince Andrew one night. He took a full drink of me as his eyes roamed up and down my body. I was looking particularly sexy that night. Though I had a nothing wardrobe, I fit perfectly into Phillipa's clothes. We were quite a team, I must say. When we went out, people knew about it. Or became aware of it. Soon.

Phillipa also got me a new job with friends of hers who had started a mail-order children's clothing business on the Internet. They were a husband-and-wife team named Nigel and Lavinia Morrison, and they were very nice people. Phillipa, of course, felt that I should move on from the B & B, to get more out of my day-to-day work experience. So I did. I learned how to use a computer, and Nigel taught me how to take orders, keep track of inventory, and mail stuff out. He taught me about the management of the business as well. Basically, I was involved in all operations.

Lavinia was a former stage actress, and she was the creative force behind the team. She designed all the kids' jeans and dresses and sweatshirts. And it was her brother who became my second boyfriend too. His name was Martin. He was a handsome young actor. A Libra like Jasper. It's a very creative sign. And Martin was creative. Especially in bed. Or at least I thought so at the time. He expanded my horizons in that regard, even though it took some time to get used to his uncircumcised penis. I wouldn't let him touch me for the longest time. I thought he had a disease. He always wanted to go down on me, and I thought it was a sign of someone who was really very sexual and generous sexually. But really all it was, was my first brush with the lick and stick. You know, guys who don't caress, don't kiss, don't touch you, and, therefore, don't try to create any buildup of passion. They just immediately taste you for lubrication purposes, then plop on top. That was Martin.

In any case, I was actually very happy those first few years in London. I learned all about computers and the Internet, I learned about English literature, I learned to speak the language properly, and I even developed a slight London accent, asking questions in a funny way, the way they do it. In addition, as I passed from my teens into my twenties, I became more attractive physically. I mean, I hadn't ever been unattractive. But now, the baby fat had all but gone away and my figure had popped out, perilously so. I had no shortage of nightly invitations. I don't think I'd bought a drink for myself in nearly a year!

But I must say I did begin to feel homesick, and Martin had been getting on my nerves. He was a bit jealous and passive-aggressive and a mild control freak, though I didn't know what any of it was at the time. I just knew I didn't like being with him as much anymore.

Besides, he'd freak out whenever Phillipa took me out alone. I can't stand control freaks. When in the presence of a real flame douser, the door gets bigger by the minute.

But it was the movies that killed me the most. We'd go to the theater in Leicester Square, sit down, and view some picture based in New York City or Los Angeles or Florida or somewhere in the States, and it would make me yearn to go back. It was affecting me more and more. Until I couldn't take it anymore. I wanted to go home.

One evening at Annabel's, Phillipa and I were seated at a cocktail table with a banker friend of hers named Crispian. He was very conservative and cheap, but funny at the same time. He had a funny face. You know, the type of guy who says normal things other guys say, but when he would say it, combined with his funny clown face, it made it hysterical. And he'd get you laughing right up until the bill came. Yet you were so overjoyed and glowing that your generosity was sparked. I don't think I ever saw Crispian pick up a drinks check.

In any case, another man joined us, a friend of Crispian's. His name was Arnot and the *t* was silent. I only noticed the *t* when he slipped me his number later. He was French, of course. But Arnot was a traveling businessman who talked a very good game. He was my first encounter with the playboy type. I sensed it immediately too. It's the way they look at you. Or don't look at you at all. He did both. You could tell he was always trying to draw you in, to get him to tell you his global stories and invite his personality to the fore. I fell in love with Arnot after half a glass of champagne. He wasn't handsome but he had tremendous charisma, which is what I looked for in those days. He was an Aries Rat like Marlon Brando. Now I demand the combination – charisma and bank.

I'd never met anyone like Arnot. He was so worldly and knowledgeable. I felt I could learn a lot from him. And I did, eventually.

When Arnot went to the loo, Phillipa told me that she had had a thing with him, and I sensed she still had some residual feelings for him, though she denied it. Crispian then remarked that Arnot had homes in St Tropez and St. Moritz and was building a villa in St Bart's.

A few years later, I coined these three locales the Saints-and-Sinners Triangle, and I'll tell you why right now. Though all three towns are named after saints, the actual lifestyle of these places couldn't be further from religion and all that is pious and religious. The only piety is a sincere reverence for big-time money, the likes of which you rarely see so concentrated and overtly displayed anywhere else in the world. And it's not all good money – far from it. Professional scandal men from all over do their best to yield exorbitant profits from secret little places and niches worldwide, running sweatshops included, places you'd never know about. Then these captains of dark industries would arrive at the doorstep of one of these towns with a sack full of money. And nobody really cares where it comes from, just as long as you have your island villa, mountain chalet, or yacht that sleeps ten in a coveted slip at the port – and invite everyone over once a season for lunch. Because these are vacation places set up for nothing more than having and sharing a good time together.

When Arnot came back to the table, Phillipa blurted out, 'You know, it's Bo's birthday.' She'd been saying it all week, actually, another reason we weren't paying for drinks.

'It is not.'

And no one believed me. No one wanted to. Especially Arnot. It was just an excuse to have another basket of bubbly.

'So – when is her birthday?' Crispian asked Phillipa.

'Saturday.'

'How old?'

'Tell him, Bo.'

'Twenty-one,' I said with a laugh.

'Why don't we have a party?'

'A party?' I asked.

Phillipa jumped on it. 'When?'

'Saturday, of course.'

'Where?'

'At my place,' Arnot offered.

'In Mayfair?'

'No. In St Moritz.'

'This weekend?'

'You ski, don't you, Bo?'

'I can try.'

And then Crispian started to grumble. 'Well, I'm not so sure. I might have to—'

'Don't worry, Crispian,' Arnot interrupted. 'I'll pay for your ticket.'

And we all laughed.

'Since you put it that way . . .' he said while raising a glass. And they all toasted me and my fake birthday.

And that evening was the beginning of a two-year detour of my life. It occurred right at a time when I was all set to return to America. And it just didn't happen. The first year I spent with Arnot. We had a wonderful time. He really treated me well. We traveled the Triangle. I became quite a no-fear skier. I even picked out tiles and fabrics for his St. Bart's house. And I met so many people – mostly wealthy, of course.

In the end, however, our relationship didn't last. It couldn't. Arnot was too much of a playboy. And knowing that, I purposely didn't give it all away. My emotions, I'm talking about. It was my first exercise in emotional restraint. It's become one of my greater talents. And I learned it through my experience with Buddy Farrell, and I began to perfect it in my handling of Arnot.

One July night in St Tropez, after Arnot had left the Cave de Rois Club with some stadium-pleasing stunner, a friend of his named Oskar invited me for a late-night drink on his boat. That was a Friday night. I didn't see Arnot again until Sunday afternoon. He was angry, of course. But he knew it was his own fault. Besides, it was only his ego that was upset. He moved on to the next new hot dish. And so did I.

I lived with Oskar on his boat for the rest of the summer. And, well, my life just took off. I became part of the affluent Saints-and-Sinners Triangle, traveling from spot to spot with all the playboys who were in search of nothing more than new girls to conquer. And when the feminine tugs of one leg of the Triangle would grow barren or dry up, they'd be on to the next stop. They were seasonal stops, actually. As one would cool down, another would heat up. It was a year-round thing. And it was during those Triangle days that I decided I was not going to be a pawn. I was going to be a player. And make my living.

And at the time I made my decision, I'd amassed quite a wardrobe, quite a roster of influential friends, quite an appetite for sex, and quite a desire to do nothing but enjoy it all. And it all began in London, where I picked up the term *quite*.

But I wasn't a fool. I was selective. And I made those whom I selected pay. For me, for my needs, and for my future. Capricorn Snake, remember?

And that's how I knew how to run in affluent circles. After all, it had become my circle. I'd made it my circle. And I soaked up all there was to learn along the way. By the time I returned to America, I wanted to be one hell of an educated, traveled, quoting, refined, cosmopolitan package. And I was.

But the best part of it was, in America I was still relatively unknown. My apprenticeship had taken place abroad and no one had a track on me. I could be anything I wanted to be. And that's precisely how I wanted it.

the bradley edit

Now, you should be wondering whether I told Brad everything I just told you, in the way I told you. Obviously, I did not. Of the years I spent in England and Europe, there are certain things I recounted to him and certain things I left out. I edited down my story. For him. I didn't want him to get any wrong ideas.

I told him how hurt I was when Buddy Farrell broke up with me. I told him I did not get on well with my mother, something he had experienced in his own life. I told him I'd moved to Chicago but not that I'd run away and lived in a church. I didn't want to be a gossip. I employed the word *we* as if it were my family with whom I still lived. I told him about my first encounter with tactless, male sleaze in the person of Rufus Biggs. I didn't mention that I'd been a grocery clerk. There was no point.

Of course, I told Brad about Virginia Lashley, but I never mentioned her last name nor that her name had been adopted by me and taken as my own. Why bother? I didn't want to bore him with details.

I never told Brad the real circumstances under which

I went to England either. I just told him I went to study abroad in London. Sure, there was some fictional glaze involved, but so what? The truth is, I did go over there to study. It just wasn't at a university. It was in a city. And study I did. Everything. My elected courses were in the ways of the world. With an independent study in English literature. And plays. And I took some language minors. I didn't tell him how I'd learned Arnot French. Or Oskar German. Or Andreas Greek. Or Mario Italian. Or Luca Italian. Or Rocco Italian. Or Vincenzo Italian. Or Emilio Spanish. I wasn't going to be a stickler for facts. Why waste his time? I just told him I'd studied Romance languages.

I told him I'd had a favorite professor, but I didn't tell him I called her **Earning Every Penny**. I told him about my vacations to Ireland, Paris, Germany, Athens, the French and Swiss Alps, Capri, Rome, the Amalfi Coast, the Saints-and-Sinners Triangle, etc, but I didn't tell him with whom I'd gone. It would have made my pitch too long-winded.

And besides, he didn't ask. Instead, I think he was enjoying learning that I was well educated and well traveled. And I was.

Now, if he had asked, I would have gladly told him about the three boyfriends I'd had in my five years based there. There was Martin, Arnot, and Oskar. I truly feel I hadn't done anything wrong in presenting the material the way I did. I only gave what everyone else in this world gives new loved ones – an AP. That's precisely what I offered Brad. An approximate past.

And just remember. As a woman, there are things

you know just never to tell anyone. Ever. You know it can only be used against you. And it will be.

The Bradley Edit may be considered dishonest or less than up-front, but in the end, I really felt that the person he liked – me – in the now would not have been that same person unless I'd had all those previous experiences. You are the sum of your experiences. Or so I've always thought. In the final analysis, all was cool with Brad and my AP. In fact, it was better than cool. He liked that I'd been around – the world, that is.

And to this day Brad has never considered me a bore or a gossip or a stickler or long-winded or a grunt for facts. And *not being* any of the above I've always considered crucial elements to a winning character profile.

and i ran – to greenwich

That third weekend in December it snowed. Bradley's parents invited us up to their Greenwich estate. It was in the horse-farm section just off Upper Cross Road. It was such a beautiful drive there. The landscape was whitened over, and thin roads ribboned around, all rimmed by white three-paneled fences that ran, in some cases, the entire length of the roads themselves. That's how big the farms were.

The Lorne-Augusts had stables as well. The first thing we did when we arrived was head straight for the barn. Mr Lorne-August had been an accomplished polo player, and they still had some polo ponies in addition to riding horses.

I was scared, of course. But Brad coaxed me into it. We took two polo ponies. He didn't tell me they were a little testier than normal horses. All the better. I was helped up by Ron the trainer, and almost as soon as I got hold of the reins, the ponies took off. We had the greatest time. Brad showed me the property on horseback, the lake included. It was about fifty square acres. It was so wonderful to be on the animals in the snow.

We were prancing around in our own postcard.

When we returned to the barn, I was sore. But I was on such a high, it didn't matter. I had finally gotten over my fear of horses. Partially, anyway.

And I was enjoying Brad's company immensely.

The Lorne-Augusts had three other couples for dinner that night. It began with cocktails in the living room. It was quite a living room, in fact. Beyond the château-like furnishings, there were two Sisleys, two Matisses, a small Monet, a Picasso, and a Gauguin, as well as others in the room's collection. I didn't study art or know it that well, but the masters I was familiar with. It's funny how masterpieces in private homes can take the air out of a room almost in the same way a celebrity at his or her height of worship can.

I wore a classic navy suit by Dior. I'd bought it in Paris several years before and hadn't worn it much. Only once, I think. I'd been wearing lots of toned-down, inconspicuous clothing lately, clothes I'd long since forgotten. With Bradley, my tastes shifted in a more classic direction for obvious reasons.

The dinner was pleasant. Brad drank freely and let loose somewhat in front of his parents. He teased his father about his inability to remember anyone's name. And his father teased Mrs Lorne-August about her brother Ned, who was a farmer of sorts. From what I could surmise, Brad's mother, Adele, did not come from money. How little money, I didn't know. I did know her eyes were giving me special attention whenever I looked away.

The Bancrofts were New Yorkers who summered in

East Hampton. They were members of the snooty Maidstone Club. I'd been there once – grass tennis courts; claustrophobically married, matronly women; cocktail-party pettiness; and green blazers. Mr Bancroft was a sweet man. He was a partner in a formidable New York law firm. They handled big corporations. But he had a soft side. He had six bloodhounds he cherished. He smoked a pipe too.

The Hales had a place in Greenwich and another on Nantucket. Mr Hale was a retired Wall Streeter, and his face had a lot of stress streaks that showed the wear and tear. He'd worked the financial district when it wasn't so easy to make money. I'm talking before the eighties. He sat next to me during dinner and even talked about it.

'These hot shots have no idea what it's really like. You could have been blind, stayed home, and mailed in orders, and you would have made money in the eighties and nineties.'

'But what about the recent crash?' I asked.

'Well, they felt a scare, yes. But only people with real big money were hurt by that. People who could afford to lose it. And they rebuilt. Nope, Wall Street has never been fair. But all in all, it's been good to us.'

I told him I'd never been to Nantucket. And he invited both Brad and me to stay with them anytime.

The Corcorans, however, were a different story. They actually made the dinner chatter a little unsettling. For me. It was Mrs Corcoran. When she heard I was from Shaker Heights, she hit me with a heart-stopper.

'Really? So am I. Where did you live?'

I was caught in the middle of the road with oncoming traffic. 'Uh, I'm from Ohio, yes. Did Brad say I was from Shaker Heights?'

All eyes were on me.

'Yes,' she said bluntly.

'Actually, we were only there a few years. My first few years – when I was a child, I mean to say, then we moved farther west.'

'Where?'

I couldn't lie now.

'Fort Lowell.'

'Ah,' she said. And nothing more.

I glanced over at Mrs Lorne-August, who was glaring right at me with something gnawing away at her mind. I didn't enjoy her look. She was no doubt night-goggling me, wondering when I was going to stuff the silver salt and pepper shakers down my pants.

After dinner we retired to the study, and brandy was served. I didn't have any. But Brad did. He had been drinking right along and by now was feeling no pain.

Then we heard a round of dirty jokes. And they were quite dirty. And politically incorrect. There was a Clinton joke, of course. Mr Hale told one using the word *pussy*, which surprised me. Brad told a couple with bad language. Mrs Bancroft even told one. Then Brad mercilessly told everyone I had a good one. They begged me for it.

'Okay, okay. A young Indian brave and his Indian chief father are seated in a tee-pee, and the young brave asks, "Father, our names are so original. How did you come up with them?"

' "Well, my son, I always gave names to you children by the first thing to cross my line of sight at the time you were born. When your sister Two Bears was born, I saw a mighty grizzly and her cub running through the forest. And when Half Moon was born, I looked up to the sky and saw a crescent-shaped moon. Why do you ask, Fucking Dog?" '

Cute. They all laughed. Except Brad's mother. You know what she was doing. Looking for more places to chip away at me.

After I gave a few more polite laughs to mediocre stories, I told Brad I wanted to go to bed. He understood. I was feeling tired and sore from riding. I bid everyone else good-bye. When I offered thank-yous to Mrs Lorne-August, she gave me her finest, icy 'good night.'

The guest room was magnificent, of course. It had a big-posted hand-carved antique canopy bed. The wood was a deep brown-stained oak. It had pillows and rolls and more pillows extending all the way to the foot of the bed.

As I washed up, I gave some thought to the evening. It had gone pretty smoothly, except for that little hesitation I'd displayed when reciting my Ohio roots. I found Mr Lorne-August to be aloof but charming. The Mrs, however, gave me the willies.

As I was about to take off my makeup, Brad came storming in, grabbed me, and gave me a French kiss. His tongue was soaked in brandy. I didn't mind. It was cute.

He knelt low and stretched down the elastic of my panties and dug in. But for only ten seconds or so. He then rose up and said, 'I want to dance.'

'What?'

He grabbed my hand and dragged me out of the room.

'Wait! I need my clothes.'

I quickly put my suit pants back on and followed him downstairs. Brad put on an eighties New Wave compilation CD, and we took over the living room. 'I Ran (So Far Away)' by A Flock of Seagulls blared through the house.

The group eventually migrated over from the study to see us whirl, twirl, and spin to a song that wasn't overtly danceable. But Brad found a way. I was rusty but improvised the best I could.

'And I ran, I ran so far away . . .'

We made it through about four songs until Brad flopped on the sofa from exhaustion. I was exhausted too.

The group gave us an ovation, and then they all went to get their coats to leave. I said my good-byes again and returned upstairs. Oddly, Brad didn't join me for another forty-five minutes. When he did, he looked pretty ticked-off. And drunk.

'She's such a bitch,' he said, and dropped on my bed, back first, still balancing a snifter.

It didn't need to be asked unless I wanted to be polite. 'Who?'

'My mother.'

'Oh . . .'

'Can't you tell?'

'She's somewhat reserved,' I said.

'Reserved. She's a bitch.'

'Why are you so upset? Did you just have a discussion with her?'

'Discussion? There's no discussing with her. She's from the Always Right Society. Discussions are lectures. And viewpoints are silly unless they're hers. You need backup when you talk to her, in the form of recent newspaper articles or texts. She's constantly second-guessing me. On everything.'

'Mothers do that,' I said. And I thought about my mother and all that garbage she'd thrown at me without ever giving any reasons.

'She thinks that genetically,' he continued, 'two and two makes four. And it can. But not always. Sometimes two and two makes three. And other times two and two makes five. I don't want to compete with her. She's my mother.'

I decided to take a risk. 'Well, don't take this offensively, but I don't think she's in your league.'

'How do you mean?'

'You're a five, she's a four – in terms of intelligence.'

I immediately wished I hadn't said it. Family, remember? Not mine, his. And *mothers*. But it was a competitive thing with his mother. And I wanted to praise him. He rewarded me soon after.

'She actually holds the notion that my entire intellect came from her. An article in the *Times* came out claiming intelligence was maternally linked. But I thought it was bullshit. I'm an accident. I'm genetic paint thrown on the wall.'

'You just happened to come out handsome and bright and a great athlete,' I quipped.

But Brad was serious. Like he'd actually come to that conclusion. 'And rich,' he added. 'People hate me, you know.'

'Why?' I played dumb.

'I'm everything *to* hate. What's there to like?'

'Jealousy, yes. Hatred, that's strong.' I petted his forehead. He jerked away. 'She's probably just bored.'

'No.'

'It's what you said about her the first time I met you.' If he believed it before, he didn't any longer. 'Or maybe she just wants to be a part of it all.'

'Of what all?'

'Of you. Maybe she fears you're slipping away. And it increases her feelings of her own mortality. Parents love to pen us in, don't forget. To make us feel like we're still in that baby chair and still dependent. And they're still in their mid-thirties. It makes them feel younger. And needed. I mean, what do they have to get excited about at their age? Other than socializing and their kids?'

I had to thank Napoleon for that last blast. He had taught me a lot about psychology. Especially from the higher socioeconomic orders. I mean, bored parents feeling their mortality didn't apply to my personal family apparatus.

Brad leaned over and kissed me. Then he rose up unevenly from my bed.

'I have the whirlies,' he said.

And then he rushed out the door. He never returned that night. That surprised me somewhat.

The following day, I woke up at nine. Sun was beaming into the bedroom and illuminating all the beautiful colors of the exquisite fabrics that had been professional-decorator-chosen for the room. I looked outside the bedroom window. The snow was melting fast and the icicles were dripping quickly. I got dressed and slipped into Brad's bedroom. He wasn't there.

I went downstairs and found him reading the Sunday *New York Times*. He looked up. 'Hi,' he said evenly.

'Morning, Brad.'

'Sleep okay?'

'Fine.'

And he just hung a dead look on me for a second. 'Listen, Bo. I have to go up north with my father this afternoon. Is that okay?'

'Sure.'

'I mean, do you mind taking the train back into town?'

'Not at all.' And I would not have minded, had his tone been warmer.

We had a late-morning brunch. And Mr Lorne-August did most of the talking. He was a morning person after all. He was miffed that the U.S. Open golf tournament was going to be played at his club that year. It was going to make it difficult for members to play. That was stress for him. I always loved to hear venting of this sort. When the privilege meter for privileged folks goes into the red zone, indicating a reduction of access to leisure pursuits. Always amusing.

Brad dropped me off at the train station. I sensed something strange going on.

'You okay?' I whispered to Brad, clasping his hand.

'Yeah. Just a little hung over.'

I knew that was not the problem. He looked antsy.

'Take off,' I said. 'You don't have to wait with me.'

'Would you mind? We're late,' he said.

'Not at all.'

He gave me a nice, warm kiss and then he drove off, sending some slush flying as he did.

There were some deep-rooted mother issues going on there still. Of that I was sure. His mother had an influence over him he was struggling with. I chalked it up to good old-fashioned family weirdness. It should never be underestimated. I certainly understood that. It was best not to interfere. I figured Brad would tell me about it eventually.

The train came five minutes later.

beware of digger mothers

The best way to describe the next three days is, Brad never called. When he did call finally, Napoleon answered. I told him to tell Brad I wasn't home, and to call back later. My stomach was churning.

It was the day before Christmas. The Lorne-Augusts were supposed to be leaving for Layford Cay. Brad still hadn't called to tell me about our travel plans – nothing.

But some others did. Morris Barton, Jim Weathers, and Howard T. White wanted to take me somewhere sunny. Warren Samuels and Digby Mathison wanted to take me somewhere snowy. Warren, of course, wanted to give me some of that good old-time religion in the Rockies.

Lawrence Dexter Fairchild called in too to take me *anywhere*, I'm sure – even Jersey – if I'd been game. **Baubles, Bangles, and My Needs** called and was in town and wanted to go shopping. But I wasn't in the mood. Finally, **At These Prices** phoned in as well. She was getting richer, of course, but increasingly homesick. After all, Christmas in Brunei – what's that all about? I didn't want to talk to any of them. I wanted to talk to Brad.

On Christmas Eve, I decided to make my own call.

'Hello?'

'Hi, Max.'

'Aunt Bo! Where are you?'

'In New York. How's Mom?'

'She's okay. She feels weak. This bug has really hit her hard. Are you coming?'

'No. I'm not. I'm not feeling so great myself. Put her on, will you, honey?'

She somehow had the good sense not to do her normal shout to some other part of the house. Maybe she knew deep down that her mother was sicker than everyone was leading her to believe.

'Hello?'

'Hi, Vick.'

'Bo?'

'Yeah.'

'Oh, I'm glad you called.'

'Merry Christmas,' I said.

'Same to you. But, uh, it's tomorrow.'

I could tell she was on heavy medication. 'I know. You okay?'

'Could be worse.'

'What are the treatments like?'

'Difficult. My hair's all gone.'

'Did you get a wig?'

'No. I wear a baseball cap. Max? Are you on this phone?' she yelled. There was a far-off response. 'You never know with that one. The doctors seem confident,

I guess. It's the treatments that worry me.'

'How so?'

'I mean the payments. I don't have any medical insurance.'

'You don't?'

'No.'

'What about—'

'The restaurant? Are you kidding?' Then she coughed. 'What are you doing for Christmas?'

'I'm not sure. You want me to come?'

'No, Bo.'

'You sure?'

'You do your thing. I'll be fine. In two months I'll be as good as new.'

We talked only a short time longer. Max got back on the phone. She told me she and Danny had got back together – for now. I reminded her of what I'd told her, that she should always be treated respectfully. She told me that he was respecting her now, that he'd changed. He was like a new guy.

Immediately, I wondered if Vicky's illness had made its rounds through town and that was the reason for Danny's change in attitude. It often takes something like cancer to make people stop being jerks.

'Hey, Aunt Bo. You got a boyfriend?'

'Yes.'

'Is he cute?'

'Very.'

'Can you send me a picture?'

'Okay.'

Two tears made their way down my cheek from each

eye. The one on the left was for my sister and Max. The one on the right was for me.

My call-waiting clicked and I said my good-byes to Max. I told her I'd visit soon. Then I switched lines. There was crackling static, the kind you get from far-off places with faulty communication equipment, like the Islands.

'Hello?'

'Hi, Bo,' he said it in that same even, deadpan, deadly tone I hated.

'Brad,' I said, though it barely made its way out. I cleared my throat. 'How are you?' My heart was pounding.

'Not bad. You?'

Jees, I thought. We sounded like two strangers.

'Okay. Listen. I hate to tell you this at the last moment, but there's been' – and I mouthed the words at home with him – 'a change in plans. My father's brother and his family are coming.'

I held my tongue with all my strength. And it took all my strength.

'Okay,' I said, and matched his even, awful tone.

'I hate to tell you so late and all, but maybe you can stay with your mother a little longer or something, huh?'

'No. I'll be coming back to New York.'

'You remember Tom and Felicia?'

'Of course.'

'They're going to St Bart's. They have a house. Want me to see if you can join them?'

I laughed slightly. 'No, thanks, Brad. Have a nice time. And – Merry Christmas.'

He repeated it back to me, dutifully. 'Good-bye,' I said confidently. And when I hung up, I burst into tears the likes of which I hadn't cried since the seventies.

Fortunately, Napoleon was in the next room to hold me. And he held me all night long.

When I woke up around five A.M. Christmas morning, Napoleon was still awake, petting me lightly. He was watching zombie TV – you know, the late, late, late-night stuff. The actors were all Japanese, mouthing English words that were dubbed in and out of sync.

I turned over, and we discussed my situation with Brad.

'It's the mother,' he said. 'She's from a nothing family.'

'How do you know?'

He just looked at me. I thought he was going to say *it's obvious* and bring up the Digger Mother stuff.

'I asked my mother,' he said instead.

'You spoke with your mother about me?'

'No. I asked general stuff.'

They know the Lorne-Augusts well?'

'Well enough.'

I asked him what else he talked to his mother about.

'To see if I could borrow some money.'

'What did she say?'

'She said what she always says – she would do what she could.'

'And what did she say about the Lorne-Augusts? I want specifics.'

'Adele Lorne-August met the father in the south of France in the fifties. At the Rainier wedding, actually.

She was doing the yachtsmen circuit. Hopping from boat to boat, screwing everyone. And she met this guy Lorne-August, who was handsome and rich – and totally dull. And she brought excitement to his life. Basically.'

'Where's she from?'

'Somewhere in Missouri.'

And there it was. The Beware of Digger Mothers theorem hitting me square in the face.

'The thing is,' he continued, 'people like her don't want to be reminded of themselves. She sees herself in you and she doesn't like what she sees. Over the years these types conveniently forget their past. They're ashamed and they block it out and they actually make themselves believe they always came from their new elevated status, like from money or high society. Because the rationale is something like *Since I married it and was accepted by it, it must mean I was worthy of it, and no one at this level had anything more than me and therefore: I must* be *it*.'

Right then I thought about my family, especially Vicky. Sure, I'd had the same ashamed feelings. I was always trying to cover up my background. It took so much goddamn energy. More tears flooded down my cheeks.

'They want to think they belong to a better heritage and always belonged to a better heritage,' Napoleon said. 'Denial takes many forms. It's just one more.'

I couldn't hold it any longer. 'He dumped me!' I cried out.

'He didn't dump you!'

'He did! I know what it feels like, and he just did it! He did!' I was hysterical. 'He did! He did! He did!'

left for dead

I hated that feeling. I'd felt it once before. When Buddy Farrell dumped me back in tenth grade and took up with my best friend, it took me a year to get over that cavity feeling in my chest. It was awful. I vowed never to let it happen again. I know it sounds silly, but I didn't have the protection others do when it comes to heartache. And still don't. I feel it more. You can cut me, beat me, hit me, and I'll bounce back. But heart stuff? Well, let's say it's the reason I turned off – and learned to turn off – all deep emotional feelings for men many years ago.

Napoleon claims this horrific episode in my past wasn't exactly why I became a Digger. But it is the reason I became good at it. And why I hooked up intially with **Earning Every Penny**, my Digger mentor. I had the ability to turn off all emotion. And be left with only equations. This plus this gets that.

On Christmas Day, Napoleon and I stayed together. We exchanged stockings. I gave him all sorts of dirty little toys. And a novel about the swinging, wife-swapping seventies in the Hamptons called *Bossa Nova*.

He gave me tons of makeup and lotions and nail polishes and shampoos and creams and conditioners and all things for beauty, face, and hair. I loved it. We watched *March of the Wooden Soldiers* together.

That evening, I watched Napoleon pack. He had a night flight to Miami. He was joining some friends in Key West. One of them was a blondie named Greg, whom Napoleon had been seeing recently. He wasn't in love with him. But he said Greg was good in bed.

At the door, we kissed and hugged. 'You sure you don't want me to stay?'

'I'm sure. Have fun. And lots of sex. 'Tis the season for giving, you know.'

'And taking . . .' he added and I eked out a smile.

'Say hi to Greg for me.'

'Merry Christmas, baby.'

One more hug. Then we said we loved each other.

For the next three days, I retired to the furniture of my apartment. I ordered in and watched TV. I did laundry. It was rather peaceful. For some reason, I didn't feel that bad. I was crushed, of course. But I wasn't wailing. Or breaking things. One night, I decided to paint my nails and toes with the new sparkly polish Napoleon had given me.

The phone rang numerous times. The Wallet Boys were constantly phoning in for New Year's Eve companionship. I received offers to go to Sun Valley. To the Caribbean. To Palm Beach. And Aspen. I didn't pick up. The calls were desperate ones. Why didn't they have their girls lined up already? Why call this late? Cancellations were the reason. I was too proud for that. Besides, I didn't really want to go.

After the sparkly polish dried, I found myself in the shower soaping up with my new lavender-scented soap. And shampooing with my new chamomile shampoo. When I got out of the shower, I found myself playing with my hair in the mirror. Then I blew-dry it. Then I decided to test my new makeup, so I put on a face. With eyeliner, lipstick, and powder. I looked pretty good. My eyes were a bit puffy, but not overly so.

I forgot to tell you about the new Ozbek dress I'd bought the first day Brad hadn't called. Nor did I tell you about the new shoes I bought on day two of Not Hearing from Jerko. I put them both on, the shoes after I put on the new stockings I bought the day Brad called and canceled on me.

I looked in the full-length mirror at my Left for Dead self in my I've Been Dumped getup. I looked pretty buttery. And that means sexy.

I then had a quick conversation with myself.

'*Where are you going?*'

'*I'm going out.*'

'*Where, out?*'

'*Out to have a drink.*'

'*Are you going to be out late?*'

'*Course not.*'

blue thumbs

It was nine o'clock. I strolled down Fifty-seventh Street, taking my time. I needed to clear my head. The air was brisk. The street was pretty empty, Christmas week and all. Anyone who was out and about was a tourist in town for the holidays. That means no one interesting.

Bobby was working that night. And the bar at the Four Seasons hotel was bustling. The tourists I mentioned were there, in from all points of America and beyond. It wasn't a good night for short-term digging. Digging at the Four Seasons is a Monday through Wednesday affair, Wednesday being the big night. It's when traveling businessmen are done with their work week. They usually head back home on Thursday to be with their missus for the weekend. So Wednesday night is the night they want to kick it up.

But this was Christmas week. It was mostly families, actually – a rarity for that place.

I sat on a chair at the bar and ordered a whiskey sour. I was in a whiskey-sour kind of mood. It was a spontaneous choice, and my mood matched it. I wasn't particularly happy. But I think I was trying my best to be optimistic, to work through the bad feeling. The last thing I wanted was to be the wallowing runner-up in my Tower apartment. Working through it also meant forcing myself to deal. And – I had a new outfit, which is probably the real reason.

Before long, a young Wall Streeter came up to me. I recognized his face, actually, and remembered what he did. Seventy-five thousand a year, tops.

'Bo?'

'Yes.'

'It's Dave, remember?'

'No.'

'David C. Lane. We met a few weeks ago.'

It's funny. He'd added the *C* to his name since I'd last seen him. I used this guy once to make my Wallet Boy a little jealous back in November. Now Dave C. Lane was just an inexpensive suit on a quasi-festive night. A pain in the ass, is what I'm saying. He started laying it on relentlessly. With a halitosis boost. It didn't take long to stoke up my fires.

So I whispered to him, 'Follow me.'

And I walked him into the corner, squared opposite, put a finger in his chest, and let him have a dose.

'Listen here, you little Wall Street guy – I don't want to hear about your big stockbroker job that's small, I don't want to hear about your weekend retreat in the Hamptons that's shack, or all your influential friends you haven't met yet, or how many Hermès ties you have. If you're such hot goddamn shit, what the hell are you doing in New York during Christmas week? You're a nickel-and-dime ticker-tape muncher. You can't afford me, you got it?'

He was stunned. I looked at him, and he was just hanging on for dear life. So I softened a bit. 'Tis the season, was my thought.

'Look, Dave – I'm going to give you a little advice. *Any* man can be a playboy. All it takes is being very generous to one girl. *One* girl. That's all. And this girl will spread the news around because she can't hold it in. No woman who's had a string of failed unions – which is the case for most women, by the way – can hold off bragging about the newfound generosity index she's found in her latest man. And then he'll get a *reputation*. That's what you want. A reputation. You want to be talked about, Dave. You want to be talked about *nicely*. Not about a few drinks you bought. Not about dinner at the River Café. Nicely. And nicely is cash. Cartier. Jewels. Diamonds. Prada. Gucci. Mercedes-Benz. And it just takes one girl, being generous to just one girl. And then every girl will want you. Got it?'

He nodded, though he was still fighting through the daze.

'That's when you add three phone lines and buy aspirin in bulk,' I added with a smile.

So did he, eventually. 'One girl,' he said, half stuttering.

'One girl,' I repeated.

And then I grazed his lips ever so slightly with mine; he might not have even felt it. But he'd never forget what I told him. I was sure of that.

I took my chair and changed liquors. I wanted to get

in a better mood. So I ordered an Absolut Citron Baybreeze. It has pineapple. It's very sweet. I wanted a little sweetness in my system.

At the end of the bar, I saw a guy who didn't belong there. He had a knee-length black leather coat on, dark disheveled hair, a heavy mono-brow to the point of having a sort of caveman look. He was actually very sexy.

The life at the bar had nothing on this guy. It just drifted by him and he didn't flinch. When the bartender asked him something, it looked as though he didn't even bother to listen. There was some strange rawness or power, if you will, to this guy.

When he reached for his beer, I saw his thumb extend and it had something stuck to the end. On closer look, I saw it wasn't a sticker. It was his thumbnail. It had blue nail polish on it. And it was only his thumb.

When he lit up a Marlboro red, the movement revealed that his other thumb was painted too. He had two blue thumbs. And yes, that conjured up a memory of a conversation I'd had with **Show Me You Mean It** a few weeks before. Old Blue Thumbs. He was the one who had done her good. Freaky good.

Then he looked my way and held on me a second, almost as if to say, *You got a problem?*

My, I thought as I turned away. I liked the look, though. It made me squirm a little.

Then my mind drifted away and I thought about my problems, literally in fact, even though he'd only silently asked me if I had one. My sister had cancer, I was low on money, I was going to be evicted, I'd just gotten dumped, it was Christmastime, and I was all alone.

I paid for my drink, left a holiday boost for Bobby, and shuffled out of there.

What a strange guy, I thought. I took the steps one at a time. I don't know why. I was floating, kind of. What a strange guy.

At the bottom of the stairs, I paused for some reason. I looked up. And there he was. The guy was looking down at me. He had black eyes, predator eyes. He kept them on me a second. Strange. I continued down the stairs.

I walked over to a pay phone and called in to my answering service. I had no messages. From anyone who mattered, anyway. After I hung up, I sat there a second. I could smell cigarette smoke wafting by. I felt myself getting, well, moist.

I slipped out of the booth and walked down the next set of stairs. I heard some footsteps behind me. Heavy steps. I continued toward the revolving doors. The steps kept coming. I turned around. It was him. He was advancing and sucking on a cigarette – the guy with the blue thumbs.

In New York City, when someone is tailing you, you take notice. When someone is stalking you, it may be the most frightening thing in the world. But somehow this guy didn't frighten me. I wasn't scared as if my life was in danger. I was scared – sexually. As to what he could do to me. He was so beastlike. And predatory. And pursuing. He knew what he wanted. And the look on his face told me that he knew he was going to get it. I was really moist.

I went to the right, down another set of stairs. I stopped and turned. He was still coming. I came to the last corridor. I saw the door to the ladies' room. I pushed through it. I didn't scream. As soon as the door shut behind me, I heard it slam back open. And then he was right there. I looked at him briefly, but I couldn't hold a gaze on him. He was too powerful. I looked down and away. He stood there not moving. I didn't move either. It was a standoff. I looked at his shiny black silver-buckled shoes. And his leather coat. I saw the thick black belt at his waist. I couldn't look any further. I retreated back a step. My arm reached behind, and I spread open the door to the bathroom stall. I stepped in, spun slowly, and turned my back to him. The last move I made involved extending my arms up and out and matting my hands flat against the powder-blue tiled wall. That bent me slightly. I stood there waiting. I was so everything, and all of that.

Less than moments later, he moved in right behind me. I braced myself. He let me imagine what was going on behind me. I felt a tug on my dress. He hiked up the back flap. Then ripped down the back of my hose. My ass was bare now, and I felt the cold air on it. Then I felt the pressure. It made my legs drift. Apart. He penetrated me, digging in slowly inside me. I writhed. The slow friction subsided. His pace increased. I smelled the scent from his neck and chest. His hands were gripping my hips like a vise. And he kept surging. My head was against the wall now. I came once, I came twice, shuddering and moaning. After a minute, his primal grunts turned to groans. Suddenly he pulled from me, and I felt the hot stream spray all over my backside.

He was that considerate, anyway.

My legs were weak. And trembling. I eased down off the balls of my feet. I just stood there catching my breath. The wall was holding me up. Then he gripped my shoulders and pressured me back to a stand. My back was still to him. I heard a zipper make its presence heard. He kissed the back of my head. And then nothing. When I turned around seconds later, he was gone.

I didn't know if anyone had come in or not. And I didn't care. No, he hadn't used protection. Like the rest of the nation who says it does and it doesn't. Sure, it was foolish. But sometimes, well, sometimes, it has to be that way. That's just the way it was at Century's End.

Of course, I was on the Pill, but that only covered the pregnancy worries.

Fifteen minutes later I found myself slowly climbing stairs to the bar. My legs were pretty weak. I maneuvered one step at a time. I ordered an Evian. Shortly thereafter, someone grazed up behind me. I knew who it was. I smelled him.

I knew he would come back around. Eventually. After all, he had just fucked me. And I sensed he knew there was more to be had.

I turned around and looked at him squarely. I wasn't surprised. In fact, I knew he'd be there. 'Hello,' I said.

He didn't say anything. I didn't expect him to.

'I'm Celeste.'

It looked as though it really made his day. I loved this guy. Under his black coat he was wearing a V-necked black sweater. A thin silver chain dangled from his neck.

I hadn't even had a chance to notice these items before. It would have been amusing, but I didn't give it further thought. There was no time. He extended his hand. I gave him mine, and he slowly clasped it. His was thick, hot, and dry. I could feel his energy still surging from it.

In the elevator I asked him a question. 'Do you know **Earning Every Penny**?'

'Yes.'

'She's a friend of mine,' I said.

'I know.'

And that was all he said. He shot an arm out and yanked my head back and kissed me. Hard. And placed his mitt on my ass, and then some. I was still so wet.

We walked down the hall. I was following him. He pulled out a room key, slid it in the door. The door spread wide. He held it for me. I slipped inside.

He took off his jacket and took me, kissing my hand. His hands were so strong. Before I knew it, I was seated on the bed.

He first placed a hand behind my neck and shoved me forward. He had me take him in my mouth. He made me take him far, all the way down my throat. He was nicely sized. After a few minutes, I heard him utter a slight groan. Then he pulled out of my mouth.

He unzipped my dress, pulled it over my head, flipped me over on my stomach, pulled my hose down again – and exposed me. He then peeled the stockings all the way off and ripped them in half.

With each leg of hose, he tied a wrist to each side of the headboard. And then he did whatever he wanted to me. I didn't tell him he could. And he didn't ask. He just did it.

Sometimes in life, you have to fuck to forget. Bo knows how to.

never happen

I was in a dreamy state when I woke up. It was two in the afternoon. What had happened? I wondered. Whatever it was, was damn good. I remembered the sex-until-nine-A.M. part. Then I got up, found most of my clothes, and limped home.

I took a nice long bath. The phone rang and I picked it up with a nice, cheery, aw-why-not? attitude.

'Hello?'

'Bodicea?'

'Yes.'

'The reluctant warrior queen?' Somehow this guy knew his queens.

'Hello, Lawrence.'

'How was your Christmas?'

And the question prompted a flash image of Blue Thumbs pounding me in a public place and me sucking on his blue thumbs.

'Can't complain,' I said, and the coast was clear to smile. So I did.

'Listen – what are you up to for New Year's?'

'Uh, I'm staying right here.'

'New Year's 1999? The night the Artist Commonly Known as Prince has been advertising since the eighties? Why don't you come to Aspen with me? I have a suite at the Jerome.'

'Look, Lawrence. I'm never going to kiss you. I'm certainly not going to have sex with you, so why do you keep pursuing me?'

'Wait a second . . .'

'No, I've got to go.'

And I hung up. Yes, it was rude. But he deserved it. I hated guys like Lawrence. The type whose only wild trick was the fact that they did drugs. It's really the only thing that made them more interesting. Other than their money. It falsely pulled them out of the dull ditch their real personality lay in.

But who could stomach going out with a drug addict? By definition, he's on the decline. The only good thing about it is, occasionally a druggy can be generous. But even so, eventually everything comes crashing back to all that is real. And reality. And when you're sitting there left with the reality of one of those creeps, it's like . . . forget it. And Lawrence was right there. I'd blown it targeting him as a Rich Rebel prospect.

Bo knows creeps too.

I quickly phoned Warren. I had to hurry. I made a quick appointment at Licari. Not only was I going to cut, but I needed to recolor as well. I didn't want to have anything more to do with Christmas Bordeaux burgundy. Ever.

I packed quickly. Just the essentials. Which included a choice of six dresses for New Year's Eve. Then I shot downstairs. Larry the building manager was there, so he helped me flag a cab.

'How long you going for?'

'Three or four days.'

'Happy New Year, Ms Lashley.'

I wished him one too. And I gave him a nice holiday tip.

queens of the mother lode

On the flight west I was sugar-champagne blond. Sugar champagne always goes great with a winter tan. And furry hats. In the mountains. With a snow backdrop. You bet I headed back to Aspen. I was going to catch up to the Tour.

As I indicated at the outset, as the seasons change, the Diggers follow the Green. And during Christmas and New Year's, the Green goes to Gstaad, St Bart's, St Moritz, Punta del Este, and a few lesser-known spots. But as for America, there is no town more celebrated for holiday Walletmen than Aspen, Colorado. And ladies in search of the Precious – men, not metals – are well apprised of the demographics. For two weeks out of the year, Aspen is the Digger Capital of the World, and New Year's Eve is the Super Bowl.

There is a long-standing historical tradition of mineral exploration in Aspen and its surrounding canyons. Ironically, the modern Mother Loders have much in common with their prospecting forefathers. But back in the 1870s, the quarry that put Aspen on the map was silver and the town yielded much of it.

Over time, Aspen became a ski resort and achieved a revitalized boost of fame for being the holiday stomping ground for the wealthy notables, Hollywood included. The word got out that Aspen was the place to be. The town promoted itself aggressively and opened up more flights. It became a first-class resort. In 1986 the Aspen Ski Company opened the appropriately named Silver Queen gondola. As more notables came, so did the country's Precious. Though the quiet celebrity in search of a private getaway is long gone, Aspen still brings in his replacements.

Large names with large bank are still there. And their presence has the umbrella effect. Where they go, their well-heeled friends go, and other Have Mores follow. And it's not that these rich men are all single, willing, and available. In many cases, they are not. They're usually linked up with Ms Right or have flown in Ms Right Now. That's me. But there are still many single Walletmen walking around.

A car picked me up at the Aspen airport and drove me up Red Mountain. It was snowing heavily. The sun had already gone down, and the town's lights shimmered away through the snowfall. Aspen really is a gem of a town.

I arrived at Warren's house about eight. He had already gone out. The house was a gigantic redwood chalet. A valet named Cristofero took my bags and showed me my room. It was huge and had a big Jacuzzi bathtub. When he slipped out, he told me the name and address of the party Warren was attending. I was to meet him there.

'And Warren's wife?'

'She didn't come this year.'

Now my invitation made total sense. I saw the brand-new white Bogner ski-bunny outfit he'd bought for me draped across the bed. Generous.

I took a nice long sudser and dressed timberline sex-kitten chic. You know, a nice blend of fur and flesh.

Cristofero drove me into the residential section of Aspen, where the houses are piled closer together. It was two nights before New Year's.

Ernest J. Rork had a nice, big modern number. He was a successful real estate developer from New York who held an annual pre-New Year's bash that kicked off the holiday week.

After checking my coat, I found myself standing on the steps looking down into the sunken living room. It was quite a frightening sight. There was a swirl of Diggers, mostly golden oldies. The mid-thirties and forty-year-old gals – the ones who hadn't scored yet. And probably never would. They looked like old athletes. It was a sad sight. *I don't want to end up like them* was my immediate thought.

They were all dressed in black, twirling, whirling, laughing, and toasting. It was a real fluff of the feathers. Let's not forget the caked-on makeup. And the faux-blond hair teased to new heights. I should have gone black-cherry black, I immediately thought.

These Mother Loders had one eye on the champagne being poured and one eye on the door. To see who on the List might enter. When I looked at them, they looked back at me and tried to melt me down. They didn't want me there. I was competition. Young competition. That meant I hadn't been as worked over by gravity's pull. I mean, some of them were doing a fine job at cheating the earth's laws. With synthetics carved into their bodies and syringed into their skin. But no matter what modern surgery techniques you employ, lasers included, you can't outdo that high-velocity facial and corporal zing that only youth can provide. How a youthful face just pops. These faces clearly had lost their pop. In fewer words, I was the enemy.

I did wave to a couple of familiar faces. **Australian, Canadian, or US** was there and so was **I'm in a Pinch**. I saw **Sure, Why Not?**, **Pop, Pop, Fizz, Fizz**, and **Pussy for Pesos**. That's kind of mean, actually. I'll call her **At Least My Toes Are Real** instead. **Food, Mansion, and Couture** was there in an Ozbek gown to round out the crowd.

And of course **The Wild Card** was there. **The Wild Card** hadn't missed an Aspen gig in twenty years. And it showed. Already I saw her jaw flapping around, no doubt due to secretive restroom intake. **The Wild Card** was capable of showing up anywhere. And she always had one objective – one more line of coke. She was a coke whore extraordinaire. She'd been in Aspen when it was cool to snort. She'd been in Aspen when it wasn't cool to snort. And she was still in Aspen when it became cool again. But her desire had never wavered. That was sad. I stayed away from **The Wild Card**. She truly took the 'fun' out of dysfunction. She usually attracted losers too. *Quel* surprise.

Lastly, I saw the diminutive **I'm Just as Good in**

Bed getting frustrated trying to push her way through the forest of people.

But Warren was nowhere in sight.

how to marry a billionaire

'B_o!'

I turned around and was so surprised. And elated. It was **Earning Every Penny**, my Digger mentor. We hugged for an extended moment. We hadn't seen each other in two years. It was really nice. My feeling for an old friend surged from me to her. And I received the energy from her embrace too. While we held on to each other, I wondered why she was in Aspen, however. It wasn't a good indicator. She looked a little older, but not much.

'I thought you got married,' I said.

'No. It didn't work out,' she said with a dour twist of the head.

'But you were pregnant.'

'I lost it.'

'Oh no.' And I clutched her hand.

'How are you, Bo?' she asked to switch the subject.

'I'm well.'

'You look great,' she said.

And right then and there, I had a melancholic dip. It made me want to get out of there. It made me wonder what the hell I was doing in Aspen. Why had I come? To avoid staying home, I guessed. But I knew that was not a good answer. Upon further reflection, it was the thought of **Earning Every Penny**'s not landing her guy and returning defeatedly to the Tour that brought on my dolor. In essence, it was what I had done too.

And where the hell was Brad?

And some big, bloated guy swooped up behind **Earning Every Penny** and vised her hand to whisk her off. 'Let's get outta here,' he croaked.

'Wait a second, we're catching up,' I said to him. And he eyed me and then her and saw that we were resolute. He moved on.

'Thank you,' she said to me. Then whispered. 'He's such a slob.'

'You staying with him?'

She didn't answer. It was an answer. And not a good one.

'So, what happened to Daddy Warbucks?' It was her name for the guy. He was Fortune 500-hot, married once, the wife couldn't have kids, they divorced, and he still wanted a family. She'd hit the mother lode. Or so we'd all thought.

'Right there.'

I looked over. 'Her?'

She looked at me and nodded.

It was **Smiles to Your Face. Smiles to Your Face** was a real Machiavellian beaut. She was cunning, smart, and very sexy. She had a face like Ava Gardner, and men found her to be quite irresistible. But she only really got off on men in one way. If another woman had him. She was the Digger version of Lawrence Dexter Fairchild. Only she had an easier time of it. Why? She was holding – and men are men. To make matters worse, I could see she was wearing Plein Sud's anaconda dress too. The one that's silver, midnight blue, and green. She looked killer.

'I can't believe it,' I said. 'One of these days, she'll get hers. It comes back around, you know.'

Earning Every Penny looked at me as if it was some small consolation, but very small.

'Come on, babe,' the slob said a second time. And he grabbed her arm too.

'Wait, Harry. Are you going to Gstaad?' she asked me.

'No,' I said. It's something we used to do together. **Earning Every Penny** and I would jet from Aspen to Gstaad right before or just after New Year's Eve, depending on the respective party lineups.

Then I noticed a blond woman across the room looking, if not staring, at me. She was a bit older and classically dressed in a black Scaasi, I think. She had an intense expression. I'd seen her before in Los Angeles. Or maybe New York. I couldn't remember. But it was always at smart parties. At first, I thought it was just me that she was glaring at, but it was both **Earning Every Penny** and me. I chalked it up as just a champagne-fueled smoocherella vibe.

Earning Every Penny then learned in and whispered it to me. 'A couple of girls are going to Brunei after this.'

I told her I knew. 'You?' I asked.

She shrugged. And Harry shoved her on. I told her to

call my service if she needed me. We waved good-bye to each other. I adored **Earning Every Penny**. She was more hands-on responsible for my day-to-day personal development than anyone. And that includes parents. I was seventeen when I met her. She taught me pretty much everything I knew about men. She'd been a mother to me. Later on, when we both were in Los Angeles, she had helped me through some difficult times. She even lent me money when she was broke herself. She didn't get a single acting job there. I didn't like Los Angeles for that and other reasons. I always got into trouble there. As soon as I set foot on the ground out there, I felt a certain eeriness.

I think in a past life I was one of those struggling actresses in the forties who never made it, yet did everything she could to make it and ended up committing suicide in one of those West Hollywood bungalows. That's how I felt about the L.A. leg of the Tour – reluctant. But Oscar time in March was very festive, and men were very generous.

Whichever, **Earning Every Penny** was now forty years old. And she was looking needy. Welcome to the dark and depressing side of my profession. There were a lot of women like **Earning Every Penny** who, for whatever reason, didn't get it done during that Ten-Year Window. And every party after became a festival of desperation that would include wild compromises no one would have ever made in their prime. And it usually got only worse. I considered a trip to Brunei to be in that category. I hoped for her sake she wasn't going to do it.

'Bo, right?' I heard behind me.

'Uh, yes, And you're . . .' And I knew the face.

'Jasper.'

'Jasper, that's right.' And I noticed he was kind of limping a bit.

'Is your leg okay?'

'Yeah, I took a bad wipe today. I sprained my ankle.'

'Ouch.'

'It's not too bad. The ski boot helped.'

'Is **Every Little Bit Helps** here?'

'Uh, no,' he said. And he shuffled a step, played with his hair, and jerked his eyes around. Uh-oh, I thought. 'She's in St Bart's,' he added.

'Oh.'

And I didn't pursue it. I could tell he didn't want me to. I knew the answer anyway. And he gave me the slightest glimpse of That Face, the one I was telling you about. Then he tried to cover it over with some cool.

'And Giles?' he inquired.

'You haven't heard?'

'No. I don't know him at all.'

I told him the news. And believe it or not, he started laughing. It made me smile curiously. 'What's so funny?'

'That guy looked like he was going to die.'

If only you knew, I thought. 'He was up there, that's true – but he lived a very active life. Right until the end.'

But Jasper's innocence and unknowing took him out of what was the dark deep water and back up to the surface. He asked spritely, 'When did you get into town?'

'Tonight, actually.'

'Really. The snow's been great.'

'I don't ski,' I said. 'In Aspen,' I added.

And he just looked at me a moment. The look seemed to have some sort of significance. But I couldn't really tell what kind. As this guy had only shown me naive colors when we first met. So when he had a flash of awareness, I didn't know how *flashy or aware* it was.

'Can I get you something to drink?' he asked politely.

'Sure. Is the champagne any good?'

'Uh, not really.'

'Kir Royale, then.'

Jasper really was a cutie. Virginia Lashley would have approved of him. Too bad my future won't, I thought.

He returned from the bar and handed me a flute, and we clinked glasses.

'Do you come here every year?' I asked him.

'No. First time. I'm actually working.'

'Working?'

'Yeah, I'm on assignment.'

'Sounds so official. Jasper Whatever-your-last-name-is: On Assignment.'

He laughed. '*Connelly*. Jasper Connelly.'

'What are you writing?'

'I'm doing a piece for *Esquire*.'

'Really? On what?' And I saw a whole new flock of Diggers and other professional nesters coming in the front door.

'Did you ever see the movie *How to Marry a Millionaire*?'

'Once or twice.'

'My piece is tentatively titled "How to Marry a

Billionaire." It's about gold diggers,' he said.

I was sipping at the time he said it, and I almost coughed up what I'd sipped.

'Ah-hah.' And I remembered one of our previous conversations. 'You were looking for something more . . . spicy to write about, as I recall.'

'You remember? Good memory.' And he got a buzz from that.

'They just assigned the topic to you?'

'Well, no. I proposed it.'

And the look in his expression told me why. **Every Little Bit Helps** had been a little sloppy. And even someone as trusting as Jasper had caught on – at least partially. He'd never know the full extent of her activity. And I wasn't about to tell him. Even though it would make everything a whole lot easier for him. Instead of heart-broken, he'd be angry. And anger is easier on the soul, and less painful.

'I'd say you've come to the right place,' I contended.

'If you have any leads, let me know.'

I nodded. 'How's it coming so far?'

'It's been pretty frantic.'

'How so?'

'Everyone's skiing or hung over or scrambling for invitations to the New Year's Eve parties.'

'Are you going to Randolph Spears's?'

'Yes.'

'That's a good one.'

'The main problem I'm having is, what woman wants to draw attention to herself if she's really involved in it?'

I just looked at him. 'That's a problem,' I said.

'And the local Aspenites don't want to damage the town's reputation. They depend on the tourism. So they don't want to talk.'

'That's another problem.'

'I guess "Not great" is the answer to your question,' he said, and smiled weakly too.

the oil baron

Just then, **Earning Every Penny** rushed up to me excitedly. She had a plan and it involved some mischief. She wanted to exact some revenge on **Smiles to Your Face**. She needed me to help her conduct the ruse. But she noticed Jasper listening in and got nervous.

'Could you excuse us?' she asked him politely.

'No. Don't worry. He's my friend,' I said, grabbing his arm and drawing him close.

Earning Every Penny gave us the quick dish. She pointed out two guys across the room.

'The one on the left is a very wealthy Texas guy, and the other is his young Mexican friend. The two are traveling together. The Mexican kid is actually the son of the maid of the wealthy Texan's family. The Texan is footing the vacation bill. But the Mexican isn't getting any girls.'

'Why not?'

'He's not playing The Game right. You know where I'm going with this, Bo?'

'You know I do.'

'I've set it all up. I've been coaching the kid for the past half hour. I've taught him to be standoffish, to smoke a cigar, say he has a controlling interest in Mobil, a mansion in San Antonio, a villa in St Tropez, and, of course, to pretend he's sooooo important.'

'What about money?' I asked.

'The Texan gave him his Gold Card too, for the restaurants and shopping.'

'Great,' I said.

'I really would appreciate it, Bo.'

'It would be a pleasure.' And **Earning Every Penny** took off.

'So – what's going to happen?'

'Watch me. I'll explain later.'

I ambled up to the bar where **Smiles to Your Face** was, and reworked my face to get it twitching and perturbed. Like I was a little drunk and sore. I began by spearing around for a glass, some ice, then barked an order to the bartender.

'What is this, a dry state?' I cracked.

Smiles craned around her neck. 'Oh, hi, Bo.'

'Hey there.'

'When did you arrive?' she asked in her saccharine way.

'Few days ago.'

'Handsome guy you're with.'

She was indicating Jasper. This one doesn't miss a beat, I thought.

'Him? He's some writer. When was the last time you went out with a writer?'

'Never,' she said flatly. 'You seem upset.'

'Yeah, well, you win some – you know the rest,' I said bitterly.

'What happened?'

'Aw, hell, this guy I had a crush on, well, let's just say it didn't work out, you know what I mean?'

'No. How do you mean?'

'He's the mother lode. Capital *M*. I mean, he's an oil baron from Texas, family owns Mobil,' I spat. I was dicing up my sentences into drunken bites. 'S'worth millions. Anyhow, we spent a week together. New York. We came here, had a nice evening. Tonight – he doesn't even know I'm alive.'

I slurred a lot too, to make her think I was truly drunk and depressed and, therefore, must be giving her a dish totally void of stratagem.

'You mean he's here?'

'Right over there.' And I pointed with an elbow. 'Hey, where'd you get that drink?' I said to no one in particular.

'Seems kind of young.' Then she asked me his age. I ignored her.

'What does a woman have to do here to get a drink? What did you say?'

She asked me his age again.

'Thirty-six,' I said. 'He's dusted every girl. No one seems to be pretty enough. I think he used to go out with Nicollette Sheridan. Dumped her too. What's worse is, he knows how to please a woman.'

'Really . . .'

'Yup. Say, **Smiles**, keep it moist,' I signed off with.

Then I bolted away – to drown my sorrows, I was

sure she thought. Jasper rejoined me by the food table. I filled him in on what had been going on. So we waited and watched.

It took **Smiles to Your Face** about thirty seconds to make a beeline straight toward him. Though it was more of a slither in that reptile dress. She did the coy thing, then the shake-hands thing, then the cutesy little shuffle, then she flashed the smile until the cutesy dimple drilled a hole in her cheek. And the Mexican – bless his heart – was playing it so cool. Like she didn't even exist. He even stepped away from her for a second and left her dangling.

'And he's the son of a maid?' Jasper whispered. I nodded. 'He has zero?'

'Nothing. He's an illegal alien. His family hopped over the fence at the Texas border. Everything he has is from the family his mother works for.'

'Look, he's walking away from her.'

'Good boy,' I said of him. 'He'll get her. Tonight.'

I looked at Jasper. 'So how's that for your piece?'

He didn't answer me. He was too immersed in the human behavioral display.

'What does it tell you about gold digging?'

'It's ruthless.'

'Better believe it.'

'This is as good as it gets . . .' he said excitedly.

'This is nothing. This is intermediate level.'

I looked around the room. Still no sign of Warren Samuels.

'I'm going to take off,' I announced.

'Me too,' he said.

I looked at his kind face. 'Jasper, I'm not here to do interviews.'

'I know. Can I at least give you a lift home?'

I looked at him and smiled.

'Look . . .' he said, pointing in a direction behind me.

The Mexican and **Smiles** were now seated by the fire, the Mexican puffing away on a cigar, still looking bored. Her posture was one direction – forward.

'I'll give you a tip, Jasper. Wait until after New Year's to conduct your interviews.'

'Why?'

'Once the hoopla dies down. Once the girls' dreams of landing their guy have died. They'll be bitter and ready to open up. And spread it wide. Like an oyster.'

I smiled in a naughty way too. And I wasn't really sure why. He smiled back.

'Thanks,' he said.

I don't know why, but I liked the idea of what he was doing. I didn't know why I was feeling a lot of what I was feeling in those crazy days, for that matter. But the reality is, I didn't mind talking about the business. It was actually fun – more fun than I'd had, well, since that bathroom whirl at the Four Seasons.

trail-map mentality

We drove down Highway 82 in Jasper's rented Jeep.

'Could you believe that party?' I muttered.

'How do you mean?' he asked. And I realized again that I was with someone who was not in the know.

I looked at him bluntly. 'Listen, Jasper, I'll help you with your piece.' He looked at me sharply. 'But no personal questions.'

'None.'

'And no names. Got it?'

'Got it.'

As we drove, I filled Jasper in on a little Aspen history. How the town used to be about sex and drugs. How cops used to do drugs with the citizens. The going phrase was 'No blow, no go.' Then with eighties greed it became 'No blow, no dough, no go.'

'And now?'

'No dough, no go,' I said. 'It's purely a business deal. Especially during the holidays. For the women it's about meeting a mate and making a merger. For the men it's about this plus this gets that. It's about manipulating a situation. And there are different levels.'

'What do you mean?'

'Some girls are better than others.'

'Is it only about the girls?'

'No, it's not. There are a lot of fortune-hunting men here too. Are you interested in them?'

He thought about it. But not for too long. He shook his head. He was working for a men's magazine, of course.

We drove a little farther and spotted a car stuck in a snowbank. A pretty girl was behind the wheel steering while her two girlfriends were struggling to push the car. We pulled over to help them. They were very appreciative and polite.

'Where are you guys coming from?' the biggest and least attractive of the three girls asked.

'Ernest Rork's party,' I said.

'Who?'

'The party's over,' Jasper remarked.

'You know what's happening tomorrow night?'

'Get their number, Jasper.'

'What?'

'Are you reporting, or am I?'

He took down their number, and we told them we'd call. They were staying at a local bed-and-breakfast.

'But call before eight,' the girl said. 'That's when the switchboard closes.'

We got back in the Jeep.

'Novices,' I declared.

'What?'

'They don't know where to go. Or how to get there. If you rent a car, you never go two-wheel drive. And you don't stay in a place that has no phone after eight. They're novices. Just like on the ski slopes. There are novices, intermediates, experts, and pros.'

'That's it,' he said excitedly.

'What?'

'I'll use the ski-trail thing to show the different levels of proficiency in gold digging.'

And he kissed me on the cheek as a thank-you. 'Join me for some tea?' he posed.

I looked at my watch. It was just after midnight. I pondered the situation. I didn't really want to have sex with Warren. Or anyone, for that matter. I just didn't feel up to it. But if I came back early, I knew he would be waiting up for me. If he was out later, he would wake me up. I decided to stay with Jasper a little longer.

Besides, Jasper was a good guy. I didn't mind that at all. And I didn't mind that he wasn't after me either.

And you wonder how it takes women for ever to make up their mind? Weighing options can take for ever. And if any of the previous preponderances and analyses don't work or they self-destruct, therein lies the formula for a woman changing her mind.

'Sure,' I said finally.

greens, blues, and black diamonds

Jasper was staying at the Little Nell, my favorite hotel. It was right at the base of Ajax, the town's main ski mountain. Very convenient. Everything in town was within walking distance and it had a great bar. The Diggers flocked there every evening for a little après-ski mother-loding.

We sat at a cozy table by the fire. I had hot apple cider; Jasper had a beer. And I proceeded to give him a clinic on the fine art as I knew it. We employed the ski-map coloring system, as he'd suggested.

'The typical Green novice types come to Aspen in groups of three or four, like our two-wheel-drive friends. They're on a budget and are powerless to reduce costs. They don't know how. They've all been with their parents for Christmas, and their moral fiber is still pretty strong. Usually two of the Greenies are attractive and the third, the leader, also known by male dogs as the "spoiler," is the ugly one. She's the engine who uses the other two as bait. But the reality is, she isn't going to get anything. And her personality is strong enough to ruin it for the others. One of the pretty ones could have just broken up with her boyfriend, though she claims she came to Aspen "to ski." It's conceivable that one of them links up with a seasonal playboy or a ski instructor or a college student with a gift of the gab. But it's not likely.'

'The novices eat at low-budget places, the franchises like the Red Onion, the Chart House, places they've heard of before. They live in inconvenient B&Bs and have standard skiwear, like a parka and mittens. They aren't good skiers and usually rent equipment. They ski Buttermilk, the easiest of the town's four mountains, and the most socially drained.'

'Jees, Bo, you should write. . . .'

That got a smile from me. 'You like?'

'I like.'

'Another type of Green is the one who has been brought to Aspen by her boyfriend. He's a young guy with little money and he has no access to the right parties. But he exposes her to the scene. If the girl has any Digger in her at all, her eyes start to wander and she gets frustrated. And she won't return, not with her boyfriend anyway. She'll come with a guy who can take her to the next level. Or she'll come back alone, knowing all this, as a Blue. In the end, the Greens are trying to get some real satisfaction. And what they get is mental masturbation. They're afraid. They're unequipped. They're vulnerable. The Greens need support.'

Jasper asked if he could use a tape recorder. I told

him he could not. So he resorted to copious notes instead.

'The Blues are more savvy. They actually come with an agenda. They know the right parties. And they're working on getting in. They've been to Aspen before, or towns like it. They may be part of the town's workforce. They know the high cost of living in Aspen and they hustle to curb costs. They may have secured lodging at a private house or have held out for a plane-ticket invite. Their agenda could be anything from wanting a boy-friend or a husband to a new career in Hollywood. But whatever it is, they've come to work it. They have dates or can get them. And certainly, if they're going to rent a car, they're going to opt for a vehicle that has four-wheel drive.

'The Blues also know about the hip places. Like Mezzaluna or this place for après ski. But it's not a requirement. If they ski, they have their own equip-ment, maybe one designer outfit, and they'll ski Ajax Mountain. They'll show up at Bonnie's, the mountain restaurant, at one o'clock for lunch. They know it's where the action is.'

'What's the difference between a Blue and the next level up?'

'The thing about the Blues is, they don't let their agenda run their lives. They're more savvy, but not necessarily committed to action. They don't run in a fast crowd all year round. They can be from down South or the Midwest. They're used to a less competitive environ-ment. They're not in the same league as the Black Diamonds. Besides, if their interest is to link up with a fat cat, they're known to hold out for someone they're in love with.'

'Keep going,' Jasper said. He had a half smile pasted on his face. It had been that way ever since I started talking.

It's funny. Yet, as I let go of some of this 'knowledge' or whatever you want to call it, I felt a sizable burden being lifted from my shoulders. I felt lighter. And freer. And I wasn't so set back by the setback with Bradley. I wasn't even thinking about it. Maybe that was the reason. Whatever, *everything is going to be okay* was my feeling. It was a good feeling.

And the more I did it, and the better it felt to do it, the more I wanted to do it. Yes, this unheralded writer Jasper Connelly was using me, which was thematically correct for the Aspen holiday spirit. As innocent as he was, he was resourceful enough to locate a gem like me. Maybe it was just dumb coincidence. But I had to hand it to him.

At the same time, I was using him too. To vent, to blow off steam, maybe even to purge myself. We were manipulating a situation, the both of us, but it was positive for both of us. That's how I saw it that evening.

'Tell me about the pros,' he barked while still taking furious notes to keep up.

'Wait a second,' I said. 'The *experts*. Then the pros.'

Suddenly I noticed several clusters of people within earshot of us. I didn't want an audience. I leaned in and whispered, 'You're staying here, aren't you?'

'I have a suite upstairs.'

'Why don't we finish up there? It's a little crowded here.'

So we did. Jasper did have a nice suite. It was a big one-bedroom with a great view of Ajax. I could see the little lights of the Snow-Cats grooming the mountain way up on top. We settled into his soft couch. Once he had his pad and pen ready, again he said, 'Shoot.'

'The Black Diamonds are the experts, the seasoned veterans. They target. They go for the gold. They know the Fortune 500 List. They study it. They already know members of it personally. They have their ticket to Aspen paid for, or they have been flown in on a private jet. And they are here to do nothing less than land the Precious. Men I'm talking, not metals.'

'I know,' Jasper said with a smile.

'Ideally, the Black Diamonds would love to be one of the town's *grande dames* and host a holiday party next year. They already have friends in affluent circles, as they have traveled to various stops on the Digger circuit: Los Angeles, New York, the Hamptons, Gstaad, and the south of France. And their international travels have taught them to kiss both cheeks.

'These experts already have a knack for living off men. Their personal expenses are minimal. Their lodging is covered. At the nicest hotels. Or private luxury homes. If they ski, they get a private instructor. They have at least one Bogner outfit and they'll likely have another by the end of the trip. Or an Emmegi. Or a Lilly Farouche. But many don't ski. Some just ride up the gondola in their furry boots and dine on the mountain. Or they don't bother to come up at all. In which case, their daily routine is one of pampering and preparation for the night. They're Chanel. They're Bulgari. They're Prada. They're dressed fashionably as if they've already scored. And they have. They can rumble effortlessly with the rich. They eat at the town's finest restaurants – Abitone's, Piñions – with their host. Or they tag along on a dinner that some other Walletman will pay for, and not committed to him, they'll operate from there. They have total access to the big New Year's Eve parties. And love is not a requirement.'

'You're kidding me,' Jasper said sarcastically. He was cute. He was feeling less anxious and more confident. He knew he was making severe progress on his assignment. He was also starting to understand the Digger world a bit better.

'The experts know love is something they can't necessarily afford. Good line, huh?'

'Love it,' he said.

that face

'Know what, Jasper?'

'Tell me.'

And he extended his hand and it matted atop mine. But I didn't pull away. It didn't make me nervous in the least. It was sweet.

'I'm tired,' I said.

'Let me drive you back,' he said.

I looked at him. I was saying something. Without saying it. I wanted him to.

'You can stay here, of course.'

I thought about it for a second. 'I don't want to go back out in the cold. I don't want to go to that house.'

That was all true. But my mood was more severe than I was letting on. I was sure that once I got to Warren's, he'd have an after party going on in full swing with new acquisitions, meaning new heathens who he just had to straighten out and purify with that good old-time religion. And his brand of religion was the last thing I wanted that night.

I looked over at Jasper as he was folding up his notepad. It was so nice to be with someone who wasn't so far gone already. That's why I didn't want to leave. I didn't want to leave the comfort of Jasper and his home. I needed that much.

I sort of nuzzled into a deep pillow. All was quiet for a while. Jasper did some straightening up in the kitchen. I dozed a little. When I woke up, the lights were on. Yet it was still the dead of night. I must not have been out that long, I remember thinking.

I raised my head out of the pillow nest and saw Jasper standing in front of the window, looking out into the blackness. And I could see it. He had That Face. That Face is a mixture of heartache, depression, paranoia, and humiliation. Nothing about That Face is good. Women get That Face. But guys get it a whole lot worse. The death of a friend or family member is about the closest thing to it. Because there's nothing that you can do to get rid of it. Other than get rid of it yourself with your own psychological defenses. Occasionally, intensive immersion into some mind-altering unrelated activity helps. But that's more of an escape. Time is the best cure, but as we all know, time never happens quick enough when you're suffering from massive heartbreak.

'What happened with **Every Little Bit Helps**?'

He didn't turn around. It was almost as if he'd been ready for my question. Maybe even hoping for it. 'She's down there in St Bart's.'

'You told me. With who?'

'Some cocaine movie producer,' he spat bitterly. 'You know, I interviewed three girls before you. Two were from Los Angeles and one from Las Vegas. All three reeled off stories about this same producer. You know, how he gives the girls cocaine and follows them into the bathroom to make sure they do it. One girl got hooked. She ended up in the hospital.' His tone lowered. 'That's who my girlfriend is spending the holidays with. Nice, huh? I'm not even talking the low-budget irony.'

'The what?'

'Here I am, doing an exposé on this breed and what they do, while my girlfriend is down on some boat doing it. I can't get away from it. Every time I interview someone, I break out in a sweat.'

'You knew she was up to something, didn't you?'

'When she told me she was going down there instead of coming with me, I lost it. I didn't call her. And I didn't return her calls. We separated for a while. But that lasted only a few days. I was weak . . .' he trailed off disgustedly.

'Does she call?'

'She called today.'

'What did she say?'

'How much she misses me, you know, she bought me a new bathing suit – the usual.'

'She's thinking of you,' I said, and then wished I hadn't. It sounded sarcastic and cruel, even though I hadn't meant it that way.

He spun around and faced me. 'She's pregnant, you know.'

I remained silent a second. But I had to ask. 'With whose?'

'She says it's mine, but who the hell knows.'

'You miss her?'

'Yeah. And I hate her at the same time.' Then he

stood there a few more minutes just pondering. I didn't say anything. There was nothing I could say.

'I'm going to go to bed,' he said. 'You want to take the bedroom?'

'I'm happy right here,' I said, and let my cheek settle back into one of the pillows. I thought about Jasper's awful and ironic predicament for a while, and then I was out.

the sin twisters

The next day, we both awoke about noon. I wasn't in any hurry to make it over to Warren's. He'd be out by now anyway, I was sure. It was a gorgeous day. Ajax Mountain was standing tall right in our living room, and the sun was slapping it directly. You could see the little ant-sized skiers making their way down. We enjoyed a nice croissant-and-coffee breakfast and watched the ants.

'Want to go up?' I asked.

'Where?'

'The mountain.'

'To ski?'

'Course not. To catch some sun.' Jasper wasn't sold. 'It'll be good for your research.'

'Really?'

'Your story isn't a story unless you catch Bonnie's at one.'

A half hour later we were stuffed in the Silver Queen gondola with the rest of the skiers. Jasper had his Timberlands on and I had my moon boots.

'This is a little embarrassing,' he whispered.

'Why?'

'I mean, riding up in the gondola, and not ski? It's so superficial.'

'You ain't seen nothing yet. What did you say the title of your piece was?'

And that made him smile. It should have. The reality is, on the level of superficiality, the scene at Bonnie's was world-class.

We arrived at Bonnie's Restaurant right after the first rush of the lunch crowd had come and gone. We found a nice table outside and just staked out our territory. Jasper joined the food line and came back with a bottle of wine. And then we just let our sunglasses ride our faces, sipped on some California red, and let the people do all the talking. And gossiping. And table-hopping. And schmoozing. And seducing. Bonnie's was a blend of the crowd from Morton's restaurant in Hollywood; itinerants from the Peninsula and Beverly Hills Hotel; Four Seasons hotel guests; folks from Cipriani's restaurants and the Au Bar Club in New York; and members of the Saints-and-Sinners Triangle who wanted to do something more 'American' this year, rounded out by a few thousand girls from all over the world hoping, hoping, hoping to be met by thousands of single guys wanting to screw, do, and screw. There was schmoozing and seducing inside and out. Everywhere you looked, there was a supermingle going on with sexual and financial undercurrents. It was a very sexy scene.

And we just became trusted voyeurs of it all.

Jasper was quiet for the first ten minutes. 'This is amazing,' he said eventually.

I was a little less shell-shocked. I spent my time wedging open the clothes atop my breast and smearing some fifteen SPF on my face. Then I greased Jasper too.

'You get freckles, don't you?' I asked. He told me he did. 'Cute,' I added.

'Bo!'

I heard it behind me. I looked around and it was *them*. Both of them. The **Sin Twisters**. They were sidled up to the outdoor bar ordering their favorite food. Their nickname was a play on the term *twin sisters* when they got drunk. And they did that a lot. Yes, the **Sin Twisters** loved to party. They both had been living in Aspen for a few years. They were resort-hopping Diggers by trade.

As they waited for the bartender to slide them their beers, I gave Jasper the rundown.

'They're both in their mid-twenties. Jean lived in the Virgin Islands and now manages one of the mountain lodges. Beth works as a cocktail waitress.'

'How would you classify them?'

'They're intermediates. Blues, through and through. They want to marry rich but they'll let love screw it up.'

Jasper was in for a treat. When the **Sin Twisters** sat down they just did their thing. They started firing off war story after war story. The beer went right to their heads, and you could tell it was mixing with whatever was still in their systems from the night before. In addition to the altitude factor. This was the way they lived it. Jasper witnessed it for himself. When I told them he was 'on assignment,' they went nuts, yelling, 'Jasper on Assignment!' From then on he had a new nickname.

The fun started when some scruffy guy who looked like he just finished grooming the mountain in a Snow-Cat uttered a greeting to Beth.

'Oh, hi,' she said, somewhat surprised at his sighting. But he didn't linger for a chat. Jasper asked who it was.

'I'll tell you straight, Jasper on Assignment,' she shot back. 'That was Off-Season Boy.' And the **Sin Twisters** both split a gut in unison.

'Off-Season Boy? Who's Off-Season Boy?' he asked.

Beth tried to explain through her snap-cackling laughter. 'He's the guy you fuck in the off-season. Before the tourist season hits.'

And of course it made me think of Off-Season Boy's cousin, Low-Season Boy, whom I'd already tagged and coined.

When the laughter died down, Jean rounded out the profile.

'Off-Season Boy is young, innocent, and has hardly any facial hair, so you have to pencil in a goatee with eyebrow pencil.' More cackles. 'He doesn't like to read, he likes ESPN, he smokes pot, he likes everything that's within arm's reach of his couch, like his beer, his bong, Doritos, and the remote. And he has large hands, and you know what they say about large hands, Jasper on Assignment.'

Jasper looked at his own. So did the girls. When they saw his hands were somewhat stubby, Beth looked at me and placed a gentle hand of solace on my arm. 'My condolences,' she offered me, as I was obviously the one suffering from Jasper's substandard showing in the hands–male anatomy correlation.

And they busted another gut.

'But don't forget,' Jean continued. 'Off-Season Boy is a real homebody. And that's important.'

'Why?' The question came from me.

'He stays close to home. So he's there when you call in at one in the morning and you haven't . . .'

'Found the Bigger, Better, Deal?' Jasper finished off.

'Exactly. And then he fucks your brains out. He's very dependable. And his name is usually Kevin.'

'Why's that?'

'Have you ever heard of a tycoon named Kevin?'

We were all laughing now.

'And he comes recommended,' Jean added.

'Explain.'

'Listen to him,' she mocked. 'Jasper on Assignment knows all those news reporter words. *Explain.*' They were on a roll. 'You find out about a good Off-Season Boy by word of mouth. You don't just do one of these guys. That's risky. That's a grab bag. You don't know what you're going to get. You have to know in advance.'

'So,' Beth added, 'when one of us finds a good one, we pass him back and forth.'

'What does Off-Season Boy do?' Jasper asked.

'He might tend bar or work the chairlifts,' Jean said.

'But what happens during the holiday season?'

'Then he becomes like a pain-in-the-ass brother. 'Cause you're not giving him any more attention. And he doesn't understand. But he gets over it.'

Then Beth nudged me, indicating Jasper. 'He's cute. Can we try him out?'

We laughed at that too.

'They *must* be intermediates,' Jasper said openly in front of them.

'Why?' I asked.

'Because they're interested in the writer.'

'Hey, what's that supposed to mean?' Beth asked.

'Inside joke,' he said.

I liked the fact that Jasper teased them back. His comment was playing off that old joke: 'Have you heard the one about the Polish actress who comes to Hollywood? She screws the writer.'

Obviously, the **Sin Twisters** were not letting their agenda run their lives. After all, linking up with a writer was digging in the wrong mine. I was enjoying Jasper's self-deprecating sense of humor. It was charming.

Before the **Sin Twisters** took off, Jasper provoked them a little.

'But I hear Aspen's not about sex and drugs and rock and roll anymore . . .' he began with.

'Who told you that?' Jean asked.

'It's about mutual manipulation,' he continued. 'It's about "I give you this you give me that" – and you know what's being given.'

Beth just looked at me and puffed on her cigarette. As if she'd been challenged. 'You don't think there's any good sex here anymore, Jasper on Assignment?'

'I didn't say that.' Jasper gave a quick look at me but didn't hold it. He was too much of a gentleman.

Then Beth offered finally, 'Have you ever heard of a Mindblower, Jasper on Assignment?'

We both said we had not.

'Say you meet a guy you like, for whatever reason,'

she continued. 'And you want to have sex with him. So what you do is invite him over to your place – but tell him to come in ten minutes. Then you go home quickly and freshen up. Then when he rings the bell and is waiting outside, you stuff two Hershey's chocolate kisses up your puss. He comes in, you have a drink, you make out, you get naked, and if you've chosen the right kind of guy – the kind who wants to please a woman – he'll go down on you. And if he does, great. He'll get a mouthful of melted chocolate as his reward. But if you've chosen poorly and he's not the right kind of guy, and he's selfish and only into pleasing himself and he doesn't want to go down on you, then – okay – you'll let him do it to you. In and out, in and out. But when he pulls out, he'll see that his penis is all covered with this brown goo. And he'll be confused. He'll think he missed. He'll think he did you up the ass instead. Then what you do is go down on him. And he'll think you are into your own feces. And that will blow his mind. That's a Mindblower, Jasper on Assignment.'

We looked at each other, mouths agape. The **Sin Twisters** were that good. A reporter's dream. Whether Jasper could use this kind of reportage for his exposé was another matter. But, in the end, he needed no more convincing that Aspen still had some good, raw, unconditional and unconventional sex up its sleeve.

dangerous business

Late that afternoon, Jasper took me up Red Mountain in his rented Jeep. I felt a healthy burn on my face. Jasper had gotten some nice color too. A few freckles even popped out on his nose. I thanked him for the wonderful time spent together and gave him a big kiss on the cheek. We planned to talk later.

I opened the front door and entered the house. I heard talking in the living room. A youngish girl, maybe nineteen, with auburn hair was sitting there. She was in a bathrobe, watching TV. She looked up and saw me standing there. 'Are you Bo?'

'Yes.'

She stood up. And when she did, the bathrobe flapped open. This girl had a body. She was soft-spoken and very polite.

'I'm **the Young and the Needy**.'

'Hi.'

We shook hands. And she quickly averted her gaze in a guilty way that bordered on shame. Of course, she wasn't feeling too good about herself. I knew the drill. She'd been up most of the night chanting about what a bad girl she's been, how she's been trying to do better but hasn't been able to help herself, and how she needed to take the Lord into her heart – as well as Warren Samuels into her privates. Because that was the way to the Promised Land. You know, standard Warren stuff. And she was just young enough to believe it all. Part of it, anyway. The other part – well, hence the ashamed look.

'Daddy – I mean, Warren – is upstairs,' she said, catching her flub. 'He's been looking for you.'

'Where the hell have you been?'

The voice had a nasty tone. I pivoted and saw Warren standing there – also in a bathrobe. His face had that flushed look, the look he always gets after he's just had sex.

'I went to Rork's party looking for you.'

'Well, you obviously didn't find me. What did you find?'

'Excuse me, Warren?' I said. The comment irked me. I'd had a nice evening and a nice day and I wasn't in the mood for his crap.

'Oh, hell, Bo. I know your tricks.' And he went over to the wet bar and tossed some ice cubes into a glass. '**Young and the Needy**, you want a drink?'

'Sure.'

'What will it be?'

'Whatever.'

Then he eyeballed me. 'Want something?'

I declined. It wasn't a cozy offer. 'Look, Warren, I'm sorry if—'

'Don't insult me.'

'What are you talking about?'

'Everybody saw you leave with some young writer guy.'

'What?'

He delivered it in an ominous way. 'When you are a guest in my house, you act like a guest in my house.'

He eyed me viciously, then marched over to **the Young and the Needy** and gave her a drink.

'Wait upstairs,' he said firmly to her. 'I'll be right up.'

And he patted her on the ass as she went.

We stood around there for a moment not saying anything. He eventually made his way over to me. 'Warren, you're making something—'

Smack! He open-palmed me across the face. I went down to the ground. The hurt was upon me instantly. My eyes immediately watered. He knelt low and grabbed the back of my hair, yanking my head back. Veins were tubing on his forehead. His lips were positioned right next to my ear. He whispered harshly. It was then that I smelled the overpowering scent of blended liquors on his breath.

'I'm going to teach you something, Little Bo Peep,' he began with. 'You know why a man pays?'

He twisted my hair for a firmer hold. My whole head stung from the tension. My eyes were stretched like a Chinawoman's.

'You know why a man pays for a woman?'

I shook my head as much as it could move. Which wasn't very much.

'He pays to get *rid of* her. A man can get it from anywhere. That's easy. But when you're done getting, what's not easy is dumping. They want to cling. If it's an hour, if it's two hours, if it's a day, if it's a week. You pay because you want to get rid of them, not because you want to keep them. And the more powerful you are, the more you want to be in control. You pay for when it comes, when it goes, and what it looks like.'

His verbal tirade continued to travel in circles, but that made it no less frightening. I was so scared, content didn't matter.

'That's what you want. Because when you're in a position of power, it's what you're used to. You pay to get it, you pay to make it go away. It's all about control. It's all about power. You follow me?'

I nodded.

'We pay so we don't have to get emotionally involved. So we can have the prize on the arm – the arm piece – and then tell it what to do, on our terms. Not *yours!*' he shouted.

I was sobbing now.

'And the little lovelies who do this – the whores like you – they're the ones willing to compromise their emotional integrity. It's not physical integrity, it's emotional integrity you're compromising when you get laid and paid. Those are the girls who were starved as kids.'

Tears were flooding my eyes now.

'Because they didn't have any emotional integrity in the first place. I'm talking about you, Bodicea. The bottom line is, the men who really want it don't pay for it. You're a whore, Bo.'

'I have emotional integrity, you bastard!'

He smacked me again. And twisted my hair harder. It was pulling strands out. It hurt. 'And though you may be a goddamn whore, don't you ever *act like one* when I'm around. Don't you *ever* make me look foolish again! Got it?'

I busted loose from his grasp, tripped, and ended up at the foot of the wet bar. I rose up slowly, steadying myself against it. He lunged from behind me, grabbing my shoulders. I spun around and grabbed his hair, yanked his head back from behind, bent him backward, and pressed the serrated blade of the lime knife to that fat vein below his jaw. I was trembling. But I said it slowly. In nine pieces.

'Don't ... you ... ever ... touch ... me ... again ... you ... sick ... creep!'

I held the knife there a moment. And another moment too. And I had a flash of bad life before my eyes, that it had all come to this pitiful, miserable kind of conclusion. I shoved him forward and away from me. I continued to look at him searingly and tossed the knife onto the floor. We both stood there, stunned.

No one moved for thirty seconds or so.

He made a step toward me. Then another. I stepped back once. Then he extended his hand slowly, like he would to an unfamiliar dog he wasn't sure about. He softly clasped my forefinger and tugged slightly. He started to move off slowly, holding my finger ever so gently as he did. He walked me down the hall. I was in a trance. We entered the bedroom. He locked the door behind us. I stood there at the end of the bed. He took off my clothes piece by piece and left me standing there.

I looked out the window and saw the late-afternoon shadows on the snow. The sun had been so hot, and now it was so cold. I felt chilly goose bumps rise all over my body. Until I felt him underneath me.

He placed a soft hand on my bare ass and eased me forward onto the bed. I collapsed down onto it in what seemed like slow motion. I felt the icy sheets gather around my breasts. Half my face was dug into the bed. The open half allowed me to breathe. I was just lying there naked. A pillow was placed under my pelvis. I raised myself slightly, helping it slide beneath. Tears welled up in my eyes. I was raised up now. There was a series of dead seconds that seemed to take longer than normal time.

When he went in, it hurt at first. And then it was like anything else. You get used to it. Tears slid off my face and soon got lost in the white-white sheets. The seconds weren't dead anymore.

I closed my eyes and just felt my frame as it was getting stamped into the mattress at a regular pace. It went on for another few minutes. Then it was all over as I heard his sounds of release. It was his same middle-aged music I'd heard many times before.

The only thing I remembered after that was being awakened out of a dreamy fog minutes later. It was happening again. He was behind me, pounding away. I was actually quite surprised. Warren didn't usually have that type of regenerative ability. His norm was once and out. But then I thought about the new drugs on the market. Viagra was giving him a second at-bat.

His hands gripped my shoulders. And his rhythm was

steady. He was actually more fluid. Less animalistic. I guessed he had gotten over my disobedient exhibition. And had used up all the juice of that passion play. Now he could be a little more sensitive.

And once again, I couldn't have been more wrong. I swiveled my head to the other side, as I'd been developing a crick. The pace was steady still. The hands were still grasping my shoulders. But when I unsealed my eyes momentarily and took in that side of the room, Warren was seated in a chair with his legs crossed, puffing away on a cigarette. He was watching me. Us.

I cried out hysterically. And the rhythm stopped suddenly.

'No!' Warren yelled. 'Keep going!'

'No!' I screamed.

Warren flew out of his seat, charged over, and whacked me in the head. And again. It shut me up.

'*No*, sir,' the man's voice said with tonal traces of mercy and regret. I detected a South American accent too.

Warren smacked him too. Since the man didn't react, didn't say anything, didn't beat the shit out of Warren, and certainly didn't relinquish his mount on me, I knew exactly who he was. He was just another whipping boy on the Jesus payroll.

The rhythm resumed. I cried dry tears. I had no water left. I just lay there for minutes more on end, my ribs heaving silently into the bed.

horror on hold

A couple of hours later I woke up in the very same position. He was gone. They both were. I didn't know who the other man was. But I guessed it had been Cristofero.

There was the sound of far-off commotion in the house. There was rumbling and movement. And that's when I felt it. I craned my neck around and saw a tall, thin, white daisy with a yellow center rising up behind my back. I didn't know how it was able to stand freely like that. Until I realized it was coming from me. It had been placed there and was growing right out of me. I pulled it out. And I felt the lowest low I'd ever felt. You remember when I told you how anyone can feel like a whore? And it's never fun. I cried again, of course.

It was one last awful moment in an awful place.

I couldn't move. I was very sore.

Perhaps for reasons of mercy and pity for me, there was an urgent knock on the door.

'I'm sleeping!' I called out, and scrambled beneath the sheets.

'Ms Bo!' the maid exclaimed loudly.

'Come in . . .'

Her expression was frantic. 'You must go! Everyone must go!'

'What's the matter?'

'Mrs Samuels is on her way from the airport.'

I got up. There was no time to dwell on the humiliation of it all. God had given me a task. It was a blessing of sorts. I could put all the horror on hold.

I quickly got dressed, went upstairs, got my things, called a cab, and waited for it by the mailbox at the end of a driveway two houses down the road. I saw the sun dip past the rim of Ajax Mountain. Everything was drowned in blue-gray shadows now. A minute later a sleek black Range Rover with tinted windows cruised past me. I looked the other way to avoid showing my face. Then I watched it pull into Warren Samuels's driveway.

The cab came about five minutes later. A real mountain man-type was driving. He had a bushy red beard and wore a red hunting jacket.

'Where you headed?' he asked. I don't remember giving him an answer.

It's no surprise that the ride into town was a silent one. I thought about how dangerous my life really was. I had been hanging around people whom I'd known in every sense of the word but, in reality, knew nothing about. Whatever was driving them to be involved with women – and women like me – wasn't a mystery, but it wasn't always explicable with the simple explicables like *He's lonely, he needs variety, he needs to be humiliated, he needs to dominate*. There was often a lot more severe psychological stuff going on that made it scary. And dangerous. I knew Warren was self-delusionary with all that religious propaganda, but the violence? I hadn't seen it coming. And maybe I should have.

I hadn't had an episode like that in a long time. And nothing ever as bad. I'd been slashed on the arm once with a knife. I hadn't protected myself that time. I never thought the guy could have done it. But this was out-and-out gang rape.

When you get involved in passion pursuits, you just never know what will happen. The jealous, control-freak types are the worst. Add some booze or cocaine to that, and what do you get? Another Brentwood murder, played out all over the country in little hotel rooms – stories you never hear about. No doubt, my business was a dangerous one.

And believe it or not, his *emotional integrity* line kept playing in my head. He'd been off-base with almost everything he ever said. But he'd been right about that. And it was another hurt piled atop all the rest.

The cab slid up beneath the awning of the Little Nell. I asked the cabby to pull over. I told him I'd be back shortly.

The door opened and Jasper was standing there facing me. Just seeing him flooded my eyes.

'Bo?'

I fell into his arms. He asked me why I was upset. I shook my head. 'I just wanted to say good-bye' made its way out.

'Good-bye? Where are you going?'

'Back to New York.'

'Why?'

'I have things to do.'

'What things?'

'Things,' I said, and broke down. It was a real waterfall. He pulled me inside and sat me down. I was a basket case.

'Honey, what can you accomplish? It's the day before New Year's Eve.'

'I have to organize. Oh, shit, I don't even know if my ticket can be changed.'

'Listen. You can't get anything accomplished tonight, right? Where are your bags?'

'In the cab.'

He got up and dialed the concierge. And arranged for the bags to be sent up.

'You wait here. I'll take care of the cabby.'

Then he was gone.

And I just slumped back into the pillows of the couch, still stuffed in my big heavy coat. My nose was running and clogged from crying. I was breathing through my mouth. I stared at the dumb Ansel Adams nature-photo poster on the wall. All nature looked ugly to me. I felt sick.

What the hell am I doing in Aspen? I wondered. Why did I come in the first place? Of course, money was part of the answer. Forcing myself not to think about Brad was another. The psychological impact of not getting away for the holidays and thinking my life was in gridlock was another. Those were enough reasons. Good reasons. But still . . .

As I pondered further, I realized it wasn't the place

that had changed. It wasn't Aspen making me feel this way. It was me.

Telling Jasper about the gold-digging activities, which were in fact my activities, was making me come to terms with them. And it was making me ill. I guess I'd been feeling that way for a long time. But expressing it to someone else was putting it right out there on a plate for me to see before my eyes. I didn't like what I saw.

I had spent years sweeping those feelings under the rug. I guess I'd developed a subconscious desire to rid myself of this scene. Calling myself on it and sharing it with someone else was my way of doing it. And if there were any doubts left over, I let Warren Samuels rid me of them.

I felt lost. I was crying and sad and feeling as though the world held no more goodness in it. I hated it. There was nothing to look forward to. Everything was bleak and black and depressing.

What was also painful was the money issue. Obviously, the money I'd been counting on from Warren would no longer be coming. I didn't know what the hell I was going to do. I had to call Napoleon.

So I did.

And he was a dream. I told him everything. Jasper stayed out of the room, sensing I needed privacy. Basically, Napoleon assured me that I had needed to come to Aspen. That it was my destiny. That as awful as that experience had been, it would probably yield something positive, eventually.

And that's exactly how I processed it. In the end I felt

it had been my destiny to come to Aspen. It was something I'd needed to do. And if I hadn't gotten this experience here, I would have gotten it somewhere else. Where it could be more dangerous and unforgiving. Sure, this kind of thinking allowed me to cope. But I needed to cope.

But having said all that, the pep talk with Napoleon did nothing for the anxious thoughts I had concerning my dwindling finances. They plagued me intermittently for the rest of the evening.

Later on, Jasper made tea. I didn't want to tell him about the fight with Warren. But he got it out of me. I didn't go into detail. I'm not a stickler for details, remember? I said Warren was just a friend.

Jasper was beginning to catch on, however. It was in his face. It didn't sport that schoolboy glow anymore. Between **Every Little Bit Helps** and me, he was getting a glimpse of life he hadn't really known existed. Or at least to the extent it did. Gold digging is an old story and an ancient practice. But it takes many forms, some of which even I had a difficult time believing.

Like all those girls headed to Brunei. To 'model.' It's not gold digging, of course. It's prostitution. But still. You can believe there's darkness out there without really believing – until it jumps up and bites you in the hand. Or calls you on the phone.

We sipped on tea and didn't talk further. I didn't want to.

Everything was happening so fast. My apartment problems, my romance with Brad, my sister's illness, Giles's death, that weirdness at the Four Seasons bar.

What the hell was that, anyway? Some random beastly interlude . . .

Now, Warren had gone bonkers on me. And I'd put a knife to him! And then he . . .

'What do you want to do?' Jasper asked.

I pondered the question. 'I'll tell you what I don't want to do,' I said. 'I don't want to talk about that other stuff.'

He looked squarely at me. 'Me neither,' he said with conviction.

And I understood what he meant.

I finished my tea and, mercifully, passed out. I slept until two the following afternoon.

snowballs

When I woke up, Jasper was gone. I found a note explaining that he'd gone off to interview some people for his piece.

Finally, I had some downtime all to myself. I had no one to talk to, no one to answer questions to, no one to give or receive attention from. It was great. It was precisely what I needed.

I felt much better. That was the day I figured out that for a woman, *every day is a new day*. In the course of twenty-four hours, your likes, dislikes, favorite songs, men, political beliefs, bad events – everything – can totally change. And for me, it had. I wasn't dwelling on what had happened at Warren's. I wasn't worried. It was a new day.

And what a difference a day makes.

Jasper returned late that afternoon. He gave me a warm hug. He asked me if I wanted to take a walk. I thought it was a good idea to get some fresh air. So we did.

The town had the usual après-ski bustle. And there were a lot of nonskiers as well. Add to that the fact that it was Saturday. Sugar Daddy Saturday. That included the Walletmen squiring their imported girls around town, fulfilling their shopping dreams. And added to that, it was New Year's Eve. People needed to make their last-minute moves, whatever they were. The town was active, to say the least.

We continued past the public skating rink. Buses were grumbling by on their way back from Aspen's other mountains farther east. I kicked a snowbank and freed an ice chunk. I used to love to do that when it snowed in Ohio.

I wondered how Vicky was doing . . .

The temperature dropped as soon as the sun went down. But the snow was still wet and packable. I don't know what possessed me, but I found myself molding a little ball of snow. Jasper was playing with his jacket zipper at the time, so he hadn't really taken notice. Then, *pow*!

I hit him directly in the side.

From then on, it was all-out war. He got me in the shoulder and the leg. I got him in the knee, the back of the head, and the arm. The snow was just heavy enough to make it hurt a little.

At one point, he had me cornered in a parking lot behind a delivery truck. I pleaded. I offered to give him whatever he wanted not to hit me. He asked for a kiss.

I looked directly at him. Then I looked away. He dropped the subject. And the snowball. Not surprisingly, I wasn't in the mood for affection.

And then I hit him with another snow bomb. He

chased me all the way down Galena Street. This went on for twenty minutes or so.

Finally, I felt the exuberant feelings of a little girl again. It had been so long since I'd felt normal and natural and not in my Digger or Fake Modes. Giggles had returned. Hallelujah!

'Would you like to accompany me to Randolph Spears's party tonight?' Jasper asked me.

'I don't think so.'

'Why not? Your flight isn't until tomorrow afternoon.' He looked at me, and funny wisps of warm breath were coming out of his mouth. 'You might as well,' he added.

The truth is, I was feeling better. 'I don't feel very together.'

'What would make you feel together?'

It was the wrong question to ask me. When I told him the answer, that's when he really gave me a shocker.

'It's on me,' he said.

Here was this guy, a *writer*, and broke as could be – relatively speaking – offering to pay for my wax, massage, and facial. It was so nice. I demanded that he come too. He declined.

'I pay for you, and you pay for me,' I posed.

He smiled. He'd never had a facial before. And he didn't need the wax. The massage he loved. And, of course, I loved it all . . . .

All in all, it turned out to be a wonderful afternoon. Jasper had been instrumental in making it that way. I liked Jasper very much. He'd successfully grown on me.

like it's 1999

There are a couple of New Year's Eve parties in Aspen everyone is desperate to attend. And they are a must for the Mother Loders. But they are not pile-in affairs. They are monitored by teams of professional security that require check-ins, ticket stubs, and escorts to the front door. In the case of this millionaire industrialist Randolph Spears's party, there was a receiving line with the host waiting to greet you. Crashers, beware.

Consequently, these party invitations are like Super Bowl tickets. And the women, and the men as well, will do anything to make it in. If there is gold to be found, that's where it is. And getting in to the right parties is one of the criteria that separates the expert Diggers from the novices. Simply put, connections are everything. If you're not in, you're out.

There's no question that the Mother Loders have their work cut out for them if they're going to score. The limited-access setup is grueling. Let's not forget how expensive the town is to get to, and stay in for a week. Holiday rates are exorbitant. So if you're not connected, you might as well stay home and do your holiday digging at Au Bar in New York or Barfly in Los Angeles or your mine of choice.

I explained all this to Jasper as we drove up to the Spears house. Speaking candidly again was a testament to how much better I was feeling.

The valet parkers took our car. I almost slipped on the ice getting out. I was wearing a long, slinky midnight-blue velvet custom dress from Richard Tyler and Jourdan heels that were too thin for the conditions.

We all stood in the long receiving line, which was covered by heated tents. The line extended up to the front door. Randolph Spears and his wife, **Why Her, Not Me?** greeted us with their usual charm and style. He'd known me for years, even before he'd gotten married. Don't forget, I'd been on the Walletman road since I was twenty-one.

And we were in. The party was partially spread out in his home, but it also extended into a huge tent where the band was located.

'I'm hungry,' I said to Jasper. I was still clutching his arm. I was really enjoying the time we were spending together. All it takes is one person to brighten your life, and your world can change. At least for a while. I was in that mode where I didn't want anyone to touch me. Nor did I want to touch anyone. But Jasper was an exception. He could put his arm around me. I felt safe with Jasper, and he was a gentleman in every sense of the word. I was convinced he had a great mother.

'She was a wonderful lady,' he remarked. 'She died several years ago.'

'I'm sorry. How?'

'Cancer,' he said.

I left that alone. But I thought the personal thoughts you might imagine.

Randolph Spears's New Year's Eve party had it all. Ambience. Great champagne. Exquisite food, including shrimp so large they must have been genetically altered. A thumping dance floor. Let's not forget all the Haves. And the scores of Have Mores. And the Have More Than Thats. As usual, the affair was incredibly well produced. Jasper and I made our way through the food line and, with full plates, took a table one over from the host.

'I know some of these faces,' Jasper said. 'It's like a *Who's Who* in American wealth.'

'And you know what that brings,' I said. 'And if any girls aren't here, they've registered with their friends as "sick", meaning they weren't invited.'

I had the salmon. Jasper had steak. And a lot of shrimp. Every time I finished a glass of champagne, there was a party penguin there to refill it.

Just then Paul and Betsy, a married couple who were friends of Bradley Lorne-August's, came by and said hi. I was surprised, though I shouldn't have been. The Spearses were their crowd, after all. Just like the star and celebrity circuits, most rich people in these circles knew one another.

I guess what stunned me was that whole December thing I'd had with Bradley. What was that? It almost seemed surreal. Like he'd breezed in and out of my life.

'Tell me about the Double Black Diamonds.'

I looked at Jasper and smiled. I took in a deep breath. 'The pros, right. These gals win. They get the long-term financial arrangement. They've mastered the qualities of the experts – but the pros have that little bit extra. In fact, the group is so empowered, you might not call them Diggers.'

'How do you mean?'

'Well, what would it take for a wealthy man to open up his life, and his wealth, to a young lady in this day and age and in this crowd? Beauty and smarts would be a start. Fame would certainly help. Or independent wealth, or some kind of dowry. But then you'd have to wonder who's digging in whose mine?'

'It's more of a merger,' Jasper interjected.

'Exactly.'

'What do you mean by *empowered*?'

'By *empowered*, I'm talking accomplished actresses, famous models, high-profile socialites, and successful career women. That's what it takes to do it. It's much easier to make money with money or make money by possessing some commodity. Certainly, if the Double Black Diamond has already gotten married once and won big, meaning received a big settlement, her chances of linking up with another wealthy guy are much greater. Women who've succeeded in this way are like legends.'

'Does it really happen?'

'Sure. But not very often. And not here.'

'Why?'

'There are a finite number of men with the money. And of that group, only a fraction are free, willing, and ready to play, if for just the weekend – let alone a lifetime.'

'That's one thing I've learned from my interviews with the men,' Jasper said. 'Every wealthy guy I ask returns it with the question *Why should I?* Almost as though they've adopted an Am I a Sucker? mentality toward marriage. Because of its financial implications. They're in a resort. They're having fun. They just want to get laid.'

I didn't like hearing that. It was almost as if, if I'd said it, it would have been okay. Because, of course, I knew it was true. But since Jasper had said it, somehow it made it more definite, certain, and true. In a brutal way. He was a guy, after all, getting the straight scoop – from guys.

'If you're not as empowered as you say – you don't have the beauty or the smarts or the dowry – how do you do it?'

I looked at Jasper straight. 'You have to get pregnant,' I said. 'It sounds harsh, but what the men are doing is harsh too. Getting pregnant is the only way.'

I took in a deep breath.

'Okay, listen,' I continued. 'And take notes. The woman who really wants to do this right? She's got to be young or have never been in this crowd before. She's got to have a nice face and body. She doesn't have to be totally thin or beautiful, but it helps. She has to dress right. The top designers. If she's poor, she can always buy fake Chanel. They sell it all over the country. No one knows it's fake. She can put Chanel buttons on her clothes. Then she attends the wealthy parties in New York, London, Aspen, wherever – but she has to hang out by herself. And stay away from the girls with reputations. Don't talk to any girls, for that matter. And she'll meet the guys. But don't sleep with anyone. Once you do, you get a reputation. You've got to not sleep with them so you become their girlfriend, and then you're respected. You're only respected if you're a girlfriend. And you've got to get pregnant.'

At this point, Jasper was looking at me intensely. And right then That Little Voice made me realize I'd been using second person – you – in my delivery and thereby had been implicating myself. Certainly, my narrative approach was due to the champagne. I quickly revised it.

'So – if a girl sees a guy she wants, and she knows he's on the List, she has to get pregnant to keep him. Otherwise, she won't get him.'

'The List?'

'The Fortune 500 list. All these girls know it by heart. Some even have it on them.'

'No.'

'I swear.'

'The person Randolph Spears married? **Why Her, Not Me**? Most women are wildly jealous of her.'

'Are you?'

'I'm happy for her,' I said in all honesty. 'If a woman is with a guy of stature, everyone respects her. But when she's alone, people are more standoffish. No matter what happens to Randolph Spears's wife, she will always be respected. Because she was Randolph Spears's wife. A woman is treated based on the type of man she's with.'

'Sounds like getting a college degree.'

'Doctorate,' I said. 'The richer the man is, the more legitimacy you get.'

I looked around the room and saw the Digger Tour girls were there in full flock. I saw **Cease and Insist**, **I Don't Fly Coach**, **What's Yours Is Mine**, and the very famous **Ms Fellatio Alger**. **Half** was there too. She'd actually hit the mother lode with a wealthy rancher in Idaho back in '96 – you know, got pregnant, got divorced – and now she could just spend, spend, spend. At that point I changed her name to **Spending Every Penny**. *Way to go, girl!* was my thought.

I saw **Turn Off the Lights, Please** and **Operation: *I Do***. **Turn Off the Lights**, Please was, of course, with yet another rotund type. She always sold herself short. She once told me how tired she was of bedding down with fleshy men who loved Tony Bennett. At the same time, those fleshy men had usually been very generous. *Quit complaining* was my feeling. **Wait Your Turn** was a tad too slutty. To come up with an accurate list of men she'd bedded, you needed an accounting firm. Too bad. And then there was **Operation: *I Do***. Well, poor **Operation: *I Do***.

She'd had it all. She'd been given the finest thirty-carat diamond ring and was engaged to be married to a wealthy European banker. But the engagement dragged on too long. So they started fighting a lot as she kept pressuring him. And every time they fought, she'd throw the ring back at him. The fourth time she did, he switched it and threw back a fake, only to dump her a few days later. It devastated her. And when she came back on Tour, she was too desperate. Her schemes were too transparent. And it showed in her eyes. They were the greenest eyes you've ever seen.

'Look,' Jasper said suddenly. And, sure enough, at the next table **Smiles to Your Face** was tightly gripping the Mexican 'oil baron's' hand and was proudly introducing him – rather, showing him off – to everyone at Randolph Spears's table. We burst out laughing. Jasper raised a hand and I high-fived him.

For the next twenty minutes, Jasper fired off questions. And I gave him answers. I told him about the Tour, the Ten-Year Window, the fine line between a Digger and a prostitute, and short-term and long-term Diggers. I even told him about the False-Pregnancy Brush.

'When a rich man is about to undergo some serious financial misfortune – like his business is falling or he's going through a divorce and will have to pay off his wife hugely – a Digger has to bail. What she does is tell him that she's pregnant and that obviously it's his child. She also explains that she can't have the kid, he will no doubt concur, and he will give her one final payoff. To have it taken care of, of course, and all the related stress. It sounds coarse, I know, but it's what these girls have to do to keep surviving. There's tons of little ways to cash out on men.'

'My God,' he said. And I detected a little judgmental thing lingering in his tone. Maybe it was the champagne freeing him up and letting him cut loose with his beliefs. Previously, he'd just listened without comment. 'What else?'

'There's always the rent thing or the car-problems

ploy. What the Digger does is simultaneously tell her entire roster of men that she's having trouble paying her rent. Or that her car broke down on the highway, that she forgot to put oil in the engine, and that it seized and she needs a new engine. Now, if you multiply a thousand dollars by ten guys, she's made ten grand in the course of an afternoon. The next time, she flips the story. If she's already done the rent thing with one guy, she goes with the car ruse the next time. Jasper?'

'Yes?'

'Let's dance.'

Dutifully, he led me out onto the floor. Once we started dancing, he began to laugh. And it wasn't an exhilarated laugh from the exercise. There was pain in it. Like it wasn't a laugh at all.

'What's so funny?' He doubled over, he was laughing so hard.

'I can't tell you the number of times she's hit me up for car-problems money. And this new pregnancy? It's the second time.'

'Sorry to hear that.'

'No, I'm laughing.'

But I could see the traces of That Face beneath the plastic jolly mask.

Over Jasper's shoulder, I saw **Smiles to Your Face** and the Mexican dancing hip to hip, as if there was nothing but a bed beneath them.

Just then someone grazed up behind me and wrapped his arms around my stomach and whispered in my ear with a deep, sexy voice, 'Hey, baby.' I spun and I should have known who it was – Lawrence Fairchild.

I just smiled.

'You look amazing,' he added.

'Thank you.' And I introduced him to Jasper.

'We've met,' Jasper said.

'May I cut in?' Lawrence asked.

'Sure,' Jasper said. 'I'll be at the bar.'

I was a little tipsy, I admit. Lawrence and I danced for a couple of songs. When I spied our table, Jasper was talking animatedly to **Spending Every Penny**, no doubt looking for more dish. Though he didn't have any money, he had a nice work ethic, I thought. I watched him guzzle another glass of champagne.

At that moment, Lawrence held me from behind as we danced. He let his hands drift a little, just below my belly button until his finger arrived at the elastic band of my panties. Then he stopped the search. I didn't do anything. I found myself wrapping my arms behind me and clutching him close to me.

The music changed to a slower number. I spun around. I put my arms around his neck, he put his around my waist. We leaned into each other. I could feel the heat off his body. His thigh was aligned with my most private seam. He was pressuring it somewhat. He had a strong leg, like he was a runner or something.

'Do you jog?' I asked.

'I run the park a few times a week,' he said.

Then I let my head collapse onto his chest, and we just swayed back and forth. He let his hands roam around a little. He felt my hips and then grazed the upper crack of my ass. He palmed one cheek briefly. It felt nice. I was tipsy too. To be aroused and tipsy is a great feeling. I don't know which comes first – but I let my body be held up by him.

When the dance was over, he kissed me on the lips and I let him. I looked over and Jasper was looking directly at us. I thanked Lawrence. 'Where are you going?' he protested.

'I'm going to sit back down.'

'Come get a drink with me.'

'I came with Jasper.'

'He's doing fine.' I looked over and Jasper had That Face on. No doubt he was thinking about things. Envisioning the dirty movie that was going on down in the Islands. The poor guy, I thought. There I was, apprising him fully of the dark side of all this, right in the middle of all his heartbreak. It was beating him up.

'I'll see you later,' I said to Lawrence. With that, he yanked my hand to come with him. 'No, Lawrence.' And he saw my no-way face and got the message and moved off.

I rejoined Jasper. I tapped his lap as I settled into my seat. 'How are you doing?'

'Great,' he said in a hollow way.

'What did **Spending Every Penny** have to say?'

'Oh, she just spun off a bunch of lies, then took off,' he said with a bitter edge. The alcohol was getting the best of him. His normally good-natured sarcasm was now sprinkled with acid.

'Like what?'

'Like how she was a student, got her degree, wanted to teach history, but got married instead. She dropped her ex's name about three times.'

'And . . .'

'I told her I was a writer and – surprise, surprise – she found a way to drift back into the crowd. As if I would ever be interested in *her*.' He took another sizable gulp from the flute. 'Wow,' he said after swallowing. 'How could any guy take these girls seriously? If I had a lot of money, I would never marry one of these girls.'

'Why not?' I said.

'They're all whores,' he spat. And he seemed to be directing it, at least partially, at me.

'And the men aren't?'

'The men are' – and he thought about it – 'just using them, yes. But what should they do? Marry one of these schemers who has no interest in him, his well-being? They're all clawing for a security blanket. Human sentiment has absolutely nothing to do with it.'

'Sometimes it does.' And I was surprised I'd said it.

'When?'

'Hey, every one of these girls would love to fall in love. But love is bad business.'

He looked at me sharply. 'You think we'd be better off with arranged marriages?'

'It has its advantages, that's for sure.'

'And no freedom of choice.'

'Take your freedoms after your food and shelter are covered.'

'So then what, endless affairs and such?'

Right then I realized I never should have divulged any of this to Jasper. Though it was helping me to let go of it, it was killing him to hear it. He was the wrong guy at the wrong time. For his assignment, I was a dream.

For his heart, I was a lot less. Our conversations were adding more stress lines to That Face by the minute.

I stood up. 'Jasper? Let's get out of here. I've had enough.'

'No!' he snapped. 'I'm on assignment. I want to hear more about whore living.'

I stared down at him.

'Come on, Bo. Tell me more.' It came out as a challenge. And his provocative expression matched the tone of the comment. I walked off.

On the way to the coat check, I wondered what I was going to do. I was staying with Jasper. As I passed out of the big tent and into the living room, I was intercepted by someone who immediately threw his arms around me. Again.

'Where's my kiss?' Lawrence added.

'What kiss?'

'It's New Year's.'

'Uh, oh, is it midnight?'

He nodded. It caught me by surprise. And I felt disappointed – that in Jasper's fit of bitterness, he'd neglected to offer me a kiss. But now, Lawrence's eyes were all glazed over as he drifted into dream state and his face fell into mine. And we kissed and kissed and kissed. And behind me I heard the band strike up 'Auld Lange Syne.' And the high-pitched sound of those horns being blown. One snapped close by and went rolling into my ear. And we were still kissing.

When I opened my eyes briefly, I saw Paul and Betsy spying us. I just smiled stupidly. What else could I do? Besides, I hadn't heard a word from Brad on my service. To hell with Brad, I thought.

'Hold on,' I said. 'Do you have a mobile phone?'

'Sure, baby.' He handed it to me. I dialed.

'Is it going through?' he asked.

I nodded. 'Machine,' I explained. 'Unfortunately.' Then I turned my back to him and delivered a message. 'Happy New Year, baby! I miss you. I love you. I hope you're all tan and sexy and yummy! I don't know if you're back yet or not but . . . Give my love to Greg. Oh, I'm in Aspen . . . Lawrence says Happy New Year too. If Jerko calls, tell *him* . . . Love you!'

I handed the phone back to Lawrence. Then he took my hand.

'Let's get out of here.'

'Wh-where?' I asked.

'Where are you staying?'

'At a friend's place.'

'We'll go to mine.' The wild thing is, I didn't object.

We got our coats, the valets got Lawrence's rented four-by-four, and we drove west, just out of town past the Aspen Club. On the way, Lawrence kissed me again at a traffic light and fondled my breast over the dress. He was a great kisser, actually. But his breath tasted funny.

The house was small but nicely appointed. We ran up to the door, and I nearly slipped on the steps.

'You forgot the headlights,' I said to him, and waited in the doorway. He ran back and turned them off. But the car buzzer was still buzzing. 'Keys,' I said.

'I never take the keys. It's Colorado!' he said in his defense.

Once inside, I let go of my heels. My toenails

were dark blue – to match my dress.

Lawrence took me by the hand and guided me through the house. It was pretty messy, actually. Towels and socks were lying around. We moved on to the back porch. He seemed pretty anxious.

'Should I make us some drinks?'

'I'll stick with champagne,' I said.

'Or do you want wine?'

'Champagne.'

'Vodka?'

'Champagne.'

'Champagne,' he processed finally.

We stepped back into the living room. And he popped a bottle. He took a sip from it, kissed me, and passed it to me in my mouth. We kept the kiss going awhile.

Then he grabbed his drink and my free hand, and we went back to the back porch area. He pushed a button and I heard this sudden surge of water. I looked over and it was a Jacuzzi frothing away. Excellent idea, I thought. 'Yaaay!' I yelled like a dopey cheerleader.

Lawrence kissed me again. And his hands went all over my body, but mostly my ass. I must say, it's my preferred item. I have a great one. He unzipped the back of my dress, and it fell to the ground. I had on sheer black panty hose. He peeled them down too. And kissed me on my mound over my underwear. He started to peel those down.

'No,' I said.

He then took off his jacket, then bow tie, then cummerbund, then pants. That's when I noticed he'd been freeballing all night.

'No underwear?' I asked.

'Never.'

He had a tall, slender body. Like a swimmer's body, and they're the best. I think so, anyway. But he had no chest hair, which was not a plus. It made him look a tad underdeveloped. It's a long way from Rome, I amused myself in thinking.

We hopped in the Jacuzzi and sipped on champagne. And kissed some more. He sucked on my breasts, and it felt nice. I just gazed out through the skylight above at a starry sky. We stayed there awhile.

And I got to thinking about Jasper. I was missing him. But I'd needed to bust out and do something a little crazy. I hadn't been feeling so great, remember? I needed to forget.

Lawrence found me a bathrobe and one for himself. He took my hand and we settled into a couch. He drew out two little packets. Then he dumped some on his hand and sniffed.

Then he poured the contents of one packet into the other.

'What are you doing?'

'Combining,' he stated. I could tell that the textures were different. 'Give me your hand.'

'No, thank you,' I said.

Then he did another sniff and grabbed me to him and kissed me. It was that same funny chemical taste he'd had on his mouth before.

Then he held my hand and raised me from the couch. He guided me into the bedroom. We paused in front of the bed. I reached low and touched him. He was half hard already. I changed that. I was surprised, actually. My experience with cokers had taught me to expect very little, that they were real underperformers when they did drugs. Not Lawrence. Not yet, anyway.

He untied my towel knot. The robe fell to the floor. He reached around and grabbed both my globes over my underwear. I kissed him lightly on the lips. Then I undid his robe. And had him stand naked before me – with his proud stem angled up. I shoved him back on the bed.

'Be right back,' I said, standing above him.

And then I ducked out of the room and into the bathroom, where I took a quick pee. Then I returned to the Jacuzzi room, grabbed my dress, threw it on, found my shoes in the living room, scratched him a quick note, slipped out the front door, hopped in the four-by-four, and never talked to that motherfucker ever again.

Combining, he'd said. I'm so sure. He was doing the Ruhypnolcocaine mix – the one that had made *willing and unable* out of thousands of girls. Creep.

It's not as though that was the only turnoff and the reason I left. I knew I was going to bust out on him from the beginning. I'd planned it. But the white-powder one-two gave me even less respect for him.

I left the car with the valet guys at the Little Nell and told them that a guy would be coming to pick it up in the morning. I gave them the name. And told them not to give out my room number.

I knocked on Jasper's door. There was no answer. So I leaned up against the wall of the corridor in my dress and stocking feet, and dozed off.

A tap woke me up a little while later.

'Hi,' I said with a dreamy smile.

'Hi,' Jasper said with one of his own. I stood up and gave him a beautiful kiss, the best I had to offer. He received it well. He opened the door to the apartment and we slipped in.

I took his hand and he lagged behind me at a slower pace. After all, he didn't know where to go. I did. I led him into the bedroom. I took off his clothes piece by piece, kissing his lips in between each article. I knelt down and took him in my mouth for several minutes. He leaned back. I drained his disturbed expression line by angst-ridden line, wrinkle by wrinkle. Until he had a comforted look on his face. Until his skin was as tight as a baby's. Until there was no sign of That Face. Not anywhere. When I finished, he was a newborn tot.

I took off my clothes and made love to Jasper until dawn. At which time I said:

'Happy New 2000, Jasper.'

He smiled. 'And just think,' he said. 'I spent it with The Millennium Girl.'

We resumed again until nine. For what it's worth, and it was worth a lot to me, I had this wild sensation while I was making love to Jasper. It felt like everything I'd done previously, everything I knew, faded into some far-off play that was someone else's. Not mine. Maybe it was all protectionary and diversionary and delusionary. But with Jasper, making love felt like a new thing. A really good thing.

Then we went to sleep in each other's arms. It was a beautiful ending to a very long night.

just a girl

We woke up in the late afternoon. And made love again. I looked at the clock. It was nearly five o'clock.

'You missed your flight.'

'Oh, well,' I said. And we made more love.

Eventually, about seven, Jasper dragged himself into the shower. And I took the blanket from the bed and wrapped myself in it and walked out to the living room and plopped into that couch I'd grown so fond of. It was an ugly maroon color. But it was a safe couch. I felt as though nothing could hurt me there. Oddly, it was a hotel-room couch.

I turned on the TV and found out a smattering of things I didn't know. And didn't care about. Then I called the airlines. I booked a morning flight for the following day. Then I called in to my service. I hadn't done it in two days. There were fifteen messages. I skipped over most of them. The last four had come in that day. Three of them were from Brad.

The theme of the first one was a simple *Have a Happy New Year*. The second was *I've been thinking about you*. The third one was *I've been thinking about us. . . .*

When I got off the phone, Jasper was standing nearby toweling off his head, with another towel wrapped around his waist.

'There's one thing, Bo, I'd like you to explain.'

'Sure.'

I knew what was coming. He was going to ask me a personal question.

'You've mentioned this term *The Game* a lot in passing. What exactly is The Game?'

Of course, I was surprised by the question. That after all the intimacy we'd just shared, he was going for something so callous. As though he'd slipped out of the emotional very fast – too fast for my liking.

And then I thought about how quickly I could turn off the emotional when I wanted to. Along the lines of, like a light switch. I didn't give it any further thought.

Besides, when you've just made love to a guy you like several times, you'll do anything for him for the next twenty-four hours. Including answer callous questions. But I lit up a cigarette first and collected my thoughts.

'The Game is, for a girl – you grow up with this low self-esteem. Why? Usually because of unavailable fathers. Fathers are the key. As a result of a father's absence, a girl finds herself able to get her self-esteem only from men. So The Game is to find the guy to take care of her so she can have her daddy again. These women who live off of men? That's how they get their self-esteem, that's how they get their pleasure. The only way women can feel their power and beauty is by attracting men who want them. And it's not just any man, it's the wealthiest they can get. The phenomenally wealthy. The richer the man they get, the more jealous everybody is of her, the higher self-esteem she attains. In the meantime, she is doing nothing but getting her nails and hair done. And since her relationship is going to be over fairly soon, she tries to get as much money as she can during that time period. That's the whole Game. And the women keep thinking, *Oh, I'll meet the man I want to marry and everything will change.* And it never does.'

'Why not?'

'Women in this society are very confused. Often they have few, if indeed any, family values. A mother can only do so much. She loves and nurtures. But it's the father who instills the value systems in a child. And if he's not around, she has no guideposts. And she loses her emotional integrity. Her physical integrity comes with that. She becomes a balsa-wood boat floating on water in the wind. Anything goes. It's very similar for the men.'

'Is there a Game for the men?'

'Men often create a life based upon low self-esteem too. The playboys, for instance – they try to bed as many girls as they can. It's often a case of having had unavailable mothers. It sounds simplistic – and it is – but it's what I've seen.'

'What about your family?'

There it was. A personal question. I'd asked him not to go there. But you couldn't blame him. We'd become more than intimate, and though that had never been a reason for me to divulge before, with him I felt okay with it. Certainly, I'd spent a lot of time offering him very private material already, which had, in effect, indirectly put the finger on me anyway as part of this breed. The sum total of what I'm saying is – I didn't feel threatened by opening up to him.

Besides, it was a show of interest in me, rather than cold, straight, and clinical reportage after sex.

I thought about his question thoroughly. And before I knew it, I was spinning off into a trance. I remember looking across the walls of the room. Past the television, past the Ansel Adams poster, past the cuckoo clock, and when my gaze drifted past the dark mountain vista with the sprinkling of little lights, I was able to lock on and concentrate and enunciate what I had to say.

'He never gave me my privacy. Little girls need their privacy. And the doors to their rooms shut. And off-limits. He would just walk into my room at any time. He had no respect. It was like I was a pet dog. He'd read my diary and at dinner bring up passages he'd read, and make fun of me. He talked to me about my period. Fathers should never talk about their little girls' periods. He potty-trained me. He never should have potty-trained me. When I didn't do it well or missed the bowl, he'd rub my nose in it like that same pet dog. And when I rejected his ways and standards of behavior, he would just walk away and not pay any attention to me for days. Like I said, a father is supposed to provide the values. If he's not there, you don't know what your values are.'

Jasper sat beside me and held me close. I barely felt his presence, though.

'He didn't treat me like I was his princess. He didn't treat me like I was his special girl. He didn't treat me like I was his treasure. And that does nothing for you. Other than make you wander around the world to find that man who will treat you like you're his treasure. To him I was just a girl. And being *just a girl* kills you.'

I snapped out of my near-catatonic condition. When I did, I was surprised at what I'd said. Later, of course, I realized I'd subconsciously wanted to let go of this.

'That's what it boils down to,' I said finally. 'Unavailable parents.'

Jasper didn't ask any more personal questions. He didn't ask any more questions at all. We sat there in silence for a few minutes. It allowed me to leave the thoughts of that pungent Brown Couch and climb out of that godforsaken house on Searchlight Lane in Fort Lowell, Ohio.

'I'm going back to New York with you,' he declared.

Of course, I managed a smile hearing it. And he gave me a kiss. This guy Jasper had gotten under my skin. I really enjoyed being with him. He was so easygoing, sensitive, and down-to-earth. Bradley was less warm and more complex. By *complex*, I don't mean any more intelligent than Jasper, because he wasn't. He just had more baggage. Mother issues, etc, that wrapped an exoskeleton around him that was difficult to penetrate. Jasper was right there; what you saw was what you got. He had that Libran ability to make you feel comfortable. And open. And honest. It was weird, and I wasn't sure if it was entirely true, but Jasper had a way of making you be, and want to be, a better person. That I considered a rare characteristic, if not talent.

A phone call interrupted us. Jasper went for it. I stepped into the bathroom and took a long bath. I was actually impressed by the Little Nell's selection of in-house bath products. I used them generously.

That evening we went to dinner at Abitone's. We both claimed it was 'on me,' so again, we'd invited each other. It was our little vacation splurge. The food was amazing. The ambience was great. The service was fabulous. And the company was – well, I was feeling strongly for Jasper. And him for me.

But it became more than that.

That night at Abitone's was an evening that held the biggest surprise of my entire life. In fact, it was a night that would change my life for ever.

It all started after dinner when the check arrived. The bill was a big one, but that wasn't the problem. Unfortunately, I had left my purse back in the suite at the Little Nell's. And Jasper had left his credit card too. So, Jasper had to run back over to the hotel. I remained there at the table for goodwill purposes.

After a short while, my gaze drifted around the dining room. And at a corner table across the room from me, I noticed a woman wiping her eyes with a tissue. At first I thought she had something in her eye. Well, she did. Water, of a personal nature.

I averted my gaze but couldn't help but think about all the sad stories out there. How I was always dwelling deeply on my own setbacks, but other people had theirs too. Some stories, I knew, were much worse than mine. This woman made me curious as to why she was upset.

She was elegantly dressed, with nice gold earrings and a beautiful black cashmere turtleneck. And then I saw her eyes lock on mine. To my amazement, she uttered something that seemed to be directed at me, but I couldn't hear it.

'I beg your pardon,' I said.

And this time I leaned over and was able to hear her husky voice, a voice that was cracked with emotion. 'Bo . . .' I heard her say.

I was stunned. I had no idea who it was. So I got up and walked over. As I approached, I didn't enjoy what I was seeing. The closer I got, the more apparent it became that the poor woman had gotten some horrific plastic surgery on her face. Her face looked as if it had been stretched back like Saran Wrap over a bowl. It was awful. And painful to look at.

'Hello,' I said.

She just looked up at me and smiled somewhat sadly. 'Please sit,' she offered warmly.

I looked at her squarely as the candlelight from her table illuminated her face. It was the eyes. The eyes were telling me something. I could see something trying to make its way out and communicate. To link up with my past, my memory, anything that could help me process this vision and identify it.

And then it hit me. With the most profound joy – but at the same time the deepest regret.

'Hello, Virginia,' I said.

We hugged like the long-lost mother and daughter that we were to each other. Tears streamed down my face. And more ran down hers. Until we were laughing and holding hands like two little girls.

'Look at you,' she said. 'You're such' – and her voice cracked again – 'a lady,' she continued.

I told her she'd made me that.

'You're so beautiful and well dressed and . . . I'm just thrilled. My God, some things in this life do work out.'

I wondered what that meant, of course. 'You gave me a chance, Virginia. I traveled all over the world. And learned about the finer things. Remember what you told me? *America is like a little boy who still doesn't know how to dress up yet.*'

'That was so long ago. How long? Ten years?'

'Twelve this March,' I said.

'My word.'

And as she spoke, that sadness kept trying to creep back under my belt. That Little Voice was vying for attention. How could she do that to herself? She had such a beautiful face. But each time, I swatted the thoughts away like horseflies. I never let my radiant, happy, overjoyed smile leave my face. I couldn't.

'Tell me everything. Where's Don?'

She wiped her eyes again with tissue. And then said, 'We didn't make it, Bo.'

'What happened?'

She cleared her throat and took a sip of wine. 'Well, you know Don received a big contract. It's why we moved to San Francisco. Don was the star of the team. Endorsements, everything. We had a beautiful house in Marin County. But he was spending more and more time out. Drinking and such. You see, we didn't have kids. We couldn't. His count was low. Well, I don't want to get into it, but the real story is, we weren't right for each other. We came from different worlds. And eventually the sex died away – and he fell in love with a young girl. A waitress in the city and . . .'

'I'm so sorry,' I said.

'So, well, that's what happened. It's funny, she looks exactly like I did twenty years ago.'

And if hearing about their breakup was bad, hearing this was worse. Don had traded in Virginia, the classiest woman I'd ever met, my heroine, my role model, for a younger version.

'She's actually very nice. And they have a lot in common.'

And there she was, complimenting her replacement. Virginia Lashley. Being a class act even in a situation as devastating as that.

'When you're from similar socioeconomic backgrounds,' she continued, 'there's nothing to explain. Stick with your own kind is not a bad philosophy.'

'Do you know what my full name is?'

'Bodicea Adams, right?'

'It was, back in 1986. As soon as I set foot on English soil, I became Bodicea Lashley. It's been that way ever since.'

Another tear welled up in her eyes.

'My God, look at me. I'm a mess.' And she laughed. Through the tears.

'Are you sure you're okay?'

'Fine.'

'You look beautiful, Virginia.'

She quickly looked uncomfortably off and away. I

clutched both her hands and held them in my lap. Like I said, it was the greatest surprise I'd ever had. 'Well, bring me up to date,' I suggested excitedly.

'I got married again about six years ago.'

'What brings you to Aspen?'

'My husband and I have a place here. I'm waiting for him now, actually.'

And then her chest heaved again slightly. She was very sad, I could tell. And seeing me didn't help. It gave her an intimate sounding board for all her sadness that the unfamiliar room had been neutralizing and holding back.

'Should we take a walk outside?' I proposed.

'No, dear, I'm all right. It's been tough, though.'

'Tell me.'

'Well, relationships can be difficult. Maybe you've been luckier than me.'

'No. I've had my difficulties. I've found out the hard way.'

'It's the only way. Have you married?'

'No.'

'Marriage can be tough too. We're going through a difficult time now, my husband and me. It's hard when you get older. As a woman. In this society. And, well, I married him because he was from a similar upbringing as me. But it was more than that. He seemed different from most men. He seemed so pure. And caring.'

Then she went quiet for a second. Almost as if she was preventing herself from saying anything too negative about the man she had married. Virginia was a great lady.

I looked at her expectantly. And, of course, I had to wonder why she was so upset if he indeed had such positive qualities.

'My husband has affairs,' she said flatly. And she took another sip of wine. 'And I know the sex can get dull with the same person. But, well ... look ...' And her chest cracked. But she had to finish it off. '. . . at me, Bo.'

And her expression contorted, and the tears streamed down her face again. And she collapsed forward into my arms. I held her tight. I knew what she'd meant. She was referring to what she had done. To her face. The surgery. In a desperate attempt to try to keep up with all the young chicks buzzing around. To keep him interested, to keep him satisfied. After all, her first husband must have alerted her insecurities. And then more of the same the second time around? Shit. It made me hate the world right then and there. Again. In ways I'd ranted to Napoleon in Palm Beach.

I calmed her and wiped her face. And clasped her hands gently. We just sat there a few moments. Then I took her away from herself by telling her about me. About my travels. About my education on the road. I didn't edit my story down for Virginia. Virginia was family to me. I told her how she had made a difference in my life. That I had made mistakes and was still making them and would be making more in the future – but she had helped me out of a lifetime of what would certainly have been more pain and trauma. And that she had restored my faith in people. That she had given me something to look up and aspire to. That she had given me a dream that I've held ever since.

'You were the mother I never had, Virginia.'

'I'm so proud of you,' she said glowingly. And then she looked up. 'Here's my husband.'

I spun around. He was walking right toward us. He saw me and smiled somewhat, or he didn't. I couldn't really tell. It seemed like a smile, though. And I knew he was the type of guy capable of one under those circumstances.

I turned the most common shade of white.

Virginia had married Warren Samuels. The pure and pious one. And it ripped my guts out to see it. And all the other ugly thoughts came with it. Like he was the guy who made her carve up her face. Because he'd been roaming around screwing girls like me. On an ongoing basis.

Don't forget all the murderous ironic twists. Like what a 'lady' I'd become. How 'proud' Virginia was of me. How 'caring' Warren had seemed. How much I truly loved Virginia. How much I thought about her. How much she had been a mother to me. And for all that uncut goodness – look what I had been doing to her. Letting her depraved husband screw me in airplanes and stick a daisy in my ass. It all smacked me right across the face. There was no letting me off easy here, and I didn't deserve to be.

'Warren, meet an old friend of mine, Bodicea.'

'Hello, Bodicea.'

I stood and shook his hand.

I bet in the history of the world there have been a few million or so people who ever felt the way I did right then. It was pure devastation. And I'm sure most of them had ended their lives soon after.

Then I heard it behind me. 'There you are.'

It was Jasper. And I was thankful for that. 'Come over here, Jasper,' I said.

I let Virginia introduce Warren and herself to him. He shook hands with Warren. After all, I didn't know their last name yet, right?

'Virginia is my oldest and dearest friend,' I remarked as proudly as possible.

'Is she now?' Warren said nonchalantly. 'Well, how nice. A reunion. Why don't we order a bottle of champagne.'

And Warren didn't look at me, thank God. I thought how God can completely destroy you to the point where you don't want to live. And then he can show you small mercies soon after.

'We have to be going,' I said.

'Bo, please. Have a drink with us,' Virginia protested.

I smiled at her. How could I turn her down? I was going to have to take it right between the eyes.

'Have you eaten, honey?' Warren asked Virginia.

'I'm not hungry,' she replied immediately.

'Well, I sure am.'

He beckoned the waiter. 'A bottle of Cristal and the menu for me.'

It was bad. It was as bad as it gets. To see my favorite woman in the world in front of me, and to know what she had done for me, to know how well she had treated me, and then to see how men had treated her, and that I was, though unknowingly, directly responsible as well, right down to the bad surgeon's knife to her skin making less of that once-gorgeous and proud face. It killed me. Of all the lows and difficult times and tragedies I'd witnessed and experienced, this was by far the worst.

And to this day it has never been topped.

Sure, we finished the bottle. And Virginia and I chatted about everything. I loved her. It was as if we'd never been apart. And, of course, I pretended that Warren wasn't there. I wished my life could have been different. I wished, all the while I talked to her. And after.

Warren and Jasper discussed politics and business. And I couldn't help but hear a few of Warren's religious buzzwords. Jasper, I think, was torn between knowing how powerful and impressive and charismatic Warren was and, at the same time, knowing what a demented sicko he was too, from what I'd told him.

I came away from that night a different person. I could only think that God puts you in situations like that to force you to reconsider your position. And orientation. And philosophies. It was like a wake-up call. Napoleon had been right about my return to the Aspen leg of the Tour. As awful and painful as it had been, I'd needed it.

My love for Virginia made me want to tell her everything and pour out my damaged soul to her in the same way she had exposed herself to me. I truly did. But she had been too kind to me. I could never inflict any more injury on her. She was the greatest woman I'd ever met. And I was proud to know her. And in the end, I thanked God for letting her cross my path in this life.

We exchanged numbers and addresses, and she claimed that she was going to look me up when she came to New York. Of course, I had ambivalent feelings about that. Certainly I wanted to see her, but, well, all the dark I'd done would certainly make it uncomfortable. But in the end I said *so what?* to those selfish feelings. I'd see Virginia Lashley Samuels anytime. And if it hurt me and made me feel guilty, then so be it. I was accountable. It was just something I'd have to live with.

I never returned Warren Samuels's calls ever again. Including the perverted one he'd put on my machine that very night after they'd left the restaurant. He'd called me Yolande. He wanted me to come over for a Three-Way. Him, me, and his wife. He put Virginia on the phone too. She said hello without much enthusiasm.

a course in madonna-ology

The flight back to New York was difficult. I couldn't let that encounter with Virginia go. And I couldn't tell Jasper about it. But he knew I was adrift in my own melancholic stupor. And he sensed why. We barely spoke for the first couple of hours. Three-quarters of the way through the flight, he handed me his notepad.

You happy to be going home? was written on it. Then he handed me the pen and broke a pleasant grin. It was absolutely the only way I could or would communicate. Jasper was very insightful that way.

I am actually. With vacations like this, who needs awful experiences? I wrote.

He read it and smiled. Then I handed him back the pad and pen.

What was your best moment in Aspen 1999? he wrote.

That's easy – running into you. Without you, I don't know what I would have done.

The white knight – is that what I am?

I don't know, are you?

You're very sexy when you write.

I'm listening . . .

I think it's the fancy script you have with all the squiggles.

Is it confined only to when I write?

Hardly. When we first met, did you ever think we'd be sleeping together?

Hardly. And I smiled too.

Why not?

I thought we were both cut from such different cloth.

Like you outgoing and me shy?

No – like you naive and me not.

I guess I am naive. And that may be why I write.

How so?

Because I didn't grow up with, and am not used to, the dark side of life. So I've made a conscious effort to understand it. I have an odd attraction to it. I would say it holds the key to writing for me. You can't be a good writer and not understand the darker shades of the human behavioral rainbow. If you know only yellows and pinks and baby blues, the writing will reflect that. I'm rambling.

Good ramble. I thought you were cute, though. And I told **Every Little Bit Helps too**.

Really . . . She wasn't very fair when it came to you. But I sensed she was jealous.

Ah, women . . .

I had always thought that writing letters and such added distance or formality to a situation. You're advised not to write things you really feel strongly formally in a letter, because you'll end up regretting them. But by passing the notepad back and forth, Jasper and I achieved an on-the-spot, no-holds-barred, blunt personal-thoughts exchange. What I'm saying is, in writing we were able to reach a heightened form of intimacy. It was very enlightening. Those little tense insecurities that come up in conversation, the ones that can ruin or detour communication, did not. I guess the writing took away the immediacy. When you are in a conversation with someone, you force that person to react immediately, just as you are forced to react. When you write, the dramatic elements are taken away. So you're much more in control. And maybe more honest.

So I asked him:

Does writing give you a sense of control?

I've never seen it that way, but – I guess. By telling stories and trying to explain the world, it helps me understand it. Writing is very therapeutic.

I know. I keep a journal. What have you learned from your research in Aspen?

That men aren't getting married these days.

Why not?

In many cases, they've already been married, in which case they don't want to get hit with a settlement again. And the single guys are holding out for ever. There's not as much societal pressure on them to get married anymore.

And the women?

For them, it's a desperate situation. Because the women are not going to get any long-term commitment. These guys on holiday just want to get laid. They'll give a string of pearls or a ski outfit or a plane ticket but a long-term commitment? No way. Any kind of commitment? No. I would say landing a wealthy man in Aspen is fool's gold.

Good work, Jasper.

Then he started writing more about his piece, and I snatched the pen from him.

Let's discuss something else.

Like?

Like Madonna.

That's fluff.

Go deep with it. What do you think of her?

Personally or the phenomenon?

The phenomenon, of course.

I think she's a competent songwriter. I think she's a genius marketer. And all art today is marketing. May the best marketers win.

Do you think she's a positive influence on women?

I think she's done both. I think she's helped in some ways. I think she's also had a negative impact.

You're such a Libra. But I agree in certain ways. She's been a role model. But I think she's also set women back.

Explain.

Because no matter what you do as a woman, you're not going to change the biology. The fact that we as women must give life – and all the life that comes with that. She's going against nature. Against biology. It's something she can never win.

Are you talking about Madonna now or just feminists in general?

Both.

But she's made women feel less inhibited and less constrained. She's promoted expression of self. That's important.

She's made women objectify themselves even further than before. She's turned women back to being sex objects. She's had us dress up in bras and lace and panties and embrace erotica, and most women don't know what they're doing it for.

They're doing it for themselves.

No. Only the real Madonnas are. That little girl out in Bowling Green is doing it for men. To get men. To make an object out of herself. Madonna and those who understand her – let's call them Madonna-ologists – do it for themselves and say to hell with you all, I'm going to let it all hang out, *but they hand off the message to people who aren't strong enough to carry the torch. It only sets them back in the end. Before they know it, they've been had every which way and back, and they've gotten pregnant and derailed their lives. Madonna-ology is fine if you're strong enough to handle it. But if you're not, which is the case for the majority of women, forget it.*

I don't agree with you.

Then we don't agree. But I tell you, if you're going to live by her rules, you'd better have the strength to back it up.

The world has always been a Darwinian place. Should Madonna-ologists not speak up just because there are some frail people out there who don't get it? I think any time you break down the bonds of repression, you're doing a positive thing. I think thinking like yours sets women back. It sets everyone back.

How?

Well, no one ever evolves over time that way. Things stay static.

But look at the time line. You're talking about minuscule changes in the big picture. You're just changing colors and hues. Women will never change enough in your lifetime to warrant this different type of behavior. The woman Madonna proposes to be has a different biology. She can change as a woman only if you change her biology. And that has not happened. She is still the childbearer, and until that changes in evolutionary terms, until there's a mutation of sorts, you're not going to change the fundamental dynamics between men and women. Madonna's offering to evolution is nothing more than a little shout heard on life's time line.

Well, even if she's made people think, that's positive.

Thinking always is. But societally, she's been no more than a dresser. She's changed nothing but clothes styles, hairstyles, hair colors, and some sounds. All superficial crap. Accessories. That's all. Nothing lasting, nothing permanent. All she's done is make a shitload of money by making the sheep follow her for a while with ingenious but very simple, even base marketing strategies. Madonna is a marketer. No more, no less.

So, does anyone's contribution matter according to you?

Yes.

What?

That we continue to produce life and evolve. That you do what you're supposed to do. As a mass of flesh composed of molecules. And seek out compassion and understanding along the way. Or if you don't like the game, the deal, the situation, the planet as it is, then you don't procreate. You have that choice. To do or not to do. Depending on your beliefs.

So, in the meantime, should women just lay down?

No. The problem with all this millennium thinking is that it doesn't really advocate change. That's what I'm saying. It all plays right into men's hands. A woman is not supposed to rule the planet. Not yet, anyway.

How can you say that?

Because she wouldn't be saddled with reproductive equipment and she would be physically stronger. Men haven't decided this. Nature has. Evolution has.

So what should she do?

It's a woman's job to influence. Not rule. Ruling is only an ego thing anyway. But it's those who influence who actually make the changes in society. Like Eleanor Roosevelt. Like Hillary Clinton. It's the women who rule indirectly. Because they feel life. And they protect it. And they know how to protect it. Women know how things should be. And men should carry it out. But if women try to be the enforcers, the ones to carry it out, they go right up against the men. And it becomes a competition they can't win. And they get chastised. And alienated. Women should use men to enact change. And they can.

How?

They are holding.

You mean sex?

Of course. Women have always had the upper hand. Men will do anything for the right woman. Madonna-ologists don't enact change. They go head-to-head with men. And that's why her contributions are a flash in the pan. The way to change is through men. And there's only one being who can make them do it. And that's woman.

I paused for a few minutes. Eventually I looked over at Jasper. He was thinking about something.

So, do you have enough material for your article?

More than enough.

Are you sure?

You're smiling. I love your smile, by the way.

Are you going to use the Mindblower?

In what way? It's the most depraved thing I've ever heard.

Well – the kinky-sex portion of your article. There is going to be a kinky-sex portion, isn't there?

Sex, yes. But I don't know how kinky they'll go.

How kinky will you go?

Good question.

Is it?

Will you meet me in the bathroom in two minutes?

Good answer.

Life presents so many twists and turns. And once you've rounded a bend, you had better be prepared for the next turn. I know it sounds crazy. But I think I was falling for Jasper Connelly.

the news

Jasper and I took a cab from JFK. We planned to meet that evening for dinner at my apartment. We kissed and I got out of the cab in front of Trump Tower. As soon as I entered the building, Larry was there to greet me.

'Excuse me, Ms Lashley.'

'What is it, Larry?'

'I don't have good news.'

'Do tell . . .'

'You've been evicted.'

'What?!' And I freaked.

'The locks have been changed. You were in the apartment illegally. Mrs Hamilton had a locksmith come, and that was it. There was nothing I could do. I'm sorry.'

'How about, show her my lease?'

'It's an illegal document.'

'My lease is?'

'Yes.'

'How come?'

'Only Mr Hamilton signed it. And you haven't abided by it. You weren't paying any rent. Mrs Hamilton knows that.'

'Giles paid the rent. Not because I was delinquent. It was his choice.'

'Her message to you was, contact her lawyer. But I'll let you know something else. She indicated to me that she already has the city's newspapers on alert for a sensational story called 'The Hookers of Trump Tower.' She's not playing around. She knows all those people.'

'How would they like to hear about her sham marriage to Giles?'

'I suggest you let it go, Ms Lashley.'

'And that bottle-blond boy toy she'd been with before and right after his death?'

'You had a good run here,' he said gently.

I spun in totally stunned, abject fear. 'Where's my stuff?'

'Napoleon came by and grabbed his things, some of yours, and the rest is at this storage facility.' He handed me a card.

'In Jersey?'

Larry nodded. 'Here's a note from Napoleon.'

I opened the envelope and quickly read the message. It was difficult through the tears welled up in my eyes. The only thing I got out of it was the phone number. Larry handed me his mobile.

'Hello?'

'Bo, can you believe that bitch?'

I walked a distance from Larry to talk. I was hysterical. 'What am I going to do? I have practically no money.'

'Baby? Meet me here right now.'

I handed back Larry his phone and started for the door. He started to come with me.

'Don't bother,' I said, dragging my suitcase on rollers.

'Ms Lashley? I mean it when I say we enjoyed having you.'

I turned around partway and tried to smile for him. Larry had always been nice to me. But the smile never came. Just more tears.

I thought about taking legal action. I went through the list of attorneys I knew. I hailed a cab. But during the ride over to Napoleon's sister's, however, I calmed down about the lawsuit. I realized, what for? Rationally thinking, we'd had a great setup at the Tower, as Larry had said. I couldn't complain. And I couldn't really blame Giles's witch of a wife. Besides, Giles was dead. Why cause trouble for a man's family – a man who always treated me gentlemanly and with respect? And was overly generous. Time and again.

I didn't need any bad press either. Not that she'd actually stoop to it. But you never did know.

But maybe the press would be good. In this day and age, no press was bad. I thought I could make even more money off my scandalous fame. Like all those Russian and Eastern European girls were doing. But I realized that it would attract the wrong kind of money. Just a bunch of short-timers who would want to get laid. If I was going to set myself up the way I wanted, I needed to keep a low profile. Those dreams had not died. Not yet, anyway.

But what overrode everything in the end were the thoughts I had of Virginia Lashley. I hadn't been feeling good about myself for my involvements with married men. The thought of those liaisons made me cringe. I felt for their wives. I decided I didn't want to be with a married man ever again.

I noticed a discarded newspaper on the seat beside me. I saw the date. It was a date I was familiar with. It indicated I was now twenty-nine years old. Yes, it was my birthday. And I'd just been evicted. And I didn't know what the hell I was going to do with my life. That's always a real picnic.

new digs

Go Go's apartment was on East Seventieth Street and Third Avenue. In the heart of the married-with-a-mistress district. Yikes. When Napoleon opened the door, he gave me the kind of hug I needed. He didn't wish me a happy birthday. He didn't know. That was fortunate because I didn't want any futher reminders.

The apartment was pretty big. It was only a one-bedroom, but the living room was large.

Napoleon brought me up to date with everything. He'd arrived New Year's Day and had spent the following day getting his clothes out of Jersey storage. 'If my sister sees all my stuff here, she will go crazy.'

'How did you get her to agree to let you use it?'

'My mother talked to her.'

'How much longer is your sister away for?'

'Another month.'

He then told me I could stay as long as I wanted, of course. He also made the rule that whoever got home first at night would get the bed. The other would use the pullout couch in the living room.

Napoleon had had an awful New Year's. Greg had

been a monster. He was such a neat freak, it annoyed Napoleon. He ended up hating Greg and not having sex with him. It was Napoleon's worst New Year's ever. 'In history,' he underscored.

'New Year's is always overrated.'

'Yes, but it was 1999. I was hoping, well . . . I saw John, you know.'

'Where?'

'Miami. We stayed there one night. He was down there with some girl.'

'No surprise there.'

'He was all sunburned on his forehead like a lobster. I wanted to sleep with him so badly. Especially when Greg started to get weird. He even got jealous.'

'Of you and John?'

'Yes. Can you believe – it was marvelous. It made me feel so good all over.'

I then told him the Virginia Lashley Samuels story. It was just about the most shocking thing he'd ever heard.

'So, how do you feel about this Jasper? Is it an affair, or what?'

'I don't know. We're a very unlikely pair. On top of that, he's broke. Leave it to me.'

'And Brad?'

'I don't think I should see him.'

Napoleon lit a cigarette and thought about it. It was a requirement for him when we gossiped at length. 'You're probably right. But if you're going to see Jasper, you might as well see Brad.'

'Why?'

'Bo, baby. Need I tell you?' he stressed. 'Have the

love romance with the poor guy and have the like romance with the wealthy guy. Don't put all your eggs in . . .'

And he didn't finish it off. As good as Napoleon's English was, sometimes he got the clichés mixed up, so he had a tendency to give up once he knew I knew what he meant.

A little later, Jasper called. He canceled on dinner. He was tired, and so was I, actually. We planned to meet for lunch in SoHo the next day.

Brad phoned in to my service again. The theme was *Are you still away or are you avoiding me?* The usual venting of insecurities associated with a lover or ex-lover who's not getting his calls returned.

At These Prices also called to wish me a happy new millennium. She'd spent hers driving into the middle of the desert in a Hummer and shooting machine guns into the wide-open space. Weird. She also had traveled to Saudi Arabia with the prince's entourage and visited the site of some Arab sheik's giant mobile home. It was the world's largest mobile home. It had thirty-two rooms and had been constructed just so the man could make it into the *Guinness Book of World Records* – which he did.

The Arab/Brunei thing sounded so bizarre. She said she'd call again. You see, she wasn't allowed to receive calls.

I had difficulty falling asleep that night, so I read my astrology texts and did a delicate study of Jasper. I read some things I already knew; that his sign – Libra Rat – is capable of creative genius. At the same time, he is known for his 'wily sunshine'; he is a crafty one; and you'd better watch out because before you know it, he's the type who can take his, only to leave you standing there empty-handed. That I considered interesting news. Or propaganda. See, I never took any of this astro stuff as gospel. I would give life its chance to confirm or deny. You had to.

Still, I didn't sleep well. I had anxiety. I was worried. It was a money thing. Nothing ties your stomach in a knot like financial problems. I remembered them in my youth. It was the worst feeling. I hadn't had any in such a long time. It was new to me. But I could never forget the place from where they came.

Since my teens, I'd always taken care of money concerns first. It was ingrained. But to switch my aims from the short-term payoff to the long-term conjugal union, I had to relax a little. And be less money-conscious. You see, the long-term stuff is much more risky. But the payoff can be huge.

The following morning I got acquainted with my new neighborhood. Then I telephoned Vick to wish her a Happy New Year and to see how she was coming along.

'Hi, sweetheart.'

'Hi, Aunt Bo.'

'You don't sound so good. You have a cold?'

'Yeah.'

'Everything okay?'

'Not so great.'

'Is your mom all right?'

'Mom's in the hospital.'

'The hospital? Why?'

'She hasn't been feeling good. They took her on New Year's Eve.'

I could hear her sobbing. 'Oh no. Max. Oh, baby.'

'Bo?'

'Yes?'

'Can you help us a little?'

'Money?'

'Yeah. Mom's been paying all the doctors. She'd never ask you but . . .'

'Don't say another word, honey.'

'I miss you.'

'I miss you too.'

'I don't like her being sick, Aunt Bo.'

Of course I was crying. But I didn't let Max know. 'You be strong, you hear, Maximilia? Max?'

'Yeah.'

'Mom needs you to be strong.'

'I know.'

'The stronger you are, the better she'll feel.'

'Are you coming?'

'Not yet, sweetheart. But soon.'

I called Vicky at the hospital, but she was asleep. I told the nurses not to wake her. Then I overnighted a thousand cash to the house in Fort Lowell.

When I returned to the apartment, I learned that Jasper had called in to my service. I phoned him back and he said he couldn't have lunch. He had to drive up to Vermont to see his parents. In the afternoon, some flowers came for me. They were from him. The note said, 'Sorry we couldn't get together. I miss you.' He signed it, 'Love, Jasper.'

Earning Every Penny called as well. She had awful news. **The Wild Card** had overdosed on cocaine and had died. Her heart had had enough. **The Wild Card** was dead. And they buried her right there in Aspen. **Earning Every Penny** was the only one in attendance at her funeral. *Christ Almighty*, was my feeling. I wept.

The next spot of cheery news was that Go Go was coming into town in two weeks. And that I had to move out. So did Napoleon. We didn't know where we were going to go.

Brad continued to call. I continued not to return his calls. If I was going to see him. I wanted to be in a position of strength. Not needy, broke, and desperate. And homeless. And sad. I needed a plan.

live from the desert

'Hello?'

There was lots of static, then the phone line was clear, then more static.

'Bo?'

'I can barely hear you.'

'How's that?'

'Better . . .'

After some holiday-gossip exchanges, mostly mine, I asked **At These Prices** to give me the specific details of how everything worked down there. Or out there. Or over there. Wherever the hell she was.

After telling me again how much she'd missed Christmas in America, she launched into it.

'It's so great. Michael Jackson just played here. Anyway, once you meet the talent scout, then you do the videotape and interview, then tapes are sent off.'

'What for?'

'They screen the tape at the palace and decide. It's not just a shoo-in deal. You have to be invited. So you wait for the talent scout to phone you to let you know if you're in or not.'

'What's the minimum amount of stay?'

'Six weeks. And every girl is promised twenty-five thousand dollars a week. And receives a gift at the end. A nice gift. You can't beat it, Bo.'

'What about getting there?'

'If you're picked, first the talent scout gives you a written contract.'

'What's it for?'

'To say you're there for entertainment purposes.'

'And you sign the contract?'

'Yes. Then they send you a ticket – it's always business-class. All flight connections are made through Singapore. Then you stay in Singapore for a day or two. And all the girls meet there. All the girls who have been selected from all over the world, from every country. Are you interested, Bo?'

I told her I was. 'Maybe,' I added.

'Right now it's kind of difficult, though. I hear they're not taking any Americans. Or Filipinos.'

'Why not?' And there was some tension in my voice, I admit.

'Because of the problems that last American girl caused. You know, the beauty queen? Another beauty queen from the Philippines did the same thing. American girls are bummed-out right now. They aren't being invited. Do you have another passport?'

'Yes. English.' It was a phony, of course. But it was done so well, it was practically legal.

'Great. That'll work. Every other kind of girl can come. Fat, thin, tall, beautiful, ugly – every type. Since you're gorgeous, they'll love you here. I don't think there's anyone – well, maybe a couple – who is as beautiful.'

I always loved **At These Prices**'s candor. There really wasn't a filter between her brain and her mouth.

'You're going to love it. There's so much money. You know the sultan pays Michael Jackson, Whitney Houston, and others millions to perform for him? Every performer has been to Brunei. And they get cash. And the sultan sends a private plane for them. You're not alone, Bo.'

She was so excited at the prospect of my coming. She was lonely, of course. But I suspected it was also that misery loves company. That she didn't feel good about what she'd been doing, and it would brighten her spirits to know someone she liked was doing the same thing. All part of the womanly self-esteem wars. You get it wherever you can.

no blue jeans

'Oh, wait a second. Before you get to Singapore, you're given a list of what to bring by your talent scout. And on the list is *no blue jeans*, okay? Prom dresses or evening dresses, the tackier the better. They don't care about class here. It's cheesy. But you cannot leave the compound of the palace to go shopping. You bring all your clothes with you. If you don't bring the right clothes, they have rooms full of clothing you can purchase, or get. You can buy clothes in the palace. And they'll just take it out of the money they give you at the end.'

'There's a sophisticated accounting system?'

'Oh yes.'

'What are the living arrangements?'

'Okay, I'll tell you. The whole palace is videotaped. Each girl stays in a bungalow with one other roommate. If you're not getting along with the roommate, it's kind of stressful. But there's this elaborate security. Videotape, tape recordings.'

'They tape your conversations?'

'Yes.'

'Can you choose a roommate?'

'No, it's random. It could be anybody from anywhere in the world. I mean, some girls have been here for three years. Then they can choose. So – they give you a list of what you can and can't wear. No blue jeans.'

'I got that.'

'They want you always to have makeup on, always to look good. You have to bring your own phone card. Because you can't make any international calls without one anymore because so many girls – the phone bills – were getting so outrageous that they said no more. I know a girl who was spending seven thousand dollars a month calling her boyfriend.'

'What was she telling him?'

'She told him she was modeling in Europe. Every girl tells her family, her boyfriend that she's modeling in Europe. My girlfriend was having some snapshots taken in different poses and was sending them back home. They were really bad. But your family doesn't know. People don't even know Brunei is a country – people are so stupid, Bo. Don't worry. Anyway, this girl was spending seven thousand dollars a month calling her boyfriend. I mean, what's the point of being here?'

And I thought about Max. And how I would communicate with her. 'What about mail?'

'You can send mail, but you can't put a return address on it. And you can never give the phone number where you are. And they've limited the amount of time you can call. It's only for a certain number of minutes. Right now? I'm on an English businessman's World Phone.'

'Okay, go on . . .'

'So – you get to Singapore and the first thing you do

is, you have to open a bank account there. Because you don't get your money in Brunei, you get it in Singapore.'

'Afterward?'

'Yes. You get all your money afterward. Nothing up-front.'

'So you do this for months on end, and then fly back to Singapore, and you have to depend on their total honesty that the money will be wired to your account?'

'It's to ensure your proper behavior while you're here, Bo. I'll be honest. Some girls might not get paid. Because they're bitchy or unwilling or have a bad attitude. But the Prince is very fair about money. Very few girls haven't gotten their money. He has to be, or the word would get out.'

'Okay, okay,' I said.

'After you have a bank account, they send a private plane from Brunei to pick you up. And there are assistants – I mean, the Prince and his family make a hundred million dollars a day, you know what I mean? He gave his daughter an eighty-million-dollar wedding. He has assistants galore. And these guys are like inden-tured servants. So they don't do anything bad. They would never hurt you. They obey. Brunei is a dictator-ship, Bo. It's not a free country. What I'm saying is, you're in good hands. It's safe.'

'Right . . .' I said hollowly.

'So you take the plane to Brunei, and as soon as you get off the plane, you have to go for a medical checkup. They make you take an AIDS test and all the STD tests – protease, blood, all of them. So you're in quarantine with all the new girls for the first twenty-four hours getting tested, to see if you have anything. You sit in this room, you can have any food you want, you can order room service twenty-four hours a day, you can exercise, anything you want. If your test doesn't come back negative, you have to go back to Singapore and you're sent back home.'

'What's the daily routine?'

'There are only two requirements. Every day at seven o'clock, you have to be at dinner. And on Sunday afternoon, you have to go to the polo match.'

'What happens at these dinners?'

'You go to dinner totally dressed up. The prom dresses I was telling you about. And, oh yeah, you have to sing karaoke. You have to.'

'What?'

'If you want to make it big here, you have to sing karaoke. The Prince and all his friends love karaoke. That's their big entertainment.'

'How many people are at dinner?'

'The dinner is huge.'

'A long table?'

'No, different tables.'

'How many guys at each table?'

'Sometimes fifty, sometimes ten. It depends on the night. Of course, the Prince has the biggest table, the nicest table. But there are tables all over. And different rooms too. It's not just one room. It's a palace, remember? They have different events.'

'Who's there?'

'It's all the Prince's business partners. All of his male

relatives. His brothers. It's all the men. Anybody who's doing business with Brunei. It's an international crowd. Japanese, English, Americans – whatever. And your sole responsibility there is to be like a geisha girl, to entertain the men. And any man who wants to fuck you, you have to fuck him. If you say no to anyone, if you say you have a headache – you get sent home.'

'What are these guys like?'

'They're all young playboy types. Other Arabs from other countries. And they're all friends. The guys don't have to get dressed up. And some of these guys are totally nothing. It's every kind of crowd. From the most amazing to the most, well, lowly.'

And at that point I wondered if **Earning Every Penny** had gone there after **the Wild Card**'s funeral. She'd mentioned it to me at that party in Aspen. So I asked **At These Prices**. And I got my answer.

'We just had dinner together the other night. But I think she was taken on a trip to London. She'll be back, though.'

That hit me hard. **Earning Every Penny** had gone to Brunei. My palms started to steam. And my questions became more direct. 'You have no idea who you're getting involved with? It could be with one of the servants, right?'

'Yes.'

'How many guys do you have to screw?'

'Well, a lot, Bo. But you're getting paid a lot.'

'You have to go with anybody?'

'Yes.'

'Do they keep you for a few days?'

'It's different every night. And some nights, Bo, nobody will pick you.'

'What about birth control?'

'You are required to be on the Pill.'

I digested that a moment. But I had more to ask. 'What do you do during the day?'

'Sleep, go to the pool, work out, hang out. You can go horseback riding. Whatever. It's very luxurious, very beautiful. It's like a big hotel. There's a McDonald's too, actually, but you have to pay a staff worker to get it for you. But every night at seven you have to be there for dinner, decked out, ready to go. Sometimes you'll get there and nobody will show up until ten. But you have to be there. It's totally strict. It's like finishing school. They train you on what you have to do, and when you prove you can do it and do it well, then you are rewarded with more and more freedom. And every Sunday for polo – you have to be there. And no blue jeans. You have to be decked out and you cannot be in a bad mood. If you're in a bad mood, you get sent home. So many girls get sent home. Because you're there for entertainment. That's what it says in your contract.'

'What's he like, the Prince?'

'He's like five feet tall and weighs a hundred pounds. And his dick is small. Let me tell you.'

'It's got to be if he's five feet tall,' I responded, and I couldn't believe I'd engaged in this part of the conversation.

'He is no sexual monster, that's for sure.'

'Were you with him?'

'Once – but I didn't even know it was him. Someone

told me later. He won't tell you. He keeps his distance. But he's very sweet, very well educated, very gentlemanly.'

'How did it happen?'

'You're just told what room to go to, you take off all your clothes, and you just sit there on the bed and wait. But that was a rarity. He has his own girls who have been with him for five years. Those girls have so much money now. They're his favorites. But you know what? The girls the Prince likes are really not attractive. You'd be surprised. They're a little tubby, they don't have boobs, they look a little dark. You know why? He likes girls who kiss his butt. He wants a geisha girl – one who washes his feet, so they treat him like a total king. He doesn't go for the really beautiful all-American girls. He doesn't like American girls. The American girls are for his friends.'

'How do you make it into the Prince's close circle?'

'You're evaluated by your performance. By how well you're doing, which means how nice you're being.'

'Nice, meaning *compliant* . . .'

'Yes. As long as you're willing.'

'What's *willing*?'

'Willing to do whatever they want to do. There's a lot of butt stuff, Bo. I'm not trying to scare you, I just want to give you the real story. So you know what you're getting into.'

'Thanks.'

'It's just like a harem. The women are treated inferior. If you want to stay and make your twenty-five thou a week, you've got to do whatever they want you to do.'

I started getting uneasy. It seemed so ... I didn't even have a word for it ... risky. 'But how do you protect yourself? You don't know these guys. They could do anything to you, and what recourse do you have? These girls have been telling their families they've been modeling. What happens if they disappear? Who could ever find them? Aren't there stories like that?'

'Calm down, Bo. I'm being honest with you. I don't want you to be scared. And I don't want you to come if you don't feel right about it. No, I've never heard of any murders, but I have heard of girls getting tied up, beaten up – but not very often. The normal punishment is getting sent home. If you piss them off, if you do the wrong things, all your stuff gets packed and they send you on the next plane to Singapore. They kick you out. That's as bad as it gets. How are you feeling about what I'm telling you?'

'Not great.'

'Listen, I'm totally happy. It's great, it really is. And if you do well – you sing the karaoke, have a positive attitude, and prove that you're loyal and can be trusted and don't talk too much – you'll move up and become one of their favorites; then you go on trips with the Prince out of Brunei. I went to London and Madagascar. But they also go to Borneo, the Seychelles, the Maldives. Even business trips to Beverly Hills. That's what you want to do. You want to get into the exclusive harem. Not just the overall big harem. But the only way you can make it into that group is if you don't talk to anybody. They record your conversations, remember.

They know what you're saying. You have to be tight-lipped.'

'So there's this hierarchy?'

'Yes. I knew one girl who had her own servants. She'd been there five years, though. She always stayed in the nicest suites. She was draped in jewelry. She would just, like, sit there. She didn't have to do karaoke anymore. And when she'd walk into a room, everyone respected her. She was one of the Prince's favorites.'

'How do you travel?'

'The Prince always flies alone, meaning on a separate plane from the girls. And the girls have their own plane.'

'How many go at a time?'

'Fifteen or so. It depends. And then you meet up. In London you stay at the hotel the Prince owns. And he has a house too. And you'll go to his house to have tea with him and his brother every day at two o'clock. And it's not always sex. I didn't have sex once in London. You talk about what you've been reading, like intellectual stuff. And they'll give you shopping money. In London we got a thousand pounds a day.'

'And the girls always travel together?'

'Yes. You're the entourage. You fly together, you all go shopping together, you can't leave the hotel, you don't have any independence. You're their property and you do what they say while you're with them, or else you get sent home. I'm telling you straight so you won't be misled, Bo.'

'I know. Thanks.'

'In Beverly Hills they take you around in minivans.'

'So what happens at the end?'

'When it's all over, you fly back to Singapore. And they wire you your money to the account you've opened. The girls who stay longer usually work out their own deals. But – and then you wire your talent scout her forty percent to her bank account.'

'Do you have to honor that?'

'The smart talent scouts have a representative at the airport waiting for you. Or they get it directly from the Prince. There are lots of different ways.'

'And you can stay as long as you want?'

'As long as they're happy with you. As long as guys are still picking you. And you're doing the karaoke. Some girls stay for five years. Others – three, two, one. I know one girl who made one and a half million dollars.'

'Where's she now?'

'In L.A. She wants to be an actress. And she's living off of that money now. She enjoyed it. She didn't think it was that degrading. I think she's going to be a big star.' She paused a second. 'Oh yeah, there're so many jewels going on here. Girls come back to America with these elaborate pieces of jewelry. Cartier watches, everything. He gets everything, the Prince. He gets anything he wants. So they have every type of jewelry. At the end, you're given a gift. You can choose the watch or the jewelry. I'm going to pick the watch. The diamond-studded Cartier watch.' She sighed. 'You coming, Bo? Just think of all the financial freedom you'll have – oops, someone's here,' she whispered suddenly. 'I'll be in touch. Bye, baby.'

We signed off just like that.

the good-bye

The call came about seven the following morning. It was a backbreaker. Max told me the worst news of my life. My sister was dead.

Vicky, my only sister, had died. Two nights earlier. But they hadn't been able to locate me. They'd been calling the Trump Tower apartment instead of Go Go's.

How I wished I could have been there. How I wished I could have held my sister's hand. To tell her I loved her. But it was too late for that.

The flight couldn't take off soon enough. Napoleon came with me. Without him, I wouldn't have made it. And all I could think about was Max's little voice. On the phone. Forced to do something that was way beyond her little head. To tell me about her mother's death. The only mother she would ever have. And now she would never see her alive again. I wished to God I could have been there with her.

Though I felt run-down and sick, getting to Max meant everything to me. We arrived in Fort Lowell about eight hours later. The funeral was that afternoon.

We went to the house, and I took a shower and

changed quickly. Then we took a cab over for the service. As we pulled up to the First Church of the Nazarene, I saw Max standing out in front all alone. Although this had been our church growing up, for Max it would be her first time inside.

I jumped out of the car as it was still moving and ran to her. We hugged and cried into each other's cheeks. We hung on for about three minutes.

'I'm so sorry for not having come sooner.'

Max said she couldn't believe how everything had happened so fast. When I met the doctor, I told him I'd thought they had cancer under better control these days, with recent breakthroughs and all. That was not the case for semi-advanced lymphoma, I'd learned. Vicky lasted only three months. He also told me that Vicky had been emphatic about not notifying me as to the extent of her illness.

'She didn't want to upset you and your life,' he said. 'She said you had enough worries.'

My mother was there too. She was in the back of the church, in her wheelchair. I went over and kissed her, held her hand, and talked with her for a moment. I buckled somewhat. I couldn't help it.

'What's happening, Ma? Can you hear me? This is too much. I'm not that strong. I need your guidance.'

She didn't know what I was saying. I think she thought she was just out for her afternoon tour of the gardens of the nursing home. If she even knew she toured the gardens daily. So I held her hand and looked to the altar and prayed.

And then after my stomach was hurting from crying,

from all those heaves, and my face was red and as swollen as a plum, I felt a push somehow in my spine. I felt some force carry me up and straighten out my back. It was this one push that gave me the strength to stand and walk.

The pastor hadn't come out yet. I surveyed the church. There were about twelve people seated in the pews. There should be more, I thought. That was the entire number of people Vicky affected in her life? It made me angry.

When the pastor emerged from a side door, I intercepted him on the way to the pulpit. I asked him to wait another ten minutes. He hesitated and then said he would.

I wasn't going to have my sister sent to heaven that way.

I ran out to the street and started to direct traffic, meaning I began waving people into the parking lot. Every car that passed, I stopped and explained to them briefly who my sister was, and asked them to join us.

'She was pretty, and very bright, and she worked at Western Sizzler as the hostess and she seated thousands of people over the years. She was polite and caring and a great mother. And I am proud as hell to be called her sister. And her only daughter is waiting in that church to say good-bye to her. But there is no one at the funeral.'

And would they like to come join us?

Well, about twenty cars just motored on, thinking I was a zealot or a bag lady or just crazy. About ten cars told me they wished they could come, but they had some other engagement. And about thirty cars pulled right into the driveway and attended the funeral for my sister. I guess it was my swollen, crying face that did it. It worked on them in a cheap way. But I didn't care. I wasn't going to have twelve people see my sister laid to rest.

One old black man named Eldridge seemed interested, but he felt that he wasn't dressed nicely enough. I told him he was, but I thought he just wanted to take off.

At the same time, some passersby I think realized they had nothing better to do; some others thought that it would be a nice thing to do for somebody. Still others I think wondered about themselves and how they'd feel if no one came to see them off in that untimely hour.

First, Max read some scripture that the pastor had selected for her. She had never gone to church, after all. Next, the pastor gave the eulogy, and as he did, I held Max's hand in one hand and Napoleon held my other hand.

I thought a lot of things about Vicky as I listened to the pastor. But most of all, about how we all have such a short spin. And it is our business to try to get beyond our differences as soon as possible. I wished, of course, I had the chance to tell Vicky how sorry I was for making her feel less about herself than she might have. I remembered times when she'd angered me so much because of her bitterness that I increased the hurt by rubbing stuff in her face. Sure, I wished I could take those events back. All of them.

The reality is, however, I had nothing on Vick. Maybe a few high-school crushes separated us. But what's that?

The problem is, how something as silly as that can adversely affect someone for life. I may have been a better judge of character and was more street-savvy, and I was definitely more of a live wire, but she was way more gifted than me in terms of writing and vocabulary and the ability to understand algebra and chemistry. She had more raw mind talent.

I felt so alone. Even though Napoleon and Max were there. I was alone without her.

As we all moved out of the church, there was a sight that brought some joy to my eyes. Even though it ended with the same result. Tears. The black man named Eldridge who I'd thought had been giving us the brush by claiming to be underdressed was now standing in the back row looking as fine as fine can be. He had a beautiful old gray antique suit on from the forties, a starched white-white collar, and a paneled tie. As we marched past him, he held out his hand, and when I extended mine, he kissed it. I stopped right there and leaned over and kissed him on the cheek.

It made Maximilia smile, actually, and seeing that – well, it was beyond worth it. We told Eldridge to come back to the house for a little reception after the funeral. He said he would.

'You can come just as you are too,' I said.

He laughed. It was the nicest moment for me in what seemed like weeks.

that little walk

Back at the house we had some food that Vicky's restaurant had sent over. Some of the people who worked at the Sizzler came. The pastor came. Vicky's former boyfriend, Eddy, came to the funeral but not to the reception. I didn't speak to him at length. I didn't find it odd that their relationship had soured once she'd gotten sick. It was all in character for him.

Eldridge came to the house too. And several others whom I'd forced to attend the funeral showed up. It was nice. Max's best friend, Cindy, was there too. Max was going to stay with Cindy and her parents until the end of the school year. Max, of course, wanted to come join me in New York. But I knew that wasn't a good idea. I couldn't take care of her properly. I had to get my life in order. Besides, she needed to finish the school year. Vick had always hoped that Maximilia would go to college. And I was going to do everything I could to fulfill those wishes.

People are so much nicer in the Midwest, I thought. Only here could people be rallied for a funeral, not knowing the deceased.

When I thought about it further, I realized that wasn't true at all. Wherever people feel, something like that can happen. It's the love. And if you show it and give it and send it, it comes back.

One couple who didn't know Vick but had attended the service couldn't make it to the house afterward. But they had a wonderful flower arrangement sent over.

After I took a bite of food, I saw Max sitting there on the Brown Couch all by herself. Her eyes were about as puffy as mine. But now she was staring straight ahead.

So I went over and asked her if she wanted to join me for a little walk. We held hands and went outside. We didn't make it very far, actually. We were immediately absorbed in what we had to say. We didn't want to walk any farther.

'She looked so beautiful, Aunt Bo. She looked at me and said, "You stay strong. I need you to be strong." Just like you told me on the phone. Then she made me promise I would go to and finish college. I told her I would. Then she went to sleep. And that was it.'

I wiped another stream from my face. I was trying to stay strong too – not to go to pieces in front of the little girl who now had no guideposts. Except me.

'Maybe we can get together this summer,' she said.

'Sure, baby. I'll take you anywhere you want to go.'

'And Mom also told me this. She told me to tell you she loved you.'

'Oh, God, Max. Couldn't you tell me that tomorrow?'

And Max burst out laughing and I burst out crying, and seeing her laughter, I laughed too. And cried some more.

And we just fell into each other and started hugging. And I looked up. And there was my old friend from what seemed another lifetime standing over me. One of her branches was hovering over my shoulder as if to comfort me. It was that old maple. Where Joan used to live. All those summers ago. I had turned my back on that maple. Many years ago. I had turned my back on all of nature, in fact. But now, at that moment, I never appreciated that old maple more. I let go of Max, walked up to it, and kissed its bark. And wished it the greenest of leaves in the spring.

'What are you doing, Aunt Bo?' she asked.

I told her I was kissing an old friend.

At that moment Eldridge came up to us and handed Max an old record album of New Orleans jazz favorites. We went back inside and put it on the phonograph. It bopped along, and the wailing horns seemed to take some of the gloominess out of the get-together.

'I've never been to New Orleans,' I said.

But Napoleon had. He told a very funny story about a lover he'd had there. Of course, he made it sound as though the lover had been a woman. It was a funny story. And it cheered everybody up just about an inch, which was really a mile from where we all had been.

'You must go to New Orleans, Ms Bodicea,' Eldridge said. 'You must go.'

'Vick went,' I remarked.

'Uh-huh, see? She knew,' Eldridge said. 'She knew.'

twenty-four-dollar ride

Harry Cipriani's Downtown restaurant was a long haul from my temporary apartment. It was a twelve-dollar cab ride, and I was counting. When I arrived, Brad was seated at the table already, with a wine basket placed beside it. When he saw me, he stood up and gave me a very warm hug. One that understood the upset I'd been enduring. If I failed to mention it before, he had sent a beautiful bouquet of flowers to the house on Searchlight Lane.

The flowers weren't the reason I met with him, however. And it wasn't because of what Napoleon had said. That it was just as easy to date the rich guy as the poor guy. I didn't want to date Brad. I'd never wanted to date him. I'd wanted to marry him.

In the end, I saw him because I wanted to know what had happened. I never did understand it. Our union had been severed abruptly. I didn't have any expectations. I just wanted some closure. That was the reason I accepted his invitation to lunch.

He began by asking about the funeral and how Max was holding up. I thanked him for the flowers he'd sent.

Then we settled into our chairs.

'Bo, I want to apologize for what happened in December.'

Yes, it sounded predictable. But it had to be covered, at least. He launched into an explanation of the holiday vacation debacle, and how and why he'd disinvited me. He blamed it on his mother's pressuring, which wasn't a surprise either.

'There are a few things we've had to iron out between us. We've done that finally.'

'Like?'

'Well, she's never been very fair. She talks authoritatively on subjects she knows little about. She'll hear something at a table and ingest it as gospel. Then you're always fighting off some platform of hers, and she doesn't even know whether or not it's accurate. She's a caring person but intellectually tyrannical. She makes snap judgments about my friends.'

'About me?'

'About every girlfriend I've ever had. Like out of some old-winded A. R. Gurney play.'

'What did she say about me?'

'It isn't important.'

'Tell me.'

'She just felt we weren't right for each other – the usual. It's never different.'

'Who are you right for?'

'That's just it. It's a state of mind for her. My being with someone is Pavlovian for her to reject that person. You can't take it personally. And I try not to.'

'So, what was resolved in the Bahamas?'

He hesitated. I guessed he was attempting to best summarize the discussion he'd had with the Always Right Society. As if the wording was significant.

'I told her to let me live my life the way I saw fit. To stay out. She said she'd comply,' he said. 'It's hard for her. She has front-row tastes but was raised in the upper deck.'

'That's funny,' I said.

He liked hearing that. It broke up his serious posture.

And as Brad was speaking, I never pictured Adele Lorne-August more clearly. She was just another Dairy Queen Elitist. You know, the kind of woman who worked the cash registers at the franchises in her youth, selling thousands of gallons of soft-serve, wore bad clothes in all Slurpee colors, like me, and ate at places with only laminated menus – then as an adult, because of marriage and a quantum class leap, becomes an intense elitist and social critic, pooh-poohing anything plebian, nouveau, and trendy that came her way.

Brad leaned in and held my hand. I left my hand there to be touched for about five seconds. Then I pulled it away. It wasn't an artificial move or gamesmanship. It just felt awkward to touch him.

And then I thought about touch. And how much the slightest touch can mean – and then there's Brunei. Where touch is more like a flesh rumble riot for six weeks or more. Wow, I thought, and let that one go.

'What's that look for?' he asked.

'Nothing,' I said. 'So, what's next for you, Brad?'

'I didn't get that job at *National Geographic*.'

'Sorry to hear that.'

'Yeah, well. I'm thinking of working for another magazine. *Outside*. Or *Men's Outdoors*. Or *Smithsonian* . . .' he said, trailing off. And took on a serious expression. 'But, Bo, I invited you to lunch to talk about us.'

I just looked at him squarely to see where he'd go with this.

'I care a lot about you. I do. And I realized it while I was away. I thought about you all the time.'

And he clasped my hand again, this time very gently. His hand was very warm, almost sweaty. I liked that. It meant he meant what he'd been saying. Or was at least tense about saying it. Whichever, I was somewhat surprised.

'And that's not easy for me to say. But you're unlike any of the girls I've ever gone out with. I mean, smart, funny – all my friends like you. Since we've been apart, they've been saying to me, *What are you doing? Don't let her get away.*'

I felt a smile pressuring my mouth. It was nice to hear. But I didn't let that smile show itself.

'Will you accept my apology?'

'Brad, it was disappointing. I was hurt. We had all this . . . good feeling going, and then it was like nothing ever happened.'

'I'm so sorry. Let me make it up to you.'

I didn't say anything. And then I did. 'Did Paul and Betsy tell you they saw me?'

'Yes, they did.'

He then fidgeted. It was a test. But he didn't say anything more about that avenue of thought.

'What do you say about coming to Antigua with me?'

'Antigua?'

'First week of February.'

I sat back in my chair. 'I don't know, Brad. I'm not a trusting person. And what happened took away my confidence in you.'

'You can't forgive me?'

'I can forgive. But I rarely forget. That's just me.'

'Will you think it over?'

'Brad, what do you want of me?' He squirmed in his chair somewhat. 'You think we have a future?'

Then he leaned in.

'I wouldn't be sitting here if I didn't.'

'What are you telling me?'

'That I love you. That I want to be with you.'

I still wanted him to say something more. Though I wasn't going to ask *him* if he wanted to get engaged. But I was fed up. I said it anyway.

'Yes,' he said.

'For how long?'

'Not long. Until we get married.'

I took my first sip of wine. I felt a bit easier. But not by much. It was nice to hear what I was hearing from him, of course. Whether he was totally serious or not, I couldn't tell. But he seemed serious.

After lunch, Brad dropped me off in his car. We kissed cheeks and nothing more.

When I thought about it further, I realized that I couldn't depend on Brad anyway. Not yet. Not with how much I needed to. He'd run away in a puff of prairie-dog dust if I leaned on him the way I needed to. Financially. And emotionally. I needed to be able to stand alone on my own two feet. I needed to be empowered. I would be much more attractive that way. Not just to Brad. To everyone, in case it didn't work out with Brad – something that raw statistics and experience told me it may well not.

That night I got my answer. The **Three-Minute Princess** rang me from London. After I gave her the dismal rundown of my life since Christmas, the conversation went just like this:

'How's it going for you?' I asked.

'So much better, Bo. I mean, I can't thank you enough for sending me here. Your friend Crispian has introduced me to the nicest guys.'

'*Nice* meaning *generous*?'

'Of course I mean generous,' she said without hesitation.

And I believed her. There was a snap in her voice coming from a confidence that had grown. It was clear that her self-esteem had been given a push. No doubt from endlessly fawning Walletmen overseas.

'You didn't get involved with Crispian, did you?' I asked her.

'Of course not. After he made the deal that I cover the cab if he covered the drinks, I knew not to get near. But he does know well-heeled guys.'

'Yes, he does.'

She'd even met Arnot, who was still doing the same womanizer thing but with less hair. And less often. It's that way with the greatest of playboys. Eventually, they have to pick and choose their nights.

'I want to send you the money for the ticket, Bo.'

'What ticket?'

'Well, the ticket you bought for me to come here.'

And I was about to say, *Don't be silly* or *Someone did it for me once, forget it,* but somehow neither response made its way out.

'If you feel compelled to,' I returned. And she asked me the new address. And I told her. Then she told me how many flights she'd taken in the past six months. She'd even gone to hot spots during high season. She'd gone to Gstaad for Christmas.

'That's progress,' I quipped. 'I thought I might see you at Aspen for New Year's. It would have been proof you weren't still with Low-Season Boys. Did you stay in Gstaad for New Year's?'

'No. We went to the Bahamas.'

'Which island?'

'Nassau. I went with Neville Turnbull. We stayed at this very exclusive club.'

'The Layford Cay Club?'

'Yes, how did you know?'

'Lucky guess.'

'Yeah, right,' she said sarcastically. And I liked hearing it. It was further proof of her beefed-up self-assured quality. 'In fact, I saw **Check the Passport** there.'

'Really?' And my heart started a conga rhythm.

'Yeah. She still thinks the world owes her a favor.'

'Who was she with?' I said, all the emotion making its way up my throat.

'This guy. Handsome guy, actually. Named Brad. Or Bradley.'

My heart sank and dropped right down to the

basement. 'Did you meet him?' came out of my mouth.

'Yes. We had drinks with them. A group of us actually.'

Water began to amass around my eyes. I saw a droplet hit the floor. 'Who was there?'

'Other people. Young people. Neville was the oldest guy there.'

'You mean his family wasn't there?'

'Neville's family?'

'*Brad*'s,' I shot back.

'No,' she said with a laugh. And the laugh impaled me. It meant their activity had been so enthusiastic and fun and bedroomy and wet and beachy and bedroomy and surfside and bedroomy and wild that any parents around to witness it would have made for great humor, which would result in laughter similar to the laugh she gave. 'They were staying there at the club.'

'For how long?'

I sounded like the panicky detail-groveling journalist. And each time I got an answer, I got a kick in the face and had to readjust my jaw.

'A week or so. I mean, we were there for a week, and they stayed there after us.'

'And no family?'

'No family,' she said. 'This isn't good news, is it, Bo?'

My face buckled. 'It's not the greatest, no.'

'Oh, baby,' she said with full gentle pity. And that was another dash of cruel irony. The **Three-Minute Princess** was consoling me on my galactic stupidity. Fortunately, she didn't rub it in and scold me the way I'd done to her in the past.

So much had happened so fast. And now this.

'Is there anything I can do to help?'

I told her there wasn't.

I pulled myself together after a minute. And the **Three-Minute Princess**, bless her little Digger heart, tried to get me off the pain of it all by asking me something factual and unrelated.

'Bo, what are you up to the next few months?'

I hesitated with my answer. 'I'm going to Europe,' I said in a low voice.

'England?'

'No. France. And Germany.'

'What for?'

'Modeling.'

monica

I went up to the tenth floor of the St Regis Hotel and knocked on Room 1013. It opened, and a blond woman was standing there to greet me. She had a healthy chest that was artificial, but she wasn't thin.

'I'm Celeste.'

'Right. Monica is waiting for you.'

I stepped into another room, and a woman was sitting behind a desk. It was that woman. The one I'd seen for years elegantly mixing with the affluent people in New York and Los Angeles and, most recently, Aspen. The one who had been staring at **Earning Every Penny** and me at Ernest Rork's party. And now I understood why. She was as blond as ever and beautiful and very well dressed. She had on a gray suit and jacket and spoke in a very businesslike manner.

'Hello, Celeste. I'm Monica.' She had a Swedish accent too.

'I've seen you before,' I said.

'I recognize your face as well,' she acknowledged, and left it at that. 'Your appointment was at five.'

'I know. Sorry.'

'It's almost six.'

'I know.'

'That's the last time – if we're going to do business together. And if you go overseas, lateness is a sure way to get sent home.'

'I understand.'

I had my reasons for being late – the first was, I was scared. Second, I didn't want to see or meet or be seen by any other girls.

I looked around the suite and spotted a white screen deployed at the right wall and a video camera on a tripod opposite it.

'Did you bring a bathing suit?'

I said I had.

'And an evening dress?'

I nodded.

'Perfect.' And she then looked at me with hard, steely eyes, almost as if scrutinizing my skin or something.

'You're very beautiful,' she said. At that moment, I felt a smoocherella vibe, meaning lesbian pulsations were coming from her.

The whole thing lasted several hours. The interview, the shoot, and the little makeout session we had after she put her hand inside my bathing suit. When it was over, Monica was convinced I'd be invited. She told me she usually notified applicants in a week or so. She said in my case, however, because I was so gorgeous, she would overnight my 'application' and get me an answer in twenty-four to thirty-six hours. She then asked me if I'd like to go to dinner with her that night.

'Sure,' I said.

singapore stopover

There's just one word to describe the flight to Singapore. You know what it is. I arrived a day later. I was exhausted. But the flight itself gave me a lot of time to think about everything. The death of my sister, my finances, what was awaiting me, what I'd left behind – Max, Giles, Warren, and Virginia. And Jasper. Jasper had called once before I left. I didn't really think about Monica. She was just your average grazer getting her talent-scout skim. A no-brainer.

Nor did I forget about Brad, the latest Master of the String-Along. I couldn't help but cringe at how I'd misread him. Me, the almighty Capricorn Snake. I'd prided myself on my ability to understand and even anticipate character aberrations and recognize character flaws. And he'd totally figure-eighted around me. Using his overbearing mother – the ferocious, meddling ex-Digger – as the screen. The absolute lies he'd reeled off at lunch were quite impressive. I'd been so sure of myself. I thought I had everyone's number. The reality is, I didn't know shit.

And if misjudging Bradley wasn't proof enough, my

journey to Brunei certainly was. After all, if I knew so much, what was I doing going there?

A few questions lingered. Not that they mattered at all, however. For instance, I wondered if **Check the Passport** had told Brad about me, about my background, about my past, basically most things I'd left out of my AP in the Bradley Edit. And if she had divulged what she knew, and I was sure she had, why would he still be telling me he loved me? And that he wanted to spend his life with me? Well, there was an easy explanation. Because he wanted to have his cake and eat it too, two strong tenets of the String-Along plan. To give himself options. And backup and the freedom to play. He had no intention of marrying me, but he'd play with me for ever. Or at least while I still looked young. And sexy. And was able to give pleasure.

The thinking made me tear up once again. So I tried to avoid it.

The airport was little Asian people running every which way. I quickly made it to a bank Monica had suggested, and opened an account. Then while waiting in a hotel, I had a glass of champagne. Might as well, I figured. It made me think of Aspen. And New Year's. The year 2000. And me, The Millennium Girl. A name I considered saturated with sardonic humor at this point.

Then I thought of Jasper. As I mentioned before, I'd spoken with him before my departure. He started the conversation by saying he was still away in 'Vermont.' But Go Go's caller-identification system had indicated to me that he'd really been phoning me from California. I didn't call him on it. I knew what had happened. He had crawled back to **Every Little Bit Helps**. I wasn't surprised.

Halfway through the conversation, he did say, 'Bo, I have to be honest with you. I'm not in Vermont.'

'I know.'

'I'm with **Every Little Bit Helps**.'

'I know that too.'

'How do you know?'

'I can hear it in your voice.'

'I wasn't trying to be deceptive.'

I can't recall how many times I'd made that mile-long crawl to someone who had never been deserving of it. But I couldn't give Jasper the benefit of the doubt. After that episode with Bradley, this kind of tale-telling was difficult for me to go along with.

'I don't sound too good, do I?' he remarked.

'You sound pretty drained.'

'I am.'

'It's not getting any better?'

'No, it's not. I'm so sorry, Bo. I miss you.'

'I miss you too.' And the beat was an artificial one. At that moment I saw Jasper pretty clearly. He was in Bradley's class. But I wasn't going to grill him on it. I had my own worries.

'But I'm . . . weak. I had to do it.'

'I understand. . . .'

I had tears in my eyes now. But not for him. They were streaming down my face for myself and my predicament and what I was about to do to pull myself out of it, and what he would think of me if he knew.

'It was like the lurking unknown; I had to grab at it.'

'Believe me, I understand.'

Then I told him I'd be going away for a while. 'Modeling in Europe,' of course. He asked me to call him with a number. I told him I would. Even though I knew I never would.

While sitting there in the airport, I had a rush of anxiety. I was terrified, actually. I didn't know what the hell I was doing in Singapore. My life had come to this, and wasn't there any other way? I wanted to call home. Then I thought it wouldn't be a good idea. I could only hurt myself more. It would make everything that much more difficult. And painful. I decided to call **At These Prices**. She'd given me that private World Phone number.

But neither she nor the English businessman was answering. I began to panic. So I called in to my service.

Brad had called to tell me he had gotten our tickets for Antigua. All I had to do was tell him when I was coming back. That was a laugher. Napoleon called to give me his new number. He'd rented a bedroom in an apartment with one of Greg's business partners. And the Senator called in to tell me that he was coming to New York the following day and that he wanted to see me. And I almost forgot. Hermès called to tell me that my Kelly bag had arrived and I could pick it up anytime. Another laugher. It was also one final gift from Giles.

There was one more call. It was difficult to make out the voice at first. She was crying. Tears on an answering machine are the worst. It's so haunting. Because you know the person isn't speaking to you live. They had recorded this display in the past. And where were they now? it made you wonder. And what had happened in all those intervening hours? Haunting.

'Bo,' the cracking voice said. 'I'm having a difficult time. He's been violent with me,' she said, and broke down. It went on for another ten seconds. 'I don't know whether to call the police or not. It's so embarrassing. But I'm scared. I'm at the Beverly Wilshire Hotel. Call me.'

It was Virginia. I immediately called her back, of course. She was there, thank God, still hiding out. She told me that Warren had been unbearable. He'd hit her numerous times. I told her to call the police.

'No, I can't. I don't want it all over the press. I just want to get away from him. What do I do?'

I thought about it, short but hard. 'Just stay there, okay? I'll take the next flight to Los Angeles. I'll be there in two days.'

'Where are you?'

'Somewhere I don't want to be.'

You see, I took Virginia's distress call as a signal, warning me not to do what I was about to do. I could only see it that way. And even if it wasn't a signal, I was going to get myself back to help her. I took the next flight to New York. I was down to my last two thousand dollars. It was just enough to cover the Los Angeles ticket. But I wasn't worried about the money. I was worried about my friend. And what that creep Warren would do to her. I considered him capable of anything, even the worst. He had just the right amount of money and the right amount of sickness. Control was his game, remember? To move ladies in and out of his life.

As I was gathering my stuff, a dark-skinned Indian-looking man approached me and asked, 'Are you Celeste?'

'I don't speak English!' I snapped at him. And I dashed off. I yelled after him, 'And I hate karaoke!'

california swing

I arrived at LAX two days later in the midmorning. I was obviously worn out. But getting to Virginia was the priority. She had moved from the Beverly Wilshire to the less-conspicuous Bel-Air Hotel. I met her in her suite. When she opened the door, I was pretty shocked. We hugged, of course, and I held her. But it was her appearance that killed me. She had bruises on her face and neck. She looked as if she'd been in a prizefight.

We sat in her little garden adjoining the suite. I had some fresh-squeezed orange juice. Virginia didn't have anything. She just curled up in a chair in her bathrobe, knees to her chest.

She told me the whole story. She had moved to the Los Angeles area from San Francisco after she'd split with Don. Don had given her a decent settlement, but it wasn't earth-shattering. With it, she bought a small house in Brentwood. She then met Warren at a church function in Beverly Hills. He told her that his first wife had died of breast cancer. They began to see a lot of each other and eventually married in 1993. All was fine, seemingly, for the first few years. She had gotten to know some people at the L.A. Tennis Club and played regularly. Warren already was socially prominent in the city.

But then the relationship became more and more strained. And she didn't know why. How he was going on trips for long periods, and his behavior had become more erratic.

As Virginia told me this stuff, her eyes were all puffy from crying, and her face was swollen and discolored where he'd walloped her. I thought about my next move for several minutes all the while she was speaking to me. I realized I had to do it.

'Virginia. I must tell you, I have not been a saint in all this.'

She looked at me sharply, as sharply as a drained soul could, anyway.

And I told her. I told her how I'd met Warren Samuels, how we had continued to meet, what we did, and how often. It was difficult to say, of course, but I felt it was only right.

As I said it, she looked directly at me, and then after the initial news, her gaze just drifted off to the row of shrubs, her head hanging low. Some more water came out of her eyes, but her face didn't change its shape. The water just flowed freely.

'I'm sorry,' I said.

'No,' she said. And she told me that it wasn't my fault. That I wasn't the only one. That women would call the house. That she knew he was constantly cheating on her.

I felt awful, of course. But I knew I would. 'I couldn't

tell you in Aspen. And I should have. If I had, none of this would have happened.'

And I cried too. That's when she rose up from her chair and walked over to me. She placed a hand on my shoulder and kissed the top of my head.

'I'm so sorry, Virginia. If there was anyone . . .'

'I know, Bo. I know.'

'Do you?'

'I feel it. Love is something you feel. And when it's not being received, you feel that too. I've always felt it from you.'

'I do love you, Virginia. I always have.'

She knelt low, and we hugged.

I spent that night with her in her bedroom. We slept in the same bed, in fact. The next day, we drove up to Santa Barbara and stayed at a horse ranch owned by a friend of hers. It was just what she needed to collect her thoughts. To recover. To think about things. To swim, to take bike rides, to ride the horses. And to listen to me as I told her of my plan to extricate her from this predicament.

At first, she was wary of doing it. And then she agreed that it was the smartest thing to do. That with unsavory characters like Warren, it was the only way.

'You're so strong,' she said to me one morning.

What I didn't tell Virginia were the exact details of my plan. I didn't think she needed to know.

It all started with a few phone calls. The first was to the **Three-Minute Princess** in London. She had offered to help me if I needed it. And I told her I did. And I told her what she needed to do. With Virginia's financial assistance, I bought her a first-class ticket to Los Angeles. She said she didn't mind coming back to Los Angeles, especially now that she felt like a different person, a stronger one.

She arrived in Santa Barbara two days later. Virginia liked her very much. In fact, they played tennis each morning. We stayed there through the weekend. But before we left, I had the **Three-Minute Princess** make a few calls. The last one was to Warren on his private phone number, the number I knew by heart. This is how her side of the conversation went:

'Hello, Warren? I'm Theresa. I'm a friend of Bodicea's. Yes. Of course.' Then she belched out a big laugh. And winked at me. Warren was already tantalized and was chewing her ear off. 'Excuse me, but where am I talking to you? You're flying high? Where, high? Close to heaven? Aha. Somewhere above Nevada. Why, yes, I am in town for a few days. And, well . . . Sunday? Sure, would love to. The Burbank airport? Two o'clock. Right. Okay. Oh, I almost forgot. Warren? I have two other friends who are already very bored of Los Angeles. Really? Great. I'll tell them. We'll see you on Sunday.'

And she giggled demonically, a response that I was sure had been prompted by his own version.

And that was all it took.

That following Sunday, a limo picked up the **Three-Minute Princess**, **Smiles to Your Face**, and **Check the Passport** at the Beverly Hills Hotel and drove them to the Burbank airport. **Three Minutes** had corraled the two of them at my urging. Don't forget, she and **Check the Passport** had shared some nice, profitable

Wallet time in the Bahamas together, with Bradley
Lorne-August no less. And **Smiles** was **Check the
Passport**'s closest pal. Make no mistake about it. These
two had been carefully selected. It was a nice play,
actually. I wasn't worried about it not working. Warren
had never been able to turn down an afternoon of Three-
Way Dreams. Let alone Four-Way. He was quite
predictable that way.

tea and twenty-four hours

The next day I phoned Warren. I told him that I wanted to meet him at the Polo Lounge the following day to discuss some business. He thanked me for setting him up with my friend Theresa.

'Don't mention it,' I said.

For my meeting with Warren, I dressed as if I were attending England's Royal Ascot horse race. I wore a beautiful print floral Oscar dress with matching bonnet. I was Malibu beach blond and Virginia did my hair up in a stunning beehive with Ivana wisps. I had a new pair of Gucci black rims to fend off the sun. I was all business.

I arrived first and selected a table away from the others. When Warren arrived, his expression was glowing. He tried to give me a big squeeze, but I extended my hand instead. He kissed it.

'Bo, how the hell are you?'

'Never better,' I said.

And I told him why. I told him what the situation was, what the terms were, that they were non-negotiable, and that I had myself covered in case anything perilous were to happen to me.

As he listened, his face turned a shade I'd never seen on a man's face before. On any face, for that matter. Then it filled with blood again as he tried to hurl threats at me.

But the threats didn't matter.

I calmly ordered some tea and gave him twenty-four hours to get the gears in motion. He told me something along the lines of 'Fuck off!' I didn't use bad language. It's not that I didn't know all the dirty words. I just didn't need to.

The meeting lasted only about twenty minutes. I got up during his saliva-spitting, charged, yelling, and whispering tirade. I left the meeting pretty relaxed, actually. For someone like me, once I know what I'm up against with respect to the capacity for depravity of a fellow human being, I don't get scared. It's the surprise stuff that terrifies me. Like that difficult afternoon in Aspen at Warren's house. As I spoke with him, of course I flashed on that day. I remembered him sitting on that chair so coolly, so sickeningly, so disgustingly as he puffed away on a cigarette while I was being made a good-time tramp of.

During my limousine ride home from the Beverly Hills Hotel, I thought about **Check the Passport** and how she'd overstepped her boundaries just one too many times. And I also thought about **Smiles to Your Face** and how she had stolen **Earning Every Penny's** husband-to-be and with him, her catwalk to lifelong security.

I never considered myself a vindictive person. And to

this day, I don't think I am. But a situation presented itself that enabled me to take care of the people I loved as well as a few I didn't with one little parcel of graymail. I didn't consider it full blackmail, because of the heinous deeds that had been done to warrant it. It was graymail. It was in the form of videotape captured by state-of-the-art technology, a technology so small that it could be housed in something as light, airy, sexy, and thematically correct as a bra strap. And to work it, you didn't even need a master cinematographer. The age range for this toy was from eight to eighty. The **Three-Minute Princess** was twenty-five, so you could safely say she was in her video prime.

Sure, Warren had hurled a lot of insults my way. Let's not forget the threats on my life and my children's lives and any family member he could find, wherever, whenever. But I didn't care. I knew what I was up against. And I knew what he would do if the church ever found out about his Air Religion games. He'd suck on a revolver so fast, it would make anyone in the vicinity's head spin.

I considered that a nice insurance policy.

That afternoon Virginia and I were in the backyard of a house in Santa Monica owned by a friend of **Three Minutes**. We were sitting on a love-seat-style tree swing eating melon wedges. Late-afternoon West Coast sun was slashing right into the backyard. That's when the call came in. It came in on my new mobile phone. It occurred at the four-hour mark of the twenty-four hours I'd given him.

Warren had calmed considerably. I was happy for

that. He was actually pretty polite. But better than that, he agreed to all my terms. The transfer was to be made the following day. I'd given him the correct account number to wire the funds to, ABA data included.

It was a nice afternoon, actually. The two of us just feeding each other green honeydew and orange cantaloupe slices alternately. Me, then her; me, then her. Her, then me; her, then me. And that was how I secured a divorce settlement for Virginia Lashley Samuels for sixteen million dollars.

Like I said, it was a really nice afternoon.

the silent assassin

The Digger Sting, as I called it, gave me a strength I'd been lacking in recent months. Or maybe I had never had it at all. It was a new-found strength. But it was strong and it didn't end in Los Angeles. And that was a good thing. After all, I needed money. Of course, Virginia had offered me some for having helped her. But believe it or not, I couldn't take it. I had contributed to her pain, however unknowingly, and I didn't feel I should profit from it. Besides, I had already received sizable amounts from her husband in the past. That was payment enough.

When I returned to New York, I underwent a whirl-wind of activity. First, I phoned the Senator. It had been a couple of weeks since he'd phoned me. He was no longer in New York. He was campaigning up in Sharon, Connecticut. I was pretty blunt with him, actually. I told him I needed to borrow ten thousand dollars. 'That's not a problem,' he said. And he apologized for his behavior in the fall. He had been nervous about the upcoming election. But now the campaign was running smoothly. So he felt a little more at ease. I promised him

I would pay him back. He told me not to worry. I told him okay. When I received the overnighted check the next day, it was for fifteen grand instead of the ten I'd asked for.

That's one of the old Digger postulates I've neglected to impart. If a Walletman messes up with his behavior, with his treatment of you, or shows of disrespect to you, never fret. Like verbal abuse, a sudden breakup, violence, or painful sex. Consider it a good omen. It usually translates to money down the road. You can pressure him for it, or threaten him for it. In this case, the Senator just needed a little polite request to spark his generosity.

I arranged to stay in an inexpensive but nice hotel on the West Side. It was about a hundred and fifty a night, but the guy gave it to me for a buck and a quarter. No, I hadn't done anything for that twenty-five-dollar reduction. He just did it of his own free will. With the *hope* of receiving something for twenty-five dollars. It would never happen. And it didn't.

I had enough money for three months of inexpensive living. Bodicea living. It would be less if I got careless. I didn't expect to.

My week started with Jasper, even though he had nothing to do with my new plans. How could he, after all? My plans didn't involve warm fuzzies or preppy fiction or a two-for-one dinner at Pedro's Cantina. He'd been trying to get ahold of me for days now, making all sorts of romantic overtures. But that wasn't my interest in him. We had spent some intimate time together. And he had gotten under my skin. I sensed I needed something from him. It wasn't simple closure. Something else was driving me. I couldn't put my finger on it. I just felt I couldn't move on until I dealt with him. We had unfinished business.

'Let's meet for breakfast,' I said when we spoke.

I think that surprised him – that I didn't want to have dinner with him, or at least lunch. In fact, when we met, we never ate or drank a thing. We took a long walk down the esplanade to Battery Park. We did it early in the morning. I arrived at eight; Jasper got there ten minutes later. I'd been getting up early every morning. Just after sunrise. It was my new routine – work out in the hotel gym, then go to breakfast. I scheduled in Jasper to that.

He looked a little sleepy when we met. 'You're going to work out?' he asked in a surprised way. He yawned too.

'Already did.' See, I was still in my gym clothes. Another fist to his shoulder. Like he wasn't worth my wearing real clothes. But I wasn't trying to prove anything or be vengeful. This was me. The new and improved me.

'You have great color,' I told him.

'Yeah, we spent some time in San Diego at her friend's place.'

I didn't bother to tell him I'd had a California swing too. 'How is **Every Little Bit Helps**?'

'Same. Floating through life,' he said, looking off.

'Is that what you think of her? What does that make you?'

He looked at me sharply, struck by my directness. 'I don't know.'

'You enjoy the fact that she's somewhat light-headed.'

'We broke up.'

And I didn't give it any credence. 'Again?'

'Bo,' he said correctively, 'we've never broken up before. It's the first time.' I nodded and let his comment die. 'Listen, I didn't want to see you to discuss her.'

'What *did* you want to see me for?'

'To talk about us.'

'Us. What is us? No – wait. I'll tell you what. *Us* means two people in a mountain resort comforting each other.'

'Is that what you think?'

It wasn't really. But I didn't care anymore. So I wasn't going to let him know what my feelings were or had been. I was holding on to my own. It was an attitude I'd picked up long ago, after my traffic-accident-style breakup with Buddy Farrell when I was sixteen. Then it continued during the Tour years. Also, Vicky's death had given me some added clarity. I thanked her for it in my prayers. Let's not forget the newfound strength I'd experienced as a result of the episode with Virginia.

In essence, gushing was not part of it for me anymore.

'We were both on the rebound, Jasper. Your girl was getting shteueped down in the Islands. And my guy was, well, he had just finished eleventh grade and was heading into his senior year.'

I didn't need to tell him about Brad's duplicitous display. It didn't matter.

'You sound bitter.'

'Bitter, no. Determined, yes. Jasper, our little pitter-patters for each other were nothing but a little speed bump in our long romantic lives. I mean, we were together, what, three days?'

He looked at me sternly. 'What has happened to you?'

'Life – and a few other things.'

'And this is your attitude based on your experiences?' It was my turn to look sharply at him. 'What are you doing?' he asked in a tone soaked in judgment.

'What do you mean by that?'

'I mean – what exactly is your life?'

'Don't give me that crap,' I snapped.

'What crap? Buy yourself a toolbox.'

Oooooh. The comment stung a little. He wasn't done either. Here he was, the real Jasper Connelly coming at me live and in color. I guess it was a character trait in him I'd been sensing for a while. And it was the very reason I'd come to meet him. I wanted to bring out the real Jasper in him. The one I'd sensed was lurking beneath the surface.

'What do you get involved with people for? You run around waiting for the next enabler. And they just tell you you're great, fuck you, hand you money, and you go to the next to the next to the next.'

'That's right. It's better that way. Emotions are left out. You avoid the lies, the false promises. And you're in control.'

'Are you?'

'Yes, I am,' I spat. 'I make my own moves on my own time, and I have to listen to no one. And no one's soul-probing crap that's saturated in self-interest. Don't try to be some Mr Fix-it for my life. Take a look at your own.'

'What self-interest are you talking about?'

'Yes, you're a sensitive and feeling guy – but don't use it to mess with other people when there's nothing wrong with them and there's no reason for it but your own personal gain.'

'There's nothing wrong with you?'

'Everyone does what they have to do. And you know it.'

'Nice cop-out.'

'Look, Jasper, go manipulate somewhere else.'

'You think I'm manipulative?'

'I *know* you're manipulative.'

'How have I tried to manipulate you?'

'To start with, what you're doing here talking to me. What's your message?'

'You want a sound bite?'

'*Message*. What are you trying to tell me?'

'I came here to tell you I'd like to try it again. But I see now you could never give up that gold-digger bit and get human for a while.'

'That's your message?'

'Yeah – and that you won't be able to move on with your life until you get your priorities straight.'

'What are my priorities?'

'Do I need to spell them out? Okay, but I need to know what country you're in. Then I can call the currency by its proper name. In America it's dollars. In France it's the euro. In Japan it's yen.'

'The priority for me is called one thing – survival.'

'Don't wrap this up in some sort of Darwinian thing. There are tons of women out there surviving, not doing what you're doing. Look there. And there. And over there.'

'Well, maybe they got cut a different deck. I have dealt with my life as I've seen fit, as it has been handed to me.'

'Bo – you're lost.'

'Screw you, Jasper. In fact, I think you're lost.'

'Am I?'

'Completely. At least I've come to terms with who I am. You're just deluding yourself.'

'Oh yeah, how?'

'You're so far away from being in touch with yourself, you're dangerous.'

The reality is, Jasper was no different than Brad. He was trying to work me, another Master of the String-Along. He had used me for his writing assignment and now he wanted to use me emotionally. And it irked me. Especially since I was still smarting over my experience with Brad.

'Oh, me – *the dangerous one?*' And he laughed derisively.

'Yes. Because you're a silent assassin. You're not mean or inconsiderate or rude or tactless or impolite. You manipulate with sweetness. You're a total gentleman. And you use it like a knife.'

'How?'

'You try to control, you want to control, but you wash it in lots of poster values. Like compassion and caring and sensitivity. That's the dangerous part. Because you make people think you really care about them. When all you're really doing is looking out for your own and caring for yourself. Like now.'

'Like now . . .'

'Right now. Calling me on my gold-digging way of life. To get through to my soul. When deep down you know what some people do, what some people have to do. Your research told you that much. It's just that I'm not following your program – the one that says, "Now that my girlfriend has dumped me, I'm scared, and my self-esteem is low, I'm going to run back to Bo and see if I can have her hold me. So I can substitute her for that emotional support I'm missing. I'll tell her how screwed up her life is – to break her down, tell her what a coarse, crass, classless money-grabbing bitch she is – so she'll fuck me until I feel better."

'Then once you have the security blanket wrapped around yourself again, and you get your self-esteem back, then you can peek around slowly but surely, and see what and who else is out there. Meanwhile, I've derailed my life again for a creep like you – hoping – and then you just dump me and move on. And I've given you my heart again for the umpteenth time, and the worst part of it is, all I've done is get older.'

I needed to catch a breath, so I did.

'You told me, Bo. Never sleep with a guy unless you don't want to keep him.'

'So?'

'You slept with me on the first night.'

'Second.'

'Same thing.'

I looked at him for a moment and disregarded what he'd said – for the moment. I'd get to it. Maybe. Or maybe not. I was a woman, remember? Convenient Mood Technologies would dictate that one.

'And you know what else, Jasper? You're mean. I always sensed you were the type of guy who, when you've been apprised of something intensely personal and embarrassing and hurtful to someone, would fake at absolute sincerity and understanding, and then throw it back in their face when you needed to – to use it against them. I thought this back in Aspen. When I told you all about that stuff. You don't think I wasn't aware that you were studying me and classifying me and using that piece as my indirect biography? And I knew it would come back to haunt me.'

'I've never written it that way.'

'But you processed it that way. And I don't blame you. But now when you're not getting your way and you see I'm not available for you and your pitiful emotions, because that's all you see me as – an emotional pit stop where you're caught in between loves, and you have heartache and you're trying to pull yourself out of it by using others, namely me – when you see it's not working, that's when you get mean and resort to name-calling and boomeranging my comments and hitting below the belt. The very honesty I shared with you and respected you for, you've used against me as a last-ditch attempt to turn me around and break me down so I come crying back to you; well, it's just not going to happen that way.'

He just eyed me blankly.

'It's like my saying to you, Maybe, Jasper, you finally have something real to write about instead of dancing along the surface of life with your little preppy Upper East Side stories – hitting you with shit like that to make your self-esteem cave, so you'll feel needy of me. The breakdown in the name of honesty, when it's just self-serving trash. That's your game, Jasper. And, sorry, but I don't want to play.'

His mouth was a thin line across. It didn't show hurt or happy. He didn't know what hit him. But he knew I had hit him where he lived.

That's when I put both hands on his shoulders, spun him around 180 degrees, and gave him a little shove. He resisted at first, and then his legs started moving and he walked back down the esplanade away from me. I watched him for a while, then started off in the opposite direction.

About a minute later, I heard a 'I'm sorry' being yelled. It was the last dose of sweetness I ever heard from Jasper Connelly.

And, no, I never did get back to explaining off why I'd slept with Jasper on the second night. I did it because I'd wanted to, because I'd been feeling strongly for him, and for the first time in a very long time I didn't want to abide by the rules of The Game. But I'd never let Jasper know that. He didn't deserve to find out.

But I wasn't bitter. In fact, I was happy for him. Because once I realized how well he knew how to manipulate silently and seamlessly, that's when I knew he was going to make it. Slowly but surely, he would get to know the dark side. He was already inviting it, and all the pain that came with it, into his own living room. It's why he was with **Every Little Bit Helps**.

Though he wasn't consciously aware of it. But his subconscious was seeking out her and her type, even me. Sure, he could process his union with her as *she's deceived him* and *she used him* and *how awful* and *women are bitches*, but really, was he ever going to take her on as a lifelong mate? No way. He'd been using her too. Only her choices had been more conscious ones.

Jasper didn't know all the answers, but he knew he didn't, which is three-quarters of the battle. And he knew how to get them. He knew his limitations. But instead of trying to compensate or cover up or pretend to know, he went right after it to plug the hole. It's another way to cultivate success. Where I let my demons work for me, Jasper was letting his weakness, his darkness deficiency, work for him. He would deftly use all this knowledge to his benefit. Nope, I wasn't worried about Jasper Connelly one bit. If anything, the guy was going to become a great writer. And perhaps even he was going to make some real money. Eventually.

It's true Jasper used me to educate him, and I used him to purge my soul. But in the end, I don't think our union was solely a utilitarian symbiosis. He saw something more in me. I could feel it. That maybe even there was a future with me. But he wasn't ready. He was still in school. He wasn't going to graduate for another seven to ten years. By then, I'd be thirty-five and counting. He needed to explore. And I knew he would.

I never heard anything about him again until his 'How to Marry a Billionaire' article came out in *Esquire* about four months later. I bought a copy and read it. Jasper had done a nice job with the material. And thankfully, he didn't use real names.

double tongues

I returned to my cheapie hotel. It was a safe house now, as it had become my base of operations. I felt pretty good about what I'd said to Jasper, the silent, sweet assassin. Suzanne White was right on with that one when she coined the term 'wily sunshine' for the Libra Rat. Let him shine brightly and softly manipulate somewhere else, was my feeling.

A few days later as I was on my way out the door to meet Napoleon for a drink, I saw Brad standing across the street, waiting for me. There were no cabs to be hailed, and that was unfortunate. I walked in the direction of Ninth Avenue. He, of course, followed and caught up to me.

'Bo.'

'Hello, Brad.' I kept walking.

'Listen to me.'

I slowed and spun around. His forehead was a wash of perspiration. He had a different look in his eye. He was very nervous. Uncontrollably so. I'd never seen him this way.

'Are you all right?' he asked.

'Yes, Brad. Thank you for all the flowers.' He had been sending me arrangements almost daily. I didn't think much of it, really. He was rich and a Master. Master of the String-Along.

'How is Max?' he asked.

'Taking it as well as can be expected.'

'That's tough.'

I nodded.

'There's something I want to confess to you,' he said. 'But I gather since you haven't returned any of my calls, you know already.'

I stood there to listen to him for no other reason than I wanted to hear him phrase it.

'I wasn't with my family at Christmas. I was with a woman. Is her name important to you?'

'No,' I said flatly. And he scanned my face to detect whether I might know who it was. I gave him nothing to read.

'Because I will tell you. Not that it matters.'

'It did. But it doesn't anymore.'

Of course, I was speaking in double tongues. His downflated expression indicated that he had processed it personally, that I was implying he didn't mean anything to me anymore. When really I was saying that the fact it was **Check the Passport** did matter, and it had made me seek out revenge on her and now that I'd accomplished that, it didn't matter any longer.

But even that was half-baked. The reality is, **Check the Passport** would get hers only if Warren ever came after me. He'd already made good on the settlement with Virginia. But I never turned over the compromising material to him. I kept it as my own safety-insurance policy. So, in the end, **Check the Passport** would suffer only if something happened to me. But that was okay. I didn't feel the need to nail her. Or **Smiles**, for that matter. Like I said, I wasn't vindictive. And the episode that had inspired my initial vengeful feelings mattered a lot less anyway.

I snapped out of my reverie. With what Brad had to say to me next, it warranted it.

'And I'll tell you why I invited someone else,' he began. 'I know about you, Bo. I know your background, I know your reputation. Not the reputation you send out in your personal press releases. The silent one. The one you don't talk about. And I must say, when I first heard, I was crushed. I felt deceived. I felt, well, a lot of things, and they were all pretty negative. I was in love with you. And to find out the person you're in love with has that kind of activity going on, well, it's not the easiest thing to take.'

This surprised me. Not that it should have, however. I kept silent.

'You know I have a tendency toward jealousy anyway, so to think of you double-dealing me . . .'

'I wasn't, Brad.'

'You were living two lives.'

'Not when I was with you. I was dedicated to you.'

He just looked at me, not knowing whether to believe me, and made another flash study of my face to check for any break in its honesty.

'Until you blew me off. Then I got involved with someone. In Aspen. Do you want to know his name?'

'No,' he said.

'You meant a lot to me, Brad.'

He nodded. 'And you, me,' he said. 'But when I heard all that, I panicked. I said, I've got to get out of this, to distance myself, to not want to care for you, so I wouldn't go nuts. That's why I took a girl down there with me. To forget you. Can you blame me?'

I really couldn't answer that. There's no question I'd been spinning a web of deceit. And it's not like I wasn't aware of it. It wasn't so much that he had lied to me. I was not that righteous. How could I be? It was that he had placed himself in that Master of the String-Along category, the one who is the archenemy of women like me, of any modern woman, for that matter. I'd had my hopes set on this one, at a very vulnerable time of my life. So much had happened to me so fast. And I was needy. And I'd grown dependent on my thoughts of a future with him. And that was my fault.

He took out his handkerchief and wiped the wetness from my eye.

'Who gave me the sparkling character reference?' I asked.

'A friend of my parents'.'

'Who?'

'Does it matter?'

'Something like that always matters, even if it doesn't.'

'Mrs Merriweather. Your roommate's mother,' he said. 'And then the girl I took to Nassau knew you too.'

That was no surprise.

'I wanted to call you so badly. And I would have. If

she hadn't been there taking up my time. I did it for me. To protect myself.'

'So, Brad,' I said with a sigh, 'what are you doing here now? What's this with the daily flowers? You brought me here to bust me on my past?'

'Partially. But not exactly. I came here to tell you why I behaved the way I did at Christmas.'

And then he extended both his hands, which were urging me to extend mine. After a moment or so, I did.

'But also I came here to tell you I still love you. And I want to marry you.'

We just looked into each other's eyes. His were very sincere. And in support of them, his hand floated to his side, disappeared into the hip pocket of his jacket, and returned with a little blue-velvet box. He held out the box. 'Open it.'

A tear was welling up in one eye. Then the other. 'No,' I said resolutely.

And I didn't have the strength to walk. I ran down the street, all the way to Sixth Avenue. There on the corner I phoned the Four Seasons bar to notify Napoleon that I wouldn't be coming. Then I walked all the way to the East River. It was chilly, but I didn't feel it. I didn't feel much. I didn't know what to feel.

the package deal

It was the third week in February, and my hair was long and two-toned. The Ohio chestnut brown had grown in, making for a marked contrast with the Malibu beach blond left over from my California swing. I'd been inside my base of operations for several days straight. I hadn't gotten together with anyone, and certainly not Brad. Though I was hearing from him a lot.

I decided to drop by the Oak Room bar at the Plaza for a drink. I ordered a Cosmopolitan. Very soon I was halfway done with it. My mind was on how much I felt I'd outgrown the place, and all places like it, when I was tapped on the shoulder.

'Are you Bo?'

'Uh, yes.'

And I looked at him and pretty much died.

'I'm John Summers. I think we met at the Costume Wing Ball last December.'

'Did we?'

'Well, I was actually pretty drunk, and either we met and talked or someone else told me about you. I remember watching you dance, though. Of that I'm sure.'

I was surprised. He seemed nice. But all womanizers do. Nice is an essential part of their get-you-in-the-sack-quick charm. His self-deprecating, confused thing came off as charming too. Very charming. And his looks didn't hurt either.

We continued to chat. We swapped some names. I knew a few more people from his Late Twenties crowd, because of my association with Brad and the parties we'd attended together.

Of course, I gave a thought to Napoleon and how he would be standing in a puddle if he could have seen me now.

For the holidays, John claimed he'd gone to Mustique. But he was still tan three months later.

'Are you sun-bedding it, John?' I asked. I was pretty tipsy, actually. During the course of our chat I'd switched or I'd been switched to margaritas, which is what he'd been drinking.

'Well, once every couple of weeks,' he said smugly. 'You know what Aristotle Onassis said . . .'

Of course I did. Capricorn Snake, remember? But I pretended I didn't. 'Why, no.'

'He said the formula for success is, Wake up early and have a great tan.'

And right then I saw the vain kick in on him. Pure nicety was dwindling in his demeanor at a quick rate. He was in second gear now. His approach was in the direction of sly. He was feeling more comfortable with present company and therefore more relaxed with letting his true personality come to the fore, good aspects and bad.

'Where do you get it done?'

'My tan? The Racquet Club on Park. You know it?'

'Sure do,' I said, and a hiccup blasted out of my throat. We both found that to be funny, me more than him.

As time went on, John switched a couple more gears of his personality. And with playboys, you know how that goes. From nice to sly to provocative to fresh to aggressive to insistent.

He said stuff like, 'I have twenty-one personalities, you know. You'll like eighteen of them.'

He had become freer with his hands too, and they started to get acquainted with my back, my shoulders, then my lower back, my knees, then the curve of my ass. He thought it was his due. His arrogance told him so. His hand then grazed my breast when he inspected my Tiffany necklace. But it was an excuse to get touchy-feely with my tits.

Somehow, I might add, my hand grazed his lower area, and I felt that he was hard, very hard. Kind of like somewhere in between asphalt and cement. And my God, yes. It was e-norm. The only thing that came to mind was Bam-Bam's club from the *Flintstones* cartoon. That that image speeded to mind is also a sign of how tipsy-turvy I'd become.

He did another palm of my upper ass, then elbowed my breast and found only more softness. I'd had enough. I grabbed him and kissed him. He immediately sent in the soldiers, and we sat there at the Oak Room bar, lip-locked for half a minute or so.

We then paid up and went to Au Bar, where the room was lower-lit and more discreet. The champagne basket arrived soon after. And I was getting sloppy. So I went to the bathroom, powdered up, made a phone call, and took a pee, not necessarily in that order. The phone call was one of those crazy drink-and-dial ones.

When I returned to the table, John – in totally predictable, New York millennium-womanizer character – was chatting up **Smiles to Your Face**, who, when she caught sight of me, flashed icily. I'd heard from the **Three-Minute Princess** in Los Angeles that **Smiles to Your Face** and her 'oil magnate' lover had spent that entire holiday week together in Aspen. The maid's kid had had the greatest vacation of his life. I wanted to inquire, but she took off before I could ask her if she'd met the family yet. I didn't feel that guilty. After all, that four-way Air Religion romp I'd arranged with Warren Samuels had boosted her accounts hugely. Of that, I was sure.

The petting and fondling with John resumed underneath the table of our booth. John was in one of those later gears I described before. That meant getting inside a girl's panties in public places. He was not shy. Nor was I shy with him. I gripped him more than once. I had to. I hoped Napoleon wouldn't be upset.

Now, let's establish this right now. John was very drunk, though not uncontrollably so.

So – when I told him to get in the cab, he complied. When I told him to pay the cabbie, he complied again. When I told him to get into the elevator, he complied once more. When I told him to wait quietly in the hall as I stepped inside the apartment, he was more than happy to. And when I invited him inside, he was, again, willing.

The apartment was very dark. But candles were burning everywhere. The living room was a haphazard arrangement of big square floor pillows with Eastern I-guess designs on them. It looked like a Balinese opium den. Do they smoke opium in Bali? I didn't know. And I still don't. Whichever, since his sister had come and gone again, Napoleon had set up the place to his liking.

He was seated on one of the pillows, holding a glass of wine. He was wearing drawstring pants and was barefoot.

'Take off your shoes,' he said with a gentle smile. He was beaming somewhat. He'd already had a couple.

When we sat down next to him, he served us some wine. Immediately, I put my head on Napoleon's shoulder and became very affectionate with him. And John felt compelled to settle on the other side of me. But soon after, I got up to go to the bathroom. When I returned, Napoleon was brushing back John's bangs, discussing his hairstyle, which he called a 'tragedy.'

'You are too long in the back. It must be cut.'

'Let Napoleon do it,' I offered.

'Yes, let me do it. I can't look at it this way. You are too handsome.'

'He's great,' I added.

'Okay,' John said.

'But first, take off your shirt,' Napoleon advised. 'I don't want to get hair all over your clothes.'

John had no problem with that. To add a little energy to the room, I took off my pants and sat there in my pink La Perlas. I stroked John's thighs as Napoleon massaged his scalp, then snipped away at his hair.

'Look at all this pampering you're getting,' I remarked.

'I love it,' John responded.

I lay a slow, gentle kiss on him while he was getting cut. He couldn't move his head. He was kind of a trapped hostage. Then I played with him. Yes, there. When I released it from his pants, John jerked a bit.

'It's okay,' I told him. 'Napoleon and I were roommates together. We don't have any secrets.'

'And we don't share them with anyone else either,' Napoleon added.

I could see Napoleon leaning over every once in a while to get a peek at him. John, I must say, was enjoying it. It was all registered in his superfirm condition.

After Napoleon finished cutting him, he began to gently massage John's naked shoulders and back. John leveled eyes at me. His look was a question. I nodded. Yes, we were a Package Deal. After that was silently established, I went down on him. It was a nice reward. I was sure he'd see it that way.

John relaxed even more, of course. Soon, he found himself gliding through heaven. . . .

But I didn't do it for very long. I came off him, rose up, and peeled off my top, exposing my bra. Napoleon stood up and slid behind me. He unsnapped it. My breasts were set free. Napoleon smiled at John – in essence, inviting him. I was standing there all alone, exposed except for my panties. John, who was still erect and sticking out through his pants, moved toward me. He started kissing my breasts. Meanwhile, Napoleon moved behind John and extended his arms around his waist. He undid his belt buckle, then his zipper. And

John's pants went to the floor. Napoleon caressed John's body and ass while I held him. Then I let go and let Napoleon hold him for the first time. From behind.

John was writhing now.

We all settled back down on the pillows. We let John lie down on his back, and I maneuvered over him. I still had my underwear on, and he moved beneath me and pushed aside the air strip of the panties and went to work on me.

That's when Napoleon went to work on his lower half. John filed no complaints.

Meanwhile, John was taking very good care of me. I braced myself against the wall. Eventually, though, I got up. John had that glazed look on his face. He wasn't weirded-out at all. It was as if all his bathroom and bedroom fantasies from high school on were being played out for him all at once.

And Napoleon – well, it should come as no surprise that it was pretty much the night of his life.

When I rose off John, Napoleon stopped too. I took John by the hand and led him into the bedroom. And all that can be said is, we found positions and more positions. And Napoleon was there too, playing with John as John worked me. It went on for an hour or so. The room was so open. So free. We were under the sheets, on top of them, in the corner, against the wall. It was a night to remember.

After I praised John's anatomy, he said something that came off as arrogant but was very funny.

'You know, the best thing about having a big cock is – it's appreciated by every generation.'

'And every *gender*,' Napoleon added.

We all found that funny.

And then I left. I looked at my watch, it was five in the morning. I flagged a cab and arrived at my hotel a half hour later. Oddly, I wasn't tired. I did a quick pack. And settled my bill at the hotel. I made my way to Newark Airport. It was closer to my hotel than JFK or La Guardia. I took the next flight to Cleveland.

Call it payback. Call it what you will – a gift, maybe. But Napoleon was my best friend. He had gotten me through the worst of times. He was the one person who had always been there for me. So I delivered him John.

You see, when I left that morning, they remained in the apartment. John didn't leave until late the next night. And he left contentedly with a cool, closely cropped cut. They never got together ever again. The forecast was not for snow, and John wasn't a snowman and wasn't switching over. But in the course of that evening, everything he'd ever wanted to know or try or have tried on him had taken place. From then on, whenever they saw each other, they smiled warmly and chatted. They actually developed a very special bond. But their physical relationship was over. It was not to be revisited. Yet, not to be broken. And never to be forgotten.

tickling bricks

Of course, to this day, Napoleon feels indebted to me. Beyond what it was I'd done and what he'd received. I was worried at first that it would hurt Napoleon in the end. Because I thought he might fall hopelessly in love. He did not. In fact, he lost his crush on John Summers: what you've had and all, I guess.

One day, a package was forwarded to me from the hotel. I opened it. It was a thick fold-up thank-you card from Napoleon. Only it was sixty cards long, and it folded out into a giant penis. At the end it read, 'Thank you for the best night of my life.'

Everyone has that one night. Some have more. Some less. Napoleon had one. And that one was it.

I didn't think much about it, however. You see, I had arranged that package deal for my own reasons too. It helped me forget Brad once and for all. The same way he had used another woman to forget me. He had hit me hard emotionally that day. I was dazed for days. But I regained clarity and then made my moves.

You see, I needed to clean house. I'd let go of Jasper and now I'd let go of Brad. Finally, at age twenty-nine,

I'd learned to depend on no one but myself. And love myself. My self-esteem that had been poorly formed in my younger years had grown stronger. And I was able to make moves of strength and power, that in previous years I'd never been able to. No more getting caught up in a guy's lies or false promises or emotional smoke screens, I thought. Finally, Bo knew self-esteem. And finding that strength allowed me to do the very thing that would change my life forever.

You see, what I realized and what I told Brad my reason for not wanting to marry him and have kids was, I already had one. And she needed guidance. She needed me. Or she was going to be that same balsa-wood boat floating aimlessly and directionless on the windy high seas. I had a choice in whether or not she was going to drift. I chose for her not to. I wasn't going to become Maximilian's mother. No one could ever replace her. I could never replace her father either. But I was going to come damn close.

At one point during my meditations, I wondered why I couldn't have both. Meaning marry Brad *and* take care of Max. Certainly, we'd have an instant family and lots of cash. That was a great play by anyone's standards. But I felt strongly that Brad was being driven by two forces that had made him come back to me. First, he was servicing his rebellious fires. He wanted to give his meddling mother a facial and for ever rid himself of her curse. This was the very reason I'd selected him in the first place. The Rich Rebel. But more important, he was taking this step because of his all-consuming jealous streak. In essence, he'd been manipulating the situation just like Jasper, only his methods and reasons were different. He didn't really love me and want me. His was a simple case of not wanting anyone else to have me, which is a pretty collegiate and stupid reason to marry someone.

That jealousy dynamic would certainly grow old and sour. Once that possessive feeling for me had worn off, he wouldn't care who had me. He'd just start cheating on me, and me on him, and it would be another modern matrimonial mess. Yes, I'd have the money set up, but I still felt I had time to do that anyway. In fact, I was sure of it. Besides, look at the facts. I had a child now. I didn't want to inflict a relationship that had that idiocy as its foundation on Maximilia. Or myself.

You see, it would be another act of my not loving and caring for myself. I wanted to start out clean. And fresh. And not dive into things anymore that I knew from the outset were tainted. It was the type of weak move I was known to make before. But no longer. Plain and simple, avoiding this arrangement was an act of love – for myself.

That is not to say I didn't keep in touch with Bradley Lorne-August. I spoke with him once a week, in fact. Just in case. And that's the last Digger axiom I'll offer. And it is a significant one. Never break off badly with a Walletman. He'll always come back if you don't leave on messy terms. And you never know when you're going to need him. In life, remember, you never know.

The one other thing I said to him was, 'Hey, Brad, get a new best friend.' He said he had done that already.

One significant note on Napoleon. Soon after our

evening with John Summers, Napoleon traveled down to Palm Beach to speak with his father, Mr Townsend Merriweather. At which time Napoleon recounted to him the story of how he'd avenged the crime of Go Go's first guy – that age-old family scandal. And he told him exactly how he'd done it, leaving out no details. Mr Merriweather was shocked and puzzled at first. He had to figure it all out. And when he did, he uttered two precious stones for Napoleon.

'Good boy,' he said.

The long pause Napoleon experienced between his father's hearing what had happened and his response was understandable. Mr Merriweather was, of course, forced to decide on the implications of the sum total of the activity: he had a son who was gay, which had always been crushing; at the same time, Napoleon had given an enemy of the family his due and just deserts; yet still, his daughter had slept with a guy who obviously was bisexual and therefore had taken all the risks involved with that; and, still worse, the jerk might have enjoyed the act of revenge he'd received.

In the end, it was just too much millennium thinking for a man whose morals had been shaped in the forties. He had to chalk it up as a positive.

And a week after their discussion, Mr Merriweather sent Napoleon a check for five hundred thousand dollars. Napoleon was back on the payroll. And from then on, any reservations I'd had of giving John to Napoleon were erased.

Money is a funny thing. You can try to get your hands on it for years, pounding away, scratching and clawing for financial survival, and hitting a ceiling constantly – then sometimes if you tickle the right brick in the right way, the entire wall crumbles and the money just pours out. That's what Napoleon's tale of family revenge had done. In his father, he had tickled the right brick.

to the max

And then there was Max. She was my true pride and joy and everything I now lived for.

When I returned to Fort Lowell, she was ecstatic. Though the family who had taken her in had been good to her, she was happy to return to that house on Searchlight Lane.

For the next two weeks we fixed up the old place together and then put it up for sale the first week in March. But we lived in it until it was sold. We had a really nice time. As soon as Max came home from school, she'd put on her old clothes and help me paint the trim. I loved being with her, and I saw my sister in her too. The squint, the reserved smile, and the wit. That was especially nice.

And the spring leaves returned to the old maple. Yes, I noticed it. I was back on with nature after a long layoff. Too long.

One afternoon, when I was cleaning out the attic, I came across a long cardboard box. It was so dusty, it made me cough. I opened it. And there it was. My used-once, white prom dress from that fateful Sadie Hawkins

Dance all those years ago. It made me stop everything I was doing. I just sat there in the attic and invited all thoughts of that previous life. It's the type of deep thinking only ancient heirlooms and artifacts can provide. I think I made it back downstairs an hour later. At first I was going to give the dress to Maximilia. But I decided against it. I had my reasons.

Believe it or not, I was saddened when the place sold so quickly. It netted us about fifty thousand dollars. I also sold Vicky's old Chevy for three thousand. I gave that and half of the house proceeds to Max for her education, and I put my share into my new business, matching the contribution of a partner I'd taken on.

There was one special night Max and I had together before the house sold. We were in the living room, listening to that old jazz record Eldridge had given us after Vicky's funeral. It was then that I posed the question to Max. 'You want to move?'

'I don't know. Do you?'

'It's up to you. You have all your friends here. And senior year coming up.'

'I don't care about senior year.'

'I do.'

'No, I don't mean it that way. I mean, I don't need to finish here. I broke up with Danny,' she said.

'I know.'

'And the memories here are not that great, Aunt Bo,' she added.

That hit me hard. It was a piece robbed right out of my own life. We looked at each other as the jazz horns were wailing, and I saw her smile. It made me smile.

'I know what you're thinking,' I said.

'You've never been there, Aunt Bo.'

'I know. I never have.'

And just like that, we decided to move to New Orleans.

the visit

Before we left Fort Lowell, I had one more thing to do.

I drove to Beckwith early one morning. Beckwith was the next town over from Fort Lowell. That's where he lived, I'd heard. I turned down Hastings Street. Sure enough, his name was on the mailbox. I turned off the car and strode up the walk to the house. I stepped up onto the porch and tapped on the door. A woman came to it.

'Is your husband in?'

She paused a moment in an attempt to make sense of me. She couldn't. 'Yes, just one moment.'

A version, a swollen version, of the boy I once knew advanced to the door. He wasn't thirty yet, but he looked a good twenty years beyond. His hair was barely there, and his face had fallen. He had garage-mechanic blue on, with a name patch in red and white above the pocket. It said BUDDY in red stitching.

He paused at the screen door and looked at me and then squinted to double-check. He moved through the door.

'Well, I'll be a bluenosed gopher. Bodicea. What the heck . . .'

And I'd actually forgotten about his Kentucky accent. His family had moved from Kentucky when he was young, but he never lost that hillbilly twang.

'Hello, Buddy.'

'What brings you here?' he asked excitedly.

'I have something to discuss with you.'

'Sure thing . . .'

'I'd like an apology.'

He looked at me in a puzzled way. 'You mean . . .?'

I nodded.

'Hell, Bo, that was ten years ago.'

'Thirteen.'

And he kind of laughed. It wasn't a laugh responding to real humor. It was one that indicated real resistance.

'Come on now,' he said. 'You've come all the way . . .'

'You never apologized. You never even called. You never did anything. You just flat-out dumped me. And started up with Shari. Didn't we have those special moments? What were you thinking?'

Just then, the little girl I'd heard he had came up from behind him and teased his leg with her hand. She was very cute. Her free hand had its thumb stuck in her mouth.

'Hello, Ginger. Say hi to Bo.'

'Hello,' she said warily.

'Angel, I'll be right there.'

The little girl drifted back inside. And Buddy stepped down from the porch and started down the front walk. I followed him.

'I'm glad you have a little girl, Buddy. Just remember, I was a little girl once. And the way you treated me –

and I was in love with you – set me back.'

He looked at me a moment. Surely he wasn't ready for this kind of strange interlude. All these years later. At his home. From me. He shuffled uneasily a bit. 'I'm sorry, Bo. I truly am,' he said in a tone that wasn't artificial.

I waited to respond. 'We're all sorry now,' I said. And right then I wondered if I should have come at all. But something had been driving me to do it. It was something that was dangling and had been dangling in front of me for years, maybe impeding my development, maybe not. But it was strong, this compulsion I had to experience this confrontation. I'd thought about it thousands of times since that fateful weekend.

Buddy didn't know what to say. He started a few times to say something, but nothing came out. And then finally, his eyes cooled and fixated a moment. It revealed that maybe he had something coherent to offer on the subject. His eyes went from this concentrated focus to a certain wistfulness. And they got sadder by the minute. And the only explanation for his reaction was that I was bringing him to a place he'd thought about previously just about as many times as I had.

'Whatcha got there?' he asked.

That's when I handed him the box. He was surprised. Then he took it. And opened it. His eyes stared into it and took on a disconcerted look.

'I only wore it two hours,' I said.

He waited a long while. Then he tried to speak, but his voice cracked. 'You want me to have it?' he said eventually.

'No. I was hoping you'd give it to Ginger.'

And he looked behind to see if she was there. She wasn't. He nodded. 'Sure thing. Thank you.'

'You're welcome.'

And he just looked at me.

'I was a jerk back then,' he uttered, and he didn't say it loud. It came from some place deep and true, a place he hadn't let express itself in a while. I could tell. And his eyes just went into a scary, teary stare, off and away down the short rim of fence that held in his little yard.

'I was the star of the football team,' he continued. 'I had the prettiest girl in school – you – I was good, Bo.' And he looked at me with welling tears. 'Those were my best days. I thought I ruled the world. So I behaved like it.' He shuffled a step and tried to get control of himself. 'Have you fallen in love again?'

'Not really.'

Buddy wiped his eyes for a moment. Then he made a quick instinctive jerk back around and glanced at the house, and I saw a curtain move. He redirected his head back forward and went silent for another moment. The silence was eventually broken by a whisper. His.

'Love isn't everything it's made out to be. What I mean is, it changes.'

I just looked down the street at nothing in particular.

'You never married, Bo?'

It hit me. It wasn't what he'd said, but it was an emotional shove. I didn't answer him. A couple of tears that were on hold started to run down my cheek. I brushed my eyes.

'Look how beautiful you are,' he said, and pressed

two palms on either side of my face. And his face crumpled a bit, and his chin trembled as he spoke. 'It's not once I've thought about you. And how I . . . it.' He'd mumbled the *blew* part.

I leaned over and into him. We stood there and hugged.

'Sometimes,' I started, trying to speak through the upset, 'sometimes you just need to do things, Buddy. Like me coming here.'

He held me tighter.

Eventually, we separated from each other but still clasped hands. The corners of his mouth finally turned up to settle on a despondent smile. I'd seen looks of regret before, but not really like the one registered on his face at that moment. It was as if he'd needed this moment. Like he'd dreamed of it too. Like he'd tried to dominate his feelings on the subject for many years. And now he was relieved to see me and hear me out and let go of all that pressure. To let go of all those little lies he'd been telling himself. Sure, some sadness was there but also a look of relief that had taken over his face. He was off the hook finally. And his soul was closer back to equilibrium.

I hadn't been looking for that kind of reaction. And I didn't profit from it internally. Our relationship back then might have ended months later of its own accord. In fact, I'm sure of it. We weren't going places together. But that moment of looking into his eyes and seeing the ballad that was silently being sung, well, it did make me smile faintly. For different reasons.

There we were. Two older versions of young lovers

who'd experienced all those grown-up things and feelings for the first time together all those years before, and we hadn't said a word to each other ever since. And there we were years later, being what you might call human – saturated with vital, real, and true feelings for a brief but exquisite moment. Through the tears. I call it the best life has to offer.

'You get inside, Buddy,' I said. 'And be good to that family.'

We didn't hug again. Or kiss good-bye.

'I am sorry, Bo. I truly am.'

I then turned around slowly and got back in the taxicab that was still waiting for me.

'Good-bye, Buddy,' I said through the backseat window.

'Good-bye, Bo.'

And he stood there on the front walk, holding the box as the cab motored off down the street.

another world

Maximilia and I made our first trip to New Orleans during Mardi Gras. It was a trial run, I guess you could say. A festival week is never a good time to get a feel for a place, much less to assess its character. But there was something vital and life-affirming about the city that came through all the hoopla. We checked out the French Quarter. And saw all the beautiful flowers cascading from balconies. We visited the port. We walked down Bourbon Street. We heard all the music and saw all the smiles and the good cheer. I even opened up a charge account at the specialty store La Maison Blanche.

New Orleans was like another world. I think that's why we liked it so much. It was like another world. It was what we were both secretly yearning for. Another world was us.

We made our decision. New Orleans was going to be our new home. We went back to Ohio, closed on the sale of the house, grabbed our belongings, mostly clothes, and returned to the city. We rented a nice house on the outskirts of town. And that was that.

And, of course, my new business partner broke up

with his lover and moved down there to join us. Napoleon and I had decided to start up an Internet hair-products mail-order business. We called our concern Millennium Girl Industries. We even planned to sell cosmetics in addition to an array of hair products. After all, Napoleon knew what he liked, what he didn't, and what there was and wasn't enough of in the marketplace. We even had our own Millennium Girl perfume in the works. The slogan went *Make him pay for it.*

I found us an office space in a cute second-story flat in the French Quarter. How did I know what to do? I had profited from my experience in London working for the Morrisons' Internet clothing company. I knew what computers to buy and what software and spreadsheets to use and how to manage it all. In addition, I knew how to find investors to cover our initial investment. Make that two of us. We made Maximilia a junior partner in the company. And I have to confess, when Max and I went out on a meeting in search of financial backing, it was not overly difficult to drum up interest. After all, she'd gone Creole orange and I was Louisiana bayou blond.

So, if you're wondering, that's what happened to me – I became a businesswoman. If I was going to marry, I was going to bring something to the table. And if I wasn't, I was going to be able to stand alone on my own two feet. I was done with finding my power in others. At Century's End, I think it's crucial for a woman to cultivate her own tools of empowerment. I really do. Some hard years on Tour had taught me that.

by the way

So I had my little family and my own little company. Nice.

At the same time, I did not turn my back on old friends, especially Bradley Lorne-August. In fact, I allowed him to visit us in New Orleans, not once but three times. The first two occasions, we actually had a nice time. And Max even liked him. Brad taught her how to ride horses at the nearby stables.

The third time Brad came down to New Orleans, he came for good. It's true, I'd been in love with him and still was. And I had denied it. It's why I'd opted to hear him out after he'd lied to me. All had been forgiven. His mistakes. And mine.

That summer, we decided to get a larger house and we all settled in together. In the fall Brad got a job as a traveling news correspondent for the city newspaper and Max enrolled in her senior year of high school. And my Internet business with Napoleon took off. I even influenced Brad into investing in our new fragrance. After all, influence is where it's at, don't forget.

Of course, you may be wondering whether I married

Brad or not. Yes, he proposed to me. And yes, he offered me a ring with a large, beautiful diamond. There's no question I wanted to form a family with him, which would include Max. And I wanted to start a new family with him too. But in the end I didn't accept his proposal and I'll tell you why. I certainly didn't need to do it, which is significant. But more important, my feelings about marriage had changed over time as a result of my experience. And how could they not? I believe the 'M' word pressurizes relationships to a difficult degree. Yet the institution is clearly right for some people. It just isn't right for all people. I thought Brad and I would be better suited for each other if we did not get linked together in that formal way. I thought, and still think, there would be a greater degree of mutual respect for our union if we did not. It would keep the relationship alive and make it thrive and no one would feel tied to one another. I had a need for family, but family as a group of people who care about each other, yet who are not formally bound to one another. Which, in the end, I was sure would keep us together. Along with the love, of course. You see, for marriage, love had never been a requirement for me. But for spending the rest of my life with someone, it was. Those were the terms under which I wanted my man. And they were my terms. Not society's. And no one else's. That was how I wanted it. And that was how I got it.

A year and a half after we moved in together, Brad and I had our first child. We named her Victoria after my sister, of course. For the christening, Virginia came out from Carmel, the seaside town in Northern

California where she'd moved. I asked her to be Victoria's godmother and she felt honored and gladly accepted. And Napoleon was named godfather and Father Rollins performed the christening. We had a nice party too in celebration of it all. It was a sweet reunion.

Certainly, it was an odd collection of people that constituted my family. From different places, different walks, and different persuasions. But I think at the millennium hour it's crucial to find family wherever you can get it. That's what I did. And to this day I have no regrets.

And that's my story. If you want to help yourself, don't depend. *Independ*. Because in the end, it's all up to you. Because you're born alone and you die alone. And there are some people you get real close to along the way. But – happiness only comes from truly loving yourself and those around you. It's amazing how fast the world comes to you once you do.

By the way, about that ring? Of course I took it. I've always had a weakness for sparkles, you know.

Much love,
The Millennium Girl

The Real Thing

Catherine Alliott

Everyone's got one – an old boyfriend they never fell out of love with, they simply parted because the time wasn't right. And for thirty-year-old Tessa, it's Patrick Cameron, the gorgeous, moody, rebellious boy she met at seventeen; the boy her vicar father thoroughly disapproved of; the boy who left her to go to Italy to paint.

And now he's back.

'You're in for a treat' *Express*

'Alliot's joie de vivre is irresistible' *Daily Mail*

'Compulsive and wildly romantic' *Bookseller*

'An addictive cocktail of wit, frivolity and madcap romance . . . move over Jilly, your heir is apparent' *Time Out*

0 7472 5235 1

HEADLINE

Woman to Woman

Cathy Kelly

Best friends Aisling Moran and Jo Ryan think they have it all.

Aisling is deliriously happy with her brilliant editor husband, two beautiful ten-year-old sons and a home she's rag-rolled and stencilled to within an inch of its life. As a journalist with an Irish glossy magazine, Jo has a great career, independence and a drop-dead gorgeous boyfriend.

But that's all about to change.

One Friday morning, Aisling finds a receipt for expensive lingerie in her husband's suit pocket and Jo finds a blue line on her blue-for-positive pregnancy testing kit. By Friday night, it's all over – or has it only just begun?

'A page-turner' *Sunday Independent*

'A powerful story for the nineties woman; sharp, sexy and witty' *The Star*

0 7472 6052 4

HEADLINE

If you enjoyed this book here is a selection of other bestselling titles from Headline

Headline books are available at your local bookshop or newsagent. Alternatively, books can be ordered direct from the publisher. Just tick the titles you want and fill in the form below. Prices and availability subject to change without notice.

Buy four books from the selection above and get free postage and packaging and delivery within 48 hours. Just send a cheque or postal order made payable to Bookpoint Ltd to the value of the total cover price of the four books. Alternatively, if you wish to buy fewer than four books the following postage and packaging applies:

UK and BFPO £4.30 for one book; £6.30 for two books; £8.30 for three books.

Overseas and Eire: £4.80 for one book; £7.10 for 2 or 3 books (surface mail).

Please enclose a cheque or postal order made payable to *Bookpoint Limited*, and send to: Headline Publishing Ltd, 39 Milton Park, Abingdon, OXON OX14 4TD, UK.
Email Address: orders@bookpoint.co.uk

If you would prefer to pay by credit card, our call team would be delighted to take your order by telephone. Our direct line is 01235 400 414 (lines open 9.00 am–6.00 pm Monday to Saturday 24 hour message answering service). Alternatively you can send a fax on 01235 400 454.

Name ....

Address ....

....

....

If you would prefer to pay by credit card, please complete:
Please debit my Visa/Access/Diner's Card/American Express (delete as applicable) card number:

Signature .... Expiry Date..............